A PERMUTED PRESS BOOK

ISBN: 978-1-61868-669-5
ISBN (eBook): 978-1-61868-027-3

ZOMBIE APOCALYPSE PREPARATION
How to Survive in an Undead World and Have Fun Doing It

Cover art by Zach McCain
Illustrations by Jack Knight
www.knighttimecreations.com

PERMUTED PRESS

Permuted Press, LLC
275 Madison Avenue, 14th Floor
New York, NY 10016
permutedpress.com

ZOMBIE APOCALYPSE PREPARATION

HOW TO SURVIVE IN AN UNDEAD WORLD AND HAVE FUN DOING IT!

DAVID HOUCHINS & SCOT THOMAS

WARNING!

Reading the following publication may result in one or several of the following undesirable side effects:

- Laughter
- Priapism
- Memory loss
- A suave demeanor
- Anal leakage
- Depression
- Clarity of thought
- Sleep depravation
- Lockjaw
- Night vision
- Paper cuts
- Memory loss
- Temporary baldness
- Permanent baldness
- Genital baldness
- Mild gender transition
- Increased breast size
- Male lactation
- Bees
- Itching
- Vertigo
- Dizziness
- Tingling in the extremities
- Loss of balance

- Profuse sweating
- Heart palpitations
- Memory loss
- Sexual arousal
- Psoriasis
- Tunnel vision
- Dry mouth
- Oily discharge
- Hangnails
- Leprosy
- Hyper hearing
- A desire to take up knitting
- Slurred speech
- An Australian accent
- Apathy
- Suicidal thoughts
- Memory loss
- Headaches
- Sore throat
- Stuffy head
- Fever
- Anxiety
- Excessive salivation
- Club-foot
- Amnesia

Do not look directly at the book while reading as mental trauma may occur as understanding and comedy dawns on you.

This book has a lifetime warranty. Some terms and conditions may apply, see store for details.

Do not taunt the book.

The book may stick to certain types of skin, both inside and out. This has been tested and verified.

This book may serve as a useless flotation device. In the event the book is used as a flotation device, the warranty is voided.

This book has been known to cause blunt force trauma when hurled forcefully.

Do not hold this book near open flames. It's made of paper and that burns extremely well. If the book begins to smoke or smolder, please discard immediately. This also voids the warranty.

This book may cause memory loss.

This book has a lifetime warranty. Some terms and conditions may apply, see brick wall behind manufacturer for details.

FOREWORD/INTRO/ RAMBLING BIT

Following the first publication of this work, we felt a little bit like there was something we left out. Indeed, there are plenty of other aspects to not only survival, but the zombie apocalypse and your basic getting along. In fact, there was so much left out that we decided that there needs to be an updated version covering all the shit we forgot to mention that helps us be happy amid the zombie apocalypse. Because let's face it, that's what it boils down to. Now the first edition, for basic survival and weaponry information, by all means, keep that damn thing handy. It's good as it is, but for a more in depth look at certain aspects, well, that's why you're going to be reading this.

Anyway, for this book, we'd like to thank a few people, starting with ourselves and our overactive imaginations. A special thanks also goes out to basic paranoia and the unstable human condition. Midgets, or little people, also deserve a special bit of high praise, but they're unable to reach it, so let's not dwell on that too much. Sorry, that was a little joke. We tried to keep that short. Craig DiLouie, who is a fan of the page, a friend, and an inspiration to us both for showing what a regular guy can do when he puts pen to paper (metaphorically speaking, we don't know how he writes, but you get the idea). Dr. Dale, Jack Knight, and Sean Page, our friends across the pond who keep showing support and anti-zombie sentiments equal to our own. Also, to Jacob who initially decided to take a chance on a couple of over-eager freaks who kept emailing a book at him and saying "MAKE THIS HAPPEN" until the inevitable mental breakdown from information bombardment caused him to relent. Michael Wilson, who took over Permuted Press and has been relentless in pressing us for something bigger, longer, and uncut: sorry about the restraining order, all a big misunderstanding. Finally, to our fans on our illustrious Facebook page, who have been with us on the journey of a giant inside joke, you fine folks are a daily source both wonder and dread, but if you weren't there, we wouldn't be doing what we do when we get around to doing it. Without all of you people, we'd probably have still made it, but you helped and that can't go overlooked.

David Houchins & Scot Thomas

July 31, 2015

SECTION 1
GETTING TO KNOW YOUR UNDEAD ASSAILANTS

"The zombie infection will come from the least expected place. Scientists working to genetically engineer a pig, so that it has ten times the bacon. Sounds good on the surface. But then that genetically altered pig catches the flu, and the flu gets altered, and it infects a human. Next thing you know BAM—zombies roaming the earth, and all you wanted was bacon."

– Found on a fortune cookie

So many people tend to speculate on what will inevitably cause the zombie apocalypse and it has become almost a game with writers to invent some wild new theory. We're nowhere nearly as concerned with *when* as we are with *how*. The reason behind this is that some of these ways are totally preventable with a few well-placed pre-emptive head shots, but sadly, they are unlikely to happen as a result of the value placed on human life. On the assumption that someone reading this is unstable enough to actually take us at our word and cause widespread panic as a result of these writings, well, go for it. You can't blame us for your craziness. All that aside, let's look at what could be the eventual cause of a world full of walking dead.

Aliens

These extraterrestrial bastards have been probing our tender assholes for years, no doubt searching for our weakness. Little do they know that humanity's greatest weaknesses are mind-numbing television, fried foods, and general stupidity. Now, since they've mastered interstellar travel at greater-than-light speeds, it stands to reason that they've come up with some spiffy advances in genetic engineering, and as a result, can really screw up our plans at being the first civilized organisms (that we know of anyway) to wipe ourselves out via nuclear holocaust. Assuming we don't all freeze to death in a nuclear winter, at some point an alien species may in fact want to make our world their own.

From a military standpoint, the first thing you want to do when you establish a base is to pacify the local area. In this case, pacify means kill, and what they want to kill will be us. Well these guys have patience, and all they have to do is dump some nasty shit into our water supplies, or even just the atmosphere, and let it do its work. Some kind of aerial bombardment of pollen or spores or creature from outer space sperm could be peppering us all right at this moment, and there isn't a whole lot we can do about it. Just one variation of this intergalactic snot could turn a portion of the population into zombies without much work at all. These new walking alien pets bite one guy and he turns and so on. Then we're not only fighting what we would easily term "the undead" but we're also covered in some dried alien cock-snot. FACIALS FOR EVERYONE!!! Not a pretty picture. In fact, if this were the case, anyone not continually in a biohazard protection suit, is screwed. No hope for survival unless it happens to be some kind of short-life contaminant that loses its effectiveness after a short time.

If it only manages to infect those outside when this stuff rains down, if humanity is to be saved at all, then the world will be saved by, guess who, the nerds. Can you just imagine a force of geeks laying waste to the undead, all while shouting "FOR THE HORDE" or something of similar geekitude? I mean, this would take a few days, they'd have to lose power, run out of pocky and whatnot, but eventually, nerd-rage will grab hold, and the world will need to be put right. There's a raid scheduled. The geek shall inherit the Earth. All your base are belong to us and all that good stuff.

Bioengineers Screwing The Pooch

We really are huge fans of science in all its forms (except meteorology, those guys are some guessing game full of shit bastards) because science knows only truth. They experiment, interpret, analyze and all that good stuff and come to a conclusion and move on. Of the many branches of science, bioengineers are the only ones that really have the ability to dabble in evil. This is awesome, but it's also pretty goddamn frightening. Tampering with the parts of human beings in order to cure, fix, breed out, or whatever they're doing, has the potential to increase human longevity, make us healthier, and make us smarter as an entire species. They give people a chance to have kids when normally it wouldn't happen due to various reasons. They can clone whatever they want, and probably make a seriously awesome cup of coffee while they're at it. Well, probably, don't ask us, we're not scientists.

Then again they also make pig-dog-monkey-people and just don't tell us about it, they created the chupacabra then released it (because nobody takes the crazy ranting of third world farmers seriously), and sold us sea-monkeys. That last one being the most malicious of the lot. Their main purpose is to push the envelope with whatever they can to see what they can do and how they did it, and at some point, they're going to find it. Some guy whose wife's been screwing the pool boy and who has a child that doesn't share his complexion—he's going to be at work one day, find a chemical that interacts with human tissue so that it becomes necrotic, doesn't degrade, still allows control and movement and craves more flesh. Instead of reducing this shit to a burnt crisp, like he should, he's going to replicate it, leave work one day, and drop that shit off in a fast food place's "special sauce" bin. There you have it folks: instant pandemic. Don't let the fact that these clowns smell like Big Micks fool you; they now want your flesh. You've become a side of fries to these undead fools, and all because some feeble-minded douche bag idolized Lex Luthor as a kid. Maybe this could have been avoided if he hit the gym once in a while, or his wife wasn't a whore, but who knows? Now we got zombies on our lawn, stepping on the petunias. Now it's your job to kill these bastards. Way to screw up a weekend, science. And since we're talking about it...

The Walt Disney Company

I can hear you thinking, "How could Uncle Walt's company possibly cause the zombie apocalypse?" Let me tell you, the company isn't just cute animated shorts, and the seventh largest non-military naval fleet in the world. No, they are the fuck not. They also own most of the neat things in the world. Among those subsidiaries are a few medical companies, which we're positive are used for genetic experiments. Tired of paying college kids to play the stars of the screen, the Walt Disney Company has set out to make beloved characters like Mickey, Minnie, and Goofy into flesh and bone. Look at Harland Williams, pretty sure he was failed Goofy #1. Also, genetically engineered creations don't currently have any rights they will technically be slaves until all that legal kerfuffle is handled. Now, while that may not seem plausible to you, just think about the past successes they've had launching child stars. Countless young boys and girls starring in re-occurring roles, all with the looks, voices, and talent needed to woo kids and tweens into watching for years on end. Sure, in some extreme cases these sub-units self-destruct after about eighteen years on earth. We won't mention any names, but I'm sure you understand the ones we're pointing at here. But for the most part, the basic idea is that a perfect genetic army to rule the movies and airwaves all created in a lab to benefit the frozen overlord Walt Disney presently exists somewhere. Now it's all been smooth sailing up to this point, but all it takes is one mistake and BOOM we've got undead pre-teen stars chewing on the soft and pink fleshy bits that we covet and not in such a way that would cause joy or sexual energy, but more in the "ouch, stop that, you're hurting me, YOU'RE NOT SUPPOSED TO CHEW ON IT!" way. This is what happens when you trust important scientific processes to corporate-funded doctors who are hell bent on warping the minds of the world's youth.

The Water in Mexico

We've all heard the rumors about the water in Mexico and made jokes to our friends who go south of the border for some rest and relaxation. Well, anyone who has had the experience will tell you that it's true. If you're not local, and you suck down the mule piss that they call water in this very foreign land, you'll end up on the toilet for the remainder of your trip, wondering how you're going to make it back to the States without violently shitting on your flip flops every forty-five seconds. Luckily your body takes the intrusion of this swill as a personal affront and violently kicks your ass as a warning against further ingestion of this horrible liquid.

Which begs the question: what if you continued to drink the water? It's entirely possible that further consumption of the Mexican water could leave you on the toilet until you just about shit out your entire catalog of working internal organs and then reanimate your corpse. So there's no proof to back this up scientifically, but if you've ever experienced this, you'd know that it definitely feels like there's some kind of alien trying to violently force you to give birth to it inside your guts. It stands to reason that if it were to actually win, you'd end up a zombie. This has to be due to something in the water. Look at the shit that passes for television down there.

Remain on the safe side and avoid Mexico entirely. Not just the water, but all of it. There's nothing there worth seeing anyway. Just cartels shooting the place up, and scantily clad, obviously medically augmented women playing Jenga on TV for seven hours straight every single day. It's horrible.

God

People are always quick to thank the Lord for helping them through troubled times, win sporting events, that the light stayed green, when a test was passed, or because the new season of a reality show has been signed. However, if you look at the Bible in general, there's some pretty ominous shit in there. Quite a few zombie movies like to use that line about there being no more room in hell, the dead will rise up and walk the Earth. Well we've been to Detroit and we can say that it's already true; there's not much room left there.

Now this falls under the category of "supernatural" occurrences, and we're not huge fans of it, but why can't this be as plausible as any other reason? Despite the implications of what this may mean to the faith of certain people, it's as handy as an explanation as any other. Punishment, testing, vengeful spite, whatever the motivation behind it, being that it's of "divine" origins means that we don't have to understand it and probably never will. The only problem there is that if it happens to be the mighty reckoning of an angry omnipresence, aren't we really all fucked? That shouldn't stop you from fighting against the undead at all, but it's just a bit of wondering out loud.

Thinking on this point a bit, wouldn't just laying down and surrendering to the lack of mercy the undead will surely show be an affront to said Creator? You were given a life. It's yours to do with as you see fit. Rise up and live it, even if it means taking down just a shit-load of stinky corpses. Free will means choosing not to die that day.

Undiscovered Organisms

On this planet with us exist a multitude of organisms that are simply amazing in their diversity. Human beings walk the land on two legs, other mammals live in the sea, and some flitter overhead. We have lizards, amphibians, fish, and insects and they all share this floating rock with us. The really fun part is that we still discover thousands as we continue to inhabit the Earth we thought we knew. Sure, we have diseases and parasites and they take us down a notch every once in a while, but we always manage to fight back and minimize our total losses. It's just a matter of time before one gets really serious and tries to turn our own bodies against us in the most sinister way possible. Zombification.

There are critters of every shape and size that fit into literally every single environmental niche in the world's various ecosystems. One of them could easily be deadly to the human race, and not only that, but cause our corpses to stand up and attack the living in order to further its growth as a virus. Whether it's a virus or a parasite, or even a fungus among us, it only takes one to start the spread of infection. With a long enough dormant period for gestation, it could even infect several people who then travel before it's even discovered to be fatal. Unknowns are what make the world fun to live in, especially if you follow happenings like new species, but it's also a bit frightening to consider that something out there may just have it in for the human race. If it comes from a deep sea exploration, we'd be quick to blame dolphins. All that chattering they do sounds a bit like they're talking shit to us. We're watching you, Flipper.

So screw looking outward for a cause of the zombie apocalypse. If you look at the world around us, there's plenty of shit that wants to kill us already. From diseases to sharks and fungal growth to polar bears, if we find ourselves in the wrong place at the wrong time, death is everywhere. All it takes is some hippie to crack open some jar of concentrated zombie juice that's been buried in a rock for millions of years and next thing you know, we're fighting our friends and family because they're trying to chew on our junk. Damn nature, you scary!

The Broad Overview

So here you are, and you want desperately to learn something about the walking dead that you don't already know. Ideally this new bit of information should prove useful in such a way that may help you stop them in their shuffling tracks. Well, we're aiming to give you just that sort of knowledge. However, that's going to wait a bit. To start off, we need a bit of basic information. This book is written for the express purpose of aiding those who wish to survive a zombie apocalypse and have fun while you do it. If you wish to actually BE a zombie, just put the book down and go watch some daytime television. If you wish to know how it is that you can dismantle the undead, laugh maniacally, and continue about your existence, then please continue on. Are we all on board now with the intentions? Excellent, then we may continue. We've thrown in humor throughout the book, even when it's woefully inappropriate, in hopes that the information both before and after the funny stuff will be retained and stick with you when it's needed most. Sometimes, it's just to be sick and there's little if any redeeming knowledge worth retaining. You've been warned. Now... where to begin... Oh, OK, how about this: zombies are, for all intents and purposes, already dead. This brings about a few changes to the body, which we're going to explain so that we all know what we're going to encounter.

Those infected, once the change is completed, feel no fear of anything. They're single-minded in their pursuit of living flesh, which they consume, and thereby further spread infection. Zombies will chase down living prey, completely ignoring any threats or necrotic flesh they pass near. Attempting to frighten, amuse, or cajole the undead will gain you very little. Do not taunt the undead; this is a complete waste of time, and you'll look silly doing it. Assuming, of course, there's anyone around to see this.

The undead will not go directly for the brain; in fact they tend to go for your nice soft squishy exposed fleshy bits instead. The brain thing is a myth, and flesh makes for far easier tearing and ingesting, what without that silly skull being in the way. The consumed flesh offers neither sustenance nor nutritional value, though it is in fact Atkins-friendly. Piling flesh on top of flesh is what causes this to go down into their innards; no actual swallowing or digestion occurs, so normal functions are right out the window here. The point is, unlike your mom, they don't swallow. They will continue to feed until they actually rupture and the consumed flesh begins to spill out of the stomach and/or intestines, making for one big horrible mess. It's debatable on whether this is better or worse than an actual zombie bowel movement.

Upon first seeing the undead, you may be confused. This confusion is going to stem from the fact that you're not standing in front of an all-you-can-eat buffet at 4 PM, but there are loads of slow moving people moving in your direction anyway. These are not the elderly coming in for the early bird special. Well, it's entirely possible that it is, and if so, you'd do well to get the hell out of their way. They're just as slow moving and deadly in large groups when their senior citizen discount is compromised.

"How can this be?" you ask. Well to put it simply, the human brain is a wonderfully complex and mysterious thing. The human body is controlled by electrical impulses, which turn desire into action via signals from the brain. These pathways remain active and open even in death and are still able to be stimulated in such a way as to cause motion in the human body. All these pathways need is something inhabiting the brain that provides the little electrical spark in order to get up and walk again. Given that there are unknowns remaining in almost every part of our world, it's likely that some undiscovered parasite, chemical, or virus is what causes this expiration and reanimation. For the sake of simplification, we will refer to it as a virus. We shall name it Horatio because it sounds funny, and the idea of tiny little David Carusos running around in your head making you be all zombie-like is just great. Not really, we're just going to refer to it generically as an unnamed virus. If it helps, think of this contagion as a little taster that keeps zapping these recently deceased people in such a way as to make them want to eat your flesh.

Another thing about these foul creatures worth taking note of is that they are not subject to exhaustion. The undead require no sleep, power naps, eye resting, or any other form of recuperation. These abominable automatons exist only to feed to no good end other than infecting living human beings. This is considered an advantage they possess over us, and should be treated as such. They will walk, crawl, pound, pull, and hit without end in order to gain access to their target.

A single way exists to end their macabre time on this earth as the undead; that is accomplished by destroying the brain. Removing the head will cause the body to cease functioning, but the head will remain "alive" and still requires enthusiastic termination. You know those terribly old singers and actors that just don't want to go away even though they're so past their primes that they just make you feel sad for them, but nobody tells them that they suck now because they were cool sixty years ago? Well, it's a little bit like that. Ultimately your options are to either physically demolish the skull with brute force, or deliver a fatal shot to the head through ballistic means. "How" matters far less than actual accomplishment in regards to their permanent demise. Just split that sucker open and end the threat, smile, move on, and repeat.

Intellect

"Let me tell you, chaining your buddy who is now a zombie up inside the shed so you can get a quick game of COD on is not a good idea. Not just because they would be trying to nom you at every chance. But seriously, without higher brain function they'd be a shitty team member."

– Homeless guy outside of the post office

Though human in appearance, aside from open wounds and sagging flesh and a penchant for cannibalism, the undead retain no memories of who they were or any prior learned skills, no matter how ingrained they may have been. Only the abilities to move and attack still remain. These are basic and primitive skills, which the virus utilizes in order to spread itself with ruthless efficiency. Think of it as a means of viral reproduction on a slower, yet slightly more admirable scale that has the potential to fuck the human race so hard in the ass that it just curls up and dies as a whole. While this offers little comfort to those of us trying to combat this shambling menace, it puts things in perspective somewhat, and allows for our mental preparation in facing this type of opponent. They don't know that we know that they don't know anything. Yeah, that sounds about right.

One irrefutable fact is that zombies are no longer who they once were. There may be those among us who may end up thinking to themselves, "I know she's trying to eat my face, but I can't hurt my mommy." Bullshit you can't. OK, maybe she was awesome when she was alive; she made some badass pork chops and pineapple upside down cake, and she could drink four Russian sailors under the table without missing a beat, but that's no longer the case. All bets are off once they try to turn you into a walking steak with a bad haircut and worse personal hygiene. You saw the movie with the kid and the Indian burial ground, right? It's a bit like that little fucker, but he doesn't talk, run, use tools, or look nearly as creepy.

Your survival depends on a simple ideology: "Detach and dispatch." Forget all notions of trying to save any loved ones who've become infected; there's no way to get them back and they're totally just going to chew on you, and that's not a good way to spend your day even if you're a masochist. If they had retained anything at all about the person they used to be, it stands to reason that they wouldn't be trying to violently end your life by showing their love with their teeth and nails. Come to peace with it, say a prayer, write a song, kick a puppy, do whatever you have to do, but don't let the misconception that they're still who they were be the end of you.

Luckily for all of us, the undead are terribly stupid when it comes to doors and windows and recognizing threats. As previously stated, they are utterly fearless and will follow the living without pause. When clustered together in a huge mass the undead can seem terribly frightening, but in small groups it makes both attacking and defense far easier. In fact, it's a bit like tripping a blind kid as he walks past. Yeah, you're an asshole for doing it, but what makes it so funny is that he never saw it coming and couldn't do anything to stop it. They're no longer able to use tools or simple machines, which works out just wonderfully for us. They're more prone to the "HULK SMASH" line of thought and little else. By way of example, they're a bit like Reagan towards the end of his life once the mind started to go, with lots of groaning and bumping into shit.

If the undead should descry your location, they will flock toward you in a terrible writhing mass of groaning former-humanity. Ever see those documentaries about the siafu or carpenter ants? Those are the kinds of ants that will literally cover you and eat you asshole-first until there's nothing left but bones. Zombies are like that, except they won't die when you spray them with Raid. When this happens, it's generally not a good thing, but the up side is that this isn't some kind of shared intelligence. As active predators, zombies pay attention to what's going on around them and constantly scan about looking, listening, and sniffing for any living to become their next victim. If one spots you, chances are, it is going to moan, groan, and start to head in your direction. Once this happens others will notice you as well, and they'll all be coming in short order because they're all up in each other's business. This sort of horde-like action is another strength they possess, but it's also one that a well-prepared group can repel and use to their advantage (more on that later). Remember, they are incredibly thoughtless and easily lured to where you want and need them to be. All you need is the right bait and a bit of dazzling planning.

Yet another fine example of the intellectual void that is the living dead is their well-documented love of both reality television and Scientology. It's probably a good idea, just to be safe, to make a pre-emptive strike against anyone staring blankly at these brain-melting, un-artistic barrages of imagery or reading Dianetics. It will save you time in the long run. Now we're not saying that you should hang around the place where you bought this book and wait for people to purchase anything written by Hubbard, follow them to their cars, and beat them to death with a tire iron. That's just WAY too public of a place. Just keep an eye on them and assume that if they're not the harbingers of the zombie apocalypse, they'll likely be the first victims.

Physical Abilities

REVIEW TIME! OK, so zombies feel no fear, they don't get tired, and mentally they're a bit on the slow side. Stands to reason they must have some nifty mystical powers, right? Not at all; in fact the undead are just reanimated husks and can actually do less than an able-bodied living human being in most regards. Here is where we discuss what the undead have to work with and its limitations. You can also do the Chicken Dance, but we're not advocating such behavior, nor is it useful in any way, shape, or form.

Recognizing that the undead are, in fact, dead, they're no longer susceptible to drowning or smothering or anything that pertains to oxygen deprivation, which gives us information to work with. If you try holding the undead at the bottom of a pool in hopes that it will expire in such a fashion, you're wasting your time and crapping up your pool. If this is not your pool, that's kind of a dick move, unless you plan on cleaning it out afterwards. Hoping that the undead will go for a swim and never return likewise isn't a very good plan, and is also the lazy way out. Haven't you seen a horror movie? The threat always remains. Also, if you have sex, you're going to die, but that may be another movie, not entirely important right now anyway.

Basic overall physical strength of the ghoul is dependent upon how the muscles were trained while alive. If the newly turned zombie was a body-builder in life, he will naturally be a bit stronger than the normal guy on the street. The undead carries this brute prowess with him into undeath. We know that when a living human being uses their muscles to their capacity while working out, the muscles tear and then repair and gain in size and strength. The same thing happens with the musculature of the undead when they use theirs, only there's no repairing and rebuilding going on in their biologically effete husks. The muscles will break down over time as they get used to grab, subdue, pound, and so on. Score one for the living's ability to heal! The older the zombie, then it stands to reason the weaker they will inevitably become.

There is, however, a theory that is being debated by the writers and their intelligence-gathering counterparts regarding recent additions to the undead hordes. While they will be inhibited to the physical limitations they were stuck with in life, there is a chance they will, for a short time, have additional strength. Think of those awesome stories of guys on PCP busting their handcuffs, getting out of the back of a police car, and then beating the shit out of four cops. It'll be a little like that, except there won't be any foaming at the mouth and self-urination. This isn't due to any bit of supernatural chicanery or anything like that. The reasoning behind this line of thought is as follows: pain thresholds govern a living human to use his or her strength to a certain boundary where pain becomes an inevitable conclusion. A zombie will not be hindered by such constraints. What this means is that, conceivably, they'll push bones and musculature beyond their living limitations. In death they will be able to do more damage, but only until the bones and muscles are damaged from the strain and eventually become wasted beyond any use, as previously mentioned. Since we are of the strong opinion you shouldn't trap zombies for testing, this theory will likely never be proven, but this information may be garnered in the future through careful observation of the recently risen.

Dexterity is another area in which the undead fall short. They may have been a marathon runner in life, but once infected, toss that idea out the window. The undead shuffle slowly, only taking a step every one to two seconds, giving them around an average speed of one to three miles per hour, even slower if they've lost a leg or two. Their base motor skills are comparable to that of a small child who's gotten into the strong cough syrup shortly after waking up. Evasion of small numbers of undead should not pose a significant endeavor for a healthy and reasonably agile adult. Navigating a set of stairs proves a bit of a mess for most zombies, but it's an attainable goal in most instances. Steep grades are a bit more daunting due to this lack of coordination, and ladders are nearly impossible. Climbing a sheer surface isn't something any undead can do, but this will not stop them from mindlessly trying, and can prove a good spot to have a bit of fun with gravity. Running, jumping, and climbing trees are all tossed right out of the zombie playbook, since they fail to recognize their own ability to use these to their advantage. Passing a field sobriety test though is easily accomplished. Use this knowledge to your favor at all times.

Damage suffered by the undead goes largely ignored; the reason behind this is that they simply do not feel it. Obviously a lack of proper vital life functions has inured the pain receptors in the walking dead and, as such, injuries to the undead go completely unhealed. One of the consequences of rambling around the world in a dead body is that it fails to kick into OMGFIXIT mode, and this also works to the advantage of the survivor in many cases by slowing down our limping adversaries. The undead feel no pain at all, and as such cannot be effectively stopped by causing damage to their limbs or torso. They won't be daunted by things like a bullet to the heart or turning on horrible '80s sitcoms. Even removing the head from the body will not end the threat, as the head will still try and take chunks out of you. The undead are just fun like that.

The undead hunt the living in the same manner in which the living hunt anything else: by sight, sound, and smell. Now just how acute these senses are is a subject that is debated, but being that they become predatory in nature upon their reanimation, it's a very real possibility that these senses all become attuned to peak capacity. This would go far toward explaining their ability to hunt far more effectively than the living are able to at night. Human beings fail to use our senses to their full potential due to the fact that, generally, we're more inclined to just observe our surroundings and go back to whatever it was we were doing. There are still a good number of people though that fine-tune their senses in order to track prey in the wild. Others are just creepy guys that sit in vans across from schools, and these should be treated as the undead, and just as violently.

Zombies, it was mentioned before, have no need of oxygen at all. The only purpose that breathing serves for the undead is to allow them to use the sense of smell to hunt. It may seem a little far-fetched to think that these stupid creatures are stalking you because of your overabundance of cologne, but it will happen. If you decide to pull a double pits to chesty right before going out to do some recon, you're going to end up surrounded by women. They're dead and they want to eat you, but hey, that commercial finally turned out to be true.

In several cases it's been observed that zombies fire a stunning bolt of lightning from their posterior regions. This bolt has been noted as being able to take down a mature horse and leave it motionless for several minutes. Wait, no. You can ignore the previous two sentences, just wanted to make sure you were paying attention. That would be awesome though, right? OK so, probably not awesome so much as unfair. I mean, who wouldn't want arse lightning? Maybe Thunder Butt. We'll work on that.

While the undead are biologically inert and do not actually breathe in a meaningful manner, when they spot prey they tend to issue a very low yet piercing moan. This is recognized by other undead simply as a disturbance and will in fact serve as something of a rallying cry once something edible is recognized. The reason behind this can only be the contraction of the torso as they move. The lungs are pretty much just balloons, and air will fill the space despite lack of triggered use. Since they seem to use their sense of smell to hunt, air will move through the nose gradually filling the lungs as normal, without the additional extraction of oxygen. Compression will cause the expulsion of air, which flows over the vocal chords, causing this ghoulish call. The act of taking in air is another primal instinct; it is in no way a conscious act on the part of the undead that indicates an intelligent coordinated effort on their behalf. It's more like when you try and hide a fart but everyone notices it anyway; it's just the way the world works. These types of inane utterances can also be found among most pop music in the world today.

Another thing of note is that the undead have no significant body heat of their own which is internally produced. Without all that pesky blood flowing through their bodies, much like certain political analysts, no internal heat is generated. What this means is that, aside from the minor amount of friction-related warmth from the joints, a zombie's body temperature is going to be that which you find outdoors. As we all know, if you walk outside naked in January, you're probably going to freeze to death, but if you're dressed right, your clothing retains and reflects your body heat, and you're just fine. Not so with the undead, they simply freeze solid and wait for the ability to move to once again be granted by a nice thaw. Luckily for us, these silly creatures don't have the advantage of thermal underwear, so there's another one for humanity. Hooray for toasty junk!

Zombie on Zombie Hate-Crimes

The question has been raised in the past as to why the undead, known to notoriously devour flesh, seem to ignore the act of chewing on one another. To this end, we here at ZAP have devised something of a theory, which may go a way toward explaining this phenomenon.

New healthy cells are constantly replacing the human body's cells because they keep dying off. In fact we replace ourselves entirely about every seven years, which is why sometimes tastes change over time and good science-y shit like that. Living tissue, when deprived of oxygen, which begins to happen immediately upon expiration, starts to deteriorate with or without the presence of bacteria, which are known to aid in decomposition. Tissues undergoing this change are going to begin to give off a different olfactory fingerprint immediately, and this is on account of the change in the cellular structure that is occurring due to its lack of oxygenation. Recognizing this supports the theory that the undead retain a sense of smell, and actively use it in a predatory capacity in order to seek out living prey. They may in fact smell one another and think to themselves "rawr rawr stinky guy rawr rawr" and thus leave the other zombie alone. I've never been a zombie, so it's hard to say, but the actual process of thought or recognition there would probably be much simpler and lack quotation marks, but likely remains very similar in other respects.

The second suggestion is that perhaps the undead are able to sense our thoughts or living essence through another, as yet unidentified, sixth sense. As frightening as this thought may be, dismissal of this line of reasoning could prove a fatal decision, as it is a notorious truth that the undead are equally adept at nocturnal hunting as they are during the day. It's hard to try and rationalize that they may in fact have abilities that we do not possess ourselves, but considering the inscrutabilities of the human brain and its potential, even on the most primitive level, it's best not to overlook this idea. This would also help explain why we're unable to move about the undead freely, even masked in scent and disguised as one of their number. This may be something of an active type of ability though, because with proper utilization of stealth, wind direction, and lack of farting at inopportune times, one can conceivably avoid detection by the undead.

Another likely culprit of what may well cause this "ESP" is what is known as Jacobson's Organ. Found in a majority of vertebrates, this is utilized in order to detect pheromone signatures left by other members of the species, as well as other species, and this is also found in human beings but widely regarded to be vestigial. Contrary to this information, however, pregnant women often report of a heightened sense of taste and smell that could be directly linked to this particular organ given the heightened hormone levels present during this time. The undead could conceivably be making use of this due to an unrestricted neural pathway that they have access to, even though humans largely do not. Perhaps the virus unlocks many of the primitive reptilian skills we once had but unfortunately lost touch with.

Zombie group interactions are limited to their horde-like movement toward a target, and, in these instances, are the only times you'll see an actual physical interplay between the undead. This is not a social gathering, as bumping into each other doesn't exactly constitute a hootenanny, though it does offer us the rare bit of observation of zombie on zombie violence. In their natural efforts to lay hands on their prey, the undead will attempt to bite, claw, and scratch their way through any obstacles which bar their path. This includes the other ghouls in the immediate vicinity. The weaker of these may fall victim to horrible injuries from their ghoulish brethren, though fatal injuries are unlikely. If there's one thing nature has provided us with, it's a damn hard skull, and clawing and biting aren't likely to do the job required to incapacitate the human brain, even if it is contained inside of an undead husk.

Infection and You

"You know, I think I know what causes most men to become zombies. Cleavage. Yep, that's right, a pair of boobs staring out from inside a tight shirt, dress or whatever. Instant death sentence for most men. Much like causing earthquakes around the world. Boobs can cause the apocalypse."
– Gandhi?

Now this entire thing can only happen if one animated undead shit sucking zombie manages to infect a living human being, and they infect another and so on. You may in fact want to know how such a thing can occur. Any sort of fluid transfer, such as a bite, can cause this, or perhaps their having dripped congealed blood onto an open wound, into the mouth or eye, or having sex with one of the Disney kids not in rehab after (maybe even before) infection. It transfers from the undead to the living. The idea that the actual deceased rise from the grave is just silly, and doesn't happen unless some crazy doctor gathers body parts and sews them together and straps them to a table and lightning strikes it. No, wait; I think they already made a book for that and possibly a movie or two. Or that's Ron Perlman, I'm not too sure. Moving on, a virus needs a living host on which to adhere to, and a dead brain lacks that certain spark which it finds so attractive and necessary. Also the brain, after rotting a little bit, tends to look a bit like jelly left out in the sun on a very hot day, and who wants any of that? You can't even make that look good with extra chunky peanut butter.

So, for the sake of argument, let's suppose that someone who's reading this does in fact get infected. What should you expect? What can you do? Did Han shoot first or was it Greedo? Let's ignore that last question. Well, the virus that has infected the body pretty much causes a terrible flu-like thing to happen, after which you die and then reanimate within a period of four to twenty-four hours, dependent upon severity of initial infection. Hopefully not you, but who else would be reading it that fits this scenario perfectly? Who can tell with these things?

First signs of infection are going to manifest as something akin to a crappy summer cold. You're going to feel very much like someone forced you to listen to club music for three days straight and beat your head with a sack of potatoes. Then the fever arrives, and things are really going to suck because you're going to want to just hurry up and die. Once the fever breaks though, you're going to feel just fine, and fall into a deep, coma-like sleep. Luckily for you, that's pretty much the end. Not so lucky for your friends and/or family who now have to kill you for coming back as a zombie, though, is it? Bad survivor; no doughnut for you!

Your overall best bet is to avoid becoming infected, because it *really* screws up your plans for not becoming a flesh-craving cannibalistic viral puppet. If you do in fact find yourself infected, your one and only hope of getting out of this situation is by halting the spread of the virus. Unfortunately the hasty application of a tourniquet and removal of the limb will likely not stop the infection, but will, at best, slow it down a minuscule amount. The only way to decisively halt the reanimation process is by destroying your own brain so that the virus never gets a chance to take hold. The fastest way to do this is by reading translated transcripts of Mexican soap opera hospital scenes, but a bullet to the head will suffice if you're in a real hurry and would rather not endure that kind of unimaginable agony, and let's face it, you probably wouldn't have time.

One point worth mentioning is the exclusivity of the reanimation in regards to human beings. By no means are humans the only creatures able to incur the virus that causes this horrible condition, but we are in fact the only ones that will, as a consequence of infection, return as zombies once we expire. Animals great and small have an instinctual avoidance of this virus, which causes them to flee from anyone infected and attempt to save themselves. Perhaps it's because anything other than a human, which comes into contact with this affliction, simply dies and is no more. It has been theorized that the virus causes a cessation of life functions in other organisms too quickly, and the infection is never able to get a proper grip on their brains. Now the down side to this is that we won't be getting any immediate help from mother nature on cleaning up these undead once we put them down; the up side is that we won't have to worry about safeguarding ourselves from crazed zombie sharks, chipmunks, butterflies, and lambs, and sloths, and carp, and anchovies, and orangutans, and fruit bats, and breakfast cereals and so on.

Worried about the infection hanging around possibly in the plants, soil, or water supplies? No real need for that kind of concern, because once the host has expired in one fashion or another (like you blow its damn head off) the virus seems to die off after a couple days. The only real vexation at that point is the remaining husks left behind to rot by natural means. As with plagues of the past, the bodies of the fallen are going to be biohazards like you wouldn't believe, and will be in need of disposal. If you don't want to wait for that pesky virus to kill itself off like a sad little emo kid outside a trendy mall boutique that hasn't opened yet, the safest and most direct way to go about this will, of course, be our good friend fire. Fire eliminates all traces of the infection upon contact. In regards to the undead, total body immolation is required, which takes several hours and in some cases days; steaks, however, can be seared to preferred levels in just two to five minutes per side, depending upon grill temperature. Baked potatoes take much longer, so wrap them in foil and start them early. Avoiding contact with any of the bodily fluids and burning the corpses down to ash presents zero risk of airborne infection becoming a threat. It probably won't be a good idea to roast marshmallows over the flames though; that's just bad decorum.

SECTION 2
CLASSIFYING OUTBREAK LEVELS

"I've been noticing a new possible threat. They live on the Jersey Shore, sometimes Florida. I'm convinced they are all zombies. Or at the very least the largest source of herpes on the planet. I think those who watch the show may be zombies as well. Definitely herpes patients. Be warned."

– Overheard from a guy on bath salts

So what kind of mess are we looking at here? We're going to cover the four basic classes of outbreak from small to large and what constitutes each. It's fairly simple and straightforward, and though I know you're just itching to get to the good stuff, let's first concentrate on knowing what to prepare for. Any outbreak can be radically different, given where it takes place and panic levels of the population and so on, but let's face it; it's still an outbreak. You don't want to go out and swat flies with an elephant gun, though a gun that shoots elephants could be thoroughly awesome. I digress, oh yeah, elephant levels... wait, no... outbreak levels, let's begin.

ZED

Level 1: Just a Small Town Plague

A very small outbreak among a very limited populace, level one outbreaks are the easiest to end because there just aren't enough bodies to really be a concern. These will happen with very small numbers, anywhere from one to a couple dozen zombies, and will be limited to isolated and extremely rural settings. These are generally unreported and go unnoticed because the folks in these areas are going to recognize the threat, put it down, and then never speak of it again much like certain unnecessary movie sequels. This could take anywhere from hours to weeks to be put down, but it should prove a fairly simple task to do for an organized and well-armed group. The preferred weaponry isn't always available, and as such it will take more time to put the dead to bed, but it's still an attainable goal. The amount of living brought down should be minimal if any at all. Then again they could be ignorant yokels and just end up as a bunch of walking corpses which will lead us to the next stage.

Level 2: A Little Closer to Home

These tend to happen in coastal regions that hold cities and towns. Now the severity is a bit higher, on the order of a dozen to around a hundred undead will pop up in the span of hours due to a lack of understanding and subsequently spread infection. On the other hand, these shouldn't last much longer than a standard small outbreak because increased population precipitates greater response. The chances that these attacks will be picked up by a news source are decent, though they may be reported in such a way to be misconstrued as riots or gang activity or even civil disobedience. The outbreak in a marginally more urban area would be fairly confined at first, whereas in a rural and less populated setting the problem can extend for a good number of miles outward from the initial source. There may be state/local police and/or military mobilization in the event of a level two outbreak. If there is any official response, you may certainly feel free to offer to assist however you can; if it's not accepted, however, just stay out of their way and let these men and women do their jobs. Don't be Johnny Two-Balls trying to ride in and save the day. They hate that shit.

Level 3: Yeah, It's About Time to Panic a Little

This is where things begin to seriously go bump in the night and it's time for the brown pants. A level three outbreak is thought to be an occurrence that begins as a result of boy-band concerts; this is where the reality of the situation will hit home for most of us. The undead will be in vast numbers here, literally hundreds to thousands, and cover huge tracts of land covering multiple municipalities. This situation's a little more difficult to unfuck. There will be a clear military presence involved in this type of epidemic, and the press will hover thicker than flies at a barbeque. There will be no mistaking the threat we face in a crisis of these proportions. Even in the event of a full media blackout, there are going to be far too many victims and witnesses for it to remain suppressed giving you time to get where you need to be. Should travel restrictions, martial law, food/water rationing and *Welcome Back Kotter* marathons be imposed, this information will still find a way to get out. Those who find themselves inside these areas would do well to stay home where it's safe, and rely on their own resources for a time as opposed to going out and looking for help. Let the help find you instead. Just hope that back up arrives before the undead do. The worse situation here would be if maybe our military were all deployed overseas and there was a minimal response to the threat, which could very well be the end of things barring a swift and organized response from the populace.

Level 4: What's That on the Fan and Why Does It Smell?

Duck and cover! What equates to total Armageddon; the undead are here to stay it seems. A complete breakdown of social order will ensue, and initial attempts by the military will have proven dreadfully unsuccessful in halting the shambling menace. The lovely after-effects such as looting, riots, murder, and brazenly singing musical numbers in the streets will occur, the participants of which will most likely become among the number of undead. All major metropolitan areas will have succumbed to infection almost entirely, and there will literally be more dead walking than the living. This is NOT good. Almost all manufacture of supplies will have stopped and you're left with what you can beg borrow and steal. Think a world like *Mad Max*; now think it groaning and with a limp. OK, so the undead won't be driving cars, and the vast majority won't be wearing a hockey mask, imploring you to throw wide your doors and allow them entry, but you get the idea. Chaos will become a normal part of the daily routine, and it's going to be unlike anything anyone could have dreaded or dreamed of. The one positive note here is that, despite all that's going on, as long as you stay alive there is hope. Plus you've got this neat little guide that's going to walk you through the survival process. Aren't you a lucky little somebody?

Identifying Outbreaks Before They Become an Overwhelming Problem

"A new threat has emerged: it's the football scandal information zombie. Beware of these guys, as they're sneaky; they pose as journalists! So if you see a news crew, just assume they're infected and run the other way while screaming YOU WON'T INFECT ME, NEWS SCUM!!!"

– News Anchor That Was Really There

1. **Social networking sites:** A recent phenomenon in our internet-savvy world is the ability to constantly update our goings on and all things inane that cross our minds. These can often prove invaluable, assuming you can sort through the bullshit and discern what is valuable intelligence and what's just gibberish.

2. **The media:** While these tend not to always be entirely accurate or impartial, newspapers and television can provide subtle hints that can clue you in to a possible outbreak before it reaches your neck of the woods. Murders labeled as satanic rites or cannibalistic in nature can provide you with a bit of warning that you can take note of and follow daily. Specifics you'll be looking for are anything to do with bludgeoning, shooting, or removal of the head. If this occurs anywhere along the US/Mexico border, it's probably just the cartel saying hi to someone.

3. **Youtube:** The chances that a video found here regarding someone "climbing in your windows and snatching your people up" as being related to zombies is remote. Sadly the inundation of the video-sharing sites with rubbish as opposed to something beneficial is

simply too staggering to make searching a worthwhile use of time in regards to identifying a true outbreak.

4. **Looking out your window:** This is where being nosey can finally pay off. If you're one who looks out their window or peephole when you hear a car door or footsteps, you'll finally be earning your keep. If you start noticing people walking in an ungainly fashion, and they're covered in blood or horribly wounded, you win a prize for being observant. You may just have gotten the early warning you needed to survive.

5. **Monitoring specific sites that relate directly to the possibility of a zombie apocalypse:** Yes, boys and girls, there are a few of us who actively look for this kind of information so you don't have to. We here at *Zombie Apocalypse Preparation* do have our ears to the ground, and would like to clue you into a few of our illustrious counterparts who do the same in hopes of keeping humanity from becoming living-impaired.

Should you come across any information which you think indicates an outbreak, you should immediately begin noting the when and where. How far away is this? What number of people are reported as hurt or killed? In doing so, estimate that an infection can travel outward at about fifty miles an hour, the same as the average rate of travel by car, unless you're a lead-footed psychopath like me and then it's close to seventy. Some of those who have become infected will not know what it is they're carrying, and will surely manage to conceal their wounds long enough to start spreading it around. This isn't something most people are prepared to handle. As soon as this trips your sensors, get in contact with your group. Get everyone ready. Call in sick—tell them that Aunt Flappy-Tits is battling bulimia and everyone wants you to head to the intervention. Whatever it takes, be prepared to move when you have to.

SECTION 3
WEAPONS!

Having the right equipment when dismantling these cannibalistic automatons can make a world of difference between who ends up dead. Is it going to be them or will it be you? Once they've turned into zombies, they will no longer have compassion or mercy and, as such, it stands to reason that you shouldn't waste time harboring these emotions either. At least you shouldn't toward the undead. In addition to your new "Kill Em All" attitude, you're going to need the gear to save your rear. Now this, by no means, indicates that you should be loading yourself down and running out like Johnny Two-Balls to save the world all by your lonesome. In fact, this section should instill quite the opposite line of thought. Your main purpose is to stay alive so that you can fight another day.

This section is going to highlight pros and cons of each weapon, and should in no way be taken to mean that you simply MUST use one or another. Most of these implements of destruction were designed with stopping a living human being in their tracks in mind, not the undead, and, as such, they must be viewed specifically in their ability to cause proper physical damage to the head and brain. As we run down the possible uses, think what will best suit your style and ability. Just because we say that one thing's better than the other at something, doesn't mean that you can't use it in such a fashion; it just means that having tried and tested these weapons, or witnessed their capabilities, these are our findings. Go with what you know, use it well, and stay alive.

Basic Good Ideas Regarding Your Equipment

Well, people have just gone and screwed the pooch. Some vile shit was unleashed on mankind and somebody got infected, and then tainted someone else and so on. People got bitten, they died, then they got up, and THEN they had the audacity to try and chew on your favorite body parts. This is rude and unacceptable, and you need to put an end to it cold, hard, and fast. What should you use though? What all should you have available? Hopefully we'll be able to shed a bit of light on this for everyone and maybe even make a few helpful suggestions. Who knows? Well, let's first go over some basic guidelines, no matter what you do, who you are, or where you come from. Really this part's good; read it, unless you're listening to the audio-book version, in which case you're lazy readers. Technically, an audio book doesn't count as actually reading any more than listening to an English rock band makes you English. Unless of course you're already English, in which case the preceding statement is inadmissible. Geez, pick up a book and turn off the TV once in a while.

"So you've got your plan, you've got your equipment. Now all you're waiting on is the world to end. Which can get kind of boring. So, I suggest you buy a paintball gun and practice on neighborhood kids. I know it's cruel, but at least they're moving targets. Good practice because they're faster than your average zed. "

– Gryant Bumble

A) Is There Weakness In Your Technique?

Whatever it is you choose to implement as your tool(s) of destruction, use it well. To this end, train, train, and train some more. Your survival depends on your knowledge of and skill with your weapons, and, as such, you should be sure to handle them as deftly as a chef handles a knife. OK maybe not the drunk lady that just about took her own thumb off on that show, but other chefs that still have all their fingers and didn't attend AA meetings. Back to the point here, being able to depend on your use of these tools is of paramount importance and it should be treated as such. Grabbing a gun and firing at a target with your eyes closed, just hoping that because you're the good guy, things will fall down, isn't going to cut it. Go to the range, set up targets about half the width of the human head. This will allow you a margin of error in times of stress. Once you're comfortable with that, increase the range with all your weapons to a maximum effective range. This increases your difficulty with the practice, so that, later, a head looks like a huge target. If your weapon is melee in nature, use a coconut. Those will approximate the density of a human skull. Wear yourself out, rest, and do it again. Inch thick wood and pig skulls are also an acceptable substitution for the resistance you'll encounter. Become efficient in the utilization of your weaponry and tools and practice an economy of motion so that it becomes a fluid dance of death. (Insert evil laughter here.)

B) Is that Rust?

Take care of the tools that take care of you. This part cannot be stressed enough. Maybe if I typed in all caps it could be stressed more, but I'm not going to be that guy. The editor might though. Anyway, your care for your weaponry is extremely important in regards to being able to rely on them, and they're not going to clean themselves. Blades need to be sharp and oiled, guns need to be cleaned regularly with or without frequent use, and keep those toenails trimmed. OK, so that last part is your own personal business, but seriously, what are you, a koala? That aside, a dirty gun is likely to foul up at an inopportune moment, and in a zombie apocalypse, any time is a bad time for a jam or a misfire. Spending time clearing a jam could lead to a potential case of tooth rape. This doesn't mean you should plunk down when out and about and start cleaning your weapon in the middle of an undead kill-fest. You should have done that where it was safe to do so. Don't be a smart ass, Captain Koala-toes.

C) Did You Buy that at a Flea Market?

If the answer to the above question is yes, then don't expect that it's going to be much use keeping you bite-free when trying to use it against the undead. 100 years ago, you could walk into any craftsman's business and have a sword fit to your stance, swing, and ability. This is simply not the case any longer. Silly display-only items are not going to be able to withstand the rigors of actual combat application. They're made for sitting above the fireplaces of those who want to appear worldly without having actually been anywhere or ever used a real blade. When buying a sword, you're most likely to get a pressed blade, which is either too brittle to use as a fighting weapon, or worse, too soft. With that said, make sure you're buying items from reputable dealers and/or blacksmiths and not the home shopping channels. I don't care what you've seen on the Internet, you simply are not buying a quality battle ready sword for anything short of a grand. Don't read this and say "Johnny Two-Balls got an awesome katana on the Internet for a dollar plus shipping." If it is a true katana, and he paid a dollar for it, it was stolen and its rightful owner will come and kill Johnny and take it back. Those are very expensive, very old, very one-of-a-kind types of blades. If you're going to acquire weapons, do it the right way from the right sources. There are still very skilled craftsmen in the world that put their heart and soul into their art. Find them, talk with them, pay them, and walk away happy and confident.

D) Don't Get Yourself Arrested Trying To Be Prepared

Being prepared for the worst-case scenario is the best thing you can possibly do, but getting a visit from the cops as a result is not something anyone wants to do. So your living room looks something like a compact version of a Marine armory? That's legal in many states, but, excuse me, do you have a permit for that grenade launcher? How about that twenty-foot concrete wall? Excuse me, sir, but where did you get that tank? Next thing you know you're in jail becoming very close with a massive cell-mate, and wouldn't you know it? Zombies. Well that's what you get for being a little overzealous. Make sure you're avoiding stepping on any legal toes when putting together what's needed for holding down your fort. A little bit of law research goes a long way in regards to what's a "go" and what's a "no." Don't let yourself become what equates to canned zombie-chow on account of a minor technicality and a nervous rookie cop. Besides, with a little luck, who knows what you'll find when you're combing the zombie-strewn landscape for useful items?

E) Get to Walking

"I know, you're all ready to step on some caps and bust some wigs, and get the apocalypse off to a homicidal start. But seriously, you're going to need more than cardio training in order to be the ruthless killing machine you imagine yourself as. So, along with the dance lessons, I suggest some strength training."

– Fisherman F. Thompson

The best thing you can do is start getting in shape. I know that round is a shape, and that's a fine joke, but when the time comes, you're going to need strength, speed, and endurance to have a chance at survival. I'm not talking about rushing out and becoming a marathon runner or even having a testicle removed and riding in the Tour-De-Foreign-Country, but getting prepared now is something we should all do. Join a martial arts class, maybe pick up an old Tae-fu video and sweat to some oldies. Whatever it is, get the heart rate up, and think to your self how much better off you'll be when you're having to move at a constant fast walk away from the undead. Working already, isn't it? Nope, you're still sitting there and reading this. I suppose that's acceptable, but afterward, go outside. It's nice, or not. I'm not a fucking omniscient weatherman.

F) Fear Does Not Exist In This Dojo

Keeping control of yourself is going to become critical in all stages of the zombie apocalypse. Having lost several friends, family members, pets, your favorite Zippo, and those really nice socks that you liked so much and kept your toes all toasty warm without making your feet sweat and get all stinky, you may tend to get a bit aggravated. Don't let this take control of you. Instead, use it to fuel the cold and methodical fire that keeps you going, surviving and eliminating the undead. Who else is going to make sure that those horrible Hollywood remakes never again see the light of day? Find new friends, organize, gear up, and head out in a methodical fashion. Always be aware of your group and your surroundings. Look carefully and listen closely. Stay frosty and stay alive.

Firearms, EEEEE! GIMMIE!

"OK, so everyone's always on about this craptastic double tap rule from a comedy movie. Problems with that, and there are many, so I'll limit myself. One: ammo will be very short in supply since factories will stop. Also to shoot every zombie twice you'll have to carry twice as much ammo. So, unless you're a pack mule with a genie, this is a horrible idea. One bullet, one brain destroyed."

– Fred Rodgers

In the effort to not reach out and touch a dead someone, we present to you the most formidable beasts in your potential ranged arsenal. Here we're going to go over each type of bangy-goodness you have available as an option as a consumer of goods and services in this wonderful world of ours. So without further ado, first up we have...

The Ever-Popular Handgun

The good ol' U.S. of A. is known for big cars, bratty movie stars, reality television, fast food, Wyoming, and a gun in every home. The hand-held weapon personifies this in stellar fashion. Presently a multi-billion dollar industry, handguns are produced in record numbers and sold just about everywhere. They've been a part of American history almost since its very founding, and there's no reason to think that they won't continue to be so well into the zombie apocalypse. They're not really the route you would want to take as a primary firearm, but they make one hell of a handy backup. While they're relatively light and easy to carry, the ammunition may not be when everything is loaded up together. Their accuracy is limited both by barrel length and the skill of the one using this compact instrument of destruction. While a highly trained marksman can use a handgun at a moderate range to truly devastating effect, the average weekend-warrior shouldn't pride himself on lofty accomplishments of hitting a stationary target at the shooting range twice per year. This being said, a handgun should be used in short-range situations where space, time, and options are limited. In desperate times, putting the barrel against the ghoul's head and pulling the trigger takes little effort or skill and does a fine job of ending the immediate threat. The capacities of these weapons vary depending on your choice of semi-automatic or revolver, but the short version here is that in the wrong situation, it will never be too much, but it could just be enough.

When considering your side arm of choice, bigger is not always better. Think how awesome it would be to unload into a swarm of undead with a .50 caliber hand-howitzer. This sounds awesome, right? Not so much. The idea in preparing is to have the equipment before everything goes bad, and these kinds of guns are simply a waste of your resources. They're heavy, expensive, and the ammunition alone is just terribly not worth the price. Cranium-piercing power can be found in the much lower caliber and thus price range. Also the ammunition for these more modest weapons tends to be far less bulky, heavy, and expensive. Another thing of note is that the larger the weapon does not equate to ease of use.

Let's also explore the advantages of both the revolver and the semi-automatic. First off, we have the oldie but goldie: the revolver. Topping the list is simplicity. There are generally no safeties to disengage on a revolver, and there are far less moving parts, allowing for easier maintenance and cleaning. The revolver is the traditionally more powerful of the two due to its more sturdy construction and, as such, has greater overall stopping power. Many types of revolvers can load different types of ammunition, such as .357 magnums/.38 specials, .44 magnum/.44 specials, and .45 colt/.410 shotgun shells. Just check with the manufacturer on these specifications. Another key point is that sights on revolvers are fixed, and in theory this would allow greater accuracy. Finally we have reliability. Every heard of having to clear a chamber on a revolver because of a jam? Neither have I.

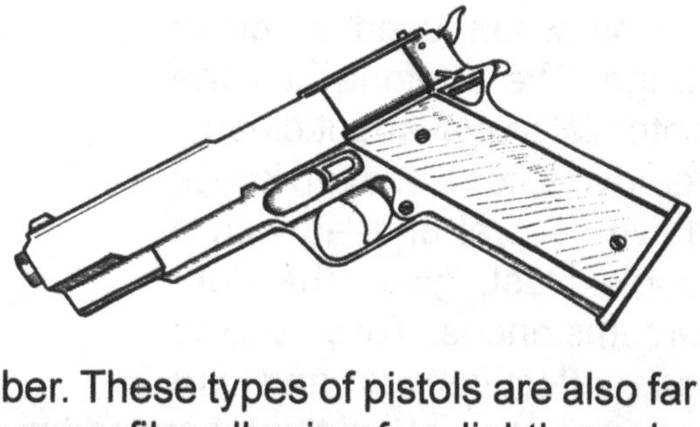

Semi-automatics do boast an increased ammunition capacity over their 5-8 shot revolving cousins. Typically these hold between 7-10 bullets in a clip and one can be slid into the chamber. These types of pistols are also far lighter and have a slimmer profile, allowing for slightly easier carrying, both concealed and otherwise. Semi-autos tend to be on the relatively quiet side, as well as having the ability to properly take advantage of a suppressor, which can be a lifesaver when it comes to avoiding detection. Another notable example of a semi-automatic pistol's advantage is the compact carrying of additional ammunition. Held in pre-loaded magazines, these take up far less room and hold more bullets than bulky speed loaders needed for revolvers, and these also decrease overall reload time, translating into faster killing times.

Of course there are the accessories, which can increase the accuracy of even the most untrained gunslingers. Most notably, the laser sight, which has the potential to turn a total novice into Billy the Kid. However these require a power source, which is, of course, finite and does nothing to teach proper marksmanship. Also, a laser sight does nothing whatsoever to stop one's hands from shaking uncontrollably and sending a round wide, missing or simply damaging the undead to no ill effect, but more on this later. Once again, keep your pistol at hand, but for backup purposes only.

The Shotgun

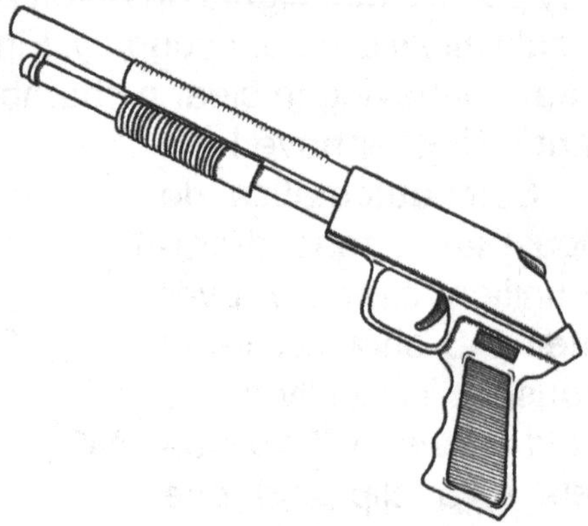

Shotguns are the all-time commanders of crowd control. These little beauties do indeed pack a mighty wallop when used at close range. The shotgun has the potential to just about cleanly remove a head or even knock down several undead with a single blast, given the right circumstances. They tend to lose effectiveness and are not very good at anything beyond ten yards when facing large numbers of zombies. Slugs have no dispersal pattern, but work quite effectively at range. However, there are better weapons for this purpose. Despite all that, these give us yet another wonderful way to deal death in close quarters. The only real drawback to these grand little devices is that they're rather hefty, and the ammo takes up a ton of space when packed for moving fast. Perhaps a member of your group could have one of these handy for a quick escape, or it can be utilized for crowd control. All things considered, they have their purpose, but there are better ways to make the undead stop following you in a hurry.

Bolt and Lever-Action Rifles

So in terms of what we have available today, these are pretty antiquated and rarely used outside of hunting and the odd bit of target shooting. In fact, if you flash one of these, the chances are you're going to be laughed at by the cool kids with the automatics, but what do they know? These elegant weapons, in use against the undead, are the bee's knees. They do tend to have a very limited ammo capacity, but these things are for starting off your undead-pickings from a moderate distance, and doing so accurately. Having to take one shot at a time causes you to be deliberate with your actions as well as your aim. Being of a more simple nature and of a kinder, gentler time, they take away that pesky little desire to throw your weapon into overdrive and potentially waste valuable ammo by panicking and missing your targets. Ammunition is available just about anywhere, and should be an easily stocked and carried item when in your chosen dwelling or when you're on the move. Additionally, older models have the solid wooden stocks and can be used, extraordinarily effectively, in a melee capacity when forced into such a situation. Utilized properly in this manner, they can easily be used as a bludgeon without compromising the weapon's integrity. Overall, these simple yet deadly weapons make a wonderful choice for a primary firearm. You can name yours Charlene.

Semi-Automatic Rifles

The backbone of the U.S. military for millions of years... OK, only about forty, but these absolutely beautiful devices are the epitome of zombie-slaying goodness. Actually, if there's a word which describes how awesome these things are while blowing apart a zombie's head, everyone should shout it mid-coitus. Brought into the military forefront to replace the slower reloading bolt-action rifle, these were modern marvels of their time. Sturdily built military models were designed with not only accuracy in mind, but hand-to-hand combat use. Many are still in production and widely available on the market today. The semi-automatic rifle first saw combat use in WWII, and were relied upon heavily as the workhorses of the infantry for decades. Since these types of rifles will automatically expel the spent round and chamber the next, remaining calm is essential. Not giving in to the desire to rapid-fire your weapon until empty will require a bit of restraint. Take your time, feel the target, and then make it stop moving with a well-placed round to the head. Ammunition is a little smaller than many other rifles, and widely sold throughout the U.S.A. making its pre-apocalypse stockpiling a little easier. Always a fine example of a choice primary firearm in your battle of survival against the undead, the semi-automatic rifle can be your best friend. Take good care of these and they'll take good care of you.

Heavy Machine Guns

In conventional warfare, these are indeed handy tools to have for our boys in uniform. They can lay down a devastating line of lead that is largely unmatched on the field of battle. Unfortunately when facing an undead opponent, this is largely without a practical use. Generally utilized to provide suppression fire against a foe that doesn't want to be shot, these metal-spitting monsters are woefully inaccurate without laying down bursts, which in a world of little production and much fighting, becomes a complete waste of ammo. Why bother with shooting off multiple rounds when one from a carbine will give the same result? Sure, the heavy machine gun can rip a human being in half with a few well-placed shots, but this won't prove the same type of deterrent to the walking dead who care nothing for themselves or their fellow ghouls. Couple with this the fact that the expended amount of ammunition is far greater than that needed to take the time to place an accurate headshot, and what you have left is a very heavy club that has a heavy damage potential without any true damage being realized against the shambling menace. Also included in this category is the mini-gun. All a mini-gun amounts to is a heavy machine gun that wastes three times as many rounds. These weapons are very cumbersome to say the least and the ammunition isn't readily available at all in a commercial setting. The heavy machine gun is absolutely lovely to hear, but terribly impractical to implement. In short, though very eye-catching and grim-looking, avoid these enchanting instruments of debauchery when combating the undead.

Submachine Guns

In recent years the SMG has begun to rival the pistol in terms of being an American mainstay. Originally designed to shoot pistol rounds at a higher rate of fire, submachine guns offer the control of a pistol in close quarters and the high rate of fire found in assault rifles. These often come with a folding shoulder stock for additional control and accuracy. Their compact nature also provides ease of use as opposed to their larger counterparts, allowing for a more inviting shooting experience. Like its much bigger brother, the heavy machine gun, the problem comes into play regarding ammo used versus undead being dispatched. One could certainly justify carrying one that shares an ammunition type with their pistol of choice, as they would be interchangeable. Doing so, and keeping this weapon set to single-shot, would help conserve your limited ammunition resources and, once again, promote the methodical placement of your supersonic projectiles. A major drawback though is the limited accurate range of these weapons. Sharing basically what equates to a pistol's range hardly puts it in another category, but it has the ability to go to a fully automatic setting (with some models), and the stock adds stability, so these traits do indeed set it apart. You can also slap a silencer on it to cut down on noise and maintain stealth when it's needed the most. All things considered, you could choose it as a primary or as a back up piece of hardware, depending on the situation, but it's not recommended. Either way, keep it off automatic.

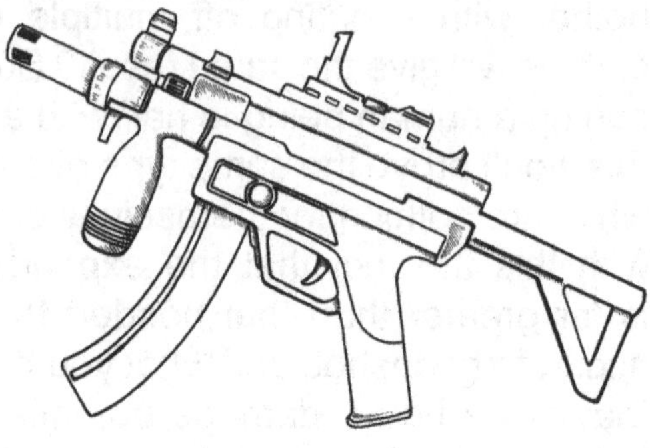

Assault Rifles

Well now who doesn't just love the good old trusty assault rifle? Well, I don't, but I'm not asking myself questions because that would be silly. Filling the chasm between the heavy machine gun and the trusty old rifle, the assault rifle has the rapid-fire capability of the former and the range and accuracy of the latter. These swiftly firing dynamos very much represent the ultimate in potential of losing self-control and going full-tilt bat shit crazy with automatic fire. Wasteful ammunition expenditure is a constant problem with these engineered executioners, unless of course one keeps their wits about them. For this reason, this weapon may not be a good idea for those afflicted with ITS (itchy trigger-finger syndrome).

Now by way of example, the rifle designed by Mikhail Kalashnikov in the mid 1940s, and implemented into service by the Soviet military in 1949, remains one of the best, most durable, and most reliable weapons on the planet. There are several variants of the AK-47, many of which equal its predecessor in all aspects, and are purchased around the world on a daily basis.

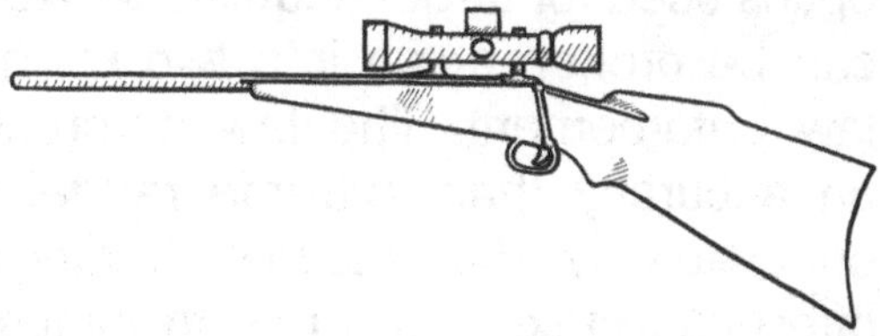

The original design required the new weapon be dependable despite the harsh Soviet landscape. Mud, snow, sand, and dirt cause zero problems with this weapon's ability to function. Produced with the idea of having to be cleaned with gloves on due to freezing temperatures, these are quite easy to maintain and keep in top working condition. However, accuracy has always been an issue with the Kalashnikov rifles, but more recent designs have vastly improved upon this early design flaw and greatly increased the exactitude of the fired round. Domestic-made assault rifles are presently the standard issue of our armed forces, and these weapons have a bit more accuracy, if not reliability in adverse conditions. Though you can always count on a problem being fixed as it arises, such is the way of the US military and its hardware suppliers. If at all possible, base your choice on availability of ammunition and ease of use. As a primary firearm, assault rifles do have potential; just don't go all wacky haywire with the option of going fully automatic. One shot should do the job admirably.

The Sniper Rifle

Here we have the holy grail of long-range awesomeness. The sniper rifle, also known as the battle rifle, first came into its own during the Civil War, when someone thought it would be a cool idea to put a telescope on an old Whitworth rifle and see what kind of damage they could do. When he started pulling 800 yard kills on Union officers, that's about when people started to take notice. Since that time there have been major advances in not only the rifles themselves, but also the optics used for target acquisition. Now our modern sniper rifles can be broken down into two major categories: military and law enforcement. The law enforcement type focuses more on accuracy than extreme range, where military leans the opposite way. The reasoning behind this is that military snipers often use maximum range to minimize risk of exposure, and thus ensure a stealthy kill without unacceptable risk. Having explored this, let's get to how these weapons can help you against the undead.

Provided you're able to acquire one of these beauties, once again, check for availability of ammunition for your model. One can't snipe without ammo. Well, you can try, but getting a zombie in your sights and then saying "pew pew" isn't going to be very effective. Now laying your hands on police-/military-issued weaponry isn't going to be something that just anyone can do, nor do we recommend trying it. This would just end very badly. Training for proper employment in these services is required and can be sought through various organizations both private and military in nature. It takes a steady hand and ability to gauge not only distance, but also wind speed and temperature as well as shoe size. Shoe size? What the hell? OK, we'll just move on. Being able to properly estimate distance and variations of the wind will enable you to dial in on the enemy form and allow you to engage in the most rewarding of zombie-slaying mantras which is "one shot, one kill." It takes time, patience, and a cool head to learn your most effective ranges and how to make these various adjustments, but doing so will allow for a much greater chance of survival.

If you're not able to get a hold of a proper sniper rifle, there are innumerable weapons in your local hunting/sporting goods store which can be just as deadly and effective when faced with the daunting task of mowing down the undead from the safety of a nice out-of-reach spot. Hunting rifles are the civilian versions of these long-distance lords of destruction, and can be found along with plentiful ammunition just about anywhere guns are sold. These fall into bolt-action and semi-automatic categories, but have longer barrels for longer ranged shooting. They can easily be fitted with a scope and sighted by professionals for an additional fee. Knowing how to go about this on your own is something we recommend you become familiar with. Accurate use of these shootin'-irons allows one to safely take an active part in dismantling the undead menace, one headshot at a time. One dedicated, barricaded, and well-stocked human being can make one fine dent in the numbers of undead using one of these rifles. Now imagine thousands of these people all supporting each other. Yes indeed, there is potential there and with that in mind, making use of a hunting/sniper rifle as your primary weapon should definitely be high on your to-do list.

BB and Pellet Guns

While these are indeed worthwhile pest repellants in terms of protecting your garden from being riddled with cat poop, discount their use against the undead entirely. Really, you're just being ridiculous at this point. They do have the ability to get lodged in, and, in rare cases, penetrate the skull, but it's a long shot that you really don't want to find yourself depending on. Using them for waking up your fellow survivors could be fun though.

Firearm Accessories

While there are many different makes and models of handguns and rifles out there, there are an equal number of accessories for these weapons. These can cover a vast range in price and legality, and once again it's best to do a bit of research. Never do you wish to wind up with anything that perhaps doesn't fit, is too complicated, or worse yet, illegal. Keeping small animals for purposes of muffling the sound of gunfire is, I'm pretty sure, illegal. Even if it's not, it's just not cool.

Scopes

These handy dandy little tools can make all but the most distant undead seem to be standing in front of you waiting to be brutally dispatched. The effectiveness and magnification of these devices vary greatly, but a little help from an expert can get you what you need to do the deed.

Regular old optics are tried and true, but can leave you feeling a bit blind in the dark, and to that end we have night-vision scopes. Just like the normal scope, but green. These are geared toward light-amplification, and can make the night a little less spooky when trying to keep an eye on the darkened horizon. The only real downside to this sort of technology is its requirement of a power source, which you may certainly stock up on in the event you choose to purchase this despoiler of night-blindness.

Finally we come to the thermal scope. Ah, technology is our dear friend. Picking up a heat signature and making it stand out like the proverbial sore thumb against the room-temperature rest of the world, you can see how this may be useful. These also require power to function and have one tiny drawback. Zombies are dead and create no body heat of their own, which keeps them at pretty much the same temperature that it is outside. Due to movement, there may be a bit of heat being generated on account of friction in the joints, but there is no knowing if this is going to give you a proper target when the opportunity presents itself. Not a recommended choice; you'll be better served going with night vision or the plain Jane telescoping sight.

Laser-Sights

Initially used for sight calibration, these little beauties were modified in recent years to lay parallel to the barrel of a firearm and allow for increased accuracy with little actual effort. As long as you keep a steady hand, these babies can keep you shooting like Annie Oakley all day long. Naturally, this is another bit of gear that requires a power source, so as long as you keep it on, it will be right there at your side (well, the barrel's side, whatever), pointing the way.

Barrel-Mounted Flashlights

One more little technological marvel which requires battery power, but it can also prove to be multi-functional. In addition to illuminating your target, some are also fitted with a gradual light field that simulates a bulls-eye effect. LED lights are useful for this purpose and could potentially prove to be a wise investment. The downside is that they could also potentially give away your position to a zombie and set very unanticipated events into motion. Trading off a bit of stealth for accuracy is a choice you'll have to make with one of these. These things happen though; such is life.

Silencers

The silencer or suppressor was created initially to decrease the noise created by firearms, with the added effect of reducing muzzle flash. This is caused by slowing the escaping propellant and sometimes the round itself. Utilizing these with a revolver is largely ineffective due to the lack of properly directed propellants, and would pretty much be a waste of time since a large portion of the gases escape around the chamber before being directed into the barrel. Moving on, these are legally attainable in the United States via ATF permission, a criminal background check, and a subsequent tax in most states. The following states have explicitly banned civilians from owning any type of suppressor: California, Delaware, District of Columbia, Hawaii, Illinois, Iowa, Massachusetts, Michigan, Minnesota, New Jersey, New York, Rhode Island, and Vermont. Just in case you wondered. Even if you didn't, now you know. And knowing's half the battle! Sorry, childhood flashbacks.

Other Ranged Weapons

So we find ourselves delving into the slightly more obscure and lesser-utilized versions of launched weaponry. While none of these equal the power represented in the firearm category, they do offer the advantage of silence. I hear that's golden, but that seems like it would make a lot of noise if it fell, since it's one of the heavier metallic compositions.

Bows, Long, Cross and Otherwise

We're not talking about the kind you put in your hair to go to the sock hop; we're talking what put our Native American and Mongol brothers on the map as serious kickers of ass. Having been around for over 60,000 years, these were man's very first ranged step toward the top of the food chain. Essentially a spring made up of a pair of elastic limbs and string which, when pulled back and released, makes a neat "TWANG" noise. Introduce into this equation the arrow and a skilled marksman, and the "twang" noise lessens, and you have what is potentially a deadly long ranged weapon that is virtually silent. As fun as this may be to contemplate, the chances of piercing the human skull at extreme range are not that wonderful. It's certainly a feat that is attainable, but it requires a consummate professional with years of training to hope to do so with any degree of consistency. The potential of a fatal headshot is dependent not only on the person shooting it, but also on the tools used to make the shot.

Great technological strides have been achieved in the art of bow making, and these can be found in compound bows that mechanically enhance the power of a shot while reducing the needed strength to draw back the string. Traditionalists can still find proper old-school longbows or even recurved bows, but these lack the power generated by the more modern models. Utilizing a bow is not a horrible idea for one highly trained in its use, but keep in mind that the chances of losing your arrow after a strike are rather great. These can, of course, be bought or made, but the making of an arrow takes time. Fletchers weren't exactly the most expedient of craftsmen, but hey, you try it and then talk shit. Arrows will take up a lot of room for a relatively small amount of firing potential. This would make it a primary weapon by default.

Crossbows were the next generation "big brother" of the standard bow. Using the same basic principles, the bow portion itself is mounted to a stock, which allows for greater draw strength, but also causes a far greater reload time. As stealthy as its less techno-savvy counterpart, these medieval masterpieces are equally able to deliver a potentially deadly projectile to the head of the walking dead. Different variations exist in the present day crossbow that aid in rapid reloading, but its basic concept remains largely unchanged over hundreds of years. Firing a much shorter version of the arrow, commonly called a bolt, these are equally precise when launched by one who knows his scaled down ballista intimately. You may consider this as a primary weapon, in fact you'd pretty much be forced to due to it's size, but you'd do well to pick your battles carefully on account of the considerable amount of time required to reload. Bolts, much like their longer siblings, take up a lot of room and grant very little in the way of bulk shooting potential. Having one of these available could mean the difference between taking out one zombie and being done, or having to take down twenty. Overall this is probably not the greatest piece of attainable artillery one could hope for, despite its stealthy properties.

There are also hand-held crossbows available that are fairly powerful for their size, but lack sufficient strength to pierce anything other than the eye or fleshy parts of the body. Because of this, discount these weapons entirely. For recreational fun, though, they could make for an amusing and energy-independent way to pass the time. Maybe this will prove a bit more fun than traditional darts; you'll never know unless you try it.

Ninja-Stars, Throwing Knives, and Throwing Axes

These are awesome ways to spend a bit of time around the homestead. I mean, who wouldn't enjoy hurling sharp objects around their living room with a dozen of their closest friends around to help catch the inevitable bouncing bit of sharp metal? These three are equally swift and silent, and all of these weapons require just insane amounts of time to master enough to even be able to make them stick into unmoving objects the right way with any accuracy. Without years devoted to studying these weapons, hitting a moving human head will prove to be a nearly impossible task. Supposing you do have the training to use these, at least a fairly heavy throwing axe has a chance to cleave the skull of a zombie, thus bringing it down. The other two are nowhere near heavy enough, or as effective, in regards to bone crushing, and should be discounted entirely as an effective means of combating the undead. Attempting to utilize these effectively in dispatching the undead would be a sure indication of your desperation.

Slings and Slingshots

Using a slingshot to take down the walking dead is impractical to say the very least. Constructed simply of elastic stretched between upright forks on a Y-shaped frame, these simple little rock-launchers are fun for kids of all ages. In fact, these were even once deemed safe by parents, and kids were allowed to shoot at each other with these things. They hurt, at least as much as a BB gun, and today's over-protective standards would have parents throwing a raving shit fit if kids still went around pelting each other with these things. More recent updates to the designs and components used in their manufacturing have greatly increased both the power and accuracy of these devices, but they still lack the power to cause sufficient damage to the zombie's brain. The slingshot has a variety of uses in regards to survival though. One can utilize these to hunt small game such as rabbits and birds, and if you're having trouble reaching the other side of that pond, why not use your slingshot to get that fishing lure out there? They have their place, there's no doubt about it, but don't try to overstep their bounds. All it'll do against the undead is let them know you're there, and then, so much for the element of surprise; way to go, Bart.

Slings are perhaps one of the oldest forms of ranged combat gear on earth. Get some cord, put a pouch in the middle, add a football shaped stone, and swing it over your head. Now that you look silly, let it go and there you have it. Traditionally used in times gone by for combating your fellow man, these bruisers are terribly inaccurate outside the hands of someone who's worked with them for a goodly amount of time. Still used by some for hunting small edible critters, they will prove to be useless when employed against the undead. I suppose you could try to make one laugh itself to death by swinging this over your head and singing lyrics to a bad '80s song from a movie featuring a then-popular actor and a large-breasted singer, but this is not advised.

Jai Alai

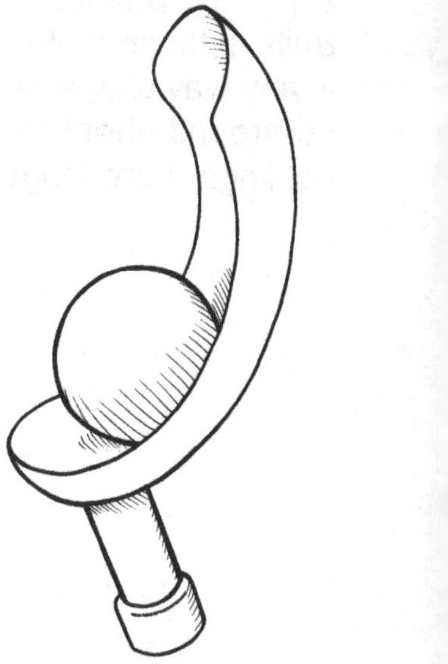

The players of this sport are just a little insane. Yes, that's science talking; look it up for yourself. They toss this goatskin covered little ball that weighs between 125-140 grams at a wall at nearly 200 miles per hour. Now, if you do the math, that has some potentially fatal results written all over it in big bright pink neon letters. The accuracy needed to make such a brilliant shot is just sickening, but it's within the realm of possibility. Using even heavier balls, maybe rocks or grenades, whatever, these could be really dangerous to the undead. It's not the most practical route you'd want to take, the gear's a little cumbersome, and having plenty of shit to throw would be a major pain in the coccyx, but just imagine using a funnily shaped wicker basket and a fucking rock to hit a zombie in the head. The twitching alone would be totally worth it. All in all, it's not a terrific choice, unless you're some kind of world-class player of the game. Not sure you'll have much time to learn once there are zombies everywhere. However, necessity is the mother of all invention.

Blowguns and Spitballs

The blowgun has been used for centuries as a delivery system of various toxins, which range in effects from causing unconsciousness to oily discharge and even to death. Likewise, spitballs have been used in classrooms to torment teachers and other students since the invention of the drinking straw began to be mass-produced for use in schools. Neither is worth a damn against the undead. Some may point out that you can modify a blowgun to fire something akin to an exploding paintball pellet. Good luck with that, Johnny Two-Balls. If these methods somehow fit into your survival scenario in any way shape or form, please be sure to let us know. We'll be around shortly to eliminate your reanimated corpse. Let's not linger here longer than needed.

Hand-to-Hand Weapons

Melee combat should generally be avoided as a rule. You don't want to find yourself inside the bite-radius of the undead, but there are times when it's simply unavoidable and you have to get your hands dirty. Doing so and walking away requires both the tools and the talent, and we're going to give you the rundown on all the good stuff. But first, DRUM SOLO! You hear that too, right? Maybe it's just us…

With any form of melee combat, you should be keenly aware of your level of endurance and effectiveness. If you can't swing for too long without becoming winded, or you simply lack the strength, either begin working on it now or stick to the firearms. Playing a support role for those who can manage a physical fighting situation can be just as important as any other part of this type of battle. A little bit of rooftop sniping, maybe just a look out role, perhaps you're in charge of the perimeter watch, whatever it is, take an active part. Your contribution could mean the difference between everyone walking away unscathed or leaving people behind and having to kill them later.

Bladed Weapons

The variety here is simply astounding, and we are going to try and cover every conceivable base. Now first and foremost, you need a blade that's complimentary to your skill, size, weight, strength, and speed. Having a sword that is not fit for your stance and ability renders the blade essentially useless. If it's just a smidge too long, you're nicking your feet, and if it's too short, you'll whiff your target. Both are very bad. If it's not balanced in your hand you can lose control, causing a wild strike, thereby opening yourself to a sure case of dead. If you happen to find a sword crafter who can make you a true blade that's fit for your body, there are other problems that come with using a sword. A good bit of physical conditioning is required for any prolonged use of these weapons, but that shouldn't be a problem, right? The biggest issue you'll face though is range. Using a sword, you have to be right next to the zombie to dispatch them in this manner, and where there is one zombie, there quite likely will be more. Basically, taking the Leroy Jenkins approach to battle will end just as badly as it did when you played WoW.

Another drawback is that blades do tend to get stuck now and then. You'll hack and slash, and **ching** now your weapon is a new zombie appendage. No time to stop and pull it out, you must make your move so as to avoid a case of the deads. If you're surrounded by zeds when this unfortunate but totally predictable event happens, there is no escape from your case of death. Also, unless the sword is tempered, sharpened, and weighted just right, it will not

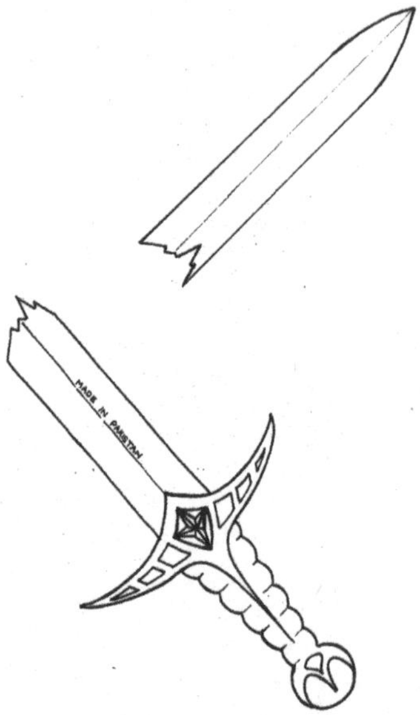

cleave tissue and bone. At best you're going to give zed a new hole to cram your pink fleshy bits into, and at the very worst? Well, have you ever played baseball and hit it just a little low on the shaft and got that painful vibration? Yeah, the same thing happens with swords. You want to avoid this. It's really a bad place to be when you're trying to fight off a horde.

What should you take from this section? Unless you're properly trained with a hand forged sword designed specifically for you, and you possess the super human ability to avoid being swarmed, I wouldn't choose a sword as a primary armament against the undead. As an emergency weapon it's fine, but in short, once the firearm was created the sword was discarded for a reason. So whatever choice you go with in regards to your blade, keep it clean, sharp and shiny, and it could just save your life.

Swords

"I know, we're promoting a lot of anger and stress over the melee weapons discussions. But we're going to continue. Because we feel it's in everyone's best interest. Today, we're going to focus on the rapier and it's less useful cousin the foil. No. Just no. No way in hell. Let's start with the foil. What are you going to dazzle them with your perfect form? Swishy poke them to death? Or do you hope a zombie has a sense of humor, and will die from laughter? Yes, fencing looks spiffy on TV. OK, well, it doesn't, it looks rather like a dance with toothpicks. It's still a rather worthless weapon. I can hear the fingers typing right now; I know you could stab a zombie in the eye to kill it. Shut up already. Are you going to be up close and personal with a group of zombies and score an eyeball shot each time? No you're going to be killed. In fact, I think your group should shoot you on principal if that's the weapon you show up with. On to the rapier.

Slightly useful, good slashing weapon. If you wish to cause damage to a human. Want to leave them with a scar on each cheek as a reminder that not only did you kill their father cause he was a crappy sword maker, but you can school an 11 year old boy in the process with your six fingered hand. But as a melee weapon in combat against the undead. What are you going to do? Hope they get a nasty infection from a slightly deep wound? Possibly stab their already non-functioning internal organs? Or aim for the eye and try to get that perfect shot in again?

Neither of these "swords" and I use the term very loosely since they are in fact a bladed hand-held weapon of length, are bout the poorest choice anyone could make as their back up melee weapon. Now, if you plan on carrying them so you have something long and pointy to roast your dinner over an open fire, hey go for it. They make great kabob makers. In short, not only no, but hell no."

– Inigo Montoya

The Longsword: One of the most widespread variations of the traditional blade, the longsword is a double-edged weapon featuring a fuller, a straight cross guard, and a one handed grip. These were used generally in conjunction with a shield, and proved very capable of thrusting, slicing, and cutting opponents. Measuring anywhere from twenty-eight to thirty inches (sometimes a bit more), these were a preferred weapon for centuries in most European countries. The longer blades would often have an extended grip to accommodate two hands. Designed for combat which involved parrying, thrusting, and the like, these were prime hand-to-hand weapons of their time. Overall, these are not the best choice of a bladed weapon one could have, but you could do much worse.

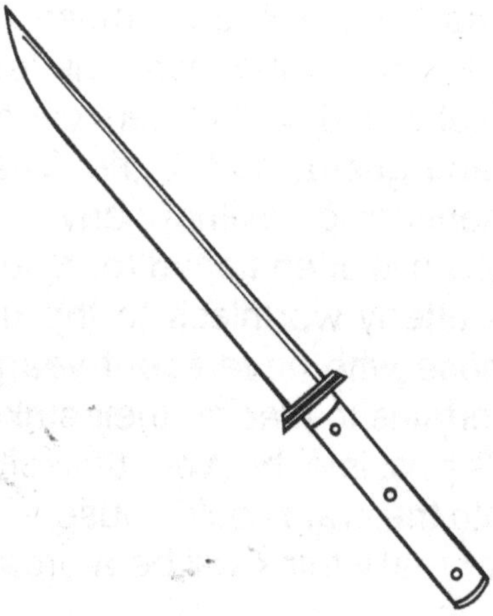

The Miao dao: This is a very long, two-handed Chinese sword that features a single sharpened edge. The blade typically measures over 1.2 meters, and, as a result, these blades have excellent range and damage potential. Just make sure you know what you're doing before you head out and start swinging this thing around like you're Babe Ruth and you really want to get back to the bar before last call. Actually, since he's dead, he wouldn't be swinging much of anything, but you get the idea. Try not to stand too close to your friends while you're hacking at the undead with this beast. You could become very detested very quickly.

The Cutlass: A short and thick curved blade favored by those beloved marauders of the high seas, you guessed it, the pirate. Able to withstand the rigors of cutting through thick ropes, canvas, and even wood, these were often utilized on boarding missions due to their ability to be used in smaller spaces more easily than some longer blades. Requiring less expertise than many other blades, they were devastating in close combat. If they're good enough for pirates, they could be a snazzy addition to your arsenal. Mayhaps ye be usin' one matey!

The Saber: A single-edged curving blade that features a hand guard as well as a thumb guard. Later adaptations for use by cavalry were straighter and double-edged. You could certainly work with one of these in order to get your technique down. These can indeed get the job done with appropriate practice.

The Foil: Used by those who practice the sport of fencing, these particular weapons feature no true blade. Measuring a total of 110 centimeters overall, these have a rounded blade, a hand guard, and a grip. That's about all there is that's worth mentioning. Without any cutting surface aside from the point, which is often tipped (or foiled) to take away its lethality, the foil is utterly worthless to the unskilled combatant. However, to those who have spent years mastering their swordplay, as it pertains to placing their strike exactly where they want it to hit, it's possible, but very unlikely, that a strike through the eye and into the brain could cause a zombie to fall. This isn't something we really think will be a great idea to try out. Ever...

The Lightsaber: Principally just a metal handle that contains a power source, which when triggered interacts with a crystal and emits a blade about three feet long, which can cut through just about any material with ease. The color of the blade is dependant upon the type of crystal used in the weapon's construction. Highly advisable for use against the undead, as the human skull will offer no resistance to the blade. Also recommended for use against the Sith (or Jedi, depending on your affiliation). You know these don't exist, right? You got all droolie fanboy for a minute. It's OK; so did we.

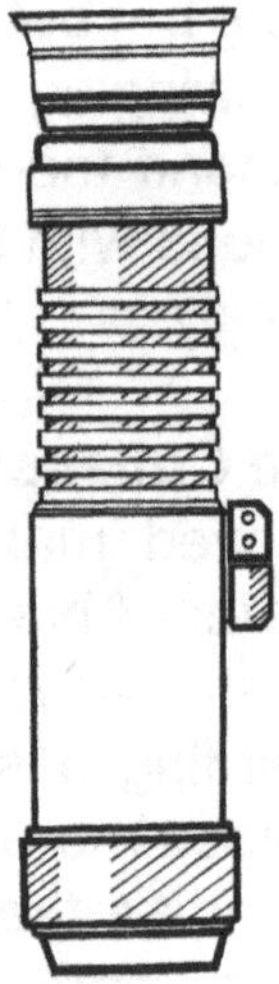

The Scimitar: One handed weapons with single-sided blades that were initially created for use from horseback for a high speed sweeping attack. Best utilized as a slashing weapon, as opposed to chopping or stabbing. This type of blade could leave you feeling very inadequate, but used with enough power and correct technique, there are shoddier choices.

The Katana: The traditional "Samurai sword," these lovely instruments of death have been in existence for over 600 years. The single edge design of this weapon allows it to be drawn and inflict heavy slicing damage in a single motion without the need for silly posturing. Those who have mastered the use of these destructive tools are ever testing themselves against targets constructed of natural materials that simulate flesh (wara or goza) and bone (green bamboo) in an effort to constantly better their skills. The blades of these awesome weapons were folded several times during the forging process to give them incredible strength. These superbly constructed blades are still widely available in their traditionally constructed style and strength. Always consider and research your source for these types of purchases. Are they reputable; will they allow testing or demonstration; is there feedback from other consumers? If you buy it at a pawn shop, you're not going to just run out like Bushido Johnny Two-Balls and start lopping off undead heads. However, if it's authentically made, you've got yourself a potential winner.

The Zweihänder: Two-handed greatswords. German and Austrian infantries carried these for the express purpose of laying waste to the ranks of enemy pike men and spearmen in the fourteenth to sixteenth centuries. Weighing in at nearly eight pounds and flaunting a frightening five feet of blade, these were used to great effect in the severing of limbs and heads. These were the predecessors and larger cousins of the Scottish claymore, which had the same overall design but slightly smaller dimensions. Claymores were typically around fifty-five inches overall and weighed about five pounds.

Take nothing away from the claymore in terms of devastating effects on the human body; these are impressive to say the least. However, sustaining a proper defense against the undead would take considerable strength, endurance and skill, but going about it with any one of these would make a great story for around the campfire. Plus you get to talk with a funny accent while you do it, if you so choose.

The Gladius: A member of the short sword family, these were favored for centuries by the Roman army and they continued to see use in the gladiatorial arena. Measuring between twenty-five and thirty-two inches, these double-edged weapons were by no means easy tools to use while staying safely out of harm's way, and they will demonstrate to be even less so against the undead. However, they're fairly heavy for their size, and could prove very useful when confronted by only a handful of zombies. Their primary use was as a thrusting weapon, but they have proved adept at heavy chopping. If you have one, use it, if you don't, well then, it is our hope you have something else.

The Falchion: Measuring around thirty-six inches in total length, a falchion is a heavy and straight single-bladed sword with a flared tip. These attributes combined the useable versatility of the sword with the weight and power of the axe. The construction of these blade types have varied greatly throughout history, but one thing sets them apart from most: they cut shit up, and they do so with authority. The power derives from the thickness and heft of the blade itself. Using one of these obviously will limit the range at which you engage your target, but the skill needed to hack away at the undead effectively is relatively little. These things have power, especially when they're kept sharp. Having one of these hanging on your hip may not be a bad idea for those up-close-and-personal types of confrontations.

The Rapier: Supposing you're a Spaniard out to avenge the death of your father who died at the hand of a six-fingered man, this is the weapon for you. Like the long sword, the rapier is straight, slender, and sharply pointed. There are some variations of this sword which feature a thicker blade, but those generally conform to the same characteristics as their slender counterparts. Unlike the long sword, these tend to have an ornate sweeping hilt which acts as a guard for the hand. While this may look like a truly elegant weapon to have at your side, it's not very practical in its applications against the undead. Rapiers are thrusting weapons, and were never widely regarded for their ability to cut. Sure, they can be sharpened and used in such a way, but in terms of dispatching a zombie through cerebral trauma, chances are low. A thrust through the eye may result in a kill or severing of the brain stem, causing the ghoul to fall to the ground immobilized, but these won't be easy to accomplish unless one is learned in the ways of this weapon. These were mostly worn by gentlemen of the time as decoration, and perhaps even used as dueling blades. They weren't designed for heavy combat even then; there's little chance they could be valuable in that particular realm in the present day against hordes of lifeless cannibals.

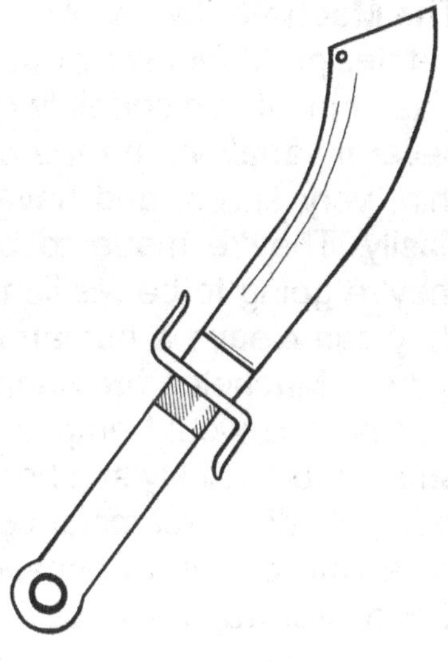

The Dadao: The literal Chinese translation of this word is "Big Knife" but it's a bit more than that. The single-sided blades on these measure between two to three feet, and are very thick toward the top, giving extra lop to your chop. The grip can be used in a one or two-handed fashion, and if they're made right, could easily lop off a head or a limb. While the skill required to use these effectively in an offensive conflict would be considerable, a novice could certainly utilize this weapon in a defensive posture and walk away from the conflict.

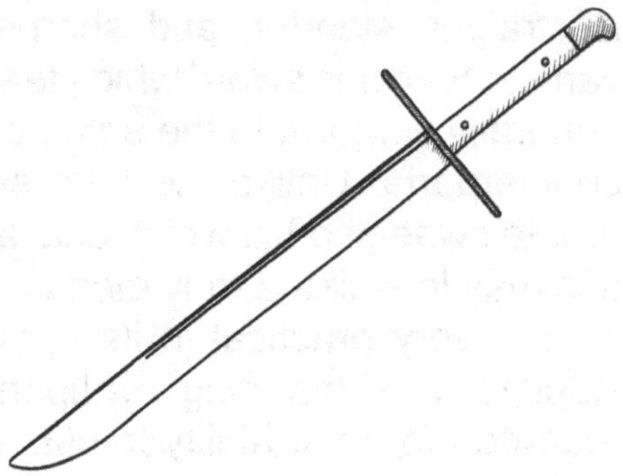

The Grosse Messer: This is a falchion that had a growth spurt. It sports a single-sided blade, a straight cross guard, and measures in at around forty-six inches total. While the blade does curve back toward the end, it lacks the overall thickness of its smaller cousin. This overall design, combined with the blade's weight, translates into superior cutting power for this weapon. These were actually the weapons of the commoner due to their availability and relatively cheap pricing. They took little skill to use compared to many other blades, and were actually used for more mundane purposes around the home. However, due to its size, it would be a good idea to work with this thing a lot before trying to adequately defend yourself from the hordes with it.

The Machete: OK, so it's not a sword at all, and is in fact a tool not designed for laying out crazy amounts of zombie hack and slash fun. It can certainly be used that way, though. There are several variations on the basic design, but all are essentially thin, very sharp, and have a sturdy handle that doesn't slip easily. They're made to be a working blade, so you know they're going to be resilient and strong. Properly sharpened, they can cleave a human body apart like a hot knife through butter. Machetes are shorter than most conventional swords that people would employ, and, as such, they're lightweight and can be quickly stashed in the rigging of your pack without worry. In dire circumstances you can use the machete to hack off a limb or two to escape to freedom. Who the hell left all these bear traps outside anyway?

Axes

While many variants of the ordinary axe exist today, they all share one general principle. Swing it, and things fall down in more pieces than they existed as in the past. The same standard that exists while using large, two-handed swords leads the way in regards to using the axe. Sharp heavy blade at the end of a stick—swing, connect, detach. The axe will grant you more power, but you drop a bit of accuracy. This can be offset by sheer viciousness, but that can also lead to death in the wrong circumstances.

Using an axe is going to be physically intense. It takes a lot of power, and you will likely become fatigued rather quickly. Sinking your blade into the undead repeatedly carries with it the added possibility of it getting stuck. Like swords, an axe head is a blade, and it's not unheard of for it to become wedged into bone. This will have to be compensated for. Start practicing now: split logs, chop down a tree, and commence working on that endurance and exactitude. Beginning now will prepare you for the undead menace.

The Battleaxe: Designed for use with one or both hands, these were specifically designed with killing in mind. Ranging in weight from one to six pounds, these existed in different cultures and styles throughout the world. These could be either headed with a single or double blade, and were more common than swords for quite some time due to their inexpensive nature and versatility. Used by someone powerful, they'll easily remove the head from the body. Finding one that's up to the rigors of combat may be a little difficult, but it's not unheard of. Making one for yourself could be an option if you possess the skills.

The Broad Axe: This is a large headed axe that, in times long past, was used for precision shaping and hewing of logs. Largely unused today due to the mill industry, they're pretty much a forgotten piece of hardware by most. We can't let this one go. On a chopping broad axe, the axe head extends above and below the poll (or butt, hehehe) and offers a gargantuan cutting surface. Taking one of these to the head or neck of a zombie is going to cause a wonderful bit of destruction. Like most types of axe, these can get to be a little heavy after a while, and engaging in a drawn out campaign of axe-induced murderous glee is not a great idea, but the potential for doing so is certainly there.

The Hurlbat: These things are pointy all the way around to practically ensure some form of damage is going to happen. Constructed entirely of metal, these were designed with the express intention of hurling it at your foe, causing them to scream like a little girl with a skinned knee, and thus, putting them down. They typically measure about eight to twelve inches and vary in blade size quite a bit. People have gotten a bit too creative with detailing this particular weapon, and we're sure to get emails about how they're bigger or smaller or smell like pine and have a nice heady aroma with a strong nutty finish, but we don't particularly give a shit. The point is, we talked about throwing axes earlier, and if you're good, by all means, take a shot with it. Having a few of these for use in melee combat as well as throwing applications could be a decent path to take, if that's what you have available to you.

The Firefighter's Axe: A long handle topped by a bladed head and backed with a pick, these are primarily used to break down doors and windows and aid in saving lives on a daily basis. You've seen these—they're large, red, and usually have a handle made of new-age materials that absorb shock and all that good stuff. You can even use them for a few different things, so it's not a bad choice. They can also crop off a head in a pinch if ever the need arises. How is that ever a bad thing?

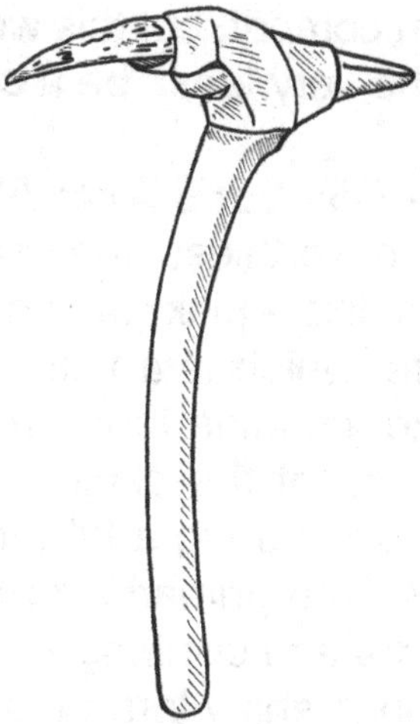

The Adze: This is an axe, technically, but get this—the axe head is turned ninety degrees and curves downward a bit. These were traditionally used as a woodworking tool for smoothing out rough trees and the like. Awesome if you felt the need to make a fort. Using one of these in an offensive capacity would feel unnatural at best, but could potentially be a devastating one-shot kind of weapon. Sink this little mean bastard into the top of a skull, and then grab something a bit more useful for multiple swings. If you plan on building something along the log cabin lines, have one handy for helping it all fit together. For constant use against the undead, there are superior weapons available.

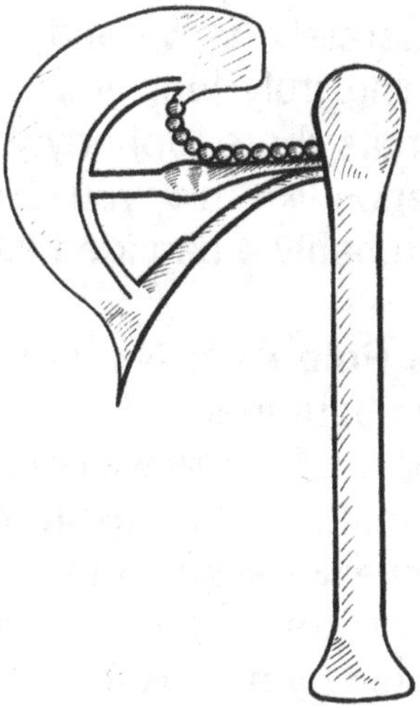

The Nzappa Zap: OK, this gets automatic points for having our group's name in it twice. This thing looks fucked up like a hooker on a Saturday morning. What we have here is a traditional African weapon which seems to be their answer to the hatchet or axe. It looks like a club (BONUS!) with an ornately designed axe-head attached. It's also pretty short, and exact dimensions weren't to be found, but it looks like it's about twelve to eighteen inches overall.

You can either throw this thing or keep hold of it and cause some serious zombie-chunking to occur. Either way you use it, this thing is sure to look awesome. Plus the fact that on a back swing you have a meaty little club in your hand, which makes this double awesome. It's probably not good for anything aside from combat, but this would certainly be something that would, at the very least, be a conversation piece.

The Climber's Axe: Also called an ice axe, these are pretty much worthless against the undead. They have a pointy end, more like a pick with added serrations, and the other side is an adze, which is a flattened wider horizontal head (just like an adze, imagine that). You may be able to whack one through the top of the skull and get the desired effect, but why not use something a bit more to the point? Puns rule. Anyway, these are primarily for assisting you with trekking through icy tundra and climbing and all that good stuff. Use it for traveling through shitty terrain, and only offensively as an alternative.

The Splitting Maul: Axe meets sledgehammer in this nifty little device. Half big fucking hammer and half axe, the top of this thing provides some serious dual purpose log-splitting and skull thumping action. Useful when push comes to crack-the-zombie-upside-the-head-then-cut-it-off. These can be moderately heavy and very good at making trees, doors, and fencing truly fear you. If you're good with it, by all means, go nuts there, Johnny Two-Balls. Just be aware that, with a weapon like this, you're going to wear down quickly. Missing is probably a bad idea as well.

The Pole Axe: No, not the people that have so many jokes told about them. Those are funny, and we may get into some later, but for now we're talking about those axe heads mounted on shafts that measure over 1.5 meters. Indeed, these were originally designed to crack open the canned hams that were known as knights. There's the standard single axe head, backed by a hook for grabbing and pulling down an adversary, and to top it off, literally, a handy poking spike that issues a forceful, pointed, and often lethal kick while the other guy's down. Not very useful in tight quarters, as it takes a lot of room to properly utilize, but it could find its niche in keeping the undead at bay. If you've had training with these and you have a good one lying around, it may make for a decent fire-poker if the need arises.

The Danish Axe: Well, it looks like a Viking axe to an untrained eye, but nope, the same folks that brought you tasty cream cheese covered breakfast pastries also came up with this little beauty. Pretty much just a single-sided axe head on a longer shaft, these look much like a pole axe without the hook or stabby bit, only a little shorter. There are variations, of course. Nobody could leave a good weapon alone. A lot more to the point than other designs, with this, you take a big swing, connect, and things die horribly. In the case of using it to dispatch the undead, they die beautifully. Not one of the superior designs you will come across, but why ignore a chance to give the Danes proper credit for this design and talk about yummy breakfast food? Oh, you should in all probability give this one a miss against the undead; you can do better.

The Bearded Axe: The term bearded often refers to carnival-based freakish large "women" with hairy faces and/or lumberjacks. In regards to an axe however, it simply means that that underside is swept downward in such a way as to better center the weight of the weapon. The theory behind this is that this design increases power and accuracy by providing an increased cutting surface. More potential WOW factor than many other designs, the bearded axe is one worth finding and putting to use in a good game of cranium high-sticking zombie head golf.

The Halberd: Think a pole axe with a much larger spike on the top. Now think about a hill covered in gently flowing green grass and the wind has the scent of freshly baked bread and the sun is warm on your face. OK, now stop thinking about that. A halberd is pretty much a spear, an axe, and a hook. Another weapon designed with anti-cavalry intentions, these are actually still employed by the Swiss Guard at the Vatican. Why, I'm not entirely sure, but they could be preparing for a zombie disturbance as well. We'll have to keep an eye on them. Zoinks, Zombie-pope!

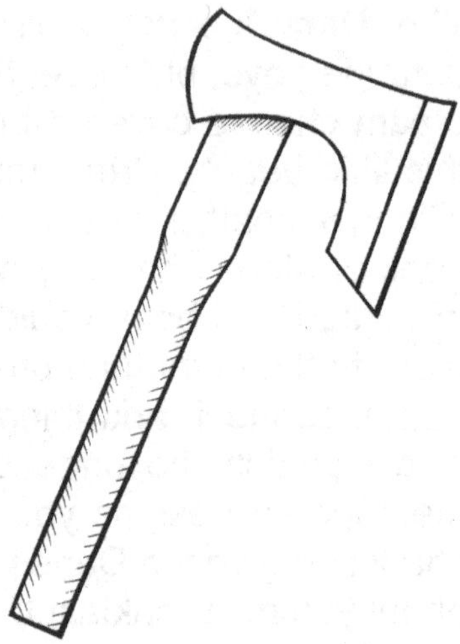

The Ono: About four feet long, this is the steel-bladed axe that the Japanese brought to the fight. This weapon was found to be in connection with warrior monks who often adapted their farming implements to become weaponry. What tool they got this from must have been connected to one hell of a daily chore, because it features a wooden handle and an oversized two-headed blade. Blending the style of the traditional axe with the bearded axe, and then giving it one hell of a metal Mohawk, this thing looks like something out of a fantasy movie. You can't look at this thing and imagine that it's not effective at head-splitting and limb removal when it comes right down to it.

The Hatchet: Measuring less than twenty inches total and weighing a pound or two, the hatchet has been a friend to the outdoorsman for a good long while. Specifically designed to be used in a one-handed fashion to cut small timber, cut wild game, and dig out roots, these provide cutting power directly where you need it. Not a recommended zombie-slaying device, but it could definitely cleave a skull if the need arose. One should definitely be kept in the campground/compound, because they also double as a hammer, and this is how they differentiate from the hand axe. Definitely efficient little tools to have around.

The Pick Axe: A bit of a misnomer, this is not really a true axe. Consisting of a spike and backed by a horizontal blade, these were used by miners to aid in excavation and acquisition of various gems and minerals. Used as a weapon though, these could easily be swung to destroy the skull and brain in an effortless manner. Recovery may be a problem though, as the penetration depth and suction could cause the weapon to stick and become irretrievable. This may be a good one-time shot kind of item, but not a very reliable tool for multiple uses.

Other Bladed Stabbing and Cutting Goodness

Pocketknives: Another bladed weapon you must carry with you at all times is the simple folding pocketknife. You'll need it for opening boxes, cutting off wire, skinning your lizard dinner, whatever the case may be. A good strong folding pocketknife could mean the difference between eating and starving that night. These are not to actually be used as weapons, but are more intended for utility purposes. There are alternatives, but we'll get to those later.

The Brush Axe: Who says we don't make a proper weapon these days? OK, this is a practical melee weapon. The tool we're going to talk about now has several uses. Not only can you use it to fend off the odd zed, you can use it to clear a path, hack down a small tree, build your makeshift camp, or what ever you really want to use it for. We're talking about the hand-held brush-axe. It's an elegant device. This tool comes in many forms, but all of them useful. There is the common one-hand yard tool as well as its much bigger brother, which is used for branches and fighting off the odd mythical flying lizard. The hooked blade on the handheld form can be used to gut a freshly killed animal in a pinch, and it can also be used to cut down fruit from trees. Hell, a resourceful survivalist could use it to jimmy doors and windows. The smaller ones have more uses than drawbacks. In fact, out of all the melee weapons we've discussed, it's actually recommended that everyone carry one of these in their pack. The blade is sharp on both sides, so you can swing two ways to take down a pesky zed, and it's weighted enough to drive the point home. Now we're not saying you should run willy nilly into a horde thinking your lowly brush axe will save your life, but should you encounter a rogue zed, instead of making a ton of noise by opening fire, drive the blade into the skull, twist it for maximum damage to the brain, and move on. Simple, to the point, and functional beyond its use as a weapon. How many other melee weapons are you going to find that are easy to carry, lightweight, and multipurpose? It's not often a baseball game breaks out in the middle of the apocalypse, so a bat has one use, swing and kill. A sword; you swing and kill. The brush axe fits in to daily life, and will help you in more ways than you can count.

The Glaive: Resembling the Japanese naginata, this is pretty much a long pole with a single, wide blade perched at its top. Not terribly useful without being able to take advantage of a full two-handed swing. In a hallway, you're pretty much not going to have much luck with one of these if you try to use it as a thrusting weapon. It's another one of those situational things, where if it's at hand and you have the room, it could work.

The Bat'leth: The Klingon long sword, these are used in duels of honor among members of the species. Though it's basically a nifty looking weapon with a blade along the front with more blades protruding from top and bottom, it doesn't seem like, were it real to begin with, it would be very useful for decapitations. We're positive someone's made one somewhere, but we don't know that guy, and we're not sure that we want to.

The War Scythe: Another leverage-based weapon that requires a wide swinging motion to do its dirty work. This is comprised of a single blade that curves inward and back out again, something like an elongated crescent moon, which is fastened atop a long shaft. Hehe I said, "shaft." This will excel at doing serious cutting damage to the undead while keeping you out of their reach. That is, it will if you're

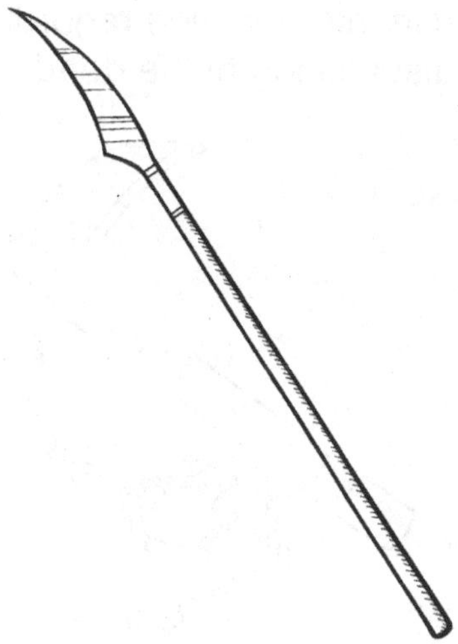

using it correctly. Like other weapons which are of the longer variety, these are only useful in open areas. Don't use this around the good china.

The Khopesh: Something of an axe-sword hybrid, the khopesh had an inward-curved hook at the end of the blade that makes the cut. Primarily known to cause slashing damage, this has almost no thrusting power at all. In the hands of an expert, this may indeed be a decapitating marvel, but its use against the walking dead isn't advised. Looks neat though.

The Kama: The Japanese hand-scythe is still used in certain forms of martial arts. Used singly or in pairs, these are typically employed in the disarming of a foe and very quick, and also lethal, counter-attack. Both the edge and the tip are used in striking, but their short-range nature brings their use into question regarding the dispatching of the dead.

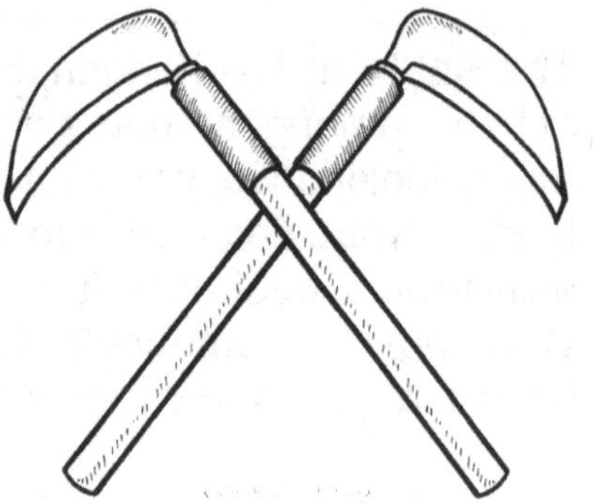

The Kusarigama: This is a kama on a chain with a heavy iron weight at the other end. Seriously? You'll put your eye out, kid. It is a beautiful thing to see these used by true masters of the art, though. To the lay person, these things are sharp and swirly suicide. It's not recommended that you grab one of these and start whipping it around without proper training. They're not the most practical weapons of the zombie slaying arsenal anyway.

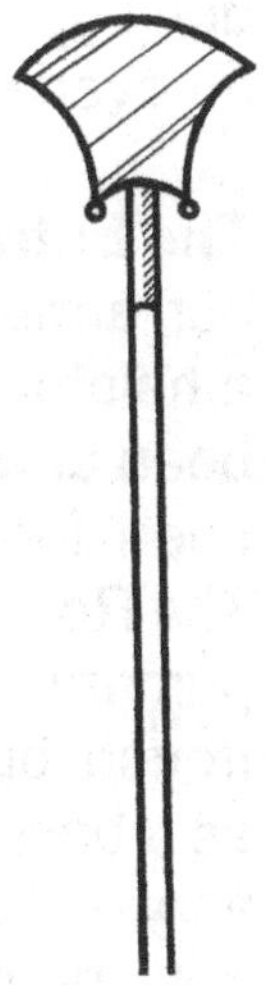

The Monk's Spade: Yet another adapted gardening tool that can be used with great lethality as a weapon against unwanted weeds and the undead equally. Consisting of a crescent moon-shaped blade at one end and spade-like blade at the other, both ends are extraordinarily sharp and deadly. With practice you can do as much harm by powerfully thrusting it forward as you can by employing this in a swinging fashion. And my mom constantly told me I'd never learn anything playing video games...

The Chainsaw: Having witnessed these being used in movies set in Texas in which there are massacres, TV shows, video games, and personal back yard deforestation, we know that these can indeed cut and cut fast. A motor-driven chain spins at high speed and literally cuts and rips through whatever it touches as long as it's softer than the chain itself. Outstanding of what its intended purpose is, there's no doubt about it. At this point though, we would like to point out that these are very loud, and then remind you that zombies are attracted to noise. Another point worth mentioning is that fuel, which these things require, is finite, and when you run out of said fuel, you're left holding a lump of metal and plastic and, very likely, looking terribly impotent and tasty to the undead. Now that being said, if you do in fact want to go on a rampage with one of these, or maybe two strapped to a pole, or even a suit made out of them, and take out some flesh eating automatons, go right ahead, have fun, sing a song—just don't dance. You're going to be making a mess and trying to shake your groove thing while spilling rotted innards all over the ground; this could get slippery and dangerous. You could quite possibly ruin your clothes, and who wants that? Settle for an understated yet satisfying booty-shake instead. You could definitely have fun ruining that now-dead-neighbor's shit with one of these, but don't get caught without gas in the can or you'll end up being an everlasting Halloween costume.

The Entrenching Tool: Carried by our armed forces, this little guy is a helpful tool to have. These have been around as long as there have been forms of militarized groups. The Romans even used these. The primary use is for digging a hole or trench, but they found a use in WWI as a backup weapon. These things vary in sizes and weights; you can get them with straight handles, T-handles, D-handles, and even collapsible models. If you sharpen the edges of the E-tool, you have a makeshift decapitator of the undead. We're fans of anything that serves multiple purposes, and this little guy could prove very useful to have.

Bludgeons

There are those among us who want to go the route of our beloved RPGs and get the damage increase of the blunt objects against the undead. Sadly there's no multiplier for blunt vs. undead in this situation, but there are plenty of options for the use of a bludgeon against the human cranium, whether it's occupied by the living or dead. Any of these will require a bit of skill and brute strength to use to their full potential, but there is one massive plus. No cleaning or sharpening is required. Just grab and smash until your target stops moving. What could be more simple or fun?

Brass Knuckles: No. Just no. Don't be that guy, please. If wrapping a small band of metal around your hand and punching a zombie in the face where the teethy parts are is your idea of survival, we implore you to reconsider. No matter how much UFC you watch, you're just not that hard. The odds are high that eventually you're going to cut some part of your hand and there's going to be a fluid transfer that occurs. Don't let this happen to you. Do you really want someone to come upon you as a zombie, knuckle duster still in hand, dangling by a limp finger, see that, laugh, and then shoot you in the head? Nobody wants that, but if you use one of these, it's going to happen.

The War Hammer: No, it's not just another game for nerds; this is actually a hammer that was, in times gone by, used in real battles. Consisting of a wooden handle topped with the typical hammerhead and backed with a spike, these had no trouble making life end for the wielder's enemy. The spike was used to pierce helmets, and, subsequently, the brain and those who lived through this assault continued to wear helmets and licked windows. You can see how this may become a useful apparatus against the undead in the right hands. One concern though would be the possibility of the hammerhead making contact, breaking through, and then a ridge gets stuck. This is a potentially bad situation for obvious reasons. Filing or grinding down these edges can reduce this chance and still leave you with a nifty skull-whacker for those intimate moments with your undead dance partner.

The Shillelagh: You just can't leave this one out; it's too much fun to say. Shillelaghs come in a variety of shapes and sizes, and aside from those which are mass-produced, no two are the same. You take a lump of stout wood that has a nice little knob at one end, turn it into a dual-action device which acts as a walking stick and a slapper of all things malicious. This takes time, if you happen to find an appropriate piece of wood, shape it, sand it, and finish it. Once it sets, you have yourself a shillelagh. Obviously its use is limited by the weight of the weapon and the power of the one swinging it, but if nothing else, you've found yourself a post-apocalyptic hobby and something for new friends to marvel over. A potentially awesome way to spend your time and fend off those who covet your lucky charms.

The Maul: You may be more familiar with its modern name—the sledgehammer. A wooden handle topped with a double-sided metal head that can vary in weight from three to twenty pounds. For prolonged use, these require a LOT of endurance, not to mention strength, but the effects against the skull would be simply awesome. One well-aimed blow would more than demolish both the brain and bone. It's been said by wise men that those that survive a blow to the head with one of these things may look complacent, but inside, they cry like a little girl with a skinned knee. They simply lack the ability to show it. Look what that one funny little guy did to all those watermelons in his act. Even a glancing blow would cause the zombie, could it speak, to talk funny for the rest of its days, if not put it down in a heap for a moment. Swing speed won't be incredible, and should you miss, recovery time won't be either. So if you plan on using this with any kind of regularity, start training now and don't miss later.

The Mace: As fun as it would be, we're not talking about Windu. No, what is being discussed here is the heavy flanged or studded head that is atop a solid metal or wooden handle. The design of the mace is such that it allows great power to be focused into a single, wide area. Sizes and weights vary greatly based on construction materials, and therefore, so will its usefulness. Two-handed maces were also utilized for purposes of battle, and could even be said to rival the maul in damage potential. Swinging a mace and connecting with the cranium is going to crush the skull like a fart bubble in a bathtub. If you plan on using one of these, avoid prolonged conflicts. The flanged variation on the head of a mace will focus the power on the flanges themselves and further focus the power at the point of impact. The only probable down side here is the head getting stuck, but luckily the design itself doesn't really allow for it. Bad designs, maybe.

The Flail: You get a studded heavy metal ball or rod, attach it to a chain, stick that on a handle, and you have yourself a flail. Swinging this in an arcing motion and connecting with your target will usually make said target feel far less optimistic about its day. Supposing you know what you're doing with this thing, the physics behind it dictate massive damage. In days of old, fights with these things often resulted in protest marches against violence and face-caving that are still held today. Not something recommended for the novice user in self-defense against the undead.

The Quarterstaff: Also known as a Bo staff, the quarterstaff was the favored weapon of poor woodsmen throughout history. You read about it in Robin Hood, you saw it used by a mutated turtle that practiced ninjitsu. Made entirely of wood and measuring between six and seven feet in length, these are beautiful to see when used by those who have mastered the art. The potential is there to use these in a deadly manner against the undead, but proper technique is needed in order to do so. The staff is definitely not a weapon one should use without knowing how, otherwise you're just begging for tooth rape.

The Millwall Brick: Fashioned from tightly rolled up and folded newspaper, these were allegedly used by soccer hooligans in the 1960s and '70s. Violent bastards felt the need to fight with fans of the opposing team, but on the upside, they got creative. Police took anything away from them which could have been used as a weapon, but hey, what's the harm in a newspaper? Well, paper is made from wood, and when you roll it up in a dense manner, it essentially becomes wood again. Fold it over or wrap it around your hand, and you have yourself one hell of a handy little weapon. Not too sure about its practical applications in regards to skull bludgeoning, but if you have nothing else, it would be better than going at the undead with your bare hands. Not by much, though.

The Jō Staff: Shorter and thicker than the quarterstaff, these were used to primarily combat against a sword-wielding foe. A little over four feet long and sometimes decked out with steel rings, these can pack one hell of a thump in the right hands. In fact, these were used in conjunction with the martial art Aikido, to illustrate its principles with a weapon. Some Eastern police forces still use these. If you can find or make one, you may have yourself a handy little thumping stick.

The Baton/Truncheon: Essentially these are just sticks less than an arm's length, and have been carried by law enforcement types for years. The baton was used when shooting the bad guy just wasn't deemed justified; however, beating the living shit out of them was fair game. Now there is some serious potential to inflict massive trauma upon the human skull, but it's going to take a few whacks, and, let's face it, you don't have that kind of time when you're dealing with rotting corpses trying to eat you. The nightstick is a variation of these weapons, and has a handle jutting out at a ninety degree angle about a hand-width above one end. This could potentially be used in a defensive capacity to ward off the bitey parts of the undead, while moving yourself into a safer position. Not a highly recommended piece of hardware which you should implement, but they could certainly serve a purpose.

The Golf Club: Submitted for your approval: the golf club. Finally a practical use for a worthless sporting good. You want to bust out your drivers and irons and really go to town on a zombie? Well, before you start yelling FORE, there are a few things you should know. First off, they're not designed to hit heavy objects. The clubs are specifically designed to act as a whip in order to help drive through the ball and send it flying faster and farther. The old metal-shafted clubs didn't have as much give as the new carbon fiber, or fiberglass models, but it's all the same effect. You swing the club as fast as possible, causing it to arc slightly, or greatly depending on your strength and speed, at the peak of the swing, which is when you should connect with the ball. Then the club whips forward, causing an extra burst of speed. This action sends the little white ball flying off into the distance, and begins your walking adventure.

The problem when using them as a weapon is, you'll never quite get that arc unless you get a full swing. If you happen to get a full swing then hit a large heavy object, one of two things will happen. The whipping motion of the club will cause your $200 driver to shatter like a glass test tube, or if you're a cheap bastard or nostalgic, it'll cause the metal to bend, thus rendering your prized collection of whacking sticks useless. You may get one or two good kills out of each club before they're completely worthless.

Now, if you plan on lugging a full bag around, you may survive a bit longer. However, you're not going to have a caddy to hand you the club when zed approaches. Your best bet is to leave the golf bag in the closet where it belongs. Besides, who wants to cock up a perfectly good walk through the park by searching for a tiny white ball you sent sailing?

In short, the golf club is a worthless choice when used as a weapon. Though it could be used in a pinch if you were dealing with just one zombie.

Pimp Cane: Carried by those who practice the art of love-brokering, the pimp cane is an uncommon yet deadly instrument. OK, so it's more common around Halloween, and it's probably not deadly. Dead bitches don't make money, now do they? In the pimp arsenal, the pimp-slap reigns supreme, but now and again, a bitch needs to have a point made in a firmer manner and that's where the cane comes in to play. They won't use the end in these cases because it leaves too many marks, the middle will do fine, and it leaves a bit pore of an impression than a hand covered in baby powder. Like any club or shillelagh though, these can be deadly in the right hands. We're not sure whose hands those would be specifically, but Ice-T and his mythical pimptacularness is a damn good probability.

The Club: Long before people used them to lock their steering wheels in positions that make it slightly more difficult to drive, clubs were used by ancient man as a means to get with the ladies. More importantly though, the club was mostly used as simple weapon for attack and defense. Not the greatest of war tools, but effective and abundant. If you can find a branch, you have yourself a club. You can simply grab up a chair, a fence post, a stick, or maybe Grampa's old prosthetic and just swing away. Use these as improvisational armaments only; you can do better than a caveman. (Editor's note: Clubs are not to be used on baby seals. Not cool, man. Adults seals though are fair game.)

The Morning Star: Simply put, this is a mace with big mean spikes all over it. When knights went from chain to plate armor, the mace beefed up too. So you're going to wear a big heavy piece of metal? I'm going to stick this goddamn thing into your chest and leave it there, so how do you like those apples? The morning star is difficult to retrieve when it's stuck in something or someone, and therein lies its principle drawback. It's a hefty tool that's very good at braining something that needs brained, but the inability to swiftly use it again puts this piece of hardware on the "dumb fucking plan" list.

The Kanabō: Have you ever sucker punched a sibling with a pillow? That's how much this thing kicks ass. The Kanabō is the samurai warrior's version of a club, and these guys did nothing half-assed. Constructed of either hard wood and studded or spiked along welded-on strips of iron, or made entirely of iron, this style of weapon was a mean bastard to have to stare down. Ranging in size from a forearm to as tall as the one who used it, they could be used one or two-handed, and it carried a lot of power in that swing from the weight of these alone. This weapon had one purpose, and that was to destroy anything it hit. Most other weapons were designed for something else and became adapted for warfare; not true of the Kanabō. This was created to smash armor, bones, and horses. Goddamn horses! While this weapon's weight could be viewed as a liability, its size alone makes missing an improbability. The whole length of this thing is studded death just waiting to happen. Going in to close combat with the undead? Find yourself one of these, or make one, whatever you have to do, but yeah, this

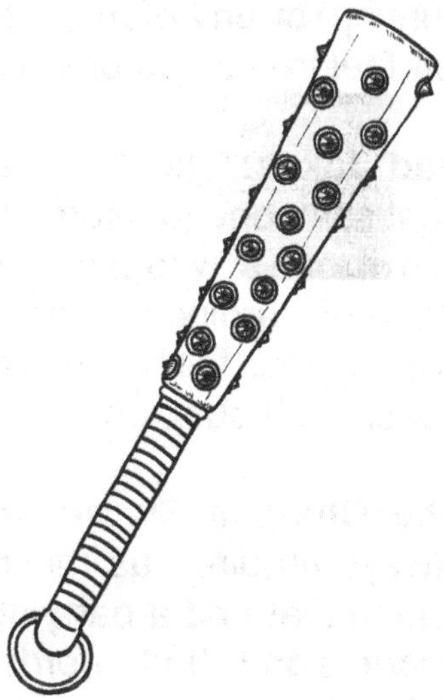

is awesome. Avoid the ones with spikes, as these tend to get stuck and make retrieval far more difficult than needed.

A Sock Full of Quarters: While known in certain blueprints to be the bane of consciousness for the mall security guard, these may not be ideal weapons against the undead. Sure it seems like a quality bludgeon at first glance, and you could possibly make a dent in a skull, but it seems that money would do more toward upgrading your present arsenal. You could certainly give it a try on a zombie, though. I'd do it myself, but I threw my back out humping your mom last night, nooch.

The Boomerang: Yes, it's technically a club—a throwing club, but a club. All right, we all know how these are supposed to work, and in the hands of one who's practiced at the skill, it's a fine thing to behold. Against a zombie though, this thing has no place. It ranks among the most useless of tools one could employ against the walking dead. If you choose to use it for hunting, or any of the various uses that they've been adapted for, feel free to lug one along with you.

Bad Jokes: These are something else that can be used to beat someone to death. Some of us enjoy them, though. Best told if one's wearing the nose/mustache/glasses ensemble. Word of warning though: choosing to use these too frequently among your fellow survivors may result in receiving a severe beating of your own.

The Chinese Sword-Breaker: Hand to hand combat has always required as much defensive skill as it has offensive, and to that end a parrying device had to be made. You'll find daggers and short swords for use in the offhand in that capacity, but nothing quite similar to the Chinese sword-breaker. While efforts to find a historical model of this weapon fell short, there's a modern incarnation made by a well-known company. This thing is a solid metal rod which is used to thrust aside or even break the blade of your opponent. It measures a total of thirty-eight inches and has a rectangular cross guard for protection of the hand.

Now if it's a deflection weapon, why is it here? Because you can smash the shit out of something with it, that's why. It's a carbon steel pole on a handle, folks, what else could you ask for when it comes to the bashing of zombie skulls? You can also jam this into the eye socket and get the desired life-ending effect. While its length isn't great in terms of keeping you out of harm's reach, you know the basic idea behind any melee weapon is as a last resort or to maintain stealth. Should you be inclined to get your hands on a nice metal smashing pole, give this one a shot.

The Crowbar: A personal favorite due to its versatility. The crowbar is not only a viable option with which to brain a zombie, you can also stab it into the eye quite nicely. It's hefty, solid, and packed with fiber. OK, maybe not that last part, but it will prove nice to have when encountering locked doors, windows, and other barriers that need to be bashed, beaten, pried, lifted or moved a bit. Crowbars were never intended for assault purposes, but it doesn't matter when it comes to having something as hefty and all-around useful as this little multi-tool. It will get the job done.

There are also a couple newer versions of the crowbar that have been released in the past few years, which have an even more diverse range in their uses. They're weighted a bit heavier, which adds to the power of a strike, but their functional additions make it a worthwhile tool to have around. You just never know where you may find a use for these things, in any incarnation.

Titties: While these are in no way weaponry, some are large enough to constitute as bludgeoning instruments. They're also wonderful to look at, touch, and be around. We are fans of their work.

Nunchakus: Popularized by Bruce Lee's wanton ass-kickery in that one movie, and later by yet another mutated martial-arts-trained shelled reptile, nunchakus are simply two metal or wooden sticks connected at their ends by chain or rope. You can create a lot of force with the little weapon by rapidly twirling and swinging it around the human body. The power of the blow which results is determined by the user's strength, speed, and skill with this particular item, but in most cases, causing the blunt force trauma necessary to dispatch a zombie with a blow to the head is not going to happen. Utilizing these in self-defense against a dojo full of students who simply stand there and wait to be hit in the face is one thing; against the undead, it's a really bad idea.

The Baseball Bat: The most treacherous of all flying mammals, these have been known to send small innocent balls (giggidy) flying for hundreds of feet with little or no warning. To that end, these are basically modern day clubs used for a dying sport, which, in the event of a zombie apocalypse, could easily become the national past time again due to our rekindled love of beating small round things with other larger things. A series of well-placed blows with a baseball bat can cause enough damage to the human body to make an underground plastic surgeon cry, puke, and shit himself at the same time. Most joking aside, these are available in wood and aluminum models, and can most definitely be used as a weapon against your former fellow humans. Wood can break under enough stress, of course, and aluminum can bend, so beware of these potential happenings leaving you feeling shortstopped.

A 2x4: Used by wrestlers in the 1980s and '90s as an effective but illegal weapon. You can use these if dire circumstances dictate that you must, but don't let the ref catch you, tough guy. HOOOOOOOOOOOO!!!

Seemingly Fun Methods

"I feel the need to go over a very basic bit of advice. Fire is bad. I don't care what you think, I don't care what you want to believe. Lighting a still animated zombie on fire is stupid. Zombies feel no pain; all you're going to get is a zombie that wants to eat your flesh that's on fire. You can use fire to destroy the corpse after you destroy the brain."

– Chief Richard Burns

FUEGO: Excuse me, but do you have a light?

When fire was first discovered, prehistoric man was delighted. When they discovered how to make it themselves, the caveman that did it carried some around on a stick and got chicks. Sounds awesome, right? It's not that easy anymore to impress the ladies, but we can still use fire to keep us warm, cook our meals, and, of course, dispose of the undead. Now using fire as a weapon is an idea that warrants some discussion. To properly discuss these uses, however, we have to look at the various ways they could be brought to bear. Keep in mind though that fire is nobody's friend when it comes to wreaking havoc and causing damage. It'll just as soon burn you as it would the shuffling monster trying to munch on your person. You've been warned, and so now we move on to how to light things up.

Flamethrowers

Two words: completely wrong. We know there's a contingent of people out there that seem hell bent on using fire as a weapon in every circumstance. While the idea of a flamethrower is awesome, using it against the undead is a complete waste of time. As we all know, using fire to kill humans works rather well. Pain causes a human to shut down rather quickly, and they succumb to breathing in the fumes and smoke, which incapacitates them. Not quite the same with a zombie.

REVIEW TIME! Zombies feel no pain, they don't need to breathe, so they won't succumb to smoke inhalation. They will just be on fire until that fire destroys them. What this means is that they will be on fire and coming after you in a new horrifying manner. Now they're going to be bringing fire with them, burning your buildings, your cars, your pets, and also, you. Some military types may argue the heat produced by a flamethrower will destroy a zombie right away. Not true at all; they will still be quite mobile for some time. It takes a high temperature and long time to destroy the muscles, fat, and tissue. Even if an initial basting of roasting goodness is applied, the undead not directly targeted will not be so quick to fall down and become crispy critters.

Also, you should consider the fuel use by the device vs. undead being affected. During the time of the zombie apocalypse, you can sure find better uses for the fuel. Hell, I'd rather waste fuel powering a generator so you could watch reality TV than waste it lighting zed on fire so they can shamble around destroying what we've

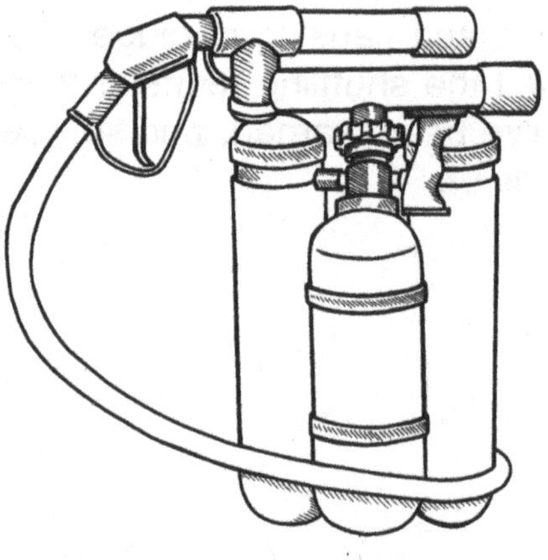

worked so hard to build. Flamethrowers are also fairly heavy and bulky for just waltzing around. "Ho de hum, hiking around, oops, zombie, roast it!" This situation is not going to work out well. It's just a burden on your physical capacities which will leave you in a state of exhaustion and terribly vulnerable to an approaching horde. Perhaps if used in conjunction with a mobile caravan of well-armed individuals these would find a better niche, but if you're planning on shooting the undead anyway, why not just do so without risking a fire while carrying around a heavy bit of equipment? Not a terribly practical weapon for every day anti-zombie applications.

Use of these weapons should be limited to general corpse disposal or last stand types of maneuvers. Fill a ditch with the recently dispatched undead, light them up, and sing Dio songs. Perhaps you know that a particular field is crawling with zombies; use the flamethrower to set the perimeter ablaze, and let it burn inward to minimize possible wildfire scenarios. Be sure to have folks stationed around as to pick off any of the walking dead who try to escape the conflagration. If you insist on using one of these, exercise all possible safety in doing so and never ever let your friends talk you into using it to conjure up a flaming fart. You could quite possibly misjudge something very badly and weld your ass cheeks together, and where would you be then Captain Uni-Bun?

Molotov Cocktails: A comparatively simple bit of human ingenuity that has been a riot cliché since its very existence was brought about. Generally used by those who don't have access to other more costly incendiary devices, their chief purpose is to set things on fire—imagine that. Made of a bottle filled with a combustible liquid and topped with a rag, which acts as a wick, these are then hurled and, upon impact, break and begin immolation of the target. Certain agents can be added to the mixture that will cause the accelerant to stick to a target and continue the burning process despite it moving from the main body of the fire. You could also employ the use of a sling to add a bit of distance to the launching of these brittle burning bombs. These could conceivably be used in a rear guard action while fleeing an area, but all precautions should be observed when doing so since, ya know, it's going to cause a fire.

The Blowtorch: Not one of the most effective means to dispose of the undead. A hand-held propane torch is never going to burn through the human skull in any kind of record time, but they are great ignition sources for combustible materials. If you're into the sickeningly sadistic kind of thing, an oxy-acetylene torch, a bit of time, and a properly restrained zombie could prove to be a fun weekend, but that's just disturbing and wrong. This will be mostly due to the smells that are going to be coming from that little plot of earth. Aside from that, what you do with the undead is your own business. Unless you happen to become one, so don't do that.

Drenching with Gas, Throwing a Match, and Running: Also known as dousing, this may not be as elegant as the Molotov or the flamethrower when it comes to spreading the flame around, but it'll work in a pinch. This is an added tactic that should be reserved for the very end of a hopeless stand against the undead. Best results would be attained from the top of a large concrete or brick structure, where you're out of harm's way and able to safely drop a road flare or some sort of ignition source onto the soaked undead, while not putting yourself at too much risk. In this way, one could conceivably taunt the undead and maybe cook yourself a few hot dogs on the end of a very long stick.

Explosives: Cool Guys Don't Look at These

In conventional battles, explosives are used in various aspects from creating a defensive perimeter to an offensively utilized hand-held weapon. The explosive's role in combat isn't just a simple throw and go type of classification at all, and shouldn't be automatically dismissed as such. While they do tend to disable opponents using shrapnel and concussive blasts, which will prove largely ineffective versus the undead, some of these have a bit more bang for their buck and do their dirty work in tremendous style.

To that end, further discussion is required on which of these are worth scrounging up and which should be left alone. Always remember that when handling objects such as these, extreme caution is warranted, and they should be treated as carefully as one would a loaded weapon, because that's essentially what you're holding. You don't really want to substitute your old pigskin with a grenade because it's Sunday and you happen to miss football and you *really* want to throw the ball around. That would simply be folly, as a grenade's WAY too heavy for a good throw, and it lacks the aerodynamics to hold a decent spiral.

Grenades

Far from a new means of wreaking havoc among the enemy line, the first incarnation of the grenade was a simple ceramic or metal ball filled with gunpowder and topped with a wick. As time went on, technology continued to improve on these hand-held devices, which has increased the effective range and power of the explosions and shrapnel. Some simple versions still remain, such as the Molotov cocktail, but these aren't true grenades at all. Modern frag grenades are set on a timer; when the pin is pulled, the spoon is released and the countdown begins, giving the thrower generally three seconds in which to get the explosive to its designated area. When these detonate, they effectively utilize the casing as shrapnel, causing horrendous damage to anything within fifteen to thirty meters. Against the walking dead, the real chances of a grenade causing a fatal wound are very slim. They may manage to unsettle the ghoul's footing and give your group time to get a head start, but expecting the undead to stay down is unrealistic. Other types of grenades are made for non-lethal purposes, such as the flash bang grenade or the sting grenade, and may in fact act as a fine distraction prior to your having been spotted by the undead. Further variations, such as the concussion and incendiary grenades, can be used for the same purposes, though the incendiary may in fact cause a fire due to its extreme heat of 2,200°C (3,992°F), and these aren't really intended to be thrown as they're more for destroying a weapon cache or vehicle interior.

In times gone by, grenades were thrown by hand or by slings in order to increase their range and better protect the throwers, but these days, we have the good old grenade launcher to do our dirty work for us. Actually we've had these for some time in one shape or another, but let's face it, the modern incarnations are the bomb diggity and can launch these volatile projectiles an awesome distance. There are simply a staggering number of potential ways to use these weapons against the undead, whether it's to trigger a landslide or avalanche or just buying time or even clearing a path to safety, but they're not going to prove the great zombie-killer, and shouldn't be treated as such. In most cases, these types of hardware are going to be difficult, if not impossible, to obtain in the civilian market, and the acquisition of these should not be attempted by illegal means, as this attempt will most likely result in your very untimely demise at the hands of rather unfriendly persons who are far better trained to use this equipment than you are.

Mines

The land mine as we know it today is an anti-tank or anti-personnel explosive charge which is generally weight-triggered and is intended to damage via explosion, concussion, or fragmentation. Practical application of these against the undead would fall into the defensive category, as they can act as one hell of a warning against incursion toward your newly chosen home. Not only will it at least take a leg off the zombie, it'll be a truly effective wakeup call to the rest of your group. Going out and randomly laying land mines is, of course, not a good idea, as these can potentially do far more harm than good when they're simply strewn about the world. You wouldn't want anyone doing that while you're out supply hunting or maybe just scouting. Then next thing you know, hey, your arm's off. That would completely put you out of the running for doing the puppet bit in the upcoming talent show.

Mortars

The big brother to the hand grenade and the little brother to the heavy artillery round, these are mobile short to long-range platforms from which to launch a nice little explosive charge.

Able to be carried by hand, you can easily lob this payload over obstacles and make a nice little dent. These have been around for hundreds of years, and they first found their niche in siege battles, but were later used during the trench warfare of World War I, where troops were able to perfectly drop their bomb into the enemy trenches and cause massive destruction. Depending on both fragmentation and concussion to do its dirty work, these have proven very effective tools in modern conventional warfare. The concussive forces caused by these explosions may in fact be enough to cause sufficient cerebral trauma to the undead. They may even result in their demise if they're within the proper range. This is a debatable premise, which will require far more testing. Just don't try to steal one from the military in the name of science.

Car Bombs

Seriously? Zed doesn't drive, so this is a complete waste of time, not to mention a very silly fire hazard. Come on now; this shouldn't even be here. Who wrote this nonsense?

DY-NO-MITE!!!

Round sticks of explodey goodness. They've been around for over 150 years, and are often a large part of the plot of some horrible movies involving speeding buses, terrorists, or rednecks. Now, dynamite has proven helpful in removing stumps, mining, leveling buildings, and fishing. These things are all proven uses for the sticks of boom. Will they be effective against zombies? Well, dynamite can be used to make a large group of the undead into a large field of pieces of still living zombie chunks. In proper situations, it will liquefy the brain as well, like if Timmy the Zombie is trapped in a well and you toss a stick down to him as a night light. However, the chances of it actually being useful as a weapon are on par with all other explosives. It's best to just use it for its intended purposes, and leave it at that.

Plastic Explosive

Common types of plastic explosives include semtex and C-4. You can pick these up at any demolition store, military base, and if you're especially handy, it can be made in your kitchen. The plastic explosive is often used to destroy buildings and hunt tricky golf course gophers. But, as Hollywood has taught us, terrorists like to form baked-potato sized chunks and kill people. They are one of the most expensive explosives to buy and make, require an outside detonator, and can rot rather fast. The upside of these types of explosives is their ability to be molded and formed into any shape you need it to be. It'll fit in door jams, cracks in the mountain, holes in the wall, or can remain as a happy little ball, making this particular explosive the most entertaining of all, since not only do you get boomy fun, but you can use it as modeling clay while bored. Sadly, plastic explosives are exactly like their explosive counterparts, and not a particularly good weapon against the undead except in extreme situations.

Poop

You may not think of excrement as an explosive, but we're not talking about your standard steamy 4-coiler. We're talking about ammonium nitrate fertilizer combined with diesel fuel. It's the same compound used to make several terrorist bombs in the United States, the most notorious of which being the Oklahoma City bomb. It's easily created with widely available ingredients, which you can use to mix up a batch in your garage. Now, having such an easily created explosive does have downsides. It's highly unstable and hard to control. When using this particular method for exploding things, you most definitely want to set it up and leave the area, and not just the immediate area; we're talking about getting completely out of the city. Another drawback would be its main ingredient, fertilizer, which does not have a particularly decent smell about it. In fact this will tend to draw quite a bit of unwanted attention if you choose to go about trying to manufacture this in the heart of suburbia. While it's a viable explosive, its use is not highly recommended, and, really, who wants fertilizer covered zombie chunks chasing after them? That's just a shitty idea.

Further Stuff & Improvising!

"Guns, blades, sporting equipment, all fine examples. But if you look around your house, you'll find a plethora of weapons. The table leg, toilet tank lid, that old bowling ball. All acceptable. Now I'm not saying to run headlong into a crowd of zed with the giant, double personal pleasure device you have in the bedroom. I'm just saying don't rule it out."

– Bob From Bob's Army Surplus

There are plenty of alternate methods that you can employ in your defiance of the undead menace. Most of these aren't the most efficient ways of dealing with a zombie problem, but each has its own merits and potential to get the job done. Some of them are simply wacky, and there are others that I'm sure we haven't even considered, probably for good reasons, but one thing you should take away from this section is that, under duress, anything can be used to your advantage. Just stay calm, look around, and get creative. An active mind that's fueled by the desire to not become a walking automaton can get crafty in a real hurry.

With that in mind, nearly anything has the potential to become a deadly weapon. That table leg may not look brutal, but wrap some chain around it and tape it on, and you have a mean club. Those old ice skates that haven't been used in a while, slap those together with a couple broom handles, and you have a potential hit. Tire irons in the garage, a piece of rebar, or anything else you see; think of how it could one day save your life. Just don't tell the people you work with that you've been thinking that the fax machine would make a great improvised flail. People start to look at you funny, and this could potentially turn into an HR issue.

BB Gun with Coat Hanger Chunks

A strong enough air rifle does in fact have enough power to lodge a BB in the skull at close range, and could conceivably end the days of a zombie at very close range. What happens if you run out of ammo for one of these? Three-inch sections of wire coat hanger? Brilliant idea! These are roughly the same diameter as your average BB and will be subject to the same amount of pressure when your air rifle is fired. Their greater mass translates into greater piercing power, and again, at short range, these can get the job done when you have no other means available. Think of this method as an extremely unprofessional late term abortion done at high speed. On second thought, don't. In fact, don't think of this at all. Ever.

Reading Bad Poetry/ Literature

Let's face it, there is no such thing as good poetry that exists outside of a bathroom stall. Trying to assail the undead with bad writing is simply not going to have any affect on them at all. No matter how horrible those books about the twinkled vampires were, espousing this crap to the indifferent zombie means you're just that much closer to being chewed on. This method only ensures your own loss of mental stability, as reading these works will simply cause your brain to shrivel up and shriek in terror. If you're unsure what the warning signs are that your brain has become unstable due to the material being read, it sounds a bit like letting air out of a balloon by pulling the open ends apart—just FYI. Another indication would be if you choose to pick a "Team" between the very homosexually oriented guy and the slightly less homosexually oriented guy. Use these warnings as signs that you may want to switch your reading material immediately. It can only help.

Nuclear Weapons

They ended Japan's involvement in WWII and scared the hell out of everyone else on the planet for a good forty years, so why not use them to put an abrupt halt to the zombie apocalypse? The simple reasoning behind this is that aside from the initial blast, the casualty rate of the undead just doesn't justify their use. Some will die, sure, but for those that remain, all you end up with is a bunch of highly radioactive ghouls walking around still trying to chew on people. Some devilish cannibalistic radioactive monster out of an old sci-fi movie. This is almost as bad as zombies on fire, which will continue trying to eat your fleshy parts, while totally oblivious to its predicament. Besides, let's face the facts here: zombies aren't going to just hang around in places waiting for people to show up, unless they're trapped somehow, and this unlikely concentration of them in a certain area just won't warrant that kind of loss of habitable land, which we're going to need in the future for rebuilding and so on. There are safer and less volatile ways to go about doing away with the undead. We'll discuss how to safely clear areas in another section, but for now, just dismiss the use of nuclear arms against the shambling menace.

Psychokinetic Powers

That's telekinesis, Kyle. Yes, using the power of the mind to manipulate matter has been a sought-after ability in human beings for many years. People have been producing illusions which appear to be actual telekinesis for a long time, but these are just entertaining tricks to amuse crowds and earn some coin. Being able to simply imagine some sort of physical happening and using nothing more than your brain to make it happen—that's awesome just to contemplate. Crushing zombie heads like ripe zits with a blink. Killing yaks at 200 yards with your mind bullets is simply such a breathtaking thing to imagine that, right now, wishing you had that power, you should be passing out. When you wake up and read the rest of this, you're going to be lost. Start over, and then pass out again. Here is where we wait.

OK, now that you've made it this far, let's point out that telekinesis is something which isn't really proven, and attempting to develop this ability, rather than finding useful weapons, is going to probably end up very badly for you. So, you can imagine it in all its tremendous glory, and then you can dismiss it. If you DO happen to possess these abilities, good for you. Stop giving mental tug jobs at the strip club, or whatever the hell you're presently doing, and go be a super hero already. With great power comes dubious feasibility. Wait, what?

Electricity

While it may not take much of a jolt to temporarily disable a living person, and even less of one to cause heart fibrillations, electricity's use against the undead is limited. Actually it's largely a misuse of time and juice. Given that, in large part, the nerves of the ghoul's body are inactive, it would take two or three times the amount of electricity to even cause the zombie to jump a little bit. This being the case, anything short of the amount of electricity it would take to fry a manatee, such as a downed power line, should never even be granted a moment of thought. Electric fences and the like would prove largely ineffective against these creatures, and would equate to nothing more than a waste of precious power. It may be amusing to hit a zombie with three or four tasers at once, just to see if you can make it do the funky chicken, but unless you're passing the kind of current which will hard-boil the brain, disregard the employment of this tactic.

Poisons

A dead body lacks the ability to circulate these, so they may not be utilized efficiently in causing a cessation of life functions. What this means is that all the time spent trying to set up and deliver these chemicals into the undead has been squandered. Even were they to be injected straight into the brain, with a lack of a proper circulatory system, the poison will sit idle and do nothing at all. Really, it's a little sad to think that we can't properly combat the undead with chemical compositions, but that's just how it is. You may not want to bother with these unless you plan on going into the hit-man business when the undead threat is ended.

Combines/Threshers

Got a field full of zombies, and you're not quite committed to setting it on fire in order to get rid of them all? Hop in your trusty combine harvester and go for a death-dealing drive. The modern incarnations of these have a nicely enclosed and air conditioned cabins, which require you to climb up to in order to enter. This could conceivably keep you pretty safe from all those dirty, grasping, and un-manicured hands. There's even a stereo in there (in some anyway) for your listening pleasure. The blades on the front will do one hell of a job ripping the bodies of the walking dead down, leaving a messy pulp and leaving you relatively safe from possible exposure. These are not recommended for use by those without working knowledge of these machines, but under the right circumstances, they could do a fine job of tearing up a decent number of these foul creatures. Plus, you can pretend you're in that movie with the one guy listening to John Denver music and singing along while writing your name in the field.

Acids

Not the variety revolutionized by Dr. Timothy Leary. Calm down, you freaks. The acids we're talking about here are the ones that eat through a fair number of materials and are horribly dangerous. Yes, they used to have jeans washed in these in the '80s, but we're mainly focusing on the highly corrosive examples. Should you find yourself in the unique position of finding large quantities or even manufacturing these chemical compounds, finding a safe and effective method in which to utilize them would prove the most daunting task. While they would prove very effective in the disposal of the undead from head to toe, this is a lengthy process in which the zombie would remain active throughout. This method is like fire in that it has zero sense of loyalty and will almost certainly prove to be as much of a danger to you as anything else it comes into contact with. Not a highly recommended method of assuring the demise of the ghouls trying desperately to get you to join their ranks, but in the right setting it could be employed in a safe and effective manner. Just don't ask us what that would be.

Wood Chipper

Probably not the most creative way to go about your business, however there's some fun trap potential here. With your standard yard-care version of these mulch-makers, one could probably cut up and dispose of a couple of recently dispatched corpses in a day. This is simply too damn slow, plus you just got your good wood chipper dirtier than you could ever hope to clean. You need to think bigger, grander, and more brutal. There are some very large industrial variations on machines such as these, and with a sadistic nature and a little planning, these could prove very useful in the realm of undead disposal. While properly armed for self-defense, stand atop one of these after building a funnel into the mouths of a couple of the tree-chewing monsters, and let the undead walk right in and get spit out. Since they're wanting to get to you, they'll take the most direct route, regardless of your lofty perch. Allowing them to do so will cause a lovely volcanic eruption of gore to be spewed forth from the back ends of these machines. Word of caution: don't let anyone stand behind these while you're going about your grisly work, otherwise, they'll probably have to die too. Enjoy!

Weed Eater with a Saw Blade

This one's not elegant or quiet, and it sure won't be pretty, but there are massive possibilities with this modified gardening tool. Simply attach a nice sturdy saw blade to the end of a weed whacker, start it up, and go to town until the gas runs out. This is certainly a fun way to do a bit of zombie clearing yard work. We're pretty sure the joy one would feel while using this improvised implement is illegal. At the very least, it's surely immoral. Sure it's a bit dangerous, it's loud, there could be bone and congealed blood everywhere, and it just screams "bad idea," but that little voice that's whispering cautioning words into your ear is just a pussy. The probability of the noise attracting more of the undead bastards is very high, but that's the chance you take. Hopefully you have more gas than they have numbers in the area. If you do decide to go this route, just make sure you get the job done before it rains or you can't go out this weekend.

Bulldozers

Something of a simplified term for a large piece of construction equipment, these come in various shapes and sizes and thus, usefulness. The common and most helpful varieties would be the bulldozer, front-end loader, the backhoe, and the road roller. The front-end loader is a massive construct, which requires you climb into the cab and operate it from a safe location while using the bucket and mammoth horsepower to great effect against the zombies that are menacingly encroaching on your territory. With a little practice in one of these, you'll get to where you can knock a zombie down and pop its head.

A bulldozer is a front-end loader with a more stationary bucket and treads instead of massive tires. Treads are an automatic plus for this thing already. The backhoe also has a bucket, but additionally is equipped with a nifty shovel you can dig with and swing around, causing all kinds of insane damage and merriment. Childlike glee is one of the backhoe's common side effects. The road roller is a road roller, and what else needs to be said there? You've seen these before, probably slowing down your daily commute. On the up side, the undead are stupid, and will try to win a game of chicken with you, so why not use this to your advantage? Maybe they'll just get pushed down or out of the way, but the potential here is just too amusing to pass up. The amounts of exquisite violence one can inflict with heavy equipment could make even Mother Theresa into a bloodthirsty fucking lunatic.

Now, any of these take a bit of getting used to when you first get into them, but they all also offer a raised, and generally enclosed, seat from which to commence your destruction. OK, so maybe not the backhoe as much, save for the larger designs, but some of the smaller ones have cages that will work in a pinch to keep you safe. Especially with skilled backup to pick off any of the zombies that manage to evade your swinging bucket-o-death. These things have potential. Find one of these and use it, and this could just lead to some wicked good times. Also, for additional enjoyment, find yourself a lovely tracked excavator. Yeah, that's the stuff. I'm starting to drool now just a little.

Cranes with a Wrecking Ball

Yep, more heavy equipment, because it's fun and we can. Given the right location and working knowledge of their use, cranes can be a lifesaver. You may not attain rapid kill ability with one of these, but there's massive potential for both practical and impractical applications here. With the wrecking ball alone, the probability of sending an undead husk flying is almost worth the effort and potential danger. Having to climb up into the control cabin gives you a safe strategic point from which to operate the crane, and when the time comes, you can easily make an exit without very much risk to yourself. Unless, of course, the undead have managed to completely surround your new toy. As always, you should have plenty of ammo on hand to work with and, in so doing, your getting out alive shouldn't pose a significant risk.

Cement-Filled Tires Down a Hill

This is primarily a defense-only type of weapon, and should be used as such. With what will surely become an excessive amount of unusable vehicles in our undead world, why not use the parts to our advantage against the undead? You could easily fortify your hill-top and set up a nice protective system with these simple and very painful devices by removing either individual tires, or entire axles with both tires, and filling them with cement or rocks, then unleashing them against the advancing hordes. Using nothing more than gravity, setting these loose down a hill toward the undead may not result in a kill, but it will transform them into one hell of a mess. Think of a knee-high clothesline on steroids. At that point, what previously looked like a slow-moving onslaught will have turned into a mopping up operation, easily finished with a good thumping of skulls. Setting your handy trap back up shouldn't be too difficult, and will almost certainly be rewarded in the future with successful defensive stands. Let's hear it for multi-useable life-saving devices! Huzzah!!!

Deep Fried

In the USA, we deep-fry everything. It's not always a good idea, but every now and then a nugget of joy appears as if by divine providence, and it quickly becomes reproduced at fairs and carnivals anywhere you go. To this end, we submit the possibility of the deep-fried zed. Not the fastest or safest way to go about assuring their destruction, to be sure, but it could be thoroughly entertaining. Since this has yet to be accomplished, we can only guess, but once they float, they're probably done. Don't eat these. They go right to your hips.

Intoxicants

At some point, there is going to be someone who thinks if they get a zombie drunk or stoned that it's going to mellow out and be their buddy. This is just stupid. First off, the undead are unaffected by chemicals in any way shape or form, aside from being bathed in acid and dissolved. Secondly, it's a complete waste of your acid, pills, booze and/or weed, and the perpetrators of this type of wasteful behavior should be slapped with a tire iron. Probably even twice. Never endanger yourself by trying to share your intoxicating methods with the undead. They're simply unappreciative and they'll continue to try and chew on you. Save it for the living who may be able to appreciate such things as getting a little narrow-eyed.

Man's Best Friend

"I will have at least one dog. Not so much for hunting, or protection, but for companionship and early warning. Animals will know the infected are around before you will. They go nuts, so be ready for a fight."

– NFL Quarterback

That's right, the dog. A dog is more of an early warning device and buddy. While not much of an offensive weapon, the canine can provide not only companionship, but also an extra moment to prepare for an encounter with the undead. They can see, smell, and hear far better than any human, and, as such, will provide us with plenty of time to prepare for an unwelcome meeting. Sure, it's another mouth to feed, they drool, and they lick their own butts, but you can't overlook their benefits. They can help distract things (living and otherwise) away from you, sniff out goods if they're trained properly, and let's face it—anything that can see you naked and not laugh is good to have around.

SECTION 4
ARMOR, TRAVEL, AND PROTECTION

"Seems many people are still confused about what clothes will protect from zombies. Those of you insistent on wearing a form of armor, well, you're going to end up being turned into undead lasagna. A general rule is if you can't bite through it, neither can zed. So stop thinking heavy, noisy armor. Use environment appropriate items that a human can't bite through, and you'll live a longer happier life."

– Edna Mode

Ever since man first began beating the living shit out of one another for purposes of asserting dominance, gaining land, stealing women, and fraternity initiations, the use of various forms of protection have become popular forms of defense. Early forms of hides gave way to more sturdy methods of construction that all served to protect the human body from various forms of harm.

Unfortunately for those of us in the business of preparing for the undead apocalypse, none of these were designed with the intention of thwarting a ceaseless horde of undead in mind. With what is presently available in the world today in regards to protective gear, there are numerous possibilities when it comes to protecting your tender backside. If you do choose to go the armored route, don't let it build up a false sense of security. Maintain the thought that you're still squishy under that material and very vulnerable to injury, otherwise there won't be much hope for you when your own stupid actions become your worst enemy. Use it for its intended purpose—to protect. It's not a safeguard against inattention or carelessness.

Kevlar: Widely known to be a component of personal body armor since the early 1980s, Kevlar has been a staple of military protective gear for some time now. This material has been known to help thwart the perilous advance of bullets and blades alike. In addition to helmets and jackets, face protection is also available, and will serve much the same function. Now due to its chemical composition, it's boasted to be stronger than steel and is a popular bullet-resistant material. However, the undead aren't going to be shooting at you, and neither will most humans you encounter. That's not to say that it won't have its place if human in-fighting begins somewhere, just that its usefulness against a zombie is open to discussion. A jacket in the military style could certainly provide protection against the nails of the undead grabbing at you, as well as giving you a plethora of pockets in which to store gear, but at the same time it offers more for a ghoul to hold on to. Let us also keep in mind that using Kevlar in the sun degrades it over time without proper protection from ultra violet rays. Heat itself has been known to weaken this material a substantial amount. This isn't bad to have when going into a firefight, but against the undead, its merits are questionable.

Leather: Certainly a fashionable choice, though it may not make you many friends of the PETA or bovine persuasion. These cured coverings can prove to be quite valuable when faced with the gnashing teeth of the undead or having to lay down your motorcycle in a hurry. Not only can it keep the wind from dropping your body temperature, leather, especially deerskin, is a fairly strong material, and has been known to offer additional protection. When without it riding, you could leave about 100 yards of your own hide behind on the pavement. Still used by some in the racing circuits today to guard largely against road rash, racing leathers, jackets, gloves, and the like should attest to leather's ability to repel the unwanted oral advances of the undead without too much trouble. Additionally, when worn at times when extreme stealth is needed, a properly fitted ensemble should remain virtually silent, and not serve as a creaking dinner bell to the undead. The wearing of this gear may get you invited to certain bars. If this is the case, and you're unaware of what the true meaning behind the invitation really is, then politely decline it. It's for the best.

Becoming a Cyborg Cop: While this may seem like an awesome idea, sadly technology hasn't quite caught up to the concept. Think of it though: armor plated junk, auto-targeting systems, an automatic pistol that reloads itself in your thigh, and a spiky middle finger that also acts as a computer interface? Just throw in kicking the shit out of alligators being ridden by a bunch of monkeys with flaming chainsaws instead of hands, and then getting to nail a bunch of hot chicks while eating beef jerky, and you have the ultimate fantasy right there. You could always go and get yourself shot up a bunch and see if they'll hook you up with some experimental tech—you never know. Something to consider on those days you're just sitting around at home bored.

Chain Mail: Invented by the Celts many moons ago, this armor is constructed of interlocking iron rings and offers protection to the head, neck, and torso. The getup can also include the arms and legs. Chain mail is not known for its stealth, lightweight properties, or ease of production, this type of armor can often be more bane than boon. Though it can offer adequate protection against the rending and tearing teeth of the undead, it can also serve as quite an announcement of your presence in an area and let zombies know you're there for the noon feeding. With a full body suit, it does indeed offer protection against the undead and mostly uninhibited mobility, though prolonged encumbrance by the suit could cause dehydration and heat-related illness. Had you been training with this for years, it would be recommended for the odd offensive skirmish, but even then, it has the potential to become an unwanted distraction. Should this happen at an inopportune moment, you'll be ending your days as human tuna. If that happens, someone else is going to be forced to kill your jangling zombie ass.

The last real issue crops up when it comes to the acquisition of this armor. The present-day variants are often crafted of aluminum rings and made for LARP types, and these are not exactly up to the rigors of a true battle. If you're planning on entrusting your life to this form of protection, make damn sure it's going to stand up to the very real damage that it's likely to sustain over time. Find a quality craftsman who deals in the creation of this medieval cock ring collaboration. Doing otherwise, you're just begging for trouble.

Plate Armor: Once chain mail became inadequate against certain threats, they began adding plates to the more vulnerable portions of the human anatomy. Then another plate was added. After that, someone went a little crazy with the idea, threw on a helmet, and thus, plate mail was born. The most popular vision when plate mail is brought into a conversation is that of the knight, resplendent on horseback, charging into single combat against a similarly clad foe. Good for him, because if the other guy wasn't also weighted down by this shit, that would have been the knight's ass. Plate armor is heavy; there is no two ways about it. Wearing this, even if you've done so for many years in mock combat, will wear you down after a short time. Due to the fact that the fellows who wore these kettles liked to run at each other on horseback with long sharp sticks, the helmets worn with these suits offered limited visibility and just about as much audio capability. These are not liabilities you're going to want to deal with when your ability to see and hear approaching undead is of the utmost importance. Add all of this terribly stifling gear up, and what you have is a case of heatstroke inside of a metal barrel just waiting to happen. Another noteworthy concern is the limited mobility you would experience in these giant soup cans. Knights weren't exactly the European version of ninjas, and when it came to being able to move quickly, none of these boys won the cake. Plate armor tends to rattle, a lot, and it does so very loudly. You won't be doing any sneaking about in this getup. Really, just think for a moment, wading out to do battle with the hordes of undead, and all of a sudden you have an itch. Not even a fun idea there. Plus on top of all that, these suits of armor were designed to repel blows from weapons, not to withstand the pulling, ripping, and tearing of unarmed and bloodthirsty opponents. Let us not forget the arduous task of getting back up should you fall. If you happen to go down amidst the throng of undead, you'll be stripped of that precious armor and bare to their teeth and nails; it's just a matter of that time. Oh yeah, those zombies are going to pry that shit off and eat you.

Yet another thing you should know when considering this type of personal defense is the suit you wear must be crafted to you exactly for proper weight distribution and mobility. Taking a suit off the stand at the local history museum and running about quoting the Holy Grail is only going to result in your being horribly killed while yelling "NI." All in all, you could probably find an armorsmith to craft you a fine suit that would be weighted and measured exactly, and allow for near-full mobility of your limbs, but it's really not your best course of action when speed and stealth are your greatest assets against the undead. It may be one thing to screw around with when you're in a controlled situation, but it's quite another to think it makes you invincible. Pass on this one, Lancelot.

Body Odor: Seriously, this isn't armor so much as repellant to your fellow humans. Wash your crack, please.

"When you're making your big escape from heavily populated areas, remember to pack toilet paper. Having a stank itchy ass is a sure way to become bait. No one likes the stinky group member, no matter how useful you are."

– Removed Answer from Trivial Pursuit

Shields: For those who simply can't get enough of the melee combat with a slower and intellectually inferior opponent (in most cases anyway), these may just be for you. While there are countless variations on the designs of these defensive deflectors, the idea remains the same: hold one of these in your off-hand (the non-dominant hand) and keep the undead at bay while preparing your next strike. Fairly simple and they can even protect from the odd bit of splatter that may occur. Should you find yourself weaponless, you can use these in a two-handed manner and simply batter your way to safety, unless of course you're completely surrounded by a writhing press of zombies, in which case, you should have known better.

Now you can go with your basic medieval iron shield, but those are awfully heavy and will wear you out quite quickly. The Spartan variation on the shield (a.k.a. Aspis) is made of wood and covered, or trimmed, in bronze. These are great at stopping arrows, bolts, and other projectiles, plus if you swing them at a zombie's head hard enough, you could kill it or even take the damn thing right off. These, too, are very heavy and a burden to carry about. You could even fashion your own out of a barrel if you're so inclined. It's better than using a buckler. Bucklers are little shields that you wear kind of strapped to the wrist or held by hand, which is pretty much useless against the undead. You should be slapped with a dead fish for even considering this one.

Using the most modern incarnation of these, the riot shield, not only do you have the protection of the old school heavy shields, but as an added bonus, you can see through them. The basic models are between four and ten pounds, with the bullet resistant variety weighing a bit more. They'll offer you a knee to neck deflector of harm, and you can see those monsters coming; all kinds of goodness right there. Don't get cocky though. These require a bit of endurance when used for prolonged periods, and you don't want to get all worn out when the need to make a hasty escape occurs. Plus you have plenty of body left exposed, and we're sure you'd like to keep that as intact as possible. Be smart, be S-mart.

Helmets: This is yet another item that has evolved as often as the ever-adapting threats presented by our fellow man have progressed. Older variants of these were heavy, hot, and cut down on our hearing and visibility to such a degree as to warrant them almost more of a danger than the attacks they were meant to deflect. More modern incarnations are stronger, able to withstand more shock, and also allow for almost unimpeded sight and sound. The most useful type, when facing the undead, would have to be the riot helmet, used by law enforcement to put down unruly groups of people. The helmet has a clear visor in front and a neck guard in the back, granting the best possible protection one can be afforded. Use of these offers little danger from possible flying fluids, and those pesky surprise neck nibbles. Hearing clearly may still be a bit of a factor, but working in groups and utilizing these forms of armor, in conjunction with the riot shield and a proper weapon, should minimize the disadvantage represented by muffled sound.

Should you find yourself making use of a motorized two-wheeled mode of transportation, you should probably consider a helmet which is build for the purpose. They're lifesavers, really. They're not worth a flying bag of shit while you're fighting the undead, but on a motorcycle, they could mean the difference between a fun bit of skidding and you becoming the zombie that everyone calls "Eggplant Head" right before they take a shot at you and your grossly misshapen melon.

Metal Mesh: More commonly referred to as the shark suit, these are essentially chain mail armor utilized to prevent shark bites to marine researchers. Used in an aquatic environment, these will cease to produce the horrible amount of noise they would when used on land. They will adequately protect from most forms of shark bites, and would thereby do an equally effective job at halting the penetration of the undead tooth. One thing they don't protect from though is the pressure, which comes as a direct result of these oral encounters. Many a bone has been broken simply from the force of these bites, while warding off the unwanted advances of marine predators. Probably a bit less chance of that happening with the undead, though who really wants to find out? If forced to engage in any sort of underwater combat with the undead, these should be worn at all times. On land though, you could give it a miss.

Keep It Cropped: Take away one more thing the undead can grab, pull, and tear at—your hair. Sure there are those out there that consider their 1984 mullet to be the epitome of fashion, what with the ability to simultaneously rock business and party, but let's be serious for a moment. Do you really want to start scaling a fence only to be yanked up by the stylish pony nub, pulled into the eager jaws of the undead horde? If you're truly stubborn about it, tie it up, wrap it up into a hat, or whatever tickles you, but keep it close to the skull and don't let it become a liability.

SPANDEX!: OK, maybe not spandex, but one simply cannot go through the zombie apocalypse with their pants hanging half off their ass and expect to survive. Making the ultimate in fashion statements by wearing size fifty jeans just so you could potentially shelter the homeless in your pant legs is not going to be conducive to a long and healthy existence. Why do you think that the guys that wear that kind of clothing and commit crimes ultimately end up in jail? Simple answer is they can't possibly get away from anyone in that silly getup, let alone a large number of undead intent on forcibly recruiting that person into their ranks. Keep the clothing close fitting and simple, so that it provides maximum mobility and minimal hindrance, and you should be just fine. Giving a zombie less to snag its meaty claws into gives you a better chance of seeing tomorrow.

Transportation

"Looking for a unique form of transportation? When the apocalypse hits, why not head to your nearest zoo? I'm sure there will be plenty of fun animals to be had. All of humanity will be dying off, might as well grab that pet lemur, tiger, and giraffe you've always wanted."
– Minnesota Dentist

Chances are good that, at some point, you're going to have to get mobile and do so in a hurry. Now this doesn't mean you should grab the first thing you see and go tear-assing down the road like Johnny Two-Balls and the Bandit; rather, you should consider your options carefully and take the best mode of transportation, which takes into consideration the largest number of variables allowable. Every option has its ups and downs when it comes right down to it, and they fill their niche in a world inhabited primarily by the undead. Choosing the right vehicle for the right situation will prove, in many cases, to be a matter of life and death.

Cars

Much like the handgun, the car is a constant of American culture since its mass production began in the early 1900s. The standard four-door car has superior gas mileage to many other vehicle types and offers a bit of protection from the prying hands of the undead. However, the typical sedan lacks the weight to keep it from being overturned by the crushing weight of undead pressing against it from one side. Also it tends to lack the horsepower necessary to run down any organic obstacles that may present themselves. The bodies on these vehicles will also tend to crumple upon any significant impact and would render the car essentially useless if such abuse continues. This means that gunning it into a crowd of those annoying neighbors is totally out of the question. Consider as well, the possibility of roads being clogged with stalled, abandoned, and wrecked vehicles, which you're unable to circumvent, and what you have for yourself is a coffin that gets great gas mileage. Given that cars offer little in the way of storage or off-road potential, they should be dismissed as a first option. "Smart" cars? BLAHAHAHAHA!

Trucks and SUVs

The good old pickup truck and its enclosed cousin, the soccer-mom-mobile, offer a wider variety of terrain versatility and the possibility of four-wheel drive. They'll go just about anywhere you care to take them, and shouldn't protest a bit. While you sacrifice a bit of gas mileage, you get a thicker-bodied vehicle and far more cargo room than what is offered by a car. Also, as a heavier vehicle, it makes the tipping of the automobile by outside influences, such as zombies, a bit more difficult in the event of becoming surrounded. Having to run down a few undead shouldn't cause major damage to your average older truck due to its superior body construction, but it's still not an advisable course of action. The major drawback here is the vehicle's size where it relates to the navigating of vehicle-clogged roadways. Nimble, these are not. However, in the colder months, once you've established a nice little safe spot, getting to and from distant places is made a lot safer and easier when you have one of these handy. As long as the gas holds out that is.

Mechs

A mech is a mechanical exoskeleton fitted with not only heavy and durable armor, but also an array of weaponry that could simply make short work of any unarmored opponent. These would represent the ultimate in anti-zombie technology. Engine driven and hydraulically powered, these constructs could easily maneuver around even the most inhospitable terrain while delivering massive damage to anything its onboard targeting computers designate as a threat. The one major problem here is these are fictional and unavailable to just about everybody. There have been some full-sized models built, a few may even move or function, but they're unarmed, slow, and unreliable. Plus, try finding replacement parts if it breaks down. I doubt you'll find any handy at the local auto parts store.

"Another addition to the things that you shouldn't do: do not say you're going to grab some overly complicated, rare, or otherwise not real weapon. 'What if the person had a rail gun and a mech?' DON'T BE FUCKING STUPID. Do you know any person with a mech? Have you ever seen one? NO! You're also not getting a tank, or a military weapon. SHUT THE HELL UP ABOUT IT!" – Old man at the V.A.

Big Rigs

These giant truckers' toys are the epitome of pulling power. Easily able to run down several undead at once without you even really noticing, these powerful road-warriors are built for pure haul and crawl action. So what if the gas mileage isn't wonderful, they take a long time to get going on a cold morning, and they're about as nimble as a doped up rhinoceros in a dodge ball game? These were made for hauling equipment, not for running an obstacle course. Their size alone makes them impossible to tip over without mechanical assistance, and this grants an enormous amount of stability.

With little off-road capability, if you happen to find yourself without an open freeway or at least a flat bit of land, these won't take you terribly far off the beaten track. While these large rigs may in fact be able to do a fine job of clearing roadway obstacles for a time, eventually the damage will pile up if you choose to go the battering ram route. One could certainly spend a bit of time rigging up some form of structural protection for these behemoths and continue to play car pinball. That's definitely one way of going about the arduous task of making all the roads safer to travel post-apocalypse. One final thing to mention is that these aren't easy to drive. Even the variety with automatic transmissions can offer a bit of difficulty to those without prior experience in the operation of these beasts. If you've always wanted to drive one, there's never been a better time to learn. Just don't depend solely on these to save your bacon in every circumstance.

Why Not Take a Bus?

Speed? Maneuverability? Stealth? Good gas mileage? A bus driver craves not these things. Forget about being able to traverse narrow, car-choked streets or even making it through a drive-thru window. While it certainly wouldn't win you any beauty prizes at a car show, it does offer a fair bit of protection due to its weight, size, and carrying capacity. Taking one of these without careful route intelligence is certainly ill advised. It does have potential however in an offensive capacity, but we'll cover that a bit later. It won't tip over, and you could run down a whole swarm of undead with a bus, but it's still probably not the best example of decision making, should you choose to go with these public transit options.

Armored Cars

Heavy and well-protected, the armored car is a rarity among the more common vehicle types, and may not be one's first choice when considering what to take and why, but rest assured, these monsters have their places. Actually, unless you're Scrooge McDuck or work for an armored car company, it's unlikely you'd find one anyway. While you may not want to utilize one of these for purposes of general travel or escape, if you can lay your hands on one, do so, and then keep it for a rainy day. This could prove more problematic than anything else, considering their relative scarcity outside security circles, but with enough looking in the right places, you should be able to find just about anything you could want. Why not put one of these on the scavenger hunt list?

Tractors

These are slow moving farm equipment and should be treated as such. They offer no protection, zero cargo space, and there's not even an mp3 player. While you can run down the undead, they can probably reach you. This is not good at all. Whose idea was this anyway?

Trains

You're stuck on a track, which is probably littered with the overturned husks of other trains, and though its size and weight makes it a superior ramming force against the undead, there are more versatile ways of traveling. Having the knowledge of how to work one of these locomotive wonders may inspire you to take to the open tracks and feel the exhaust-tinged wind on your face, but you should reconsider this mode of transportation as a means of escape or survival.

Tanks

Heavily armored masters of marauding the field of combat, these things are simply awesome when it comes to defending against and running over the undead. Quite simply, if you're in one of these, surrounded by zombies, just drive. No more zombies. Simple, right? Well the first problem comes into play in regards to the acquisition of one of these bad boys. You're not simply going to walk onto a military base and drive out in one of their tanks. You will end up dead, or at best, you will be shot a whole hell of a lot and left outside the base to serve as a warning. Second, knowing how to drive a tank isn't something the layman is going to be able to accomplish without a hell of a lot of screwing up first.

Now supposing you find one, have a pilot, and think to yourself, "Self, this is just not something I can pass up." And you decide to take it for a spin. Seriously, who could resist? Of course there's the huge ass cannon on the top that makes this so much more thrilling. It really is the crown jewel of this mammoth, and without a doubt, you'll want to use it to turn some former people into paste. Despite its size, this really isn't a great zombie-killer. Sure, you could make them scatter a bit with the explosion, but the odds of hitting the head with this aren't terribly great. What it IS good for though is clearing a path for you to go through. Those little cars, trucks, and buildings, if you choose to not simply run them over, are going to move in a real hurry if you decide to level a blast down on them. Then fuel consumption is a small factor. Without information on the actual specs, one must guess, but it's a safe bet that it isn't good. Plus, you have to find a way to replenish the spent ammunition for the vehicle, unless you plan on ignoring that problem. A tank can certainly make a dent in the numerical superiority of the undead just by running them down, but, overall, these are going to stay the things of dreams.

Hot Air Balloons

Why would you want to spend your time on the ground when you could simply float around and let nature dictate your course? Well, probably because it's not always going to be a favorable course, and eventually you're going to run out of fuel, and that's about the time that gravity's going to say "hello" in a very determined and forceful manner. Gravity's always been a cruel mistress. Not only are you going to be highly visible to the undead for miles around, but also, once you land you're going to have a swarm on your hands. These are fine for a nice leisurely float on a summer morning in a peaceful time, but as far as transportation in a zombie apocalypse goes, you may want to consider an alternative.

Helicopters

The elegant, man-made hummingbird, these can just about do it all in the air when piloted by one skilled in the art. These will definitely be a handy vessel to those with the ability and access to sufficient fuel in post-apocalyptic times. Safely hovering above the hordes, offering rescue and additional supplies to those in need once we begin to rebuild the world and take it back from the dead, the helicopter will see plenty of use as a support vessel. Fuel consumption is a major factor though, when these come into play, and should be regarded as a major turn-off as far as constant use is concerned. Also, unless you are already a skilled helicopter pilot, disregard the idea of just hopping into one of these whirly-birds and taking off into the wild blue yonder, as you will die horribly in a mass of wreckage should you attempt to do so.

Unicycles

Got a bike seat, a short chain, only one tire, and great balance? Get creative and make yourself one of these little go-getters. Easily carried over obstacles and a terribly fashionable way to get from point A to B (especially while juggling), these circus act favorites can provide great speed and maneuverability when you simply can't bring yourself to walk. Probably not a great idea at all, but how can you ignore the super fun idea of a unicycle in a zombie apocalypse?

Airplanes/Jets

Now we're simply positive that everyone reading this is a certified pilot who has spent countless hours flying simulators, and has just as many hours in actual flight time, but for those who are not, don't try this at home, especially if you plan on flying over mine. The idea of gliding overhead in one of these machines is appealing; how could it not be? The simple fact remains that it takes copious amounts of training to even begin to safely handle one of these, and this should be kept as a job reserved for those who know what they're doing. The practical applications of a fixed-wing aircraft are limited to scouting, spotting, and general long-distance transportation. Trying to gear up in a fully loaded Raptor and strafing the hell out of a city is going to net you very little in terms of actual kills, and lose you quite a lot in terms of fuel. Another horrifying aspect is there will be constant banter back and forth over who's Maverick and who is Ice Man, and who can invert first and run into a building, trying to be cute. Let's not see this happen. Eyes on the prize, folks.

Hovercraft

Amphibious craft anyone? Boasting the ability to function on land as well as ice and water, these are just nifty to see in action. Hovercrafts are supported by a cushion of air blown through a skirt, which holds the vehicle slightly aloft from the surface. This allows it to skim across flatter terrains with ease. These presently find use in military applications such as troop and equipment transport, and in civilian life they can be found in recreational circles. They're not very easy to maintain without some basic working knowledge. Over rough terrain, they lose a bit of steam, and prolonged use in such a way can cause excess wear on the skirt, resulting in an inopportune blowout, leaving you very stranded in possibly hostile territory. It may not be a terrible way to travel in certain places, but these aren't easy to make, find, or pretty much anything else.

Pogo Sticks

It may not be the fastest, safest, most reliable, or nimble method of mobility on the list, but you'll look funny using it. Let's face it, we all would. Between the loud springy sound and the fact you'll be moving at about the same pace as walking, IF you can keep it moving

forward for any length of time, these just aren't worth the effort. You could always use it as a makeshift weapon, though, if you had to. Riding your metal club could just save your ass, but we highly doubt it.

Boats

We come now to the watercraft. There are a few different variations on the propulsion systems found within this type of craft, namely motor, sails, and paddles. Sailing takes a bit of skill and know-how, paddling requires great endurance, and motors require gas. All are minor drawbacks considering the relative safety to be found out on the water, as long as it is deeper than nine feet. Initial escape by boat should be fairly successful, seeing as zombies don't swim. However, in a long-term situation, re-supplying could prove to be a problem, as well as a severe lack of available storage and living space. Many personal watercrafts have adequate storage for a very limited time at sea. There are larger and smaller variations on the design ranging from colossal ocean liners down to the lowly canoe, and what you need is something that suits your purposes but is within your ability to use. Cruise ships require a lot of people who know what they're doing to even operate, never mind trying to fill these beasts with supplies. Should you manage to find an able crew and all the gear you need, you won't want for room, and good luck. Smaller recreational boats offer little protection against the elements, and have no room for provisions to speak of. While you may find something a bit in between the two, like a yacht, and fill it with gear and safely anchor offshore, you still have to remain aware of threats. While it's unlikely that a zombie is going to find your anchor chain, and even less likely that one will find the dexterous ability to climb it, there is your fellow man to worry about. Pirating could conceivably become a viable form of self-preservation for some, and should be regarded as a threat signified by any approaching vessel. You're not the only one that can use boats and weapons at the same time, and there may be more than a few folks out there who would just as soon scuttle your schooner as go away without it. It's the eye-patches, I think, which make the idea so attractive.

ATVs

The all-terrain vehicle is pretty much just what it says it is. These things can go just about anywhere. On land anyway, not underwater, and they don't fly very well, but you get the idea. They're smaller and more maneuverable than a car or truck, they come in three and four-wheeled models, and you'll look slick riding one. Now these offer limited carrying capacity, but they can be outfitted to carry more. At the very least, they should be able to handle transporting you, your survival pack, and weapons without hindering its mobility. Snow, loose dirt, sand, rocks, and city streets are all the same to these recreational transports, and they can move a lot faster than the undead are able to manage. Fuel consumption isn't great, but for short forays into hostile and unsecured territory, they'll do just fine.

The best use of these would probably be in a skirmish sort of setting against several undead that you've spotted not far from your camp. Just load up, scoot their way, make them no more, and scurry home. Mission accomplished, unless you manage to die, in which case you just did something horribly wrong. Let this be a warning. Exactly how this is a warning is entirely up to you.

Motorcycles

A two-wheeled captain of cool, a motorcycle is a fine choice of post-apocalyptic transportation. Able to leap tall buildings in a single... wait, that's that one guy with the red underwear outside his pants. Disregard that previous sentence, please. With the abilities to take off and stop quickly, steer between stalled and/or wrecked vehicles, and get great gas mileage, these are nearly perfect to have when the world goes to shit. However, the average motorcycle or chopper lacks a bit of off-road reliability and surefootedness. In summation, they can get you out of a tight spot, but let us not go all crazy unless you're on some pavement or dirt roads.

One other point to be made about motorcycles is that you have to be careful at all times when operating these machines. You're certainly going to be moving faster than the undead, which is what makes these safe enough for use in these deadly times, despite the lack of constructed body protection. Be aware that simple accidents, not zombies, are what will be the cause of most motorcycle-related fatalities. A simple breach of concentration can become a deadly situation when you're on a bike, and the last thing you need is to lay down your ride, end up in a ditch, and all you hear is the incessant shuffling of the undead coming closer. Protection should naturally be worn in the utilization of these particular modes of transportation. Stay alert, wear the right gear, and you'll be fine.

Dirt Bikes

The dirt bike is the smaller recreational cousin to the motorcycle. Boasting better shocks, more reliable tires in off-road conditions, and a narrower frame, these are built for going off the beaten track and having loads of fun while you do it. Nimble, easily repairable, good on gas, and thoroughly enjoyable, these little guys can go just about anywhere and get there in a hurry. As with the regular old motorcycle, proper protective gear should be worn when operating these off-road beauties. Doing so should reduce risk of injury, should an error be made which causes your ass to part from the dirt bike at an accelerated rate.

Using this machine's speed to your advantage to avoid an undead entanglement can be as deadly to you as it can be advantageous, so exercise extreme caution when there are obstacles about. Maintain control of your vehicle at all times. You don't want to end up as a paraplegic zombie. Those are like clowns with sad faces. Exactly like them, in fact; destroying either one is probably a good thing.

Bicycles

Human powered two-wheeled transports of the apocalypse, these are an excellent idea for getting where you need to go with a minimum of worry. Reliable, fixable, and they require zero gas to operate. Doing all the work, you make this thing go, so the control is all in your hands. You can pick it up and carry it over or around obstacles (unless you're just a weakling) without a hint of discomfort. You can even do a few tricks if you're inclined toward such a thing. Trying to bunny-hop over zombies is probably not a great idea, but who are we to tell you what to do? These are fast enough, maneuverable enough, and gosh darn it, people like them. In the long-term, consider having one of these handy, especially the mountain bike, due to its heavy-duty construction and versatility. You can use any of the other types that you like, but for rigorous off-road capability, the mountain bike is your best bet. A second bike as a backup, or even for spare parts, probably wouldn't hurt matters either. Pick up a few. Hell, nobody's going to miss their bike anymore since the owners are largely undead. Such irresponsible ownership is just sad. Feel free to use this as an excuse for your liberation of their goods.

Roller Blades

The updated, modern incarnation of the classic roller skate, these provide you with fleet feet on any street. As long as you don't have an abundance of obstacles with which to contend, and there aren't any major cracks in the pavement that crop up, and you're going downhill, you should be able to use these just fine to escape the undead. These can certainly be used in an urban environment to not only look very cool but also get you from one place to another. In fact, using these to do so will enable you to hack the Gibson. Or so we're told. Roller blades are probably not the best idea for deft avoidance of the undead's clutches, but it's an option.

Horses

Hundreds of spaghetti westerns can't be wrong, can they? These critters can go just about anywhere on any terrain, and all you have to do is feed and groom them. They're fast, strong, and make little noise unless at a full gallop. Pretty simple right? That is, IF you know what you're doing. It's simply not likely that you're going to be able to walk up to a strange horse, throw on a saddle and ride, especially without prior experience in having done so. Let's face it, many people no longer rely on the horse as transportation as was done in the past, and as such we've lost contact with how to go about it. Maybe a few lessons wouldn't be a bad idea before setting out on such an endeavor. The difficulty aside, the chances that your horse will absolutely lose its damn mind and freak out at the first sight or smell of a zombie is very real. It will rear up, buck, kick, and bolt. If you happen to be on the beast when this happens, you're very likely going to be seriously injured as a result. A companion of the equestrian variety would prove a fine means of mobility, possibly a friend, and even an early warning system. With prior know-how in dealing with these animals, it would make a fine choice; otherwise you may wish to consider an alternative.

Walking

The shoe leather express has been our primary method of travel for millennia. Relying on our own bodies to get us to and fro, we strengthen our muscles and increase our endurance. Walking everywhere will naturally cause some fatigue, but without a serious accident your chance of malfunction is very low indeed. Your primary concern is keeping the footwear you've chosen in working order, but with people gone, finding another pair of shoes shouldn't be too lofty of a task. You should know your limits and, as such, be able to anticipate your breakdown level, thereby preventing serious injury or exhaustion. Simply keep yourself hydrated, comfortable, and full of proteins, and you can go on as long as you need to, at least as long as you remain careful and aware of your surroundings.

SECTION 5
OTHER THINGS YOU'LL REQUIRE

So we've looked at weapons and transportation, but these alone will not get you through this global epidemic. Sadly, we humans require sustenance, appropriate body temperature, and a certain measure of comfort in order to put off the inevitable dirt nap. To this end, you're going to need to travel with quite a bit of gear, or at least have it available nearby. Now we're going to detail what you're going to need for both on the go situations of moderate length and at "home." Whether or not home is your actual abode is a concern you'll need to think about ahead of time and, if it is, this should be easy enough to supply. Many people live in urban or suburban areas, and doing so will require a bug-out bag in order to hit the road in a hurry. You don't want to be caught having to gather up supplies and pack everything at the last moment. Haste makes waste, and it's very probable that something critical would be left behind. It would be a damn shame to get through twenty miles of zombie-infested territory then remember that you left behind your favorite PEZ dispenser.

Bug-Out Bag

"Lightweight equipment will save you a lot of stress. They make some awesome titanium crowbars, axes, and various other gear. While it's not weightless, you can swing them longer than their heavy steel counterparts. Remember, while on the move, what you carry will limit where you can go. The lighter the better."
– Kid at the Sporting Goods store

Now you're going to need a sturdy, large pack for your to-go bag, and you want to make sure you're comfortable with it being heavily weighted with your supplies, and that it has an easy way of being un-slung and accessed or even dropped. You can find something that is more than adequate for this purpose at sporting goods, military surplus, and various other stores. Luckily getting back to nature is a big business, and there are numerous places that enable us to do just that. Now you'll want to have information available on the pack's strength, or even test it yourself. Wear it while it's full of gear, so you can gauge your ability to wear it for long periods without the nagging chaffing and raw bits of skin becoming a factor. You don't need to wear yourself down with distractions such as these while making your way to safety from the undead.

- Things you need for being on the move:
- Broken-in hiking boots (nobody needs blisters)
- Extra socks (because you don't want stink foot)
- Hat or bandana
- Shades (for better hallway vision as well as practical use)
- Small mirror
- Compass (that one guy in that movie had one on a knife; just an idea)
- Map (we're not talking about a globe—that's just not helpful at all)

- Flashlight (if you have one mounted on a pistol, you won't need an extra)
- Batteries for various equipment
- Water purification tablets
- Water skin or canteen
- Sleeping bag or bedroll
- Waterproof lighter with additional fluid or waterproof matches, which are easier to carry
- Rain gear, which could be a poncho, maybe a trash bag; it's entirely up to you
- Multi-tool, which does away with the need for a pocket knife
- Primary firearm (with at least one box of ammo)
- Secondary firearm (another box of ammo)
- Melee weapon (you shouldn't need ammo or you're doing something wrong)
- 142 Mexican Whooping Llamas (probably not going to be easy to carry)
- Universal gun-cleaning kit (only one person needs to have this if you're in a group, but extra bits are always good to have)
- Binoculars (a scoped weapon can substitute for this in most cases)
- First-aid kit
- Entrenching tool
- Second-aid kit
- Flare gun
- Radio with earpiece
- Protein bars or other non-perishable food supplies for three to seven days

When traveling in groups though, the gear carrying can be shared and certain items only need to be carried by one person. It doesn't hurt to have back ups, but let us now make a list of group items which only need to be had by one person:

- Medium or large first-aid kit
- Silent weapon (suppressed firearm or the twangy kind)
- Crowbar (make the big guy carry this)
- Water purification pump (with replacement filters)
- Gun cleaning kit
- Two way radios with earpieces/headphones (in a group, these should be had by everyone to avoid shouting and getting everyone killed)
- Forty specially trained Ecuadorian mountain llamas (again, not easy to carry)
- Bolt cutters
- Board game or cards
- Additional ammo
- Shotgun (yes, someone in a group should be in charge of crowd control; probably something else you should pawn off on the big guy)

In the Home or Fortification

Now, in your domicile, whether it's your own home or a chosen place of refuge which you picked out far ahead of time, supplying is a bit easier since you don't have to carry all this heavy shit. You have to gather and transport this stuff, but aside from that, carrying it around with you is right out of the equation. That being the case, you can really pump up the volume on what you have available for survival gear. Having ample and dry room for storage increases the life of equipment, and it also lets you really pile it on. Now we're not talking about stocking up so heavily that you look like a leftover from that show about those slobs that don't know when to throw crap away, but being ready for anything and highly organized is never a bad thing. It does no good to have tons of useful items around and no way to get to them because it's all stacked on top of itself. What you're looking at should be on par with preparing for a siege. Granted, you're not going to be set upon by an enemy laden with trebuchets or anything, but why not prepare like you are? The enemy may not be technologically inclined, but they're numerous and wanting to eat your sweet think-jelly. Now what you're going to need is a laundry list of items, and it should be multiplied for the number of folks you have residing with you. It goes as follows:

- Rifle with scope(s) (pick your own type that you're comfortable with) with 500 rounds
- At least one shotgun with 250-500 shells
- Secondary firearm (again choose your own type with or without accessories) with 500 rounds
- Melee bludgeon
- Knives (don't use anything with a serrated edge)
- Hatchet
- Melee bladed weapon
- Axe (to be used mainly for utilitarian purposes)
- Earplugs
- Sandbags
- Canned and/or non-perishable food, three cans per day per person or the equivalent (MREs and the like; you can go nuts here if you have the room)
- Soothing music
- Tomato soup, ten tins of. Mushroom soup, eight tins of
- For consumption cold: Ice cream, vanilla, one large tub. Magnesia, milk of, one bottle. Paracetamol, mouthwash, vitamins. Mineral water, Lucozade, pornography. (I shouldn't be watching movies while I write—sorry about this)
- Hand-held water pumps
- Water purification system with replacement filters
- Portable electric or gas stove with additional fuel sources
- Batteries for various applications
- Telescope
- Flashlights

- Building materials for reinforcements of doors windows etc (lumber, bricks cinder blocks, concrete mix, etc.)
- Generator (have modifications planned for making this human-powered)
- Gas, 20-50 gallons
- Lanterns with replacement fuel and wicks/socks
- Fire extinguishers (five or more)
- Heavy blankets or blackout curtains for covering windows
- Flares and flare guns (may as well have plenty of fire hazards)
- Glow sticks x 30 (RAVE TIIIIIIIIIIIME! Not really, but as backup light sources)
- Advanced medical supply kit (you can even have your own little pharmacy if you're able to; couldn't hurt anything)
- Buckets for water collection (why not use the rain for something useful)
- Earplugs
- Solar-powered or rechargeable radio
- CB or HAM radio
- Cooking implements (pots, pans, utensils)
- Awesome tool kit (sledgehammers, ratchets, wrenches, shovel, saws, hammers etc.)
- Replacement parts for all things mechanical
- A library consisting of instructional manuals and entertaining literature
- Old school washboard (because even though there's an apocalypse, your ass can still stink)
- Lime for the covering of poo

The above lists are pretty much everything you'll need to survive, physically anyway, both on the run and in your chosen dwelling. Skill, patience, and common sense are also noteworthy traits to have in your possession in these difficult times. You may not be able to find all three in most people, but you can give it a shot. Be sure to have some form of entertainment handy, either in your compound or on the go, because levity is important, too. We'll get more into the levity part later.

Buried Treasure

Whether you're a concerned parent or just a paranoid government hating woods-dweller, you're going to need weapons. Now to keep them safe from prying eyes, one option you have is to keep them where nobody could find them without either prior knowledge of their whereabouts or ground penetrating radar. Dig a hole, and throw 'em in. It's not quite that simple, but it's close. You'll want to make them a manageable size if they're larger, and protect them in a manner sufficient to keep out the harmful effects of the various forces at play on our planet. The Earth does like to reclaim its various bits and pieces, and your job here is to thwart that as efficiently as possible.

Break down your rifles; yeah it's work, but you'll get over that. Handguns are less difficult to deal with since they're handguns and obviously a bit more friendly where confined space is involved. You'll also want to add ammunition, and if you're really meticulous, cleaning kits to your list of "to be buried" pile. Now your first line of defense against the elements is vacuum sealing the various parts in some heavy grade plastic. If you lack the means, those spiffy bags that computer parts come in, those work, too. You can use an iron to get a good seal and waterproof those things good and tight.

Now you just drop this shit in a hole, and... wait, no, that's not going to work, you need further protection. PVC is one hell of a sturdy material, and you can glue it tight enough that, well, it's used in industrial plumbing, so it has to be good, right? Pieces of sufficient size and length, along with caps and the glue to hold it in place, can be purchased without raising an eyebrow. Do so, as it's a worthwhile investment. Secure one cap, allow it to dry, drop in the weapon(s), ammo, kits and leftover '80s mixed tapes (time capsule style) and add the other cap. Once your glue has dried, you can bury the weapon. Make sure that you know the location well, and you can easily use landmarks to identify your stash spot. Failure to recall where you left your goodies will mean you fail to find them when you need them. Well, you may be able to find them, but you'll probably come near to killing yourself digging up the surrounding landscape.

Now this may seem like an extremely overzealous route to take in keeping your gear hidden and secure, but rest assured, not only will your weapons remain perfectly safe, but they'll be like a little apocalyptic nest egg. You may even have let them fallen out of thought completely. Then when things get bad, it'll come to you like some sort of ballistic epiphany. Thinking that you really need weapons, and then remembering that you have them—that's a cool feeling.

SECTION 6
OUT OF THE FRYING PAN...

"Having that overly excited person in your group may be fun. But their constant surprise will eventually lead to your downfall. You can't exactly move silently when someone is constantly excited about things. I suggest a roll of duct-tape, if that fails to silence them. A swift punch to the temple will. Silence is golden when running for your life from the hordes."
– Anyone who watches ghost hunting shows.

Well, the zombie apocalypse has indeed begun. You're decked out with equipment, loaded with supplies, and you've dug yourself a nice hole in which to wait it out. Waiting it out's not an option, unfortunately. At some point, you're going to have some sort of resistance to your plan of staying out of the way and unmolested. To this end, you need to know where you're going and how you're going to get there. So far you know what equipment there is that's both accessible and required. You've crossed that bridge and filled the backpack, RV, truck, pack mule, or whatever you plan on using to get as far away from this shit-storm as possible. What are your truly viable options? There's no perfect answer, but there are plenty of choices available to you. This is where we get to go over these in detail. First off, though, there are a few things you want to know about wherever it is you've chosen to go.

1. Is there a readily available source of water?

2. Is there a wall or fenced perimeter?

3. Will your group be able to defend it effectively?

4. Can you supply it before (or easily do so after) the outbreak begins?

5. Are there any tools located here or will they need to be supplied?

6. What supplies, if any, are available to increase fortification?

7. Is the plural of Bigfoot Bigfeet?

8. Are there several floors to work with? Maybe a basement?

9. Can it be locked down and fortified to withstand a prolonged encounter?

10. How many entrances/exits are there?

11. Lacking a fence, is the terrain going to make it difficult for the undead to reach you?

12. Will the environment be beneficial to you, or will it be a hindrance?

13. Will there be ample space, favorable climate, and fertile soil to grow your own produce?

14. What is the air-speed velocity of an unladen swallow?

15. What is the proximity to major population centers?

16. If ever there is dissention, can someone be made to walk a plank?

17. Provided enough (if not all) of the answers to the above questions are deemed within acceptable parameters, how long do you think your group will be able to hold out there?

Having explored all the possible questions about your new home, let's pour over the possibilities of where you can make it. There are many, and each has its own set of pros and cons. Always remember, though, that taking the lazy way out can often be a self-imposed death sentence, and it's very likely survival won't be as cut and dry as stating you're going to make your stand in one place and that's the end of it. If encroached upon by the undead, you will have to be ready to defend your little plot of land and abandon it if needed. Before considering defeat though, let's look at making that an improbability.

The Regular Old House

So you want to make a stand at home, and you've decided that those lousy undead bastards aren't driving you out of your humble abode. Good for you. If you're facing a low level outbreak, this is fine and dandy and you're encouraged to make a go at it. Your supplies should be easily available already, and hopefully you're not in the middle of a city or even a suburb.

Fill the bathtubs with water just in case the powers that be decide it's time to shut it down. Board up the windows, and it may be a good idea to barricade the doors with extra deadbolts; you do NOT want to limit your escape options, but you do need to remain safe. You want to keep any lights and/or noise to an interior room where it cannot be easily observed from outside by any shufflers which may show up. If your home is a two-story, you may consider heading to higher ground, and have the staircase in a state that leaves it ready to be taken down in a hurry. A rope ladder can be used for ground floor access and easily pulled up in a hurry.

Supposing that you're in a situation where shooting becomes a necessity, in a single floor home, do so where you can without compromising structural integrity of your barricaded points to the outside. If you find yourself with an upper level, utilize the windows and roof for brilliant displays of marksmanship. It's a safe way to let the zombies know that they cannot turn you into one of them.

Preparing your home for this type of scenario ahead of time may be something you can accomplish on your own with minimal effort. Bars over the windows, solid locking gates over the doors, and so on can add immensely to the security your home provides. These may be frowned upon by homeowners associations in some areas though, and, if so, you may want to consider a move, depending on how serious you are about planning for your family's survival.

Now it's important to note that there are a couple designs of the modern home which are fairly resilient all on their own when it comes to being breached. First off is the stilted house. Commonly found near beaches and rivers, the undead won't exactly be making a coordinated effort to topple these, and all that really remains to defend are the stairs leading up. Aside from a natural disaster rocking it from its perch, you should be fairly safe, as long as you pick off anything roaming around the underside of the home. Next, we have the modern mid-western masterpiece, the tornado-resistant domicile. Built with the ability to stand up to F-3 force winds, these have heavy-duty storm shutters and are essentially solid rocks with doors. Built of sufficient size, these could prove durable enough to hold out in even level three or four outbreaks, as long as you're not in a densely populated area.

Making a stand in your own home is a decision you'll have to make when preparing. The simple fact is that most homes aren't going to be able to endure the beating that being surrounded by hordes of undead is going to lay upon them, due to their being located in areas which aren't terribly far from a large population. Consider seeking safety elsewhere, unless you're living in a rural area and are prepared to the point of full nuclear fallout levels of self-reliance.

Office Buildings

Utilizing single or multi-story office buildings is a bit of a gamble, unless you've already confirmed it is both clear and constructed of materials that are able to endure the endless pummeling of undead fists. Second and third floor windows will provide a safe vantage point from which to fire accurately upon the undead that may be hovering outside trying to get to you and your companions. The real drawback here is the lacking availability of useful supplies to be had. There is not much which can generally be found in this type of setting. Office buildings don't normally offer much in the way of food, medical supplies, or armaments. Equally lacking is comfortable sleeping quarters, but these are something of a luxury, and can be set up without too much difficulty. There may be an abundant amount of water coolers though, and this is advantageous.

Being able to supply these buildings on your own could potentially eliminate these drawbacks, but doing so may not exactly be a welcome intrusion by the owners. This is something you may want to explore, though doing so may result in your sanity being questioned. Another thing to consider is, once again, the proximity to population centers. If you're going to be able to hold up and barricade the building, what good will it do to have a sea of undead at your walls all the time? Office buildings are commonly found in urban and suburban environments, and that means out of the way, they are not. You'll be right in the middle of the horde, and even though you're safe inside, it may not last forever. Supplies and ammunition will dictate how long you're able to make your stand here. If you do want to take a shot at this particular plan, have an escape route ready.

Hospitals

"Once the outbreak starts, there's sure to be shelters that will open up. I would avoid these places, unless you like the idea of being teeth raped. Someone in the shelter will have been infected. It will spread like wildfire inside the confined area. I say even if you have to sleep in the sewer avoid the shelter. Smelling like yesterday's tacos is better than being dead."

– Dr. James Brightbottom

This is the worst idea you've ever even conceived of. While some hospitals based in older-style buildings may in fact offer a potentially secure structure from which to base your operations, many newer hospitals are using more glass and open areas to create a more inviting atmosphere, which promotes comfort in patients. This is well and good, but designs such as this equate to nothing more than an indefensible structure in times when undead begin to walk the earth. The old brick and mortar style with multiple floors, like the office building, has its potential, and you have a ready stock of supplies for anything medical which ails you. Weaponry will have to be brought with you, as well as construction materials with which to reinforce doors and windows on lower levels. Most hospitals do come equipped with cafeterias though, which can certainly be used to your advantage, but that food won't last long without power. Emergency generators are also common to these buildings as patients requiring constant monitoring and life support simply will not survive in the event of a power outage. Backup power is a plus and can be to your benefit. These will naturally require gas, or can be retrofitted to allow human powering of these devices. Also, let us not forget the abundance of available sleeping apparatuses available within these houses of healing. You won't want for a comfy spot to rest your head.

Now while the above paragraph does indeed paint some hospitals in a somewhat attractive light, let's look at the major downside. In the initial stages, folks are going to be injured and gather here for treatment. Most of these injuries are going to be mundane and not life threatening, at least at first. Eventually, an injured party who has been bitten and infected will be brought in, possibly several, and within several hours are going to expire and reanimate. This horror is unlikely to gain much initial consideration, having not been recognized for what it truly is, and these recently anointed undead are going to rise and do what they do: begin to brutally infect others. Hospital staff isn't going to be ready to fight off this threat; in fact it's highly likely more than a few will become infected while trying to forcibly restrain these zombies in order to further their treatment. This is one instance where their professional compassion kills. Having spread from patient to staff and so on, it will run rampant. This can potentially happen in mere hours, turning a hospital from a place of healing into a house of horrors. If it rages unchecked then the sick, the elderly, disabled, and anyone else in the building when this transpires will become another member of the walking dead. Miserably enough hospitals will, quite literally, become zombie factories in the beginning.

Malls

Loaded with supplies both usable as armament and sustenance, these could easily provide for a large group for a time without the nagging need to look outside for gear. Clothing stores, food courts, and sporting goods shops for weapons make these seem almost ideal. Novelty shops and bookstores will provide entertainment and education, while there are even coffee shops for your morning cup o' joe. Often there is even a security area that can prove to be a sturdy panic room if the need arises. Make no mistake—the need eventually WILL come to pass. The chances are that since these have been glorified bastions of gathering in many a zombie film, more than one ragtag group is going to try and make this their new home. Let's face it—there just aren't that many malls in the US, so chances of conflict for control of these monuments to consumerism are high. The simple truth of the matter is, they're not that great, and they're just not worth fighting over. It's only a mall; get over it.

These are probably the most indefensible structures one could hope to find. Large glass windows make them easily breached by the undead, and these just so happen to surround shopping malls. On the interior you can easily close off individual shops with the retractable metal fences, but how much punishment can they truly withstand before falling at the hands of these relentless ghouls? Also consider that a majority of the larger stores have multiple entrances and exits, which are unable to be easily blocked off and secured. What this provides is not so much an abundance of exit strategies, rather a constant threat of security breach by the undead. It only takes one door, window, or wall to fail to start the hemorrhage of zombies into your building, and causes the fallback action to begin. Once started, this is going to cause panic and indecision, which will only end badly for everyone inside. In conclusion, choosing the mall as a place of refuge is only delaying your self-imposed demise.

Apartment Buildings

Many among us call these home, and while there is strength in numbers, the layouts of these structures determine their overall defensive capabilities. Some are fenced with strong steel fences, others with wood, and there are even buildings surrounded by concrete barriers. Others are completely unprotected and open. There are the four-unit constructs and large multi-floored buildings; it simply depends on the architectural style. The main advantage is that your group will be large, even if they're unprepared; organization and discipline can be spread to help protect everyone. Duties and supplies can be shared among the inhabitants. Every bathtub filled would add up to an awful lot of water stored for various usages. All the food available in each home adds up. Weapons could easily be produced from thin air once things get bad. You never know what your neighbor has in his home. A unified effort could just help save everyone's lives.

What could possibly be a major downside here is the level of training or lack thereof that is held by the various occupants you find yourself entrenched with. If your particular situation leaves you in a well-defended position, your main concern is going to be fighting stupidity and panic. Try not to let ignorance be what gets everyone killed. Keeping the fences and gates cleared of the undead shouldn't be a problematic task, as most everyone has at least one weapon in their home whether they advertise this or not. Simply walking the perimeter and picking off the undead should pose no significant difficulty for a reasonably populated apartment complex. This keeps your wall intact and un-breached and helps maintain calm among your fellow survivors. Lacking a sturdy building or even a wall or fence, you're naturally left to your own devices. Things could get out of hand in a real hurry, and the added bit of localized humanity could easily degenerate into anarchy. If this is the case, you may want to consider another place to take refuge.

Space Stations

Obviously the best possible choice due to orbiting the earth and, therefore, lacking infected humans. Space stations make their own energy, have plenty of food, they recycle water, and they're totally unreachable by the undead. However, unless you're planning to take off with the assistance of a NASA-trained crew, you'll never even see the shuttle or much less make it off the launch pad. You'd be better served thinking along more local lines, like on the planet. An even better plan would be a space station the size of a small moon that can destroy planets! Yeah! Why not just build one of those? You could call it a Hurty-Moon! If this is your plan, please stop eating paint chips. Sorry, Duck Dodgers, this is not happening.

Prisons

While you may look at these and decide you'll pass it by, think again. Prisons built up until the mid 1960s were walled fortresses. No amount of undead on the other side of a two-foot thick, twenty-foot high concrete wall is going to cause it to budge. These sturdy walls are often punctuated by towers, which will allow for maximum interior as well as exterior wall and yard coverage by trained marksmen. The cellblocks are able to house many survivors, and can be locked down individually to maximize protection, enabling organized and safe fallbacks in the event of a breach. There exist within these walls both secure areas, which may hold abandoned weapons and ammunition, as well as medical facilities (in most anyway) that are also helpful in the event of a booboo.

There are some things you should be most concerned about when scouting these locations. The first is limited access. Most of these jailhouses offer one way in, which means there's also only one way out. This can be a slight problem if things happen to go badly and there's a flood of undead coming through the very gate that you need in order to make your exit. The second issue is the prison population itself. It's a very real possibility that many prior guests of the state are going to elect to remain right where they were, comfy and safe, away from the jaws of the ghouls outside the walls. It could also be that the guards may have formed something of an alliance with their wards, and have allowed them to roam free and potentially even armed them in order to combat the undead. These are not our best and brightest, folks. It's highly unlikely to think that thieves, rapists, and murderers are going to let an apocalyptic happening bring out their most commendable personality traits. Even if you're seeking solace and come upon this type of arrangement and it seems your only hope, you may want to steel yourself and move on, especially with women in the party. Chances are your reception may in fact be warm, but your stay won't be very long.

Newer prisons, trying to stretch the almighty dollar, tend to use chain-link fences, which may or may not be electrified as a deterrent, and, as such, should be discounted entirely. A healthy gathering of zombies will eventually cause these flimsy walls to fail and allow them entry. Granted the cellblocks can be locked down, turning them into a veritable fortress, but you're limiting your space in the event that the undead horde begins to swarm your area. On the other hand, if you're going to utilize one of these newer and more modern correctional constructs, constant perimeter patrol and elimination of the ghouls can lead to a safer and friendlier environment. Naturally stacked up rotting corpses would need to be disposed of, but that's nothing a few fire pits can't take care of.

Choosing to turn a prison into your new refuge will take a bit of work even though the foundation for survival is already solid. Again, these are not small places, and will take a while to go through and check for security purposes. Rechecking after the initial sweep is advised. After that you're going to need to make a list of all supplies found therein. Weapons, food, ammunition, and armaments should all be accounted for and added to your stockpiles. A secondary gathering point should be noted and agreed upon. Everyone should know how to lock and unlock specific doors in the event of an emergency security breach. Once the training session has borne fruit, if you're planning on making this a long-term stay, have a plan to plant your fruits and veggies. Water will also be an issue not only for personal hygiene and cleaning, but for your agriculture as well, so that should be thought of at the same time. The use of barrels and cisterns that you can cover in order to collect rainwater is an acceptable way to go, if you're unable to dig an on-site well. Also consider the proximity of local towns and cities and your ability to safely get what you need from those.

If you're unable to have what you need where you are, you're going to have to organize search parties for supplies.

If it turns out that it's safe to do so, prisons can prove to be an ideal solution to your problems. The only true test will be keeping the facility supplied and vigilance at a constant high so there aren't any mistakes. With a positive attitude infecting the group, this is easily an attainable goal. You could do a lot worse than to find an empty prison and make it home, as long as you're willing to put in the effort to do it right.

Docks/Shipyards

"Fishing will become a staple of the survivor. Casting a line in order to get a bit of food will be the easiest way to eat post apocalypse. No longer will you use fishing as an excuse to get drunk with friends, so you may want to actually put some bait to the hook next time you're out, instead of focusing on beer. Just a thought."

– Bubba

While these may be overlooked by the average person when considering a place to find a safe haven, never underestimate the use of areas such as these in regards to holding off the undead. Docks can easily become islands unto themselves either by dropping one end into the water or blocking it with a shipping container or two. Products aplenty can be found in these little goldmines, and most will prove useful to some degree. Huge cranes are generally found around a shipyard, as they're often utilized for the loading and unloading of cargo. Also, you may consider utilizing these in an offensive capacity at times to conserve your ammunition. One box dropped onto a large number of undead can make the difference between finding yourself under siege and being newly anointed members of the shuffle brothers. Being rocked with bouts of laughter is another healthy side effect. Hearing plenty of squish as it pertains to a group of zombies will surely be a smile-inducing treat that nobody should miss.

Storage buildings around these areas can be used as shelter and provide advantageous lookout spots for any type of incursion, and leave you in a more advantageous location from which to defend your position. Fortification of these can easily be accomplished by using these numerous heavy boxes, which are unmovable by human hands, undead or otherwise. Creating access points from a structure that allows you to safely check all the containers for useful supplies should be easily accomplished with a little planning and a powerful crane. Stockpiling can be gone about in a similar fashion, and these buildings can serve that purpose as well.

Another aspect of holding up in these areas is the abundant source of food, which is easily accessed via the ability to fish. It's unlikely that any sort of Department of Wildlife is going to be regulating how you catch your dinner, so you can either old school it with a pole, or take up netting and try your hand at that. Considering there may be undead wandering the sea floor around your chosen area that are attracted by the noise (remember, they're stupid, and many will likely fall in on their own), you may have to boat out a ways and try your luck there instead. Diving for your dinner should not even be an option with the possibility of ghouls wandering below the surface. It will be bad enough to occasionally lose tackle, having snagged a zombie.

The major drawbacks with finding yourself a dockyard and utilizing this area as a defensible position are relatively few. Weather will be your main contention, but there's abundant shelter for your group. Heaving seas could provide danger for the structural integrity of your wooden island, as well as possibly sweeping a prone body from its platform, but it takes some massive aquatic activity for this to be a real threat. Luckily for us, waves of this scope aren't often an issue. Normal wear and tear could eventually require a bit of repair, but that would mean you've been there for an awfully long time holding your own against marauders and the undead alike. Let us hope this won't be the case. In any event, making use of a dock and/or shipyard can easily prove to be a beneficial habitat for a group of survivors. Plus you get to call each other "scurvy dog" and such, due to your proximity to the water.

Churches and Various Other Houses of Worship

Whenever disaster strikes, humans often feel the need to retreat to a place where a modicum of peace is offered. For some it's the bottle, others go the pharmaceutical route, and a number go to church. It seems a natural instinct for human beings to feel a need to belong and understand, and these theistic havens often offer such to those who seek answers, which may be lacking. This is fine and dandy, however, it's in times of crisis that these will become flooded with those seeking refuge from the horrors represented by the walking dead.

In times gone by, one could find a house of worship with open doors nearly twenty-four hours a day, as they were always willing to take in the needy and distraught. Large sturdy doors would often be in place to ward against unwanted intrusion, for whatever reason this may be warranted, but in recent years this is no longer the case. More simplified swinging glass doors are often the normal fare, and the incarnations of holy houses have become a bit less elaborate and more functional than in days gone by. Defensive capabilities are taken on a case-by-case basis. For some it's an easily attainable goal, but for others, you're just asking to end up zed-chow.

Supplies in these locations will be few, especially when you consider the sheer number of people that could be taken in during a relatively short period. Stockpiles of food may be found, depending on the activities the management is involved in at the time, but it's not something you'll want to wager on. The ability to stock your weapons and ammunition prior to the actual rise of the undead will also largely prove unlikely, unless you're in good with the on-site supervisors. This should, once again, be a major consideration in your decision.

The major problem here will be at the onset of the zombie apocalypse. It's extraordinarily likely that many of the faithful will gather at these places of worship seeking peace and answers to the terror unfolding around them. Unfortunately for these folks, the undead are very prone to follow what they perceive to be prey, and it only takes one to start a panic inside which will alert others. Clergy aren't often big on security procedures, and checking those let in from the chaos found outside for bites isn't very likely to happen. Your average church, synagogue, or mosque is going to become a killing ground for the undead unless drastic measures are taken to remain defended and zombie-free.

Police Stations

To protect and serve? This could quite possibly be the case. Headquarters to our law enforcement, police stations provide a number of desirable qualities that you could hope to find in a building you wish to inhabit. However, this is not always the case. Many are of an older and sturdier style, which can prove of great benefit to your group in the right circumstances. Obviously, modern construction will vary, but any cop shop with a block of cells will have at least one fairly secure area from which to defend. Many also feature their own power sources in the event of catastrophic emergencies; it wouldn't do to have the police station offline when lives are in jeopardy. These will be run on finite resources and should be used sparingly. These can usually be converted to function via other means if the need arises.

Now, depending on the level of the threat in an area, certain police stations may in fact have quite an impressive arsenal, which will be ripe for plundering should you find the station empty. An active station that still has police in it isn't going to be an option; naturally you'll want to avoid this situation, as they're prone to be extraordinarily vigilant and wary of potential intruders. Another drawback of these trying times is the stress these men and women are quite likely to be feeling, and we all know how that can be. This could very well result in your gunshot induced demise should you attempt to liberate items from their armory.

Much like places of worship, in the initial stages of outbreak, those seeking safety and protection will inundate police stations. For this reason, it's a very real probability that the undead will follow, and the slaughter will begin in earnest. Sadly, when people come under extreme duress, they panic, and all semblance of order will be abandoned, resulting in further tragic loss of life. Police will be hard-pressed to offer defense to these folks when they refuse to listen to reason and prove ineffectual at even aiding in their own preservation. It's a heartbreaking reality that those who gather in large groups for the supposed protection it offers will face a merciless ripping and tearing death at the hands of the ghouls.

What one should take away from this is that interfering with those who are charged with the job of keeping order is never a good thing, but if you happen to find their building unoccupied and properly defendable, you should take full advantage.

Basements and Underground Shelters

Like any good old-fashioned American endeavor, the hazard of nuclear elimination by our foreign threats of yore caused an increase in the development of fallout shelters and bunkers. In fact, these were often constructed in such elaborate styles by some private citizens that they could have once warranted a monthly magazine. Fashioned beneath the earth and shored up either by proper concrete walls or wooden beams (depending on resources available) these can prove useful in all manners of natural disaster (except floods of course) or illegal growing operations. Based in or near the home, these can provide a convenient place of storage for any number of supplies, weapons, generators, and the like.

The down sides to these types of structures are numerous. First of all you're very likely going to be restricted to one exit and entrance. This will not bode well should your subterranean abode be discovered by the undead. Second, you're effectively blinded. Being unable to see your surroundings and provide proper defended perimeters would simply be the worst possible scenario when your main goal is to avoid contact with the undead. Not knowing where your enemy is would be damn near as bad as pitching a tent in the middle of a city inhabited by zombies and hoping they don't become curious about you being there. The inability to ascertain threats encroaching on your squat spot is an often-fatal thing with which to contend.

Should you choose to take this route, it's likely that at some point leaving will be a requirement. Now, one undead spotting you is bad enough, but it's almost inevitable that if one sees you, more will follow, and then the difficulty really compounds. Without a secondary means of escape, your only option is to let the door swing wide and take your chances. This is not an attractive prospect, and your combat and weaponry skills, which hopefully have not declined during your underground experiment, will be put to their ultimate test when this occurs.

Caves

Hey, it worked for cavemen, right? Well, yes and no. Using these natural structures as a habitat when faced with a zombie uprising can certainly be a way to go. The undead have little coordination and, as such, having a home that you have to climb to is a fine idea indeed. With proper planning and a bit of preliminary spelunking, a safe and suitable cave system can be found which suits your needs. With any luck, one can be found with alternate means of exit. You'll need something deep and dry for you to inhabit, and naturally, very little will be available in the way of supplies. All your gear will have to be trucked in by you and your group and set up in such a fashion to keep it organized and readily available.

Familiarizing yourself with local plant and wildlife will naturally become essential to sustain your prolonged existence in these locations, and should be a top priority. Look in several locations and establish secondary locations that everyone can find for fallback purposes in the event of any kind of security breach. Use noticeable landmarks in the area to easily familiarize everyone with these places. Avoiding your fellow mammals and upper-food-chain predators will be your main concern, if you pick the right spot where zombie contact is almost a non-issue. Oh, and flash floods, let's not forget those, but if you pick high ground, you shouldn't be too concerned with anything aside from collecting water from these.

Tree Houses

"I think a tree house and a spear would be simple, yet effective. Like grain alcohol."
– Zac Allen

So you saw the movie with the guy who can't do accents leading his people to live in tree houses and mystify the evil sheriff. Overall, if one has the resources that make this even remotely possible, it's not a terrible idea. Building a home far above the reach of the shambling dead is a fine plan for survival. Actually, depending on where you are, this would make a perfect place from which to pick off the undead. Aside from the obvious ballistic means you can use to dispatch the odd zombie, you can get rather creative with your diabolical destructive methods. Ropes, pulleys, and ladders can be implemented in a variety of fairly simple ways to safeguard your home among the treetops. You take melee conflict out of the mix entirely, and this is for the best.

Supplies will have to be provided and stored, and an ample amount of room will be required for your group and its supplies. These are variables that can be hammered out during design and construction. A bit of research will need to be done on your part regarding the strength and other properties of different types of tree. Picking the right trees to utilize for this purpose will be a major concern, but once done, this can only ensure your safety while going about your lofty lifestyle. This would be an architectural nightmare to say the very least, but with the right materials and knowledge, it is within the realm of possibility. Don't let anyone tell you it can't be done. Except forest rangers and other such authorities, because they can shoot you or have you arrested, and this is never a good thing. While you're pretending to be a leaf, just be careful with any fires you may need for cooking. Fire extinguishers would probably be a good idea here. In fact, having a couple dozen stationed in various places would be a wise move. Also, watch out for windstorms.

Building Supply Stores

Considering taking over a House Depot or the like? You're not the only one. This may seem like an attractive prospect on the surface. Building supplies and weapons all over the place that you have but to grab and use as you will. You'll have to provide your own ballistic weaponry, but that's a given. The amount of structural reinforcement you can do here is staggering, should you choose to do so. Actually, you could pretty much make one of these places completely impenetrable if you wanted to, and had the right set of skills. Even if you don't, there are probably books in the building that can give you the information you need to make it so. There is very little here in the way of nutritional supplies, but one could conceivably stock the place to the rafters and hold out against the undead for quite a while.

Bricking up easy access points and allowing roof-only access is certainly one way to go. The problem here though, is that you could very likely become surrounded with no clear route of egress, should the need arise. Being able to keep your area free of the undead, so that you may be able to move freely in and out, is essential. Plus you don't want those bastards beating on your walls day and night. Now, one answer to that would be narrow slits that one could easily fire your weapon through. However, these weaken structural integrity if build improperly. Another answer would be using the rooftops as a safe firing position. This gives away the fact that you're walled up inside the building to other survivors, which may be an undesirable proposition.

It's likely that someone may take exception to the fact that you "stole" their idea of hiding out in said building. If this is the case, then there is a high likelihood of having to defend yourselves against these unreasonable shit heads in order to keep what you've worked hard to achieve. This is a bit like wiping your ass with poison ivy; sure, you got your ass clean, but is it worth the pain that's sure to come with it? The answer is: probably not. You're much better off dealing with a few dozen zombies than defending against armed living opponents who feel slighted because they were slow. If the contest becomes a prolonged engagement, and there seems to be no middle ground on which to build, it may be best to get out of the situation before it proves fatal. Then again, you may want to stand your ground and kick these people in the ass. This will be a decision you could very well be forced to make.

Schools

Despite being places where learning is the normal daily activity, these bastions of education are often built not unlike prisons. Frequently used in the event of natural disasters as gathering points, they are built with thick solid walls, wide corridors, and are sometimes even fenced. These constructs are very sturdily and able to take a lot of punishment. Gone are the days (mostly) of the single-roomed schoolhouse, which provided children of all ages with a bit of knowledge. Of late, these have been beefed up to prevent unwanted intrusion from outsiders that may prove undesirable.

Some schools may have trade shops on site, such as wood, metalworking, or even auto-repair, which are courses that can provide practical knowledge for students. To the survivalists among us, they'll offer a nifty source of do-it-yourself tools. Aside from these and what non-perishable food can be found in the cafeteria, you will be mostly left to your own devices as it pertains to supplies.

Another feature, which is pleasant to have available, is a multitude of entrances and exits to choose from. Most of these doors can be locked from within and provide only an exit. Designs that feature multiple floors can easily be set up to defend the building with minimal effort, depending on the layout. Main problems would be windows that were never designed with opening in mind, but you can make the call on that when that time comes.

Gymnasiums on the premises would conceivably provide a great distraction from the tediousness of the day, and any school with a football program is bound to have a weight room as well. That would certainly go a long way in working out the kinks that a prolonged defensive posture would impose. Large open areas can be used as supply rooms and fallback areas in the event of an emergency. Perhaps even heavily waxing a particular hallway can provide not only amusement, but also an unexpected defensive surprise.

Modern schools have quite a few beneficial aspects when it comes to providing an easily defended shelter for a group looking to survive the oncoming undead adversary. When the time comes to consider where to go and what to do, don't let these stray far from your mind. You may have hated school, as many of us did, but in this case, one could very well save your life.

Super Stores

Bastions of "low prices," these places have just about everything you could need while out on a shopping excursion. Food, clothing, automotive supplies, toys, and even weaponry (not as much anymore, but they still carry some ammo) can be found in these hallowed halls of consumerism. They certainly make one-stop shopping a possibility, but how will they hold up against hordes of undead?

There is no real way to fortify these buildings using materials contained within. You could move pallets of dog food or the stacked and wrapped goods, which are found in the back, out in front of the massive doors and windows; but eventually these would begin to break down and leave your defenses in shambles. Finding out that your stack of Puppy Chow wasn't quite the wall you thought it was could throw that smug sense of self-satisfaction you were feeling right down the toilet. Zombies pouring in to your place of refuge tend to have that effect.

Something else which bears mentioning is that these places have a lot of food. We already said that, we know, but the food we mean now is frozen. Without a sustainable power supply, these freezers stop working. That food thaws out and eventually it's going to begin to rot. This is going to smell AWESOME! Really, it's not, and not only will the stench become unbearable in a short time, it will also provide a nifty health hazard to those that may find themselves around it for a prolonged period of time. Nothing like a little salmonella to liven up the zombie apocalypse. Let's hear it for post-apocalyptic debilitating bouts of dehydration and diarrhea.

Like certain other locations, this is going to be a popular survival destination due to the availability of all manner of supplies. This could lead to a conflict with others over who will take the place as their own. If they're not willing to share, then a super store is simply not worth the hassle. With some planning this is an option that's decent, but not great. There are better places, with less people clamoring to them, in which you can take your shot at survival.

Recreational Vehicles

So you've decided to go mobile, and this seems like a decent plan on the surface. There are a few points worth mentioning which will hopefully dissuade you from this course of action. You keep moving and the undead can't possibly keep up, right? Partially right, because the noise you make getting from place to place will make you a target and, sadly, at some point, you have to stop. Rest, fuel, and offloading undesirable waste will all become necessities and halt your progress, and this can be the time when you're set upon. Gasoline will be your primary concern when in the wandering Winnebago, and you can only carry so much with you. Sadly there's nobody out there making more.

Think you're protected in that tin can? Hardly. These vehicles are meant to be recreational, not survival-based automobiles, and as such are hardly armored or weighted in such a way as to make them impervious to a constant barrage of meaty zombie hands. Eventually the undead will amass outside and cause the oh-so-fun tipping and subsequent access into your once-mobile fortress of solitude. Unless it lands on the door, in which case you'll be trapped and subject to die from dehydration, heat exhaustion, or starvation, if they don't get in first.

Using these as a way to traffic supplies to and from a place that has been scouted and deemed passable is just fine, if you have it to use. Otherwise, trying to keep these machines on a forward track through a world completely controlled by limping lifeless lepers is going to be one ride which won't result in you getting to where you want to be.

Amusement Parks

Don't be stupid. There's no power, which means these places are absolutely no fun at all. The best you can hope for is to encounter some living-impaired dolt in a costume which represents some cartoon character from your youth who you really want to cause some serious fucking damage to. Your best bet is to take down the evil mouse and move on. Even if there was power, I doubt you could figure out how to make those silly teacups spin.

Oil Rigs

Drilling platforms found on various bodies of water throughout the world are fine places where one could seek refuge from the voracious hordes of undead. Self-powered, well supplied, and inaccessible to anyone who can't work a helicopter or a boat, these are manufactured islands which have the added benefit of not causing you to get sand in your crack. There should be an abundance of tools and various parts for repairs in order to keep these monsters running like they should, and all it takes is a little mechanical aptitude and a manual or two in order to do it.

The immediate concern when approaching the platform should be the crew, if any are still on board the rig. They may not take kindly to your intrusion and the news you bring, assuming of course that they're unaware of the zombies now roaming the land. They could become distraught and violent and wish to go to their families. Try and talk sense to them, but if they insist on going, let them. Just don't let them take your conveyance in order to do it. Being trapped on one of these would totally screw up that whole escaping thing, should the need arise.

Normal supplies should be brought with you, as well as weapons and an abundance of ammunition. You can hold out here for a while and, while you do so, it's very likely that another group, one far less congenial than you'd like, is going to seek out a rig of their own and decide that yours looks nice. This is going to be your primary concern. Even without power, cartoons, or other contact with the outside world, people will continue to be a problem. This isn't true of all people, just the assholes. In times like these, it's simple enough; treat everyone like an asshole until they prove otherwise.

Another worry, which would eventually make itself apparent, is that the sea takes everything back in its own time. Rust is your new enemy. Oxidized metal is a constant hazard when dealing with a primarily marine environment and even the air will begin to eat away at the metal hulk on which you find yourself. These rigs need constant maintenance and new coats of paint; luckily enough, these supplies can often be found on the rig itself, since this is a recognized hazard. You simply have to love people that think of this kind of shit so you don't have to.

If for some reason the power happens to go, and you're unable to continue to store your food in a nice cold refrigerator, you're going to have to fish for chow. Not only are you able to catch and feed on the mobile critters of the aquatic variety, but also the plants found in the water can often substitute for other essential minerals, which the human body requires. This will take a bit of research on your part, but what else do you have to do with your time? If you do plan on harvesting marine plants as food, you should probably have diving gear handy. That helps a lot in preventing drowning.

We're all aware of the potential for accidents, and on a drilling platform, this is drastically increased. Explosions and the subsequent fires are hard enough to deal with in regards to similar facilities while on land, but now you're surrounded by water, and that shit's hard to run on. Recent disasters certainly shed a lot of light on the environmental impacts alone, not to mention the loss of life. Your life, as has been stated, is the most precious thing you have when it comes to thwarting the efforts of the undead, and when it comes to an unfortunate incident on one of these oil rigs, it's definitely in peril. It's not uncommon to hear of entire crews lost in these tragic conflagrations. There is little help that can be provided in short order, even in the best of times, when all our technology is being kept manned and ready to go in the event of some sort of disaster. In the middle of an apocalypse, there will be none. It may be a good idea to just shut the drill down unless you know what you're doing.

Finally, your last source of anxiety will be the vile storms, which are ever-present in the world around us. For all the good things we can take from the sea, it can exact its revenge swiftly and without warning. Hurricanes accompanied by crashing waves are the most devastating combination of natural forces you'll face, and all you can do when stuck on an oil platform is hunker down and hope for the best. Trying to make it to shore before it hits could prove just as fatal as staying put. That's a decision you have to make. A powerful storm can crush the rig as easily as it could your boat.

An oil rig is certainly one of the better choices you could hope to make when trying to continue living in the middle of a zombie apocalypse. Chances are nil that the undead could even hope to get to you when you're on one of these. Aside from horrific accidents, and the odd cyclone, if you can keep nature and undesirable people at bay, then you can certainly spend your time confined to these metal monoliths with little to fear.

Banks

Taking up residence in a bank is a sure recipe for disaster. When the undead breach the doors, your only fallback position becomes the vault. Once inside, without anyone to open it for you, you're going to end up sucking on your own wasted breath until you die. Sounds like fun, doesn't it? No, it does not sound like fun. You can do better than this.

Military Bases

Ringed by fences and constantly staffed with trained fighters, these would be a nearly perfect place to set up camp in the event that you're invited to do so. Having their own resources to work with, including power, water, food, and munitions, these are cities unto themselves and can easily operate as such. The presence of skilled marksmen makes them almost completely impervious to incursion when they're under full alert. The undead won't stand a great chance of breaching the base's perimeter unless some sort of full-scale zombie invasion takes place.

Finding your way to one of the many bases in the country should be an idea you keep in the back of your mind if other plans fall through. The odds are that the military will continue to provide protection for civilians throughout this apocalyptic happening. This is kind of what they're here for. You would naturally be subject to screening, and the surrender of supplies for collection and rationing, but in return protection would be granted. Housing and storage are available, and there's plenty of room to spread out in a majority of these places. Eventually supplies may run low, but who better to go out on a supply-gathering mission than those trained in doing so with force? These guys can improvise.

Thinking about sneaking onto one of these bases and making off with a tank or Hummer or anything else is something you should get out of your mind right now. With a zombie apocalypse going on around them, the security would be such that any intruder without proper identification would be shot on sight and nobody would blink an eye. Protection of resources would be of paramount importance, and any compromise of this would be met with violent action. Let's not disrespect the efforts of these people who have sworn to protect us with their lives. Offer your help, but don't be a hindrance.

Now we'll hit on different kinds of buildings and places you may find yourself in while on the go and what kind of items may be used for weapons or maybe amusement. Now these will all be best case scenario ideas, since we honestly don't know what people are going to loot because people, when faced with the prospect of free shit, get really stupid really fast. We're going based on our working knowledge of the places and what they contain.

Fast Food Restaurant

There could be a plethora of useful items in these kinds of places depending on which ones you come into. Look around for cooking utensils, fry baskets, parts of the grill, and even the register. Quick weapons can be made from these. Now if you happen to be in one of the ones with a children's play place, you're in luck. The slides and climbing areas can prove an invaluable place to rest. Off the ground, and complex enough to confuse a child means it'll hinder zombies. Of course if I were to crawl into one of these to sleep, I would cut a hole in the top for easy egress. Sadly since most of these places have large glass windows to put customers at ease and make them feel comfortable, it's not a place I would stay for any long periods of time. Plus, you may find decent drugs in the ball pit.

Convenience Stores

That's right: the bastions of the quick snack, soda, and smokes. Some of these can be a great place to hold up for a bit. We'll start with the basics. Beef jerky, chips, cream-filled pastries, and canned beverages can all be found in these places. Unfortunately if you get there late into the apocalypse you're going to find them low on goodies and likely stuck with crap like diet drinks, light beer, cheap wine, and no-name candy that tastes like chalk. That's all good though since it'll all provide a bit of energy. Now don't overlook the shelving, and other items inside. You could use that stuff to build medical splints, a tote box, or bludgeons. Your ability to think on your feet is definitely going to come in handy here. Take the wire mesh off the shelf and make yourself a hobo-grill: fire underneath and grill on top. You can cook up your can of beans, or your freshly killed varmint. We all know, a warm meal will make you feel more like a human and less like a refugee. You have to take your happy where you can get it.

Gun Stores

You won't find anything here but a case of death. Anyone who could get in and steal did, so I don't need to elaborate.

Laundromats

Ah, the pickup place for older singles and also a place to make skid-marks disappear. Did you know they could be used in time of need? Now instinctively, most people will avoid these places because they don't feel they can be useful. Oh, how they are wrong. The carts you put your laundry in to ferry from washer to drier? You can break those down and build all kinds of stabby and smashy weapons with them. You can pull the doors off the washer or drier and use them as a shield. Perhaps some plumbing supplies that would be useful at a later date? All you're going to need is a multi-tool and patience, and you'll be able to come up with 1,001 uses for the items inside the building. Again, these places have large windowed fronts to make customers feel at ease and comfortable so I probably wouldn't stick around forever.

Video Store

This was once the destination to everyone who was planning to stay home. Be it working mothers, teenagers, or stoners, a trip to the video store meant entertainment for everyone. That's all changed now, but these archaic stores still do exist. Inside you'll find a treasure trove of awesome. There was a time when you could rent things like "Best of Both Worlds" or "Happy Scrappy Hero Pup" in the same store. That's of course all changed. However inside the hallowed walls of these establishments you will be able to find useful items. Luckily the remaining brick and mortar stores are dark windowless buildings as to provide people who are still renting videotapes a way to hide their shame. Of course there's a million miles of videotape, and if that movie with that guy and the volleyball taught us anything, you can turn videotape into rope! And who doesn't need rope combined with pornography? Well probably not David Carradine, but I digress. Overall the lowly video store can provide many useful items, and a bit of shelter.

The Adult Novelty Shop

You may not think of tools of death and destruction when you pass by your neighborhood smut store, but it does indeed hold these. If you doubt that statement, take a walk through one and you'll see personal devices of all shapes, sizes, colors, types, and weights. Some look like an entire arm, lipstick containers, some look like an elephant's genitalia—there's something for everyone. It was like the designers were thinking, "OK, aside from sick, twisted, wrong sexual activities that should be limited to the Internet, let's give the zombie survivalist something to use from any place that offers our wares." That's right, heavy like a club, shaped like a penis. You can bash a skull easily if uselessly. On top of that there's all manners of whips, riding crops, battery operated torture devices, leather suits, ball gags, chains, clamps, chained clamps, tons of different surgical quality tools, and of course disinfectant. Like the video store, most of these places offer very few windows and exits. They're designed to hide the shame of those who are inside buying the fist-width sexual device. Luckily for most of us, others won't think about weapons when they see these stores, they're just going to think about all the dirty things they used to watch on the internet and move on. Only the truly resourceful will venture inside. It's like a box of chocolates, if they were covered in lubricant and shame.

Airports

Now since most of the large airports are in major population centers, and we all want to avoid those we'll be looking at smaller regional airports or private landing strips. Hangars will provide a little bit of shelter for a short-term rest. You'll also find all kinds of tools and scrap metals and other items that can be used for weapons. These places also have a large supply of avgas which depending on the plane models you see laying around will function as unleaded or diesel fuel. If you're really lucky you'll find yourself at a smuggler's hiding strip which could provide you with entertainment and substances. Those are always nice to happen upon, since you're going to need a release from the daily trauma of surviving the apocalypse. Now, don't try and fly the planes because you've played a flight simulator. It will end badly with a case of dead.

Subway Stations/Sewers

So you're thinking you're going to head down underground and hide beneath the world's large cities. We can almost hear the internal dialogue now...

"Hey, I'll hide down here. No one will EVER find me here. It's perfect: there's soda machines, snack machines, and miles of tunnels to escape in!"

It's an awesome thought isn't it? Living like the mole people, being deep inside the man made tunnels looking for Zion and waiting on Morpheus to come to your rescue. Sadly, this is more likely to be how it will play out:

"All right, I'm safe. Down the stairs, zombies can't work stairs very well. So I'm good.
Wait, why is it so dark down here? Oh yeah, no windows and access to the sunlight. It's cool. I'm safe.

What was that tumbling sound? What just fell down the stairs?

Wait, what's that groaning coming from every direction around me in the tunnels?

Hey, quit touching my ass, dude. Wait, I'm alone down here, what the flaming balls? Oh, hell..."

You must remember subways only exist in the bigger cities; many people will be in these wonderful death traps when they finally die. Also, while zombies do have difficulty navigating stairs, it's not like it takes mountain climbing experience or anything; they will eventually get to the top. When you're DOWN stairs from them, they'll just miss the first step and tumble down. Like a big rotten flesh craving slinky. Since we all wish to survive the apocalypse and make it to the rebuilding stage of the world. Let's just leave the subways and sewers to the old movies with crappy acting and computer simulations shall we?

One Final Note...

Wherever you go, and whatever path you choose to take, you're going to require a latrine. If you can rig up running water and a toilet, go for it, but otherwise, digging a trench or a deep hole is going to be a necessity. A few things to consider here when scouting a location would be average wind direction, distance from camp, and the possible spoilage of your garden, well, or other type of ground-based liquid storage. You should have your pooping spot at least thirty yards from where you sleep, and an equal distance from any veggies or water supplies. This is also where lime comes in handy. You don't want to smell your own shit for a prolonged period, and you certainly don't want to contaminate precious water with butt bombs. Likewise, any leftover cooking byproducts could be disposed of in a similar manner. Doing so will aid in further concealing your presence from unwanted notice. Can you imagine being tracked by a poop trail?

SECTION 7
TERRAIN TYPES AND YOU

"During the outbreak, there's bound to be weather. Let's face it, Mother Nature isn't going to stop because we're battling zombies. But the weather can be used to your advantage. High winds, rainy weather, snow, extreme heat, what have you can all be used against the hordes. My only advice is don't fall victim to the weather you're using against zed."

– Meteorologist Zippy Hernandez

Throughout the world there are numerous types of terrain in which we can find ourselves. Whether it's in a domestic or recreational capacity, we navigate one or more of them on a daily basis. You may have been in one area for the better part of your life and become so familiar with it that it's outside your comfort zone to leave it. If you're willing to make certain compromises with your environment in order to survive, then you should do fine. If you want to know more about alternate terrain types that may help you survive in even more places, good for you. Should it be that you're unconcerned with various terrain types and what they have to offer, then you're probably going to die, and should save us all the trouble of having to destroy your limping flesh-hungry corpse. When you're trying to find a suitable place to make your stand against the shuffling ghouls in the world, there are a few things you should always do:

1. Familiarize yourself with the climate range and clothing needed.

2. Get some books and manuals on the area, which tell of wildlife and plants that are edible.

3. Having become familiarized with the wild game in an area, stock ammunition and supplies that are appropriate to your potential prey.

4. Find maps that reveal topography and population.

5. Scout these areas frequently, so you have prior knowledge of what you'll encounter. Pay close attention to natural details, sights, sounds, and smells.

6. Practice the skills needed in these places often enough that they become second nature.

7. Bring toilet paper. Even if you have no toilet, you still need to wipe.

8. Restrict travel to daylight hours. Being stuck is one thing; being stuck in the dark is scary, and just some bullshit you could have avoided.

A good idea, if it's possible, would be to find a guide of some sort. Someone who is intimately familiar with the land. It doesn't matter if you're in Alaska trying to go native or if you're in a huge city which you're unfamiliar with, the premise is the same. The chances are good that they're going to have some sort of valuable insight which will allow your passage through, or staying there, a lot easier. Now that we have that straight, let's have a look at what we're dealing with here.

Swamps

Seriously, can you think of a worse possible place to try and set up shop, let alone navigate? There are numerous perils associated with these wet cesspools, and for good reason. Never mind the fact that a zombie could be laying beneath the surface of the water (counting tadpoles or whatever the hell they do while they wait, biding their time and just itching to grab something living to sink their gnarled teeth into), what about the living critters? Snakes, mosquitoes, alligators, and skunk apes run rampant through these environments, and can be as much of a hazard as any undead.

Forget being able to decently plot a route through these giant-sized petri dishes; there is rarely a safe place to even set foot. Vehicles would become hopelessly stuck in the muck, and anything short of an airboat has virtually no chance of making it out structurally intact. It's hot, humid, stinks like buffalo-ass, and is about the most inhospitable type of land you could hope to imagine.

It's not inconceivable that one could make a life in a swampy area with a bit of intestinal fortitude and an aptitude for hunting game. Fishing is probably also something one could accomplish with a bit of knowledge on the subject as it pertains to the environment. Water is abundant and could easily be processed for drinking. Your worries about other swamp-dwellers would be almost nonexistent, as nobody wants to live here unless they have already done so for the better part of their lives and it's all they know.

The positive side here is that the undead would have an even worse time of traversing this particular patch of planet than we would. Luckily for us, they're too stupid to try and use the best possible footing for making any kind of real forward progress, and this will almost assuredly result in their being firmly mired in mud, whether above or below the water line matters little because they're stuck. The best part about a swamp is that you shouldn't be in too much danger from zombies; you're more likely to be eaten by something that would actually enjoy your flesh.

Another point worth noting is that these ghouls will be rotting a bit faster due to the heat and humidity, which are both abundant in these regions. This also works on our behalf. It would certainly be a daunting challenge to most people to try and make a life in a swamp due to the risks, but the reward of living would prove to be worth it.

Deserts

"So you've got your group, you're not going to be a red shirt nobody, and you're ready to survive. You've listened so far, however, not everything is applicable to everyone. If you live in a frozen area, zombies would move slower. In the warm areas, they'd be a bit faster. So you need to remember to adapt to your surroundings. It may just keep you from becoming lunch for zed."

– Scorpion King

Pies, cakes, and candy. Er... no, that's all wrong. Those are "desserts," two S's; there's a huge difference. What we're talking about when we say desert is an arid region comprised mostly of rock and sand with little indigenous plant life of which to speak. It's HOT, seriously hot. Like so hot, your sweat sweats. It's that hot. Making it here requires shelter during the day and plenty of water to hydrate your body. I'm not sure whose idea that was, but that's no way to run a desert. The undead may have a trying time treading on sand, but they're not going to feel the effects of thirst wearing their bodies down. In fact it's possible that the dry air may act as something of a preservative to the undead. If you happen to see a zombie that's been in the desert for a while, it will very likely look like you're being attacked by a Slim Jim that wants to get at your think-jelly.

Travel during the day is recommended in other areas, but in the desert heat, it's just stupid and suicidal. Early mornings, just after the sun starts to rise, and the evenings, when the sun begins to set, are your prime travel times. Moving at night puts you at risk of being sighted by our sleepless formerly human predators, and is never a good idea unless it's necessitated by undead incursion. Even then, it's probably not going to end well, due to our inability to see effectively at night.

Making a home in this climate will be difficult to say the least. The undead will have a free pass to travel this land, and you'll have to be constantly vigilant. Wildlife in these places is not much of a threat to humans for the most part, but should still be warded against. Defending your dwelling may take a bit of doing, but it's certainly a goal that is attainable. In addition to the plentiful sand, there are also rocky cliffs to be found. Zed doesn't climb well at all, and these can be used to great advantage when looking for a place to call home. Whether you decide to make a structure on a plateau or maybe find a nice little cave system which you can inhabit unmolested by various critters and creepy crawlies, it's probably best to stay up off the ground.

Finding a source of water nearby will also be a bit of a test. There are ways to go about this, but it's likely going to be the biggest challenge of choosing this environment. Arid regions aren't exactly known for their large sources of H_2O, and collecting it can easily become a full-time job. This being the case, you could easily become distracted by this task, when defending yourself from the undead is still a major priority. Choose wisely when faced with the decision of confronting the many obstacles this terrain has to offer.

Florida

Aside from being the previous two terrain types lovingly smashed together and full of old slow people who are going to become zombies sooner rather than later, there's nothing really to say about it other than "stay out."

Grasslands

This can refer to generally flat areas where little elevation changes occur. They're not terribly common (except for Southern Texas or all of Kansas and Nebraska), but they do happen. These places are certainly the easiest to walk through, and with a sufficiently equipped vehicle, going off road, if the need arises, should pose no significant challenge. Plants and wildlife are abundant here, and searching these areas should turn up plenty of good nutritional finds. Don't wear yourself out looking for trees though. Aside from deserts, there are fewer spread around here than any other terrain.

Fields speckle the landscape for a better part of the year in the flatter parts of the country, and can be used to lay low and avoid the odd undead which you should be able to easily spot. However, the same holds true for the zombie. Sounds can be deceptive when you're making your way through tall crops. You have to set your nerves on edge and be ready to lay down a sudden zombie bitch-slap on a moment's notice. Seriously, these slobbery bastards will come out of nowhere, and if you're not careful you'll end up as one of the douche bags of the corn.

Even out in the open, one has to be fairly careful. The lack of topographical diversity means you can spot the undead from a decent distance with the unaided eye. This also means they can spot you. If this happens, it's not too out of line to consider that the one that sighted you could become several. These ghouls are everywhere, and this type of scenario will prove it faster than almost any other. See one, you hear it moan, meaning it's spotted you, then five more pop up. Not fair, and in this game, there's no reset button. Be careful in engaging them as always. Your other option is to travel faster than the undead can manage. If you're caught on foot and you need to rest, there is no good place to do it in the flatlands. Sometimes a brief engagement is a better solution.

Making a home where it's flat can offer a couple of strategic advantages. As mentioned previously, your line of sight can extend for miles, with a tower it will extend even farther, and a couple of vigilant lookouts can spot danger long before it becomes a real issue. Second, this is going to be fertile soil, so growing your own food shouldn't pose any sort of challenge at all, as long as proper irrigation can be attained. Even traveling by vehicle through these areas will allow you to spot any potential road hazard before it's likely to become a danger.

If you're here and just passing through, move swiftly, keep your head down, and don't let the wheat, cotton, and corn drive you insane and you should be fine. If you're staying, just watch out for the weather. If that rain comes down in buckets, it has got nowhere to go. Watch out for tornadoes, too. Stay low and you should be OK. Possibly.

Rain Forests

It rains often, it's hot, it's humid, and you can't see more than a few yards in any direction. In short, rain forests are absolute crap. Traveling in circles is a common occurrence, without knowing what you're doing or where you're headed. A compass will help you navigate these areas without much trouble, assuming the extreme humidity doesn't render it useless within the first month.

Medicinal vegetation can be found almost anywhere you care to look here. Edible flora and fauna are also more than copious in these regions. There is also an equal number of organic substances, both plant and animal, which will probably kill you if you so much as touch them. As far as edible things go, remember you're also on that list. Not just because of the undead, either. Everything here wants to take a bite out of you for some form of nourishment. Snakes, spiders, I'm pretty sure the birds can carry you off and fuck up your day, and swarms of ants will bring you down and strip your bones if you run across their path and linger. Obviously rain forests are in line to be the next great family holiday destination.

One would think that maybe this would be a deterrent to people wanting to live here; hell no. There are tons of little people with Beatle bowl cuts scattered all over the place that would just as soon eat your damn feet as well. As luck would have it, they're a bit out of touch, and are probably going to eat some zombie's infected flesh and turn into undead themselves. While it's true they're still ghouls which pose their own sets of problems, at least they won't be fucking around shooting poison darts into your backside and feasting on your genitals. In that regard, you're better off picking a fight with the little native zombies who have no reach.

In regards to environmental impact on the undead, rain forests are a lot like swamps. Just imagine if you drained a swamp and suspended the water from ground level to ten feet in the air. You have a rain forest. They will deteriorate faster here, due to the extraordinary hot and humid nature of the land taking its toll on the cells of these monsters.

Your gear will pretty much rot off your back in these climates. The undead aren't the only things that are going to take structural exception to the environment; anything that enters these realms is going to be subject to an extremely accelerated rate of decay. In order to remain effective, weapons will need a daily cleaning and coating of oil to ward off the eventual oxidization. Not only will you go through a lot of metallic gear, but also you'll end up going through a lot of socks. You don't want to be laid up with trench foot when the undead start their rumble in the jungle and you're on the menu.

In terms of finding food and water, a rain forest is an exceptional choice and probably ranks at the top of the heap. Regarding gear wear and tear, there's a reason the natives walk around naked. As it pertains to combating or defending against zombies, a rain forest is a huge and dangerous pain in the ass that you probably won't want to contend with. I'm pretty sure this is why we're cutting the damn things down.

Urban Areas

These will surely be epicenters of the zombie outbreak. Concrete covered commercial cadavers of the earth, cities are going to be the most dangerous areas imaginable when the dead rise up and try to bite your meaty bits. These areas offer little cover when you're in the streets, aside from long forgotten vehicles. Movement will be a tedious undertaking through these glass and steel jungles, and should be avoided whenever possible. However, since we're talking about you being there, I suppose dissuading one from this course of action by simply saying "stay the fuck out" would be a bit silly.

Defending yourself effectively inside of a formerly populous area will be extremely difficult to say the least. The undead, as mentioned many times, are relentless and not easily distracted. At some point, leaving your abode will be a requirement, and with that many zombies around, you're probably going to be spotted. It only takes one to start its guttural bitching in order to alert the rest. Once this happens, they're going to start flocking, flooding, and ripping at doors in an effort to get to you. Unfortunately, in most modern city buildings, taking out the stairs will prove to be a little more problematic than doing so in a wood-constructed suburban two-story home. So, you may have to get creative here. Block, bar, barricade, and otherwise halt forward progress that the undead are able to utilize given their mediocre dexterity. In this way alone, one can hope to survive for any length of time at all in a defensive situation.

If you're trying to scrounge and loot for supplies in a city, first of all, you've made a bad choice. There are plenty of places in which to get gear that didn't have millions of people living in them at one time who are now life-challenged and cannibalistic. The odds are simply too great of ex-people seeing you and making a fuss, thereby drawing more to the scene. Supposing this is your only option, get in fast and go out the back. Avoid using the same entrance twice, especially in an urban environment. There may be plenty of stores where you can find yourself food and water, guns and ammo, peanut butter and jelly, ham and burger, and all that good stuff, but you need to plan very carefully or have just indecent amounts of firepower on your side when attempting such a thing. Careful planning, discipline, and ingenuity are awesome human traits, especially against the undead. You'll need them here to make it out alive.

Stealth is your greatest ally inside of a city when your numbers are small. Even in large numbers, you have to do your best to avoid being spotted. If possible, utilize silent projectiles or melee methods to avoid bringing the undead to your location. Discharging a firearm in an urban area is a sure way to end your day very unhappily. Taking down a zombie or a dozen is well and good, thanks for that, but there are going to be plenty more behind those, and that's just never a good place to find yourself.

Looking for indigenous wildlife to snack on? Look elsewhere because you're not going to find any here. Any animals roaming inside a city were of the domesticated nature and have either fled and become feral or have been eaten by the undead, who are far less picky about what it is that they eat, as long as it's alive. You may be able to find some critters in the sewer systems, but you may not want to risk venturing down to where your senses are assaulted to the point of uselessness. Doing so leaves you open to attack by the undead or maybe even a flushed pet goldfish with a grudge. Sewer systems should be avoided, unless there is no other option but to go down there for the purposes of clearing them of undead prior to inhabiting these areas anew.

Traveling by vehicle through an urban area should be discounted entirely. The only exceptions here are carefully scouted routes and driving a tank. The tank can ignore stalled vehicles entirely for the most part, but you're not going to have a tank. You're just not. No tank for you. So aside from large armored projectile-firing modes of transport, freely traversing the city streets in stylish automotive fashion simply isn't going to be an option that's on the table.

Entering a city after the zombies rise and begin their ungainly march is going to be something that one may want to think twice about. Then think about it again. Then dismiss it. Until such time as a reclamation effort is made, urban areas are going to be banes of the living. Safe habitation or travel therein will be nonexistent until the undead are purged entirely from within our once-glorified metropolitan areas.

Woodlands

"So, you're now living in the forest because it offers the greatest protection, and you're looking for entertainment. Might I suggest recording your voice on digital recorders? You can raid the nearby electronics store. Record a scream of terror, randomly drop them into a group of horde. Watch them run into each other looking for fresh brains."

– Milton Wiggum

The friend to any hunter or gatherer, wooded areas provide a landscape rich with all kinds of edible goodness. Knowing where to go and what to look for are naturally quite essential to being successful in your effort to find what it is that you're after, but a bit of trial and error can certainly help in that regard. Books help a lot, too. A water source is also a common thing near many of these areas, which doesn't hurt one single bit in regards to prolonging your life.

Naturally, you're going to see a lot of trees. It's the woods; what did you expect? This is both a blessing and a curse. Like the rain forest, but with less rain and humidity, your visibility is going to be decreased due to many tall and thick obstacles.

Noises made within the forest's barky confines are also reduced, granting an element of surprise to whichever creature's not moving at the time. Twigs snap, leaves crackle, birds chirp, and none of these are helpful to you if you're the one doing the tracking. Tread lightly in these areas, listen carefully, and keep your head on a swivel. You don't want to be surprised by some zombie wearing camouflage while you're out hunting deer.

One good thing about the forested areas would be the extraordinary lack of people. This is always a plus. Aside from crazy bomb-building hermits that dislike big government and no-shoes-no-service policies in family eateries, you'll be hard-pressed to find someone out here other than yourself. You may run across another survivor, or even a filthy hippy-turned-zombie, but it's terribly unlikely. This alone should make these areas an idea that's entertained from the beginning.

Setting up shop in the woods can be done, but it will take a lot of skill and hard work. Either the old-school fort route or the tree houses are reasonable methods by which you can go about this plan. Doing so leaves you in prime zombie-warding real estate, as long as they don't show up in droves. Also, pay attention to the game in the area. Chances are if they leave, you may want to do the same.

Mountains

A sportsman's paradise, the mountains offer many attractive features to the post-apocalyptic survivalist. Hunting, fishing, hiking, causing the occasional avalanche, making snowmen, and other winter sports are all ways to spend your time in the higher elevations. Finding certain necessary materials should not pose much of an obstacle. Wild game is plentiful in almost any area, but especially the higher you go.

Those who may be unfamiliar with the rigors of even walking at higher altitudes should be warned that it's a lot different than your normal sea level wandering about. Oxygen deprivation is a serious concern to the newly anointed mountain man. Unless you're a marathon runner, heading up to the peaks and taking off on foot willy-nilly is probably going to be a bad idea. Once there though, take walks which are easy and slightly up-hill to acclimate yourself to the altitude. Once you do that though, you'll be just fine when it comes to the hard parts. You're still going to huff and puff quite a bit. You've been warned.

Temperature is another factor that should be considered when taking to the hills. For a large portion of the year, mountainous regions are covered in snow. It's not uncommon that even in the summer, nightly temperatures drop to freezing, or far below. One good thing, though, is this means zombies are going to become frozen stiff. The undead won't be making much progress up those mountains once they freeze solid. Dismissing the undead at that point would be a mistake. It's quite likely that, at some point, they'll thaw and become a threat once more. So what's the answer here? If you find yourself confronting a zombie popsicle, save your ammo and take out the head. Beat, bludgeon, and batter it any way you can. They won't offer much resistance aside from the ice-induced inflexibility they've taken on.

Water is not something you'll have to work too awfully hard to find. If you're tired of melting snow, there are innumerable streams, rivers, and reservoirs which you can take advantage of for this purpose. Anywhere you can find something to drink, you can probably catch fish as well. Without the normal annual hunting occurring at the same rate as had been popular in recent years, wildlife should be more than plentiful in these regions. One concern you should have, though, when stalking your prey is that you can become prey as well. Where the good meat on the hoof goes, so do the animals that like to eat them. You may have to contend a bit for a meal, but when you're getting back to nature in this way, that's the reality of it.

Finding an isolated and difficult to reach spot for the purposes of fending off the undead menace shouldn't pose a daunting obstacle. Once done, and winter has set in, your worries about the undead are suspended. Thaws don't often occur again until late April or May, so your main concern is going to be keeping up a proper calorie intake. Should you have the undead on your mind during the long winter though, certainly use that time to get creative in the defense of your structure. Digging will be difficult in the hard, packed frozen ground, so try other means by which to beef up the new homestead's security. Keeping busy will be helpful in staving off cabin fever, which has been known to be a problem during the prolonged winter months. Staying sane will mean staying alive. Or at the very least, not yelling at your canned peas for hours on end and covering yourself in fecal matter while singing the Canadian National Anthem, while wondering aloud about the merits of anal probing as it relates to interstellar goodwill, and how cheese should be the day of the week between Saturday and Bandersnatch socks, will keep you alive.

With the isolation, plentiful food and water naturally found, cold temperatures, and relatively sparse population that presently exists, making your new home in the higher elevations is certainly a good way to go about your self-preservation. There are numerous advantages here that can make life far easier on anyone who is willing to endure the harsh winters in order to gain a measure of safety.

Islands

Zombies can't swim and you're surrounded by water? This sounds just about perfect, doesn't it? With the zombies all stuck on the mainland, shambling and biting and infecting and smelling all funky, where else would you want to go? First, let's see what's available here before we get into why you may not want to go to where the seven stranded castaways spent their time.

Being an island, fresh water may be a bit of a problem, and this would require you to distill your own or bring a whole hell of a lot with you, which won't possibly last the term of your stay. You'll end up making your own at some point, so be prepared for this prospect. Food will be your other primary concern. Chances are this isn't an island with a wide variety of tasty native species available. Most islands aren't known for having a cornucopia of meaty critters that are easy to kill and turn into a succulent dinner. This isn't always the case, but in general, there's a reason an island is uninhabited in the first place. Suffice to say, you're going to have to bring a lot of supplies. Diversity of plant life is subject to the particular plot of land on which you find yourself. It may or may not be covered with all sorts of grown goodness. You can also certainly find tasty goodness in the water that surrounds you. This will take time on your part to learn what is where and the best ways to go about obtaining it. Just make sure to exercise all necessary caution while doing so.

Supposing you're the only one with the idea of hauling ass to an island is not only insulting to others of your species, but also dangerous to you. Don't allow yourself to be lulled into complacency because you happen to make it there with all your gear first. Anyone with a dinghy, raft, water wings, or other seaworthy craft will be thinking the same damn thing, and only take exception to the fact that you made it there first. This will in all likelihood be met with pleas, bargaining, or most probably violence. All you need is a group of heavily armed clowns who want to be among the first to become new-age pirates, looking for a base from which to launch their raiding operations, to come find you where they want to be. In this case, you're going to have one hell of a bloody mess on your hands if they don't get what they want. You're much better off fighting against the undead than armed human beings. Let's face it, with a majority of the population gone, there's plenty of land to choose from, and that means that fighting over a sandy piece of terra just isn't worth your life.

Very much like both the rain forests and oil rigs, weapon maintenance is going to be a daily thing here for your preparedness, not only because of the effects of sea air on your equipment, but also because you're in constant danger of the undead happening upon your dirt patch. True, zombies can't swim; they just sink and wander the bottoms until they find something that captures their attention. This could conceivably mean you. A constant watch of the shoreline is going to be a must, and, depending on the size of the island, it may not be easily accomplished.

Shelter will be another concern that should top the priority list. You're going to have to get creative here because it's unlikely that a tent is going to last you the duration of your stay. Tents certainly will not provide proper protection against the odd undead wanderer, human raider, or gale force winds. When you're surrounded by water, storms are an inevitable fact of life. Luckily for you, since the island is still there, it's unlikely to be swept away by a bit of rain and wind. This is not true for your tent. Hopefully you remembered to bring tools with you so you can fashion some sort of fort or hut from the local vegetation. The stronger you can make it, the better, for obvious reasons.

Re-supply will be another vexing issue that you will have to address. The self-imposed isolation you've decided on has left you in the unenviable position of having to use a lot of fuel (or sail, however you got to the island) going back and forth to the mainland for certain supplies. Yes, you forgot something, or you need more of another thing. Whatever the case may be, you now have to make that trip. Doing so exposes your position a bit, but the undead are less of a problem in that regard. What you really have to be careful of at this point is leading those pesky raiders back to your humble abode. Watch your back when looking for supplies, and also while heading home.

Choose well, supply early, and get there before anyone else does, and an island should be an acceptable choice. Obviously, making this decision is not without risk, but done correctly it can be your own little chunk of paradise. Defend it well and you will be a happy camper. Watch for sand fleas.

At Sea

"Since many of you insist on wanting to survive via boat, I've come up with a good plan for that. Don't just survive, become a privateer. That's right—don the Jolly Roger and pirate. Remember, zed can wander around under water for quite some time, so don't be climbing down the anchor chain to access the boat. Stay above water, and survive."
– Nathaniel Mayweather

You've got a boat, a good sized one, and you've got it loaded with supplies. You've thought about where to dock and said to yourself, "Self, why should I head toward anything at all? This is a self-contained safe spot." In this, you could very well be correct. Loading up your gear and group and just anchoring yourself out in the bay, safely out of harm's way, is definitely an option worthy of consideration.

The first things to be aware of are haters. Yes, even in apocalyptic times, there will be haters among us who envy your decisive actions that leave you safely nestled in the bosom of the water. They won't worry about their own poor decision-making having led to their current plight; they're instead going to covet that which is yours. If you're moored within sight of land, be aware of this possibility when you head to shore for supplies, supposing of course that you're forced to do so. If you must leave the boat for any reason, leave someone armed and guarding the vessel.

Bands of pirates also fall into the "hater" category, but they at least have their own boats, eye patches, and a little style. They also want your goodies for their own use, and guarding against them will be another concern. Fortunately the weapons you have for use against the undead will prove equally, if not more, effective against the living, should it come to that. Beware the Jolly Roger.

Weather will be something else you have to guard against and will probably be your main concern. In open water, this threat is compounded, and you can reduce the risk of being capsized by taking shelter in a bay. Experience will tell you where the best place to drop anchor is when trying to wait out a storm. Figuring this out is essential because when your boat flips, it's no good for anyone.

Choosing a seaworthy vessel of sufficient size and simplicity will also be an important undertaking. Too small, and you're going to need supplies every other day. Too large will generally equate to complexity which is beyond the understanding of an untrained crew. Ease of operation of the boat is a necessary component to survival at sea, should the normal person playing captain be out of commission. If the rest of the crew proves unable to pilot the ship when the need arises, the situation could quickly become disastrous.

Fishing is going to become a new favorite past time when enduring your life at sea. Being able to snag meals daily from the depths will either become a thing you love or a thing you love to hate. The sooner this is realized, the better. Use smaller fish for bait, and there you have it, you'll be snagging swimmers in no time. You may want to snatch a few more nutritional items from land, but you can do very well by fishing and diving for your daily repast. Just make sure that you're on constant zombie watch if you dive.

While it's terribly unlikely that a zombie would be able to muster the dexterity to do so, keep an eye on your anchor line. Just because it's not probable, doesn't mean it's never going to happen. It would be one healthy pain in the ass to wake up and find an animated waterlogged corpse on your deck trying to make you into a midnight snack. Vigilance is key, no matter where you are. You have to protect your boats and hoes.

Arctic Tundra

Ah, the great white north. Or south, depending on your preference. Either way you look at it, the closer you get to the Polar Regions, the harsher the landscape. It's cold, the ground is hard, it's difficult to look at due to the abundance of white, and there are fatty critters that are adapted for surviving there, some of which can kill you. Aside from that, you'll be perfectly safe because zombies will never make it here. They'll freeze before they reach the first marker.

Hunting here will be your only option for survival. There are no plants you can make use of, no stores to plunder or pillage, no pizza delivery, and no real mode of transport aside from dog sleds or snowmobiles. Walking won't be a great option because, let's face it, you'll probably end up dying. It's seriously fucking cold in these places.

Finding a native to the area who is well versed in survival techniques will prove more valuable here than anywhere else. There are just some things that a book can't teach you. Reading is one thing, but doing is another, and the only way to survive in such an environment is to know how to do it. Having knowledge is great, but having practiced practical know-how is even better. Take a trip up to the Arctic Circle, vacation there for a few weeks, see how you like it before making up your mind that the land of ice and snow is the right decision for you. You back yet? That was bullshit, wasn't it?

SECTION 8
COPING WITH LIFE IN ZOMBIETOPIA

"When in doubt, trip the guy in your group you don't like that much. On the flip side, make sure you're well liked in the group."
- Shane

Up to this point, we've discussed what you need, where you can go, how you can get there, and touched on the basics of what it is that we're facing. What we need to know now is how to not only deal with the undead directly, but how to cope with all this new input we're getting, as well as the human element. Drastic changes have been forced upon us by unforeseen circumstances, and damned if this didn't ruin all the carefully laid plans you had to sit in front of the television and watch all that awesome stuff you had on your DVR. You're hardly the only person that finds him or herself in the middle of this horrific ordeal. Everyone will deal with it in his or her own way, and you must find yours in order to survive. Well, in this situation, we have a few suggestions.

How to Deal with What's Going Down

"Stupidity. It's a danger to every group. Look around, and you can identify the stupid people rather easily. If you can't, chances are you're the stupid one. If that's the case, stop reading. OK, for all you non-stupid people, the first chance you get, trip the stupid one. He'll slow down the hordes for your escape."

– Vinnie Caposte

So undead ghouls have overrun the world. The governments have crumbled, the military's been forced to set up a defensive action, and most everyone you've ever known is now dead and, oddly enough, trying to eat you. Sounds a bit like a bad horror novel, doesn't it? You may be asking yourself how you can possibly make it through this. Well, stop talking to yourself; that's just fucking creepy. Facing the undead does not mean we're dealing with anything that we are unable to meet head on in terms of survival through superior firepower, rather that we need to develop a firm understanding of what it is we're dealing with in order to safely overcome the threat it represents. Remember all that keen info at the beginning of the book? Good, because now it's time to put it to use.

Adaptation is one of the greatest of all human qualities, and when it comes to the confrontation with that which is thought to be the product of fantasy, it will indeed be put to the test. Having to firmly grasp the reality of the dead walking the earth again is a taxing thought, which each person will have to come to terms with as being a new and horrible fact. It's folly to underestimate an opponent and consider yourself superior to the point of dismissal of your foe. The reason behind this is because you may then become careless when facing this opposition and end up as one more of their number, standing against those of us who will survive through careful planning, observational understanding, copious drug use, and a strict use of proven safe and useful group tactics. Having a good working knowledge about what you're facing is the best possible start you can have. Ideas can be changed to fit with what you learn and modified to help you survive. In your mind, when considering new information, be like our oxygen-making friends the trees: strong in the roots, but you know when to bend so that you don't break under pressure. (Note: Do not be like a mesquite tree. You will be ugly, and people may cut you apart to make their meats tastier.)

Over-thinking the situation can make it seem untenable, almost like it's just you against the world. This is simply not true. You're not alone in your struggle. There are going to be many others, just like you, that are working, fighting, and resisting the advances of the undead. Sadly, many won't have the intestinal fortitude to do what must be done in order to fight off these monstrosities and pull through. We call these people "pussies" because they're just sitting around waiting to get tooth raped by some wandering ghoul. Disregard those people entirely, because if they won't harden the fuck up, then they should be beneath your notice. Your best bet is to concentrate on your immediate area. Find your patch of soil and defend it until it's no longer even remotely safe to do so, then find another and repeat the process. Don't think globally; it's simply far too daunting of a prospect, at least it will be for a while. If all the others subscribe to the same ideology then, eventually, every patch is going to be clear. No more zombies, no more worry.

Surviving means a world of opportunity for you and everyone else. There will be immediate and recognizable respect for almost anyone who survives simply because they did so. That and keg parties, projectile vomiting, streaking, and lost clothing—lots of that going on, too. Everyone will know the horrors that the other had to endure in the name of survival. Plus, look at the bright side; no more homeless people begging for change. If that's not worth surviving for, then I don't know what is.

As stated way back in the earlier portions of the book, stay cool. Don't let the situation work you into a blind rage.

Instead, try to keep that fire burning low and hot and release it at the appropriate times. Don't look for trouble, it will find you, and when it does, make it regret having done so. If you're set upon by six zombies, dispatch five, and turn the last one into a chunky puddle of fucked up, unrecognizable jelly. We're talking about serious anger management here, folks. You're the one in control of your own survival.

Grouping Up

Surviving the zombie apocalypse alone is going to be nearly impossible. You'll never be really safe without someone to watch your back when rest is needed. Plus it's going to get awfully lonely after a while. To combat this lonely feeling you're going to need friends, and plotting out your group ahead of time is always a good idea. In doing so there are several questions you should ask when making these choices.

1. Who is strong enough to survive?
2. Do any of your friends or family have the skills required to aid the others? If not, can they learn?
3. Do they have any training?
4. Are they fast learners?
5. Wasn't it supposed to be Connor that won The Prize?
6. Who has their own weapons and gear?
7. How close are they if you have to leave quickly?
8. Do any of these people have disagreeable personalities?

9. Is everyone capable of following both complex and simple plans?

Answering these and finding the best mix of attributes is going to be a necessity. What you lack in knowledge at the present time you can compensate for with manuals on the topic, as well as an ability to translate word into deed. Not everyone needs to know everything, but a little knowledge in each area certainly can't hurt. Just don't make your own head explode. Having basic understandings in several areas cuts down on the level of tragedy, should one group member be lost. Yeah, it would suck that Bob the mechanic got his shit ruined because he decided to go wacky barbarian style on a group of zeds, but hey, it's his own damn fault for losing his cool. So to this end, everyone should know a little about what it is the other people do well. Read during your down time, and always keep books handy. When you're not reading them, keep them packed and ready for transport. You don't want to lose these. They help to provide a healthy and instructional understanding of the things that inhabit the world we live in.

Being alone throughout the zombie apocalypse has yet another drawback in that you have nobody to be strong for. Having someone there to defend gives you more motivation to get creative enough to survive through even the worst situations. This is our world, and we should know enough about it to get beyond even the worst-case scenarios. Having a person who can help you plan, tease you out of fear, and kick you in the ass when you're being all silly defeatist, is a good thing. A connection forged in the fires of disaster is one that can easily last a good long time. Plus, you need to have someone around that you can pull pranks on.

Group tactics will be essential for managing threats presented not only by the undead, but the living as well. To this end we recommend you having a group of four to twelve people. The larger the group is, naturally the more supplies you'll need, but with more people comes more ability to hunt, gather, and grow food supplies. Region should play a decent part in dictating how you form your party and its size. If you're in the middle of the Arctic, food is going to be far scarcer than it would be in a wooded mountainous area. Having a dozen people trying to live in an igloo isn't going to be pleasant. Just think of all the little brown stalagmites that will pepper the area. Plan in advance and make sure everyone you get together can contribute something worthwhile and function like rational people with each other.

Luxury Items

While having a couple things with you that may provide entertainment is a good thing, some things aren't going to be around anymore. Your industrial strength hairdryer, endless amounts of sugar, take-out food, hot water (at least not for most people without boiling it first), television shows, and the Internet and its plentiful porn are all going away. Now you can circumvent the loss of electricity for certain things, but you don't want to remain dependent on finite resource-based trappings. It's time to give up coffee, cigarettes, and the other good things in life that are going to spoil, go bad, or get used up rather quickly. Now, you can naturally grow your own if you so choose, but that's entirely up to you and your environment. It will be easier to quit now and save yourself the mental distraction in the future. For those who choose not to quit these things, a strong suggestion is made to start stocking up now for the future lack of steady supply availability. Nobody wants to be around Johnny Two-Balls when he didn't get his morning cup of java and a cigarette. Whiney bastard, you're reading the warning right now. You've been warned.

Assholes and Malcontents

It is an unfortunate truism that in the world we live in not everyone is a good-natured unselfish human being. In fact, vast majorities fall into the category of "jackass" quite easily. Some people are just not wired for proper interpersonal interaction. Whether it's bad hygiene, manners, or absolutely shitty personal skills, some people just suck. Even the most mild mannered among us will eventually get sick of some people's nonsensical actions, and get to the point where maybe you can do without them. This could very well be the truth of the matter. In fact, where it pertains to the morale of the group, sometimes less is more.

If you're in the habit of taking in strays that you meet along your journeys through the world of the undead, there could very well be a time when you meet Johnny Two-Balls. He knows more than you, he's tougher than you, he's smarter than you, and he's fond of telling you that these things are not only unequivocally true, but despite the fact that he just showed up, he's the boss now; at least according to him, he is. This prick will have to shape up or ship out. He's not only going to piss everyone off to the point of irrational behavior, he's probably going to pull some Leeroy Jenkins shit and get the group killed at some point. To this end it's recommended that you do what you must in order to ensure the survival of the group. Maybe it will be an "accidental" shot to the leg which leaves him terribly exposed to the descending horde, or maybe a "slip" from a rooftop into their waiting maws. Whatever is easiest for you. Just harden up, get it done, and move on. If anyone happens to ask you what happened, you have no idea, he was right behind you, then he wasn't. Whoever offs him first doesn't matter; you were all thinking about it anyway. It isn't likely that many questions would be asked either way.

We touched on them earlier, but we're now going to discuss dealing with those who want what you have. Haters or marauders, whichever label you choose to ascribe to them, are going to be an ever-present threat to your safety. Some won't be overt about their threat; they'll spot your hideout, count your group, wait for everyone to leave, and then rob you blind. How shitty is that? 98 percent of the planet turns into mindless flesh devouring automatons, and you get robbed while you're out looking for a roll of soft toilet paper. Awesome thought isn't it? To this end, the only real options you have are to spot them first and either try to reason with these people, or kill them as painfully and loudly as possible in order to set an example to any who dare try the same thing. Other assclowns may show up, wave guns around while puffing out their chests and making threats. Shoot these morons before they bring the zombies around with all that noise. They're too stupid to live. Really, if you don't do it, someone else will.

The worst kind of asshole that will share the zombie-infested world with you is going to be the douche-cock sniper. This ass hat is hiding and waiting for undead or living to present themselves as a target. It doesn't matter to him which one it is, just as long as he can shoot it. These are former FPS campers, and they think they've found their niche in an undead world. Their main problem though is that the presence of bodies will give them away. Either the need to clear their field of fire of the scattered remains, or the odd corpse here and there, will give them away. Recon here is a good thing. With a little directional evaluation, you can find this prick, sneak up on him, and make him suffer large. They're just thieves that don't have the testicular fortitude to come get your shit from you directly, so they'd rather ninja your loot and not have to deal with you. In short, these are more of a threat than the undead themselves, once you've made it a few months through the worst of it, and you should always remain on guard from a potential fucktard like this guy.

It's our opinion that the only thing worse than the douche-cock sniper would be an entire group of douche-cock snipers. One man skilled with a rifle is a pain in the ass, but a group of them could easily mean death for everything they encounter, including you and your group. Worries are similar, either they find your camp, wait patiently, and pick you off, or they set up an ambush out in the world. Now, like the lone sniper, careful observation can clue you in to the presence of these dickless wonders in the same ways. Knowing the lay of your land gives you an advantage though, and you can use this knowledge to snap a loop on these guys, get behind them, and rape them with sharp objects. You may opt to just kill them quickly, but there's a certain satisfaction in drawing out the whole affair. If you stab a man in the liver, he'll be in far too much pain to even scream. You could always start there. Just sayin'.

The final kind of raider (that rhymes with hater) is the type that will just show up, kick in your door, and start with the rape and pillage. This is where a constant watch is a good thing. Hiding in the dark and keeping an eye out, once they begin to approach, the lookout should shoot the douche bag closest to the camp right in the balls. The others WILL stop at that point and try to ascertain where the shot came from. Use this time to shoot the next one. Hopefully your cover is dense enough to stop bullets while you pick these slimy bastards apart. The rest of the group will be happy to help at this point, having been woken up from their slumber by a bunch of pseudo-Viking retards trying to forcefully take their gear and lives and anal virginity. Always be on guard not only for the undead, but for the stupid as well.

General People Crap

One must walk a fine line when it comes to your comrades in arms. You can't expect everyone to deal with everything as if they're analytical masterminds right away. Having made it to the point where they've been picked up, adopted, rescued or whatever, means that they have the skills to survive. They simply need to be cultivated. Your own nature as well has to be in balance between ability to let off steam and maintain focus.

If you're always ON then you're going to burn out at some point. People can only take so much shit, you included. Keep this in mind for both yourself, and those around you. Staying sharp is one thing, but sharpening too much the wrong way can dull any blade.

Here we're going to explore a few phenomena of the human condition. These apply to everyone at one point or another in life, and have been written about extensively, but not as they pertain to a zombie apocalypse. At least I hope not. Even if it was, screw it, we're doing it ourselves. We're going to start with the seven deadlies and then go on to specifics you may or may not encounter. Once again, we've used thought reading paper in this book, so we can anticipate your questions. So, no, yes, possibly, that's sick, and please don't. Now on to other stuff.

Lust

Kicking off our sins category is the one that ends or sustains marriages and usually just results in Maury Povich episodes being aired all over the world. Lust simply is an element of people, and there's no getting around it. When tensions run high and life is in constant peril, it's inevitably going to rise at some point or another. While it may be an essential component to matchmaking and relationships in general, it has the ability to get out of hand and cause far more harm than orgasmic good.

Should you find yourself in a sausage-fest group without any women around, you may consider a couple courses of action. You may choose to go the Brokeback Mountain route, which hey, if that's your thing, have at it. The other way to go is finding yourself a zombie with agreeable genitalia and getting your rut on. This is highly ill-advised due to the obvious risk of infection either from the fluid transfers from scratches or bites, or via your junk. This is one situation where even double bagging isn't likely to protect you. None of these happening are conducive to prolonging your existence, at least as a member of the living. Maybe the cowboy butt sex is safe enough, but zombie fucking should be right out of the running.

Now in a group of mixed sexes, you may find yourself in a quarrel over the desired person's affections. This is invariably going to lead to fights and arguments, and probably result in someone's being butthurt or killed. As a rational human being, you should be able to talk this out and come to a reasonable solution, but ultimately, all parties have to agree on this outcome. Two guys fighting over a woman who has no interest in either of them is just silly. This goes both ways, and sometimes, we can be oblivious to that fact. When emotions fueled by desire are involved, sometimes rationality goes out the window like a bucket of piss. Any thought or feeling should be weighed in regards to how it helps your survival. If it's not going to help, then it should become secondary. This may not always happen, and actually, it's not even likely to happen, because people are stupid sometimes, but this is just advice, not a living manual. It would BE a manual on how to live if people followed it, but of course, someone always knows better. Stop thinking with your junk. It's going to get you killed.

Gluttony

Excess isn't something you're going to have a lot of in the zombie apocalypse, so this shouldn't really be a problem. However, you may find that someone in your group, maybe even you, has taken to sneaking the goodies while others are asleep. Now in these times, food is as precious as water, ammunition, and fuel, and should be treated as such. We're all going to be slimming down and toning up as a result of these hardship-imposed dietary restrictions, and at some point, someone's going to want your extra mass-produced cream-filled pastries.

Being a food-stealing bastard/bitch is going to end up one of two ways. Either you're going to get away with it and impossibly maintain girth during a zombie apocalypse as it goes unnoticed by your peers, or you're going to get caught doing it and brutally beaten or cast out. Either way ends badly for you, because your group doesn't have to outrun the undead, they just have to outrun you. Granted, you've been surrounded by easily accessed food for the better part of your life, and it's just become natural to be able to eat what you want when you want it, but you're also stealing food out of another person's mouth. Just a personal opinion here, but you're going to have to get used to a routine, in that routine, is a ration that you have to make due with. If you fuck with my rations, I'd wound you and leave you for the horde. Then again your writers are both tyrannical evil bastards who happen to have the entire group's best interests in mind. Until you steal their food. Then you're going to wind up as some hobbling corpse that we get to shoot again later. Or more likely, we'll beat you with heavy weapons until you resemble a fine paste. Food stealing bastard.

Greed

Greed is probably one of the things that got the human race into this mess in the first place. Someone once said that there are the "haves" and the "have-nots." There also exists the "have-a-fucking-shit-loads-and-still-want-more" and therein lies the problem with some people. While it's true, you should be able to reap the rewards of your labor, reaping the rewards of someone else's labor, and then the guy next to him's labor as well, is the epitome of excessive wanting. With zombies walking the Earth, there's no room for that shit, at least not to such a degree.

This one's a bit of both good and bad as it pertains to survival. You have a finite amount of resources, and you can't afford to squander these. Greed in general is crap, however, regarding your continued existence, it becomes essential. Using your own judgment as to what can be spared to those in need is going to come in to play at some point. If the answer is "nothing" then by all means, move along and don't feel the least bit bad about maintaining the necessities for your own group of survivors over the odd straggler. It's one thing if you're just a bastard, but it's another if you're just trying to maintain a healthy level of function.

Taking from another group or person, well, if that person's in need of killing for whatever reason, that's one thing. If you're simply taking what's theirs to have it, and it's not necessity, well we call that jackassery, and you should probably be put down on the spot. If it's in the name of pure survival, then greed is the way to go. If it's an "us or them" situation, by all means, make it them, and then assimilate their gear into yours. Living off the work of others without doing the work yourself though, is a grievous offense against your fellow man. When people are in such short supply, being an asshole will inevitably get you killed at some point. There's no need for that when the majority of the world has been wiped out by zombies and/or infected, leaving their shit just laying there for the taking. All you have to do is apply yourself a bit and look for it.

Sloth

As you probably guessed, we're not discussing the awesome mutant guy in that kick-ass '80s movie. What we're talking about is being a completely lazy ass hat who expects others to do the work of keeping them alive. It's one thing to trade goods and services in exchange for other good and services, but it's quite another to be a selfish and lazy fucking leech. Nobody wants this kind of drag on their backs, so keep an eye on habits that those around you possess, and if they seem worthless, start making plans to get rid of them.

The odds of someone like this actually surviving long enough to integrate into a group is highly unlikely, but anything is possible, and you need to be on the lookout for these types. If someone falls ill, or is injured, then assign them light duties appropriately within their present abilities, even if it's just maybe boiling water. Whatever it is, if it doesn't get done, you've got yourself a bit of dead weight. Sure, we've gotten to a point where we all like to sit and watch a program or whatever at the end of the work day, but some people will want to carry this shit over to a new world where inaction is the same as suicide. For everyone to function, everyone has to contribute. Those that don't can fend for themselves. It's a group effort, and every part needs to function in order to thrive. Treat the lazy like a horse with a broken leg; target practice. Only in the case of this person, make sure your aim is off for the first few shots.

Envy

One good thing about a zombie apocalypse is that you no longer have to keep up with the Joneses. You're left pretty much to your own devices in regards to what you have, how much, and how you store it. Creativity here is far more useful than just wanting what you can't have and doing nothing about it. You're going to have to get inventive in order to actually have everything you want and need. By all means, want stuff, desire stuff, but don't sit idle and let that go unfulfilled. Chances are if you don't know how something is made, someone else will, and if they don't you can find out with the right books. A plethora of information is available to you, and damned if you should have your hands on it already, just to be prepared. If you seem to lack a text which provides this information, you have the chance now to get it. Don't let the fact that someone else may have their hands on something you want drive you to find them, beat them, and take it by force when you're able to make it yourself. Your survival is in your own hands. With sufficient motivation, there's nothing a person can't achieve on their own without having to resort to thievery. Appropriating the materials needed may take time, but hey, even little goals are good to have. Satisfy that wanting, especially if it's useful to everyone around you.

Where envy is applied to other things, like maybe affection, it's probably for the best to engage in conversation about it rather than implementing complicated machinations to fuck someone over to get what you want. This could only end badly for everyone involved and result in group expulsion or murder. Neither is a good thing to be on the receiving end of.

Pride

We should all endeavor to have a bit of pride. It can be a good thing. Pride in who you are, how you act toward others, in what you accomplish, maybe even in your appearance. These aren't really things one should frown upon because they really don't hurt anyone. In survival though, pride becomes a distant second to necessity. Showers are going to be scarce, good will stretched thin, and patience with bullshit at a minimum. Of course, this is dependent on the individual. Sacrificing a bit of pride in the name of continued sustaining of life functions is going to eventually become a need. If you're forced between sticking to your vegan principles or eating canned meat, you had better suck it up, rabbit-boy, you're on a snow covered mountain, and you won't be finding berries in January.

Compromising is going to be a mainstay of your existence. Navigating outside of your comfort zone will be a daily requirement. Manning up to act in an abnormal way in order to keep the peace, or make some other gain for the group, these are worthy reasons to put your pride on hold. The fact of the matter is that we're all going to have to do unsavory and mildly (some less mild than others) insane things to make it out of a zombie apocalypse alive. Get used to the fact now and accept it. It will make things easier later on.

Wrath

Pure, unadulterated, focused wrath! What could be better? While you may want to save this one exclusively for dealing with the undead, it's the perfect human condition when person-on-zombie contact is initiated. Your world has been reduced to cinders, your loved ones killed or infected, and your pet goldfish Pierre has been without food for months, inevitably leading to his untimely demise. Why the hell not center that into a narrow hateful laser-like focus when you meet the undead? Use your hate and strike them down, only then will your destiny be fulfilled! Probably not that easy or anything, but you can certainly use that anger to keep you motivated to survive and kill more undead each day. Just be sure to keep it under control when you're not engaged in combat. Going off on your little tribe may just result in your being tagged as "unstable" and put down at a very inopportune time. Being an unrelenting slayer of the walking dead is one thing, but being the psychotic guy 24/7 that everyone is afraid of will end in estrangement and isolation. This won't be fun, so don't be an utter psychopath, just be really goddamn useful in a fight.

Plain Stupid People

"The most likely threat to come during the apocalypse will be the idiots that actually want zombies to rule. They'll likely spend their time tripping those of us who want to survive. So if someone sticks out a foot, shoot it off. Then stick said foot someplace uncomfortable. No, not like the back of a Volkswagen..."
– Fred Nugent

At some point, maybe before things get bad, perhaps after the majority of the crisis has passed, someone's going to speak out on behalf of the undead. Their stance is going to be that the undead, as former living people, still have rights and feelings. This is complete nonsensical bullshit. These zombie-huggers are going to be a danger to themselves as well as everyone else, and, sure enough, at some point, they will be the cause of another small outbreak. That is, unless you kill them. This is the correct course of action when you're dealing with these post-apocalyptic hippies. No debating, do not argue, and flat out refuse to voice your concerns. Recognize the act for what it is—a pre-emptive strike. You're ridding the world of new stupidity. Somehow these assholes made it through (assuming this is after the zombie apocalypse has run its course) the worse tragedy of human history, and managed to get all sentimental and stupid in a real hurry. This needs to be nipped in the bud, and quickly. If you come across these fools, don't hesitate to drop these neo-flower-children right where they stand. Don't forget their pet zombie while you're at it.

Leadership

"The biggest problem I see at this moment is avoiding stupid people who THINK they know how to survive. There's a lot of these people claiming to know better than everyone. I suggest when you identify this kind of person, you should probably find a creative way to dispatch them quickly."

– from the (REDACTED) Customer Service Training Manual

In the emotional time of an apocalypse, it's important to consider other's feelings and thoughts before enforcing your own upon them. You don't want to be the asshole in the group, but at the same time you don't want to be a push over. A good leader should endeavor to find the middle ground which gets a little of both across. One suggestion would be pointing out stupidity by prefacing the statement with "with all due respect." For example, "With all due respect, Johnny Two-Balls, your ideas are stupid, and you kinda smell." or "With all due respect, Aunt Flappy-Tits, no one wants to see you naked, nor do we wish to repopulate the earth with you." Using these prefacing phrases or even "No offense but..." will help you avoid those tense moments during survival. On the other hand, if someone walks up to you and says any of these, remember not to violently lash out and be angry. A bit of calm conversation can prevent an excess of violence later. If they don't take the hint after the first few conversations, one could resort to a quick blow to the knee while the horde is closing down on you all. That will ALWAYS solve the problem, and it distracts the undead long enough for a clean escape.

In all seriousness though, leadership is necessary in a party. The inability to follow one scheme through to its end, having been devised and meticulously laid out, is going to result in death for the group. To lead a group of people with wills strong enough to survive in these times will take a collected, charismatic, and rational individual who is able to be a parent, sibling, and psychiatrist to those they govern. Being unable to provide these things when they're needed will result in lack of trust in both the person and their ability to spearhead the group through these troubled times. One should be able to lift morale, or at least charge someone capable with the task of doing so. A leader doesn't have to do everything themselves; in fact, many times a leader is simply one who recognizes the abilities of those around him and can set the appropriate tasks before them in order to get the job done.

Another thing to consider is that not only will folks be looking up to you when things go well, but when things go badly you're the one who shoulders the blame. Whether it was your fault for whatever failure has transpired or not, this is the instance where shit rolls up hill. It could be that the rain hasn't been consistent enough to supply drinking water, the rabbits ate your vegetables, or that two people left a week ago and haven't made it back yet. Some people are irrational, and big or small, the blame will fall squarely on your shoulders should you find yourself to be the leader. That's just something to prepare for.

Right about now you may be wondering if you're able to handle being the leader of your group of survivors. Well, since you've chosen to read this at all, that's a damn good start. There are a lot of subtleties to being a good leader and it won't be easy, but if you're unwilling to trust your life to the whims of another, you'd better be ready to step up to the plate and take control early. Keep your head clear, be decisive, and take care of your people. Managing to do that means your group will take care of you in return. If you don't, well, you could wind up being the one with a bum knee and zombies chewing on your flesh.

Whiners

We would like to take a moment out of your busy day to talk about a problem all groups are likely to face: the whiner. That's right, the person who is never happy with anything that happens. The person who expects more credit than they get, and the person who throws a fit when they think they're slighted. These can also be known as "Crybaby Bitches."

These types of people can be a large drag on any group. They tend to make morale low, and limit the chances for survival for everyone with their incessant droning. Whether it's by whining that they didn't get a chance to pick the direction, or that they were overlooked for some important position in the group, these people can ruin your group and lead you into a sure case of becoming zombie chow.

So how can we fix these problems? Well, as with most problems in the apocalypse, they can be turned into a useful tool. One option is to send them out on a "scouting" mission into what you know to be a heavily populated area. Another worthwhile plan is to make sure they're always next to you when doing battle; that way, if you have to turn and run, you can quickly put a bullet in their knee so they will slow down the advancing hordes. A well-timed trip can be the answer to many post-apocalyptic personnel issues.

A good question may be put forth as to what makes a normal person into a little crying bitch. Well, possibly they were hugged too much, or not enough. Late night visits from sneaky Uncle Slippyfist could be the culprit. Maybe they were forced to give a bra-less Aunt Flappy-Tits a few too many holiday hugs. Whatever the reason, you didn't cause it, but now you're stuck with this jack-wagon. This is a situation which simply must be dealt with. Now maybe killing someone who's poisonous to the group dynamic isn't always the way to go. Maybe it's your personal belief or there's some other reason you happen to think this way, but whatever the thought process behind it, it will be up to you to talk to them and get them to change their ways.

Battle Duress

Sometimes when in a group, during tense situations, one person will begin to panic and scream. Now, this can pose several problems for your group. Most notably drawing attention to you in a way you don't want attention drawn. We suggest this course of action when dealing with said hysterical person. First of all, using your calmest voice possible, explain to the panicked person they are causing a scene, drawing attention to the group and annoying several heavily armed people who are already a bit on edge. This will generally calm them down a bit. Of course veiled threats of death tend to do that.

However, if the first method doesn't work move right on to method two. Here you take your hand, lick the back of it whereupon you quickly and sharply bring it across their cheek in a reverse swinging whoopin' motion. The backhand or "pimp-slap" has often been used to knock some sense into an irrational person, plus it's very therapeutic for the person giving out the slap. Should keepin' your pimp hand strong escalate the situation into all out panic, it's then suggested that you move on to the third bit of advice.

Subdue, immobilize, and restrain. Some duct tape and a ball gag will be needed for this step. If you don't have a ball gag handy, or haven't ever ventured into that side of the fetish world, you can grab a tennis or racket ball and some surgical tubing. It works just as well; don't ask, and just trust us on that. Stuff the ball in the mouth and secure it with the tubing. Duct tape the hands and feet of the panicked person so they are resting in the fetal position. Once you've done this, try again to use your very calmest voice to explain they are doing silly things that can lead to the death of everyone.

If this fails to calm the person down, move on to the final stage of the calming plan. You open a door and push the already duct taped and ball gagged person into the street and move the rest of your group to a safer location. With any luck, this will provide time to escape, and eliminate the panicked screamer in the most extreme way. This final course of action is definitely frowned upon by the Geneva Convention types, but who cares? They're all dead anyway.

With a little bit of observational skill you should be able to recognize these people before they become a liability in the field. Time will help you in identifying the telltale signs prior to their becoming a real threat. You can easily utilize these people in other manners though if you see fit. Make them the "camp bitch" and leave them at the base to look after things if at all possible. Dealing with the stress of combat may not be for everyone, but nearly anyone can help you survive if they're given proper direction.

Children and the Apocalypse

So, you've got a load of ankle biters around, and you're worried that you'll be unable to keep them safe while keeping yourself protected. There are a few things which you can do to in order to assist in keeping those little noise makers unharmed. You'll need to start with a large older home. Many older homes have an interior room away from windows, and it can be sealed off rather easily, this is where most of the earliest sex parties were held because it wouldn't do to have an uninvited neighbor seeing what you're up to (Yeah, your grandmother used to host orgies, deal with it). You should start now by buying soundboard and acoustical tiles. Luckily now you can paint this stuff any color you want, so it won't LOOK like what it is: a padded room for children. Make sure when outfitting the room you take the same care to buy heavy soundproof doors as well. All the work would be wasted if you forgot the doors.

Now we will never condone locking yourself down for survival, but when you have small children it's really your only hope. Not many kids are going to have the discipline to navigate safely and quietly through a zombie-strewn landscape. Once you've built the room, stock it with toys, games, coloring books and other good stuff. Make it their "playroom" pre-apocalypse so they'll enjoy it during. Now this little safe room will serve two purposes, first of all it's going to keep your precious children safe during the apocalypse, and second, it's going to give you a break from noise while you're preparing. Once you've built it, you can lock the little darlings inside and never hear a sound. Just make sure you never leave sharp objects inside there. It would be bad.

Human Contact

It's a basic human need. Despite the strong outer appearance of some people, they are going to need someone in their lives eventually. Be it someone to be intimate with, or just someone to talk to, or in some cases, such as my grandparents, just someone to yell at every once in a while. You're going to need someone. You can say you will survive on your own, but eventually you're going to go insane. Now there are ways to combat this as seen in several movies, you could adopt an animal, or maybe paint a face on a sporting good, or you could even paint a face on your hand. All of these will provide short-term relief from the madness, as well as provide post-self-gratification nagging.

Sadly, it won't be the perfect way to survive. Eventually you're going to need someone to actually talk to. One-sided conversations tend to degenerate into psychosis, which can then lead to a general lack of concern for your own safety. This in turn leads to a case of teeth rape. Of course, you will need to choose your partners with care. You'll have to share some kind of passion with the people. Find people with common interests and likes now, so you can keep them later. It'll save heartache, insanity, and a heap of trouble in the end.

Tense Situations

They're bound to happen; eventually the excitement of fighting for your lives will turn to stress. When the pressure starts it will inevitably get between two members of any party. While some tension, like sexual tension, is good in books, movies, and TV shows, it's not that great in a real life situation. Tension born of anger is just not good for any group, and you're going to have to diffuse the situation some how. You could try humor as it's always a good way to move beyond sticky situations. A little laugh, a little fun. You could try the ever popular "hippie approach" by saying things like, "I understand your problem," or "that's interesting, what else is bothering you?" You will either slow the anger down or get shot, and either way the tension is relieved for the moment. Of course you could just harden the fuck up, and deal with your petty issues when there's not a horde of undead monsters trying to eat your pink fleshy parts.

Mercy Killings

Sometimes a party member is so injured or sick or stupid, letting them live is actually more of a punishment than killing them would be. That's when you reach into the bag of Kevorkian tricks and come up with an overdue abortion method. Now before you go becoming the morality police, and start spouting bible verses and what not, remember this is during a time of apocalypse. Sometimes it's just not wise to let someone who has a serious injury, illness or stupid go through the pain of living. There are times when it's possible to be quick and end their suffering. Quick bullet to the brain, maybe puncture a femoral artery so they bleed out fast. Of course in some cases you may just want to strap them with explosives and leave them behind for the horde to get to in their own time. Depends on the person and the situation really. Now when making the delicate decision on how to dispatch the party member in question you should use these criteria.

1. Were they at one time an elite fighter?

2. Did they contribute to the group's overall well being?

3. Should they have been a blowjob and not a person?

If one and two are yes, a discrete and quick death is in order. If three is a yes, then take your time and come up with interesting ways to dispose of the body. Might we suggest a c-4 enema and duct tape? I mean it's not exactly humane, but just the thought of it does give you warm feelings right? The most explosive case of gas ever!

Using Children For Stress Reduction

So, you're stressed out and you really want to punch a midget in the head, but you've used your last one as a club. Remember when we said that saving the kids when possible was a good idea? Well, there's a fount of renewable resources that can be used as replacements. Yes, we're talking about children. Oh, we can hear you groaning right now. Remember, we had long range mics placed in the pages of the book. We like to know what people think. Let's not dwell on that.

Where were we? Oh yeah, children as a stress relief tool. OK, so your group has been around for quite some time and undoubtedly two members have procreated at some point, and as a result, there are a few ankle biters running around, and you're all stressed out. Now, it's not the best way to relieve stress, but you can punch the children in the face. If you condition them right, they'll even return for extra punishment. That's right, if you withhold love and praise, they'll be starved for any attention; even violence. Don't believe me? Find a drunk who has kids. I bet you money his kids will allow him to beat them, and come back for more just because daddy's finally paying attention to them. You get worked up, you simply yell out, "HEY! KID! COME HERE!" and when they walk up, you punch them in the face, and they fall over. They get up all bloodied, and you say, "Come here so I can hit you again." If you've trained them right, they'll come running.

Now your humble authors don't suggest using your own children for this, they will eventually develop resentment and anger. If they're your kids they'll know where you sleep, how hard, and where your guns are. That will definitely turn into a case of the deads for you, but if they're not yours then that resentment will be aimed at their parents first. This means when the crying, screaming, and murdering starts you'll get a heads up and be able to safely escape. We know it's not a perfect plan, but we can hear you laughing, so that's good enough.

Weaselly Bastards

Do you know someone like this? He's lying, deceitful, paranoid, and totally willing to stab you in the back at the drop of a hat. While he happens to be a fictional character, sadly enough, people like him do exist, and many will survive. Anyone willing to push kids out of the way at the threat of a fire is going to find some way to make it... out of the initial press of undead. Pulling down or tripping the able-bodied is no problem for this guy if he gets the chance, and believe me, he'll be right on top of that shit. This screaming little missile of hate has no conscience at all where it pertains to his own survival; you're just an obstacle. He gives not one hot shit whether you live or die.

So how do you respond when you find such an upstanding member of former-humanity? The only way to appropriately respond is in kind. Once you're able to spot these soulless suckers of demon cock, you should move to strike them from the face of the planet immediately. They have no redeeming qualities, and really once they cross that line, they're not even people at that point. If you're unwilling to help do anything aside from further your own agenda, then you're of no use at all to anyone else when it comes to the long haul. Allowing someone like this to live, it's very likely that you'll wake up one morning to find your gear, your wallet (WHY???), your shoes, weapons, hair piece, pet rock, favorite comb, and your food are all gone. Take care, spot them early on, and rip their faces off through their assholes. You'll feel better about it immediately.

PS: Women can fall under this category as well.

Preparing, Executing, and Implementing

"You should start looking at everything as a future life saving item. Rate buildings on how well they'd provide shelter during the apocalypse. Rate items around the house based on how well you could use them as a weapon. Judge friends on how long they'd survive. Scale of 1 to 10. 1 being this fucker's getting tripped, and 10 being one of the ZAP guys."

– Graffiti on the freeway

Forewarned is forearmed, and this is your warning. Now it's time to get armed. Not only will you need weaponry and other supplies, that's only half of it, but also you're going to need to have a location in mind. Scout this place, research it, gather printed information, and laminate it for safety purposes. Camp or otherwise vacation here for an extended period. If possible, purchase land or a cabin or even a home and begin preparing immediately. This won't always be possible or even realistic, and it will be difficult, but nothing worth doing is ever easy. Rest assured, telling anyone outside your survival group what it is that you're doing will result in more than a few odd looks. Let them look silly when the undead rise and they make fudge in their pants, while you calmly collect your gear and friends then head to your sanctuary. You can certainly feel free to invite these poor souls who once mocked your belief in the extraordinary, but think of the strain that would put on the previously collected supplies. These things must be considered because it's not just you that is relying on this gear; it's your other group members as well. Having extra goodies may not be a bad plan, whether you pick up stragglers or not, and should probably be incorporated into your planning.

Everyone in the group should know what's happening before it gets really bad. If you start seeing news reports of unexplained deaths and quarantines, that should be the signal. Call in sick to work, say your cat died, punch a midget, whatever you have to do, but get the hell out of dodge before roadblocks go up or people start to freak out. This goes for everyone, and it's vitally important that you do so. Your only other option is to wait for things to calm down enough for you to get out of town; however, there's one major problem with that plan and that is traffic. Many people will have tried the same, been blocked by stalled or wrecked cars, gotten out, and subsequently have been devoured by the undead, leaving you quite stuck in dead traffic. When you've got a few hundred pounds of gear in the car, this poses something of a conundrum. You don't want to leave it, and you can't really carry it without compromising your safety. Well if you have a safe place established prior to this all happening, then the majority of your gear should be where it needs to be already, and your bug out bag is all you should have to carry from the home. You should certainly be armed, and in this case, strap on the bag, get to cover, and start making your way out of town. Once done, find a vehicle with keys inside which is uninhabited by a zombie, and make the rest of the way like that.

Start preparing a list of what you can cook with long-lasting ingredients. There is an abundance of websites and books which detail many of the foods prepared in days gone by, as well as how to go about making them. You're going to need plenty of calories on a daily basis in order to remain strong. The diversity of foods will depend on vitamin needs and so on, but you can always have books available to tell you where you can find what in your local ecosystem, right? Dried meats and breads will be staples that can be made with relative ease and carried with you on journeys out into the world. Learning to make these will be helpful and essential to say the least. Of course, making a fresh meal is always going to be something we look forward to, and that may take some getting used to as well. We've become a bit spoiled with non-stick cookware and fully stocked kitchens to work with, so going about life in a minimalist capacity will perpetuate a need to adjust. Don't get frustrated here, just keep trying. It'll take time to get it right, and if anyone bitches about your cooking, make them do it. Old railroad days rules. Don't fuck with the cook or you become the cook.

Plans aren't only for before the dead rise up to devour us, but during as well. Who is doing what and when will be quite critical for determining sleep rotation, watches, and a sense of order in these chaotic times. The chore list and so on will likely be determined primarily by location and vary greatly, but there are certain things that must be done daily. Keeping weapons cleaned, blades sharp, cooking, and cleaning all must be part of a daily regimen, and these should be shared duties. Everyone doing a little of everything contributes to the sense of community and shouldn't be overlooked. Obviously specialization will occur to a degree among any group, but do your best to learn what you can and pass it along. Knowledge is power after all, and one can never know too much. Nothing is trivial when the world goes to hell, even if what you know is simply entertaining rather than useful. It all has its place in the greater scheme of things somehow. Stay alive long enough and you'll find that out.

What You Are Up Against

"Another threat facing those of us who survive: clowns. They'll likely die in full makeup and funny clothes, which means you'll be chuckling when you have to kill them. I mean, I know you all have secretly dreamed of bashing a clown's skull in."
– Circus Makeup Artist

Zombies are the things you have to worry about the most in an undead world. Sure, you have the random ass clowns who may try and wreck your fun and relative happiness in your little corner of the earth, but those are going to be few and far between... hopefully. The undead, though, are fairly simple and straightforward in their pursuit of the living. Obstacles may not stop their progress, but they'll certainly cause delays. One thing that zombies do have in common with the living is that for as many shapes and sizes that we come in, the ghouls are also going to come in this variety, too. That means having to keep an eye out for threats below your normal eye level. It could also mean having to get inventive in a few other ways. What do we mean by that? Well, let's explore a few of the things you may encounter, and hope that a bit of awareness will save you from an untimely case of death.

Draggers

Pretty much as the name suggests, these zombies tend to drag themselves along through the world and seek prey. Why do they drag themselves, you ask? Quite simply, something which was probably funny occurred and this now prohibits the use of their legs. A bullet or blow to the spinal column would sever the nerves from the brain to the legs and cause paralysis in the undead just as it would for the living. While this may not seem like much of a threat on the surface, they're a situational danger. For instance, you go out to drop the kids off at the pool behind a bush or a tree, while doing so, you're going to scan at a normal level for any significant threat. You see nothing and you feel safe, and you squat so you can take the Browns to the Superbowl. Next thing you know, you have a bite mark on your ass cheek from a shit-covered legless zombie. Absolute nonsense way to die, but it will happen to those who are unwary of their surroundings. Don't get butt hurt over not looking at where you're going to drop your deuce. You'd be the silliest looking zombie ever, walking around with your pants around your ankles and trying to eat someone's fleshy goodness.

Midget Zombies

"I've been thinking about the threat of 'little people' zombies. I mean you really wouldn't see them coming. You gotta be extra careful around them little suckers, as they might bite your ankle or toe, then you'd be screwed."

– Yoko Ohnooooooo (street performer)

What's forty-five inches tall and trying to chew on you? These guys right here. Yes folks, little people can be zombies, too. Not only are they shorter, but just as dexterous as the regular sized undead. Though that's not very nimble, the threat comes when you think the menace has passed, and then you spot a couple of these little horrors shambling in your direction. Smaller targets are naturally harder to hit, so don't panic. Take a deep breath and blow their heads off like you would any other flesh-craving automaton. One thing you'll be tempted to do is reenact scene from *The Wizard of Oz* or *Time Bandits* with these little guys. So maybe we've thought about it, too. It's not a BAD idea; it's just very dangerous. Knowing these guys are out there, do yourself a favor and remember to shift the aim a little lower than normal once in a while. Doing so will enable you to spot these little bitey bastards, and you'll prevent a terminal case of crotchbite.

Child Zombies

"Another wily group you'll need to be aware of: the girl scouts. Yes, once the infection starts they will fall, since they're not quite as prepared as the boy scouts. However, they will be able to lure you in, because when they die they will likely have cookies with them. Everyone's a sucker for cookies. Be careful."
– Local PTA President

Yeah, as crappy as it sounds, kids can be zombies, too. Even babies, though if they have no teeth, all you have to worry about are those little razors they have for fingernails. It's an insidious truth that we'll have to face, but these guys have to go, too. It may be a bit harder, at first anyway, than shooting an adult that has been transformed by this virus into a flesh-biting monster, but it's going to be a simple case of you or them. Life isn't always pretty in the middle of a zombie apocalypse. Do what you must to survive. Remember that once they've changed into what they are, they're no longer just carefree little children; they're just a shorter zed wanting to forcefully recruit you into their mindless legions. Also, they'll sell you cookies.

Armored Zombies

This is where you may be thinking to yourself "Ah, shit," and though it may not be exactly what you're thinking, yes, it's bad. The men and women of our military and various law enforcement agencies will inevitably fall as well, and, in doing so, they will very likely still be clothed in their body armor. Bulletproof vests and bullet resistant helmets will make your job of stopping these terrors that much more difficult. On the plus side, this will make them a bit slower and easier to hit. There's usually not armor on the legs, so if at all possible, disable these and move on to more easily dispatched zombies, and then finish these off in any way you see fit.

Another aspect of this particular type of undead that is worthy of discussion is the sense of despair one may feel upon seeing them initially. Witnessing for yourself that the forces empowered with protecting us as a people were able to fall before the collective might of the un-living could certainly fill one with a feeling of utter horror. Well, don't let that be the case; some may have fallen, but many more made it out alive and regrouped in order to stand against this menace. Just like the rest of us, they're people too, and some will have made mistakes that caused a sudden cessation of life functions that resulted in reanimation, but it wasn't all of them, or else you'd be seeing a lot more of these geared up ghouls. These will thankfully be a rare occurrence. Having to deal with these too often would get to be a giant pain in the ass.

Things Not to Do

The following is a list of simple things not to do. Ever. They're silly, a little insane, and very stupid. We've been trying to prepare you for this. In fact, this is a little bit like a quiz. You have to guess what we're going to write before you read it. Failure to do so will probably mean you're going to die horribly. Or it means you're not psychic and didn't read our minds months ahead of time while we wrote this book. That's good though, because you'd be a thought-stealing evil person, and you're certainly not that, are you? Well... are you? Starting from here, precede everything on the list with "do not," "don't," or "never" and that way it all makes a lot more sense.

- Panic
- Underestimate your opposition
- Overestimate your ability
- Eat the boogers out of a dead man's nose
- Reason with the undead
- Allow yourself to be trapped
- Rub your eyes, change your contacts, or pick your nose after cutting jalapenos
- Trust produce grown in New Jersey
- Bet on the Lions
- Ending Story
- Run out of ammo
- Kick puppies
- Shout like a moron
- Go in against a Sicilian when death is on the line
- Walk from place to place whistling like a moron
- Be a moron
- Forget the importance of occasional nonsense
- Associate with morons
- Look a gift horse in the mouth
- Look a gift horse in the ass
- Close the doors if you're in the back seat of a cop car

- Chug syrup
- Choose "Armageddon" as a safety word
- Let your weapons get dirty
- Use weapons with spikes
- Allow mimes to live
- Fuck with the Jesus (Quintana)
- Swim when loaded with gear
- Drink under water
- Admit there was a sequel to *The Blues Brothers*
- Walk across thin ice
- Forget the dangers of Salsa Shark
- Rent videos from your own store. Go to a GOOD video store
- Forget your scarf
- Wear sandals when you're out killing zombies

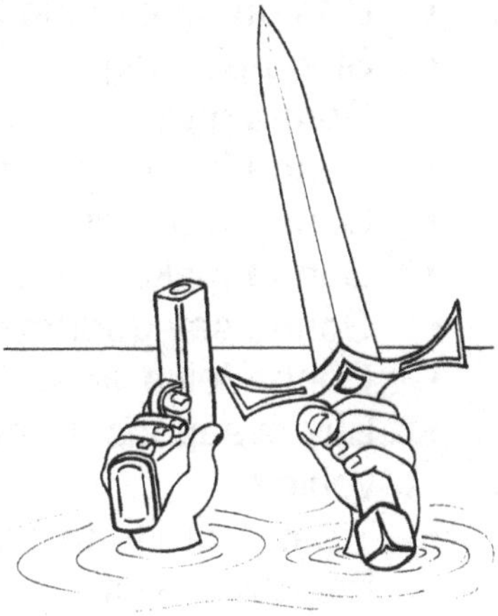

- Shit where you eat
- Use heavy machine guns
- Skip to the end of a book looking for comedy or answers to life's mysteries
- Sneeze when you're hiding from the undead
- Wipe yourself improperly
- Consider anything edible if the label ends in a question mark
- Enter cities full of the undead
- Forget to knock
- Eat fast food on New Year's Eve (NP got sick)
- Try to hug a zombie
- Forget where your towel is
- Fart while trying to maintain stealth
- Leave a campfire unattended
- Mistake a moon for a space station
- Assume
- Go ass to mouth

- Fuck with another man's French fries
- Attempt to have sexy time with the undead
- Pimp slap the undead
- Taunt Happy Fun Ball
- Piss into the wind
- Piss up a flag pole
- Piss on an electric fence
- Stop believing
- Gonna give you up
- Gonna let you down
- Gonna run around and desert you
- Gonna make you cry
- Gonna say goodbye
- Gonna tell a lie and hurt you
- Buy weapons from a dealer who operates out of a vehicle
- Trust your life to anything that has the words "Made in Pakistan" on it
- Drive drunk
- Drive angry
- Drive with your turn signal on
- Drive really slow in the ultra fast lane
- Drive sober
- Drive on the railroad tracks
- Go away mad
- Say "I'll be right back."
- Try to train a zombie
- Empty a chemical toilet into a storm sewer
- Wear white after Labor Day
- Call someone a Jive Turkey
- Run with scissors
- Look directly at the sun
- Play hockey on the roof and only bring one ball

- Bark at the moon
- Mix liquor and wine
- Ask your wife if she's hiding Jell-O in her pants
- Trust a six-fingered man who wants you to make him a sword
- Believe that Greedo shot first
- Taunt a woman with chocolate
- Trust your life to a smart car
- Set a fire you can't control
- Set a zombie on fire while it can walk
- Wade into a horde of undead with a chainsaw
- Dance with the Devil in the pale moonlight
- Mess with another man's rhubarb
- Believe vampires sparkle
- Listen to kids sing pop music of your own free will
- Doubt the power of a good psych-out
- Try to psych-out a zombie
- Trust your special cousin not to take a Christmas rant about your boss as the perfect gift to get you

- Forget to check the family tree for squirrels
- Fear shooting your eye out
- Forget number of alcoholic shots you can safely consume
- Misjudge amount of weed you can safely smoke
- Hide your stash while stoned
- Use live ammo when playing a game of Bulletproof Cup

- Trust a random stranger who says they have a plan to keep you safe
- Piss on the Dude's rug

Tactical Awareness: *The Best Defense is a Good... Defense?*

Sitting back and allowing the threat to stay away is nothing to be ashamed of. In fact, doing so puts you in a position of power that the more aggressive people will lack. Safely staying away from conflict, avoiding the undead when you're able, and not taking unnecessary risks allows you to conserve both energy and resources. Those bullets are a finite and valuable resource, which must be guarded, because it's very unlikely that you have more of those than there are undead within a 100-mile radius. Conservation will be a necessity for having these things available when they're truly needed most. This being the case, there are a few things you can do to add to your ongoing obscurity.

Try not to have bonfires. Even in the middle of jack shit nothing, that fire could be spotted by some undesirable and used to pinpoint your location. True, zombies may be stupid (so are a lot of people for that matter) but when it comes to something that significantly stands out, they will investigate. That's what they do, it's their bag; that's how they roll. Keeping a low profile is a simple necessity, especially at night; fires can be seen for miles.

When scouting your area, either for defensive purposes or recon for a supply run, make sure you step lightly and keep a close eye on everything around you. You don't want to be sighted first for obvious reasons. Nature can help you accomplish your stealthy mission, especially in the more rural areas of the world. Birds chirp, crickets make their noise, and so on, and if you hear none of this, that means either they're spooked by you or avoiding something else. Assume it's something else and start to look around. If you find yourself alone, continue on, but keep those ears scanning for anything approaching. Move slowly and utilize cover when you're able; this should aid in your endeavor to remain unmolested.

If you find yourself out looking for more gear and you're in a house or store and you do see zombies nearby, follow the same rules you would if you were making a stand in the home. Stay to the interior to muffle any sounds, make sure lights are dimmed or doused completely, and do not engage the undead unless you're positive that it's safe to do so and the odds are in your favor. Don't make the mistake of assumption here, especially when you're out and away from the rest of the group (which you shouldn't be to begin with). You also don't want to make a break for it and find out an hour later that they've pursued you to your camp; this will not make the other survivors happy, and popularity is always important.

Utilize the technological advantages you have at your disposal as a member of the race with the highest intelligence on the planet (assuming, of course, that those books were wrong and we're not third after mice and dolphins respectively) and scout with telescopes, binoculars, and riflescopes before deeming an area safe to approach. Set yourself in a tree or something with a good vantage point and scan—simple as that. Spend time watching, and see what you can from where you are before rushing right in and having some sort of ill-timed adventure that could easily result in someone's demise. One good thing about a zombie apocalypse is that you're no longer on a clock. When it comes to safety, patience is a virtue.

Defending your encampment from encroachment is something else that can certainly be of benefit to the group. Now we're not suggesting planting a mine field out in the yard leading up to the hideout or anything drastic, though if you have the option and everyone's fine with that plan, knock yourself out. However, just think about having to hurry through it in the dark. That's always fun. With mines though, zombies, being stupid, don't require you to bury these explosives, so you're able to leave them in plain sight. Think about simple early warning ideas. Trip wires tied to cans full of rocks, a couple of dogs, a spotter on the roof, or whatever you have available; these can be fine ways to rob the undead of the element of surprise. Of course, a mine blowing up would be a very loud indicator as well. It could also let undesirable elements know where you are.

Having incapacitating defensive measures in place is also a good idea. A simple log rolled down even a mild slope toward the ghouls as they approach may not dispatch them, but it can certainly take a few (probably a lot, but we're going with conservative estimates) zombies out of action, and then you just get to clean up. Shooting a target is a lot easier when it's immobile, and you can do it from five feet as opposed to 150 yards while it's moving. In these cases, a nice melee weapon is king. This not only saves on ammo, but also it's amusing to see the damage caused by large chunks of speeding lumber followed up with a sledgehammer. Defensive applications are where creativity can really be put to good use. Not only is it a spectacular way to spend your time by staying active, but it stimulates your mind, allowing for something of a distraction from the tedium of daily localized occupation. Think of the maniacal giggling which will occur while building traps for the undead. It's OK; it is very natural for plotting destruction to cause happiness when it's in the name of self-defense against lifeless monsters.

Rotating Watches

We all need to rest in order to function properly; sleeping is a basic human necessity. There's no real getting around it without a constant supply of detrimental chemicals, and even then you'll pass out eventually, and this would be bad. You need to be alert, focused, and aware at all times. This is a dangerous world we now find ourselves in, and from a simple moment of inattention, things can turn to shit in a real hurry. Luckily you were smart and decided that going with a group would be a wise choice (HINT-HINT, NUDGE-NUDGE), and you're able to have people on watch throughout the day and night so that everyone can get some shut-eye. Set it however everyone feels most comfortable. Three to eight hour shifts are general timeframes that can be used, and should be set so that everyone has equal time for work, rest, and relaxation. When on watch, you should be focused outward at all times. Eyes and ears trained on your surroundings and always ready for action. Otherwise, you may not see that zombie horde coming through the surrounding tree line, or the glint of sun off some marauder's rifle scope as he's checking out your digs. An eye for detail will be crucial in order to maintain the safety of yourself and those you've allied with. Getting your rest keeps you from nodding off at your post, and does the same for others. Except narcoleptics, but they may prove useful as bait at some point.

Contingency Plans

Just because you've decided that you want to be somewhere does not mean that it's impossible for someone or something to piss on your cereal, even though you don't want it to happen. Actually, when you're in a kill-or-be-killed world such as this, you may find that your flakes are moist right out of the box. That's just how things work sometimes. To this end, you're going to need a back up plan. Whether you've been overrun by the undead or just some group lead by Johnny Two-Balls, you simple must have your plots in place. At the very least, you must find a nearby area for gathering, set an appointed time frame, and have a scattering signal. Make sure the members of your group know all these, then it cannot be claimed that they did not know. Beyond the meeting spot, a secondary shelter should be located and secured. It may lack charm as well as any hint of sophistication, but it's a start. Starting over sucked the first time; this time won't be any different. At least this time, you have some added experience in doing so. You may be able to do a whole hell of a lot better than just having a meeting place and secondary location, and if so, go for it. However, a simple plan is better than no plan at all.

Books

With any bit of proper planning, you've remembered to bring books, manuals, porn, and basic instructional guides for furthering your understanding of essential daily needs. These will prove invaluable in the ability to grow food, fix things, make new items, and remain stimulated mentally. That is, of course, unless you lack the ability to read, in which case why do you have this book? That's just nonsense. For the duration, we'll assume you are literate and continue on. Now, you can utilize these wonderful collections of words to specialize in a specific area or broaden your general knowledge base. Either is a grand undertaking, and you're applauded for doing so. Being able to help out in all facets of survival will make you the super hero of the undead world. There's no real prize or anything, but you could possibly get away with wearing a cape. We strongly recommend that you try—the cape bit anyway, though the reading thing is good, too.

Making Happy-time

"So you're probably all sitting there thinking to yourself, "Self, when the apocalypse happens will I still have chances to enjoy life?" Ah yes, much like in the movie that shan't be named, we encourage you to learn to

embrace all the small things. Be it a good song, or your favorite processed cream filled treat. Embrace it and love it. Just don't make it your life's mission to find it."
– Blarney the Dinosaur

All work and no play makes Jack a dull boy. All work and no play makes

Jack a dull boy. All work and no play makes Jack a dull boy. All work and no play, makes Jack a dull boy. All work and no play, makes Jack a dull boy. All work and no play makes Jack a dull boy. All work and no play makes Jack a dull boy. All work and no play makes Jack a dull boy. All work and no play makes Jack a dull boy. All work and no play makes Jack a dull boy. All work and no play makes Jack a dull boy. All work and no play makes Jack a dull boy. All work and no play makes Jack a dull boy.

See? That's what happens when you don't get a break in the mental tedium that is involved in the constant defense of your refuge; whole chunks of nutcaseness. While vigilance is a constant requirement, and the need for sleep is essential, the benefit of recreational time is yet another necessity. Whether you choose to read, write a poem, get stoned, sing a song, hunt, juggle cats, clean weapons, or chew on tree bark, you need to relax once in a while. It won't be simple in this world, and our former dependence on outside stimuli may compound that difficulty. We're going to be going from a world full of Pac-Man, Hula Hoops, and record players, back into a darker time. No longer will you be able to just press a button to cast aside the outside world.

Your entertainment is going to be up to you and those around you. Take up an instrument, bring board games, learn to sing, or maybe try your hand at sock puppets. Whatever it is, the more of it you can share with others, the better it is to do. Maybe your friends will help, maybe they'll just poke fun, but if they're entertained at the same time, so much the better. Don't let your former inhibitions enter into play here, as there's no longer time for them. If you wanted to be a stand-up comedian, why not give it a shot? True, your audience consists of your fellow survivors, but who else deserves to be entertained? Always wanted to write your life story? Tell me this wouldn't be awesome material, plus the critics are all dead. How much better could your timing be? As long as you keep your mind busy in some way, shape, or form, you're going to be in good shape. Get the others involved, help where you can with their ideas, then it's a simple matter of relaxing and enjoying what you have.

Find Your Own Beauty

Whether you can paint or not, have a green thumb, or you're handy with a pencil, make something nice that can be shared. There's a distinct psychological advantage imparted to those who have that, which can represent a symbol of beauty worth fighting for. It doesn't have to be anything that's overly extravagant or took a year to do, but something that comforts your group and serves as a spiritual rallying point. It's likely that this will be something as simple as a rose bush, or maybe a "liberated" painting found in a nice house you passed on the way, but whatever it is, preserve it. Use it to your advantage. There's not going to be an excess of things that inspire us in this world, and it becomes an effort to find them. Then again you could just maintain a violence-based love for destroying the undead in all their forms and use that. To each their own; it's just an idea.

Become Self-Sufficient

You've gone as green as green can be, maybe not willingly, but what's done is done. The supplies you've brought, however, are finite, and must be supplemented. How do you go about doing this? Raise, plant, and grow your own food supplies. This takes the right environment, or perhaps a greenhouse, or a combination of the two. Either way, you need your vitamins and minerals in order to remain healthy, and those 7,000 cans of potted meat aren't going to fit the bill. You can go about growing and harvesting your own crops in a number of ways, and all of them are situational, but it will become an essential part of your diet. Depending on location, a grow room may need to be built for year-round edibles. Once again, this is dependant on where you are and how you choose to go about doing your whole survival thing.

A barn or something similar will be required for critters. You can raise cats and eat them if that's what you want to do, but you may prefer more traditional sources of food, and if so, research, grazing land, and space will be required. Animal husbandry has been accomplished throughout human history for thousands of years, and there's no reason you can't pull it off, too. Keep in mind that the average cow consumes 1.4 to 4.0 percent of their body weight in food on a daily basis. Water consumption is between six and fifteen gallons each day, and even more if they're nursing. A nearby stream, pond, or other body of water will be needed for successful keeping of these kinds of animals. Is that steak worth it? You're damn right it is. Let them graze, give birth, nurse that little meat-slab, and then shoot the damn thing and eat it. The spoils of war are very tasty when cooked over an open flame.

Stragglers

"Remember, there are two types of people who will approach your group: the stabby stealy kind, and the helpful addition type. Avoid the first if possible, but the second can be handy. Every once in a while, there's the total nympho-slut kind who just wants to have sex with everyone regardless of sexual preference. They can be nearly as bad as stabby stealy, but as fun as helpful addition."

– Scribbled on a Denny's Menu

Suppose, for a moment, that you've set up your happy little home in the middle of nowhere. You have plenty of food, water, shelter, and all that good stuff. Now a couple new guys show up and they want to be let in. You're faced here with what we call a moral dilemma. Several questions must be answered here before making any kind of decision. First off, will it stretch your current supplies to a breaking point? Probably not, if you're doing so well to begin with. Secondly, what valuable skills do they have to offer? Can they bring anything to the table, or are they simply vagabonds in need of a place to flop? Finally, are they willing to duel each other to the death to earn a spot in the group? Let's ignore the first two questions and focus instead on the third. That's right—bum fights. What could possibly be more entertaining than having your own modern day version of the gladiatorial arena? Give each of them a melee weapon and let them go at it. You only want the strongest and smartest fighters anyway, so why not let them prove their worth without having to sacrifice one who has already earned their spot in your band of survivors? Of course, you could go the boring-as-shit route and consider the first two questions asked earlier then decide based on those instead. Whatever you want to do is fine. Just always remember to be cautious of outsiders until they prove that they're no threat to you and yours. Sometimes new blood can be a good thing, but spilled blood is always more entertaining.

Microwave Your Cats for Fun and Profit

With a distinct lack of widely supplied power, this one may be difficult to do. It's unlikely that a microwave would be a worthwhile device to rev up the generator for, but if one were sufficiently motivated, it could be done. See, the majority of profit would stem from recording this and making the video a viral success, but once more, due to a lack of power, there's not even an Internet anymore. Plus, cats are kind of fun to have around. Especially if they're a little spastic. Putting your cat in the microwave is pretty much not cool. In fact, that's fucking hateful. I mean there are some amusing possibilities, but I don't know that they outweigh the negative aspects. So... you know what? Scrap this idea entirely.

Getting Intoxicated

"Rednecks and cowboys will indeed be a good asset. Anyone who can make moonshine, hunt dinner, and fix a 4x4 has uses. Also, they can help with their lean-to

shacks in the country. Nice place to hide out for a bit. Problem is, they tend to get all overly macho and run headfirst into danger with guns blazing. At this point, grab their hooch and run."

– AA's hidden 13th step

Alcoholic beverages and cannabis have both been around for just a bit longer than every single modern convenience that we presently enjoy. That's just a simple scientific fact. So, why should we be without these substances when zombies roam the earth? There's no reason for that to be the case. It's even possible that there will be more of a demand for a little blissful release once the apocalypse is in full swing, and why shouldn't there be? The primary concerns though become supply and demand. No longer will you be able to swing by the corner store for a six-pack of frosty goodness, or visit that shady dealer in a fast food place's parking lot for an ounce of red hair. These days are long gone. You can grow your own weed and brew your own beer, though, if you really want to. Numerous books are widely available on both topics, and should be included with the rest of your instructional manuals. You presently have the ability to pick up a guide on just about every topic imaginable, so why not do so? Preparation is the key, folks. You're not allowed to cry foul and say you weren't warned.

The only aspect here, which warrants any kind of warning at all, would be when to imbibe. You have to remain responsible, what with the defense of your lives being a priority. It's likely that limiting yourself to certain times and days would be a wise choice. Actually, that's a good idea anyway, but you'll do what you want to and nobody's going to stop you. If you do choose to partake with more frequency than is prudent, then surely whoever happens to come upon what remains of your camp will be pleased that you were kind enough to leave them your bag and/or brewery. Getting a little lean is all right, but try not to let it interfere with the welfare of yourself and your fellow survivors.

Reclaiming Our World

Eventually we're going to get really damn tired of the odd ghoul shuffling around, coming into our corners of the world, and at that point we're going to decide that enough is enough. It's been safe enough to scavenge and loot our areas in order to amass a decent number of weapons and an ungodly amount of ammunition, so you're thinking of going from amateur to pro on the zombie killing circuit. Well, you've had enough practice, cast indecisiveness aside, so let's take back what's ours. Don't just rush off and go on a kill-crazy rampage. Taking back the world will require a lot of thought, planning, and effort on the part of everyone involved, and, no, it can't be done alone.

Like any good idea, there has to be the right amount of manpower and resources to get it done. Taking your six-person group and trying to clear out Houston, Texas for example, will only result in a couple hundred corpses (unless you absolutely suck) and six new zombies (even if you don't). You have to think locally before you can think globally. Rash action has no place in the planning forum, and any machinations devised should be thoroughly detailed and within the realm of possibility.

Even taking back a town of a few blocks will take time to plan and the implementation of proper tactics. You certainly don't want to waste ammunition on just a few undead, and you'll have to improvise. Notice that we like the idea of improvisation. This is where scouting becomes a big thing. Knowing what is usable in an area is an advantage that cannot be an overlooked. Always keep in mind that our greatest advantage over the undead is our ability to use strategy. All they can do is swarm toward you, if their numbers are sufficient, and rip you apart. You really don't have to allow this to happen, so the simple solution is; unless it is part of your plan, don't. If it IS part of your plan, that's a shitty plan.

Tactics will take time to develop, and you have to see what works best for your personnel. Unfortunately trial and error is the only sure way to find what suits your group best. Design plans; find out who's comfortable with what and who's capable of certain roles. You can't expect the little waif of a girl to be the one lugging the heavy equipment, throwing barrels like a cracked up Donkey Kong to serve as a diversion. Then again, maybe she's wiry and all super strong, like some android chick. Whatever, it's not going to be a common undertaking to depend on the smaller group members for acts of physical power. Besides, you can do better than that.

Battle Buddies

In an offensive campaign, you never want to be alone. Having someone to back you up and help keep you safe is essential to survival. Reciprocating this act is also a necessity. If you're not watching out for each other, who else will? Teams of two or three are going to be the way to go when you want to put a hurting on the undead and not take one yourself. Become familiar with hand signals and gestures that convey the need for action. Don't try to use military signs unless everyone's familiar with them. Make up your own—you have time. The fastest way to get to know your teammates is to do everything together. Even poop in pairs. Nothing is stronger than the bond formed out of dookie bombs. Know in advance whose job it is to take the lead, who is going to watch the rear, who is best suited for door kicking, and who is the most accurate shooter. Carry different weapons, both melee and ranged, so that all bases are covered. Shotgun, rifle, and silent options are the best trio for maintaining the ability to kill, remain undetected, and control any random groups of zombies you may encounter.

You will be forced to vary your methods based on your equipment for obvious reasons, but making the best out of what you have will make you that much better with those tools. Unfortunately, not everyone will have access to firearms; maybe you're just unlucky, and perhaps you don't know how to search. Whatever the case may be, you are forced to use what you can find that's effective. Obviously keeping range between you and the zombies is preferable, but it's not always an option. A combat buddy works well here. One can defend, the other attack, and you switch to conserve energy. This isn't recommended for a prolonged conflict, but it gets the job done.

Teamwork will get you through a conflict. Inability to coexist with other people will prove to be your undoing. Undesirable personality flaws and petty conflicts over who said what, or someone farting in their sleep, aren't worth losing your life over. Your choice is either to get over it or end up dying alone while having your think-jelly tooth-raped. The simple fact of the matter is that surviving alone in an undead world isn't probable; and this can not be stressed enough.

Safety Tips for Going on the Offensive

You know you need weapons, a crew and a plan. What else is there? The following are just basic good ideas that increase your probability of survival by decreasing the chances of unwanted and unhealthy surprises. I'm sure you will probably come up with some things on your own, which is just dandy, because necessity is the mother of all invention, and at some point you're going to have to rely on your own creativity.

Knock

Even in the middle of a zombie apocalypse, let us not forget our manners. Not only is it polite to announce yourself before entering a room, but also it could very well save your life. Just because the last 420 doors you opened revealed an empty room doesn't mean the next one will be vacant as well. Knocking on the door will let a zombie know you're there, and it will come towards the door and make its presence known to you in return. The undead are without a sense of guile, and if they've become trapped in a room, they're eventually just going to stand there stupidly and wait. That knock will cause them to react and, in doing so, prepare you for the threat. So be safe and polite all at the same time; knock on doors.

Prepare Properly

The worst possible thing you can do is rush forward only to find your gun is unloaded, shoe is untied, or thong is riding you raw. Sharpen, clean, polish, primp, and preen according to the situation. This falls under basic preparation, and you should be doing all this anyway, but it's possible to get overexcited and overlook something. Don't allow yourself to be the guy who has to borrow ammo or something in the middle of an undead OK Corral.

Utilize Backup

Highlighted in the battle buddies section, going off alone shouldn't be an option. Unless you're 100 percent sure that it's a secure area, going anywhere solo should be an idea that is dismissed immediately as unsafe. Do not allow yourself to feel a false sense of security anywhere. The world is crawling with the reanimated bodies of human beings that happen to crave your tasty flesh, and should be treated as such. If that's not some inspiring shit, I don't know what is.

Focus

"While you're out taking care of daily business, be it school, work, or chores, I want you to take a moment to take in everything around you. It may not mean much now, but later paying attention to the tiny details will prove to be a life saving hobby. You never know what you're going to learn doing this, or what you're going to find."

– The Practical Guide to Being Nosey

Discipline in these times is essential. Your primary objective is to stay safe and clear the area of the undead. Finding your partners giggling because they found the battery operated personal massager in a dresser drawer of a home featuring pictures of old folks isn't really what you want to come across. Understand that sure, it's a little funny, but not enough that this should distract you. Pay attention to the task at hand and you'll stand a better chance at surviving.

Identify Your Target

When you're in an area without a clear line of sight and your primary objective is the hunting, destruction, and subsequent disposal of the undead, tensions may run high. Make sure you don't shoot at everything that moves without properly identifying it. Friendly fire is bad enough in a video game, but in real life it can be fatal. Besides causing the accidental fatality of your zombie-killing brethren, you may find yourself far less popular after the act has been committed. One certainly does not want to be considered a liability when you have to depend on others to watch your back. This doesn't mean you should steer away from group endeavors; it just means calm your ass down and look. Don't be the trigger-happy unreliable person that's likely to end up getting themselves fragged.

Tread Lightly

Heavy steps are a noise that can carry quite a bit in the right environment, so tromping about isn't a good plan. Step softly and stay out of plain sight, if at all possible. Yeah, your objective is to seek and destroy, but you want to do it on your own terms. Don't just stomp around and expect things to go your way. This is another thing which could potentially make you very unpopular, not only in the field, but around the new homestead. Waking people up from their valuable rest can get you killed in some circles.

Search for Treasure

"When you're moving from place to place, make sure to check all the usual hiding spots in any building you hide out in. You never know what some poor sap has hidden under his bed. Could be sex toys, could be a fully automatic AK-47. Some of these are more of a win than others, but at least you can have fun with anything you find."

– Maid at the Motel 6

While you're clearing zombies out of stores and homes, you may as well see if you can supplement your supplies with freshly found loot. People store all kinds of good stuff around their businesses and homes. You know it, I know it, and since you're there, you may as well see what you can find. Stay focused on your primary task, but give a quick look around, maybe toss some drawers once you've cleared the house, and maybe you'll turn up some sort of weapon cache. A shiny new .357 is worth far more than gold in a hostile world filled with the walking dead. For that matter, a nice soft roll of toilet paper is too. Luckily, we live in a world of excess, and nearly every home has got everything you need to aid in your prolonged livelihood. You just have to find it and pee on it so that everyone knows it's yours. Maybe just throw it in the truck or a backpack, and that will suffice as far as a claim of appropriation goes.

Getting to Work (Tactics)

"Step 1: Remove Head
Step 2: Destroy Brain
Step 3: Repeat Until Hordes Are Gone." – Leviticus 6:66

Now we get to the fun part: dismantling the undead and ridding the world of their foul existence. Let me just point out, this is not all-military grade goodness that will help you save the world single-handedly. Some are simple but effective plans, others are just plain silly, but as you know, that's how we do things around here. If you can't have fun with the witless undead, whom can you have fun with? Most of these are designed with groups in mind and shouldn't be attempted alone. It's always good to have a plan of action when going into any situation, and combating the undead is no different. Be sure you fully understand your advantages and disadvantages in regards to these creatures before formulating any type of plot that involves your exposure. You can count on the undead being single-minded in their pursuit of you until you are either overrun, infected and converted, or they've been destroyed. Not even the slimmest glimmer of craftiness exists in these creatures. They have no tactical sense of their own and can easily fall victim to a well-laid plan. As with any plan, keeping it simple is probably for the best. Make sure that whomever you work with can be trusted to do their part in these machinations. Without your team's ability to rely on each member to be competent, you're not going to make it very far.

Basics

"Without teamwork we're going to be screwed. Whether it's in a co-op game or in life, we need to learn to help each other out. With that being said, it's still OK to totally frag someone who pisses you off online."
– Master Sgt. Bilko (may have been Sun Tzu)

How you go about your task of destroying the undead is going to have to be tailored to your group's unique style. Some simple techniques are suited for everyone and should be utilized because they increase safety for everyone. Before we get into the other goodies, we should go over the simple things first. Close combat techniques are your friend. Learn them, live them, and love them.

Choosing the Right Group and Assignments

Attempting to clear a house, or any other building for that matter, should never even come into consideration if there's another option. Luring the undead to where you want them instead of going in and looking for them is always a preferable method. It's simply not always an option. To this end you have the unenviable task of going in after the undead. Sweeping and clearing any type of area should be done in groups of three or four. Two are always looking ahead, and the others are watching their backs. Even with just two, this is immeasurably safer than trying to go it alone. If your group is of a considerable size, pick a few to remain outside, or just inside the doorway, and out of sight. This prevents an overlap of the search, potential friendly fire, and odds of someone fucking up.

Stay Together

Splitting into groups may become a necessity at some point while inside a structure. If you should have to do so, keep one group in a designated area and have the other search and clear. Having a secondary group running around in the same building as a sweep team is dangerous to say the least. Tensions will be high, nerves will be on edge, and fingers will be on triggers. This is a potentially deadly situation should someone pop up around a corner. However, if you do have a wiseass who seems very intent on getting himself shot by fucking with the members of the searching team, oblige him. He just served as an example and it shouldn't happen again.

Take It Slow

Utilizing proper tactics does not demand speed. In fact, your objective is to remain as silent as possible while checking for threats. Being careful is far more advantageous than trying to zerg rush the damn building. Take your time, be thorough, and be stealthy. Doing so will keep you and your group safe while you wander through potentially hostile ground. Also, avoiding making undue noise will keep your position secret from the undead that may be lurking inside the construct with you.

Holding Your Firearm

Being properly prepared when going into a potential close-quarters combat situation is a crucial thing. You should be holding your weapon (in this case, we'll say it's a pistol) with both hands with your arms in front of you. As you look around, your weapon should remain where you're looking at all times.

This leaves you prepared to fire a lot faster than having your weapon in a safety position above your shoulder pointed up. Keep it ready and it will better serve to protect you from any threats you may encounter.

Corner Clearing

Corners are common in a home and most buildings, except those dirty hippie office plans that don't have walls, where everyone gets a window and a mid-day yoga/joint break. In the rest of the real world, there are shit loads of corners and blind hallways. Just barreling around a turn can lead you straight into the arms of the undead. This is an undesirable position to find yourself in. Just a quick peek can also land you in a world of shit. So, to avoid this, you can use a sweeping arc to increase your visual range around said corners, while leaving yourself room for a proper reaction.

Start out your visual recon a few feet back from the corner itself, with your shoulder near the wall (make sure not to scrape up against it and make noise). You're only going to be able to see a bit around the other side. Confirming that it's clear from there, take a step out to your left, and continue to scan to the limits of your visible horizon. Continue taking a step away from the corner, moving a bit forward, and slowly side-stepping out around it so that as you can see more. Ideally, you should be putting yourself farther against the wall opposite the corner. This provides you full visibility of the contents of the area and grants you maximum reaction time, should something undesirable enter your field of vision. It's not much more, but we're dealing with life-saving fractions of seconds here.

Doorways

Handled a bit like corners, your shoulder should be near the wall of one side of the doorframe initially. Remembering to knock first (we're dealing with the undead here, not a group of people wanting to shoot at you), swing the door open if nothing makes itself known. You should be able to see into the room directly across from your position. Stepping away from the wall and toward the opening will increase your field of vision into the room. Next, continue a full 180-degree sweep before entering. In this fashion, you can hopefully avoid surprises.

Hallways

Clearing a hallway can present a few difficulties, especially when they contain several doors which may or may not be open. First of all, you want to stick to one side or the other. Don't walk down the middle of the hallway, because this creates unnecessary exposure. You want to see the undead first, not the other way around. Proceed slowly, watching and listening for movement. If there are open doors, clear them visually in the appropriate manner and continue on.

Should you come upon a T-junction in the hallway, you're faced with a dilemma, if you're alone, which you shouldn't be. You have to pick one side or the other. Put your back almost against the wall, then swing yourself out wide and into the hallway itself to confirm it's clear. Doing so, you're forced to pull a complete about-face and scan the opposite side. If you're working in a group, you and another person can clear both sides at the same time. This is the best option for obvious reasons.

Lead Your Target

Don't be confused here with the necessity to aim forward from your target's projected direction. With the undead, your bullet will travel faster than they walk. So, if you're not 500 yards away while taking your shot, this is totally unnecessary. What we mean here by "leading the target" is totally different. This is a close quarters technique which should be employed for the simplification of your target's assured destruction.

Should you come across a zombie, but you're not able to take a clear shot, back away and out of the room, into the hallway where the rest of the group is. The ghoul WILL follow. It's this predictable behavior that makes them fun. Make it known to the others that you're being followed, and that you're going to be taking the shot. Let the zombie enter the fatal funnel and then execute the ghoul. When your target makes its appearance in the doorway, light it up. One shot to the head should be sufficient. If you happen to miss, you have back up who can finish the job. Using this technique helps you avoid injury, undeath, and keeps everyone aware of the situation. Staying in a confined area with the zombie could result in your becoming infected, so let's not do that. Safely engaging targets reduces the risk of any mishaps occurring.

Marking

As you're going about the task of clearing homes, offices and so on, it may be a good idea to let others know that it's been deemed safe previously. Spray paint a smiley face, put up a sticky note, or use something more fun and/or sadistic, like a Bratz doll nailed to the door through its head. Whatever you use, make sure it's easily recognized as a sign that the area has been secured.

The Slinky Technique

This one can be done alone or in a group, because it's just fun to observe. All you require is a simple sturdy pushing device such as a rake and a set of stairs; the higher the better. Allowing a pair of undead to reach the top, you forcefully thrust the rake forward, causing the zombies to tumble down the stairs. Unlike the traditional slinky, these will keep coming back up to you and provide you with hours of entertainment. Like the beloved childhood toy, the undead aren't good for much, but when you push them down a flight of stairs, you can't help but smile. This could go on for quite some time. If your zombies become overly damaged, inhibiting their ability to climb the stairs, then it may be time for new ghouls to play with. Put them out of your misery.

L.A.P.D. Riot Squad

For this one you'll need two groups of two people each, minimum. Equipment can vary, but riot gear is nice to have if you can find it—shields, helmets, optional vests for two people, and melee weapons for two people as well. Ranged, blunt, edged, or whatever your preference. Now whoever has the protective gear and shield is in the front, with the weapon wielding person to the rear. Lure the undead into an alley so that both shield bearers are next to each other. Then the undead cannot swarm in around your flank. While the defending pair is busy deflecting tooth and nail, our offensive strikers level cranium blows to the undead, causing a cessation of life functions. This is a decent tactic against zombies numbering from two to twenty or so, depending on the stamina of all parties involved. This can be done on a larger scale if you're feeling particularly badass, but it's not highly recommended. If using firearms, earplugs may be a good idea.

The Red Rubber Ball

OK, you've decided to take a hospital as your personal little safety spot, and now you're looking for a way to defend it. We have a suggestion. Before the apocalypse is too far underway, you could take up residence in a "special needs" hospital, or a "special needs" school; either will work for what you're going to do. Once you do so, your next step is to befriend all the "patients" or "students." You're going to want to spend some time fortifying the windows, doors, and hallways. Pretty much shore up everything but the main entranceway. You will want to fortify the secondary entrance, but not the main doors, and we'll explain why in a bit. Now this is a long-term plan, and you'll have to begin early for it to be effective. You will have to take ten minutes every day to take each "patient" or "student" into a separate room for some quality time. During this time you are only to play catch with a red rubber bouncy ball. You must give positive praise, and show affection at all times during the ten minutes. It's imperative that each and every student associates the red rubber ball with all that is good and happy in your relationship. They each also must feel as if that red rubber ball belongs to them. Really sell it to the muscly bunny-huggers. If you can't seal this deal, this tactic will be utterly useless, and you might as well move on and find another way to keep safe.

Now, while you're spending your time working on windows and doors keep the ball hidden so they can't get it and screw up all the associative work you've been doing.

Luckily there's normally a heavy-duty fence around these kinds of facilities so in theory it should provide you enough time to make all of this happen. The horde will slowly build up along the perimeter, and eventually they will slowly crush in on the fence and ultimately bring it down. This is where all your hard work pays off. You've fortified everything but the main and secondary doors. You've spent time making every student associate that ball with love and praise.

Here's where your soul needs to die just a little bit. Just a little. OK, probably a whole hell of a lot, but whatever. Once the horde breaks the fence and starts making their way to the front of the building, open the secondary doors, and the front doors. Gather all your new friends around, and pull out the red rubber ball. Now, if you've successfully conditioned them they will focus in on the ball and think of nothing else. Reach back, and hurl it into the middle of the horde. Your new friends will show a burst of speed you've never seen before. They will run, limp, crawl, or wheel (depending on how they get around) right after the ball. Since each child believes the ball is theirs and it's the source to their praise and happiness, they will fight and claw and destroy until they possess it.

After the last of your special little warriors makes their way outside, quickly barricade the secondary doors. Run to the second floor and take up your guarded position in a well-fortified room and watch the Great Kerfuffle.

There are three possible outcomes from this scenario:

1. The undead horrifically slaughter your special friends and then wander off.

2. Your own horde destroys them and each other getting to the red rubber ball, and you keep the strongest as your personal sidekick.

3. Or, everyone dies and the horde, now larger, and not speaking a whole lot differently, traps you inside your dwelling and you die.

Two of the three are very positive. The third is not so fun. At least the odds here are good.

The UT

AKA the Charles Whitman Sampler, this is one of the most simple and straightforward tactics you can make use of. Doing it solo or with a team works, as long as you're calling targets. We don't want to waste ammo, now do we? Situating yourself on a roof or water tower or anything that gives you a 360-degree view of your surroundings (maybe a clock tower?), draw in the undead and fire at will. How you draw them in is entirely up to you; whether it's music, live bait, or even just shouting, they will come, you will shoot, they will fall. Unless of course you can't shoot worth a damn, in which case you may want to give this idea a miss.

Sunday Stroll

You and your closest new friends gather up, bristling with weaponry, and walk through town in a circle shooting anything that appears unkempt. A fairly sizeable group is needed here and an escape plan is essential, in case things get too hot to handle while going about this silly bit of grisly work. With the right people, it's an option you may choose to utilize. Just walk, stop, aim, and fire; communication is key here. We don't want to leave anyone behind. Or maybe you do…

The Piñata

Got a tree, a single zombie, someone who can throw a lasso, and a sadistic streak? This one's for you then. Rope up the ghoul, run him up a tree, and beat the ever-loving shit right out of him. Just watch out for the "candy."

The Pimp-Slap

Since the dawn of time, those few among us who are tasked with keeping the women who practice mankind's oldest profession in line have relied on a smooth rap, bright and off-putting clothing, and the pimp slap. These love-brokers are proficient in the speedy distribution of hand-to-bitch face. While you may find a certain bit of appeal in the idea of dressing in outlandish fashion and slapping the undead into submission, please disregard this plan of action. It's not that you wouldn't look awesome (you won't), but more to the point that no real damage will be done to the undead, which will in turn result in your demise. You can keep the hat though; it's far too stylish to throw out. Not really; I can't back that up.

Squad Sweep

This is an actual tactical idea, so be afraid. Groups of six or more are needed here, as well as an out of the way spotter. Everyone needs to be heavily armed and have a silent means of dispatching the undead; silent armor (not shit that rattles) is also an option if you have it. For this you'll need coordination, one person to do the spotting, and either a great familiarity with hand signals or radios with earpieces. If you're attempting this at night, a low light scope will be needed. Got it? Good. You will be moving in a covering formation toward a target area using all the stealth and care you can muster. Your groups will be clearing multiple buildings at once, and the spotter will be watching the exterior for hostile movement. This is a dangerous endeavor because the group has split. Keeping the group together is also a fine idea and it greatly expedites the search of a building. However, you'll recall the possible problems with multiple teams in a single structure. Either way, clear it, close it, mark it, and lock it if it's possible to do so. This ensures that you won't have to worry about checking a structure twice and end up wasting your people's time. Several groups in a coordinated effort could easily clear several city blocks in a day with minimal risk, provided the main undead population has been cleared ahead of time. Do not try and depopulate an entire city in this manner. It won't end well. This is a clean up operation tactic.

Bring the Rhames

Yeah, he's so awesome we named a tactic after him. Big whoop, wanna fight about it? For this you'll need a bit of mechanical engineering and artistic savvy and enough people to fill the bus. Yes, I said bus. A smaller bus is fine, but you have to armor it. Weld a nice cowcatcher on to the front, remove all the windows, wrap the whole thing in barbed wire, and go out killing. It's pretty resource and labor-intensive, but it could be fun in theory. Get everyone in the back, aim out of the windows, and mow down the undead. Make several passes and then clean up. Since you're going to be making one hell of a spectacle out of yourselves anyway, this is an instance where a chainsaw will not be frowned upon, were you to maybe hook a couple to the sides of the bus and go

Leatherface ape-shit. Imagination is your best friend when it comes to this method; have fun.

The Drive and Drop

This one requires several people who are proficient marksmen (or women), lots of ammunition, a truck or similar style vehicle, and a driver. Riding through a town, you simply let the undead follow you while keeping at a slow pace, and pick them off from the bed of the truck. Sounds simple, does it not? It is. As long as you're playing Pied Piper and picking off zeds, you're in good shape. Just hope that you don't suffer some catastrophic mechanical issue, otherwise you'll end up in a highly unbecoming position. Move at a steady pace, fire, reload, repeat, and you should be fine. Makes for an awful lot of clean up, though. You may want to consider that before you try this one. Snowplow and a fire pit maybe?

The Dallas Hitchhiker

Once again you'll need someone proficient with a lasso, a vehicle, and plenty of open space to drive. Just lasso a zombie and drag it for several miles, then when it's pretty much a long skid mark, retrieve your rope. End of story. This isn't fancy and is probably a bit inappropriate, but that's just our style. Employment of this method is extremely inefficient in the expeditious removal of undead from an area.

The Mow-Down Hoedown

This technique requires several drivers, a lot of large sturdy vehicles, one or more rooftop spotters, CB radios, and more than a bit of craziness. Here you're going to use these vehicles to run down the undead. This is more than a little dangerous and can easily result in personal injury, property loss, and many giggles. Run through the streets, honking, shouting, or blasting music in order to get their attention, then working with your spotters, try to round them up for the run-down. This isn't as simple as it would seem, and there will be a phenomenal amount of mopping up to do once it's done, but it sounds like a fun idea. Try not to hit too many at once for your vehicle to handle, otherwise you may find out in a hurry that getting out of this vehicle is a bit harder to do quickly when the undead are bearing down on you. Also your fellow drivers, in their zeal to offer protection, may just ram into you. Sure it looks like that guy was laughing, but it could have been a bit of concern as well. It's pretty hard to tell when they slam into you broadside at forty-five miles per hour. Assume it's maniacal laughter though, because in all honesty, it probably was.

The Lone Gunman

All you need here is yourself, a lot of weapons, and a lacking sense of self-preservation. Load up heavy, wade into the fray, and try to take down as many undead as possible. This is not a recommended method of attempting to eliminate a copious amount of zombies unless you've been previously subjected to infection. You may be able to do untold amounts of damage once your inhibitions are cast off. Even then, those weapons may become lost if you fail to destroy a large number of these ghouls on your way out, and that leaves everyone else wondering what the hell you were thinking. If you happen to consider this route when you're healthy and unmarred by the undead, reach your hand way out and bring it toward your face with as much strength as you can manage, and slap the shit out of yourself. You should know better.

Burn It All

Just what it implies; all you need are people to set the fire from the outside and let it burn inwards. Hopefully it doesn't rage out of control and start some sort of evil country-sweeping conflagration that consumes all of our lives. This isn't a great idea; in fact it's stupid and terrifying, but if you happen to be dying anyway what will you care?

Funneling

This is a straightforward tactic that works in most any situation, and should in fact be used every chance possible. Using the natural layouts and features of our world, we can create a bottleneck in which the

undead are forced to follow. This should be a narrow area that only allows for limited numbers of the ghouls to be seen at once as targets. Depending on where you are and how you plan to do away with these creatures should help dictate the way in which you lay this out. You can use stalled vehicles, buildings, natural topography, and even piles of the undead to help direct the flow of zombies to where you need them to be. Even a simple alley can provide you with the tactical advantage you require. As you drop the undead in their tracks, you can start to relax. Their footing becomes unsteady and they're notoriously lacking in dexterity, so between the bad terrain and having to mount piles of their undead brethren, you get a little breathing room. A two-row firing line is the most efficient way to go using this tactic.

Most likely, a similar funnel system will be used leading away from the bigger cities in order to clear them of zombies. This will be a huge undertaking that will require organization, hefty amounts of munitions, and an awful lot of manpower. It's also going to take hours or days of doing nothing but leading the undead out and firing upon them. It will be hideous and glorious all at once.

In Countries Other Than the U.S.

We're aware that not everyone has the same rules and regulations regarding firearms, and this compounds the difficulty. Some of the tactics aren't really applicable when this is the case, so to that end, there's not a lot we can do for you on that count. However, when you're faced with a purely melee-based set of defense mechanisms, the use of group tactics becomes extremely important. In fact, they're going to be essential. One person alone, even with the use of firearms, can't survive the undead hordes.

You have your own native weaponry, and should know where to begin with that. With any luck, we've detailed enough so that you have a damn good idea where to at least start fashioning or finding your own means of zombie-bashing goodness. If not, well, use your imagination. We're going to try and run down some good ideas for each continent, because there happens to be a lot of countries, and that would just take WAY too long. Either way, we're pulling for you guys. We don't want to see the rest of the world wiped out by the undead. When we rebuild, we need other places to point out and laugh at.

Africa:

Toto sang about this place and we're fans, but let's look at what could go on here. Populations are concentrated in very few places inland, and, as such, this could leave the majority of the populace in the interior regions largely untouched by infection. Coastal towns and cities with higher concentrations of people, however, are going to be quite handily shit upon by this whole thing. Until the folks get a grip on what they're dealing with, things are going to be messy. In many parts of Africa, there is still fighting, and that's somewhat good. It sucks that people are killing each other over whatever it is they're fighting about, but they've got weapons. Even the simple tribes out in the middle of fuck all nothing have spears and whatnot, even if they choose not to mingle with those who have embraced the technological advances of the modern world. They survive on little, so the lack of power and trucked in food won't amount to shit for these guys. If those on the coasts manage to fall, then I wouldn't be too surprised to see the folks inland make some heroic stands against any undead that make it their way.

Antarctica:

Who the fuck lives here? Since zombies are going to freeze solid and probably never thaw again, the chances of serious horde activity are nil. Stay warm, folks.

Asia:

One of the most awesome bands of all time, and framing their poster is an indication of sexual orientation. That aside, Asia is a big fucking chunk of the world's land mass, and has just a shit ton of people all over the damn thing. As far as gun laws there in the East, we're woefully uneducated, but we happen to know, thanks to World History class in high school, that these are some tough people. Pretty much every group at one time or another has decided that they wanted to take over the world and has given it a shot. We're sure that your average person isn't going to have the recurve bow hanging over the mantle or a cavalry steed available, or even an AK-47 next to the stove, but some of these people will have some weaponry. There are cold regions in which they can take shelter and thwart the undead as they wish. In fact, the geography there pretty much covers the entire spectrum, much as it does in the US. Due to some heavily populated areas, the casualty rate may be awfully high, but then again, they could have some measures in place that will put a stop to this shit in a hurry.

Australia:

The island of displaced British prisoners is in good hands. Not many folks have firearms readily available. A few do, but it's uncommon. Some folks actively shun firearms, such as our friends at TAZAA. They have been working to keep the Australian populace informed and aware of the zombie threat and have a stable of ideas in regards to your maintaining the ability to remain un-undead. That being said, we happen to know that Aussies are scrappy folks who won't go down easily. Even the Kiwis are likely to throw down at the drop of a hat. These folks live in a place that pretty much crawls with shit that will kill you. If we had half as many deadly creepy crawly things in the US, people would demand carpet bombing just to exterminate the things. Either that, or they'd wrap their kids in hamster balls and bubble wrap. Australians though? Hell no! They tell their kids to go their little asses out and play, and if they see a black mamba, to eat the damn thing. Between the huge and sparsely populated inland part of their landmass, and the ability to take to the sea when needed, they should do fine with some organization and crafty planning.

Europe:

You guys don't have much in the way of guns, and that's quite all right. You have some pretty dense populations, and that's OK, too. Luckily you've got the guys at *How to Survive a Zombie Apocalypse* looking out for you. With a bit of ingenuity, proper utilization of group efforts, and many *Shaun of the Dead* references, you can make it. It's a shame that the undead are immune to toxins of any kind, because British food could be hurled at zombies and probably causing them to melt just by contact. The French won't be able to rude them to death. The Irish may try to get them drunk, but then having their offer refused, will go all IRA on their asses. The Scots, well, we've all seen that movie with the little crazy Aussie guy pretending to be Scottish. It's not guns that make the difference in survival; it's going to be using your strengths against the undead's weaknesses. Though, guns do help an awful lot, I can't lie.

South America:

Party people and revolutionaries, these people are serious about work and play. When the undead show up, it's going to get messy. However, in these countries, they're well practiced in surviving on very little already, so they're ahead of the curve. Plus, they have all kinds of blades and guns and a ready-to-die-for-liberty attitude. The people here won't go down easily. They can retreat to the jungles, the water, or head north to open areas, and they'll do just fine. Living off the land is what they do, and this could easily be their saving grace.

SECTION 9
REBUILDING OUR WORLD

"Survival isn't the only thing you should worry about. Eventually the zombies will all be dead. Where will you be then? Do you have an after plan? What role will you play in the new world? You can't plan on just repopulating the earth. Chances are you and your partner will get tired of sex and child birth after the first couple years or so."
– a 43-year-old virgin

Eventually one of two things will happen. Either we're going to be eradicated as a species, or we're going to hunt down and destroy every single undead creature on the planet and begin to rebuild and repopulate the world. Let's assume we're going to win out in the end and have to restore humanity to its former glory. This gives us a magnificent chance to put things right again, since the resources remaining at this point are now in such abundance that there should be more than enough for everyone remaining. It's going to take an awful lot of work, patience, and combined effort to get it done. Even then, it's not likely that the world will be unscarred as a result.

Re-Establishing Contact

"Once this is all over, the survivors will have to repopulate the earth, which honestly sounds fun as hell. However, there's bound to be the group who wants to breed a perfect race. We must avoid these people. There's nothing worse than an inbred mouth breather clan. I say diversity is our key, and incest is bdong."
– Answer given on a Customer Satisfaction survey

Little factions will eventually become larger as folks begin to scout around and wander. Call it natural curiosity about the world around us, but it's simply bound to happen, and when it does, the sense of community will once more be established. Through use of radios, smoke signals, or just taking a walk into the surrounding countryside, people will start to find each other and integrate. It will probably be very slow to start initially, but that's to be expected. There will be initial mistrust and hesitance. Hopefully, though, people will realize the value of life and let the violent reactions take a back seat to more rational thought. Human beings crave interaction with one another, so expect that effort for reunification at some point in order to further humanity's growth as a whole. Being more integrated with nature may be more commonplace than it has been in recent years, due to a newfound respect for the world we live in. Then again, the majority could say, "fuck that—give me air conditioning."

Conversely, some people and smaller groups may choose to remain outside the reach of others. Noting the toll that increased social interaction can take on some groups of people, they'll simply opt out and stay apart from any attempt at reintegration that may take place. Some folks want to be left alone, and this should be their right. If you come across these people, make contact, discuss what's going on, but respect whatever their decision may be. After a good deal of time spent fighting off intrusion, these people may be more of a threat than anything else if provoked.

Reconstruction

"With most of humanity killed off, you'll pretty much be able to just choose the home, building, whatever you want, and take it. You want to move into a bank so you can hide in the vault? No problem. Personally, I'm going to take over a combination go-kart mini-golf facility. That way I can play eighteen holes and have drunken races with my friends."
– Frank Drebbin

Considering the shit storm that everyone's just made it through, it's possible that communities will take on a very old style. Walled cities and forts may again become the norm. The safety aspect here is apparent, and could very well be warranted when one considers how ill prepared we were to face the recent undead threat. Having tall, powerful walls erected around the living areas could very well be a saving grace, should zombies ever again pop up among us. The problem here would be eventual population increase and insufficient size of these designs. That's what happened before, and people being people, it's likely to happen again. Of course the easiest solution would be to move fifty or a hundred miles up the road and start another one with a similar design in mind. Future security will be of great importance to those who make it through this disaster.

The cities that were left in ruins may be salvageable, but perhaps their present design should be reconsidered. They were likely the sites of the worst losses of human life ever to be imagined on the face of the planet. Open designs made it impossible to contain the threats that stemmed from them, and only further served to fan the flame of infection with their overpopulated nature. Just like building a fire out of a stacked up pile of sticks; you stack them nice and neat and all it takes is one match to make the pile burn. Keeping the local populations smaller, when rebuilding, will create more of a sense of community among the inhabitants. Enabling them to be locked down and self-sufficient would provide a more secure feeling among the people and contain any possible rekindling of the undead hazard.

Naturally, it is possible that people will be happy to go back to the way things were, without any significant changes. The prospect of working to build something more secure and old-fashioned could fail to appeal to the public. Sometimes it's easier to just use what's there. We all know how well it obviously worked out the last time.

Assisting the Emotionally Scarred

"Sometimes your biggest asset will be the person you least expect. The quiet guy in the corner who's been rocking back and forth may just be a mad killing machine when you remind him his girlfriend slept with his uncle."
– Anonymous cruel therapist

So maybe killing untold numbers of flesh craving dead people isn't everyone's idea of a good time. Different strokes and all that. Certain people, though they managed to put aside their passive ways and survive, will be traumatized to the point of incapacitation. To these people we say: Harden the fuck up! You're not the only ones that lost friends and family and your favorite fish. Stop being a pussy and move on. Sure, you'll have the odd nightmare of the time you had to shoot your meemaw point blank with a shotgun because she tried to chew on your leg. Who wouldn't? Life sucks—get a fucking helmet. The simple fact remains that some people went through far worse in order to get where they are now, and you don't hear them complaining. Be prepared to tell these people how, in the zombie apocalypse, you had to shoot fifty zombies, with a BB gun, in four feet of snow, uphill, both ways, all while stabbing your own mother and sister in the face with a pointy stick, after cutting off your own feet for food. That will shut them right up. If it doesn't, slap the taste out of their mouth. Pansies...

If you happen to be reading this and know someone who's likely to suffer a complete mental breakdown as a result of being forced to use violence in order to survive, the best thing you can do for them is give them this book. Prepare them in advance; let them know what could possibly come to pass. There's humor in tragedy, if one knows where to look. The most excellent weapon that human beings have is the ability to conceive of an issue prior to its coming to pass and prepare for it. Don't let your friends be whiners later on. It's been said before—forewarned is forearmed. Friends don't let friends be spineless wussies.

Cinema

"Another upside to the apocalypse will be no more bad Hollywood movies. Those of us who survive will never be forced to accept they're remaking a movie that sucked the first time and is bound to suck the second time. Yeah, it also means no more good Hollywood movies either, but if it means Free Willy 18 won't be made, I accept it."

– Page 14 of Screen Actors Guild contract

This is going to be a golden age for the world of cinematic achievement. Not only will the genre of horror have to step it up a big notch, but also, here is our opportunity. No longer must we endure another 96-minute abortion that is a movie starring a rapper who can't act. Never again will you be forced to sit through that man-hating chick flick. Your need to satiate the desire to watch that sequel which throws the whole world out of balance no longer has to be placated. All those remade films, all those silly sparkly vampire movies, everything that's intellectually demeaning to us all can finally be destroyed for all time. When it comes to this, we're passionate, because the only thing worse than a bad movie is a goddamn remake of a bad movie that's even worse than the first version. Classic cinematic endeavors should be preserved; by all means, keep copies of good films. You know the ones we're talking about. You, in Hollywood, you're close enough that you can save us all from visual damnation. Please save us from these artless lengths of trash. This is certainly one endeavor in which fire can prove helpful. If you don't do it, then damn it, we will.

New Government

"We're going to have to establish a form of government after the apocalypse. Since there hasn't been a watery tart to hand out swords in a while, we'll go with elections. In order to keep things fair, we should have a bracket system every year, like college basketball in the states, only we're going to play games of Monopoly™. That way we know the leader knows about money."

– Discarded from the Declaration of Independence

While it's likely that the major heads of state will be spirited off to a safe location to wait out the impending doom that is the zombie apocalypse, there will be no way for them to be swiftly put back into a position of governing power. Largely, we will probably be left to our own devices for a time. Let's face it—the ways we find to govern will probably be a hell of a lot better than the mess we presently find ourselves in. The reassertion of a governmental entity will be another long and slow process, as lines of communication are forged throughout the world again and military resources are consolidated. While we're not advocating anarchy or full on revolution, the chance to get back to basic democratic ideals will be presented. The United States was formed as a government by the people and for the people. Getting back to that seems like a good idea. It's highly probable that some shady under-the-radar jack-wagons caused this whole mess to begin with. Do you really want the same mistakes to be made twice? Think it over, be ready to be active, and share your voice. If we make it through this, we can only be stronger for it as a whole.

Staying Aware

With the immediate threat having been eliminated, it's easy enough to lose focus on a lingering threat from the undead. Many minds will turn to rebuilding our world back to the way it was rather than allow the mind to wander on "what ifs," and that possibility of another zombie apocalypse could easily be forgotten. Without being able to account for every zombie corpse around the globe, it's impossible to dismiss the threat outright. In fact, many bodies of water, inland and otherwise, could hold these decaying predators, and at any time they could find their way to the surface and the whole thing could begin again. Those in and around coastal towns, as well as those set near rivers and lakes, will require added vigilance. It is in these places that the likelihood of an undead resurgence is of the highest probability. It may never come to pass, and if not, wonderful. It's not as if we lack the ability to suppress these threats if the need arises. Simply keep the probability in mind that this could happen at any time. Be ready to hate-fuck anything that looks remotely undead with a shotgun the second you see it.

SECTION 10.2.1A
ARE WE HAVING FUN YET?

"When out killing the hordes, remember the best thing you can do is have fun with it. Find nifty ways to kill the undead that will bring a smile to your face and glee to your heart. Remember style points will be awarded later."
– Alex Trebek

So you're bored and just sitting around with your group, hiding out in a world full of zombies, and what the hell is there to do? I hear your cry. The answer is simple: you have to entertain yourself. You're no good at playing the banjo, you're sick of Monopoly because somebody lost the battleship (and nobody wants to be the shoe), and how many times can you really clean your rifle? You need a break in the tedium. We've come up with a couple suggestions which will not only make time fly, but make the laughs flow freely as well. See, our basic premise is, if you're going to survive the zombie apocalypse, what then?

Killing the odd shuffling undead creature doesn't pose as much of a thrill as it used to, so why not move on to bigger and better things? The following section is for those who are a little more daring, possess the ingenuity, and the semi-psychotic/sadistic element needed to take it to another level. Now, even though we've taken the time to think this shit up, we in no way endorse it by saying it's a good idea. In fact, some of it is pretty stupid and all of it is dangerous. OK, they all fall into those categories, but it's entertaining either way. If you choose to engage in any or all of the activities listed from here on out, you do so at your own risk, as well as the potential risk of the other people involved. As they say on *Mythbusters*, "Don't try this at home." You've been warned. Having said that and effectively alleviated ourselves of any and all legal responsibility, we can move on.

Winter Games!!!

Zed-Sledding

This can only be done when you're in a hilly or mountainous area during the winter months, so it's a seasonal sport, much like underwater extreme nude mud wrestling (wtf?).

To properly Zed-Sled, you will need just a few things:

- A well planned-out downhill course
- Snow

- A very frozen zombie. They cannot be slightly frozen, or slightly mobile. They must be frozen to the core.
- A fire pit and disposal site

Now you've got your supplies, you've plotted your course. From here on out it's rather simple.

Take your zombie sled, throw him face first into the course, and ride down. The proper technique for the best ride is not unlike riding a course on a snowboard. You lean forward on the nose to go faster, bank left and right to turn, lean back on the tail to stop. The more creative people among us will be able to do spiffy things like ollie, nollie, kickflip, and grind their zombies. Once you've progressed to an advanced stage of Zed-Sledding, you'll be able to pull some sick grab tricks and muted airs. If attempting these or any other tricks, exercise caution. We don't recommend getting too high off the ground in case your sled regains mobility. A quick flip around the back could pose a different problem, and as a zombie killer you should always have a visual on your target, even if they are frozen solid.

Now on to the risks of this particular sport.

After prolonged use, the friction caused by the sledding will begin to slightly thaw your sled. This can cause either the undead's mobility to be regained, or wounds on your sled, and these can cause a chance of infection for the rider and possibly others. Also, when your sled gets pounded up, you start to lose speed. The best way to avoid this is to make sure you have no open wounds on your body, and you are wearing your winter leathers under your thermal gear. When you wipe out, and you will until you master this sport, you run the risk of taking a bite out of the zombie. It's a reverse infection at this point, being that you're the one that bit the zombie instead of it being the other way round. The best way to avoid this is simple: a mouth guard or full-face helmet. No open mouth, no chance to bite down on your sled.

The biggest risk involved in Zed-Sledding will be crashing into a pile of discarded and slightly used zombie-sleds at the bottom of the run. You can simply avoid this by properly disposing of your sled when you're done riding it. Cut its head off, bash the brain to bits, then burn what's left in a near-by burn pit. Make sure the pit is far enough away from the course as not to prematurely thaw your sleds.

When Zed-Sledding, safety should be your number one priority. Wear all your proper gear, and carry your close range shootin' iron. You never know when one of the sleds will display a burst of movement and require re-deadification. A slug to the brain should put an end to that bullshit. Outside of that, enjoy this particular fun game.

Zombie Statue Theater

Yet another seasonal favorite of ours. In freezing temperatures, you can also create your own static life art display. We simply call this one Zombie Statue Theater.

Here are the supplies you need:

- Frozen solid zombies
- Trunk full of clothes and costumes
- Small blowtorch
- Digital camera
- Nice open area for posing
- A fire pit and disposal site

Now that you've got your supplies, we'll get into how to have fun.

1. The first thing you want to do is go through your trunk of clothes.

2. Pick the best outfits for the particular still life scene you wish to create.

3. You're going to have to position them in the various poses your particular scene will require, and that is where the small blowtorch comes in.

4. Gently heat the joints up so you can move them without allowing free mobility to the undead.

5. Dress all the frozen zombies in said clothes, and now you've got your actors.

We DO NOT recommend posing the head, since thawing it brings a potential happy burst of bitey death. Once you've gotten your actors into their costumes, and the joints have re-

frozen, you can start moving them into their respective positions in the scene.

The possibilities are limitless with this game. You can re-enact the assassination of John F. Kennedy, or the death of Caesar. Your favorite band could come back to life for a last show. And while we frown on it, we know at least one of you sick twisted people will dress up a group like the thriller dancers, with a Michael Jackson look alike. Don't lie—we know you thought of it right away.

Now that you've got your scene set, take a lot of pictures. Remember the pictures are what will be judged later. Once you've got pictures of every angle imaginable and feel you've completely recaptured your masterpiece, sadly, your creation will have to be destroyed.

It's time to start disposing of your subjects. IMPORTANT TO REMEMBER: they're frozen. You do not need to waste ammunition on them. Once can simply grab the handy dandy baseball bat from your pack, take aim, and smash away. Always remember to completely destroy the brain. Having done that, drag the corpses to your fire pit and dispose of the bodies.

While it would be funny to set up a scene inside an urban environment, then let them sit until the thaw and watch the fun that ensues, it is just bad form amongst survivors to play those kinds of pranks. Good on you for secretly dreaming about it while you read this. Yes, I can read your mind while you read. It's special mind reading paper.

Zombie Bowling

Because sadism toward the undead is the real reason for the season, we bring you more wintertime fun.

The supplies:

- Dozens of frozen zombies preferably standing upright or nailed to a thin base
- A downhill icy slope with a flat graded surface at the end
- A score keeper
- A small blowtorch
- A "ball"
- A fire pit and disposal site

Now, go through your frozen zombies, find the ones that are most likely to slide with the least resistance. Look for ones who are flat across the chest or back, use the torch if necessary to warm up a few joints and position them into a sliding posture. Take ten zombies, make sure they can stand upright, and line them up on the flat surface at the bottom of the slope. Make sure to use the standard bowling pin configuration so the game can be as accurate as possible. Standing the frozen zombies upright can be bit difficult, so you'll likely have to position these guys, too. Remember, avoid the head. Thawed head = potential bitey death. If they won't stay upright, screws and plywood will do the trick. You'll also need a team of "rackers" to reposition zombies after each bowler has a turn.

Now that you've set up enough "pins" for a few games, let the "bowlers" go to the top of the hill. Your bowler will slide the zombie down the slope into the ten standing zombies.

The rules and scoring are exactly as they were in regular bowling.

- All of them knocked down is ruled a strike.
- Knock some down and leave some standing that's an open frame. You get a second throw to close the frame. That would be called a spare.
- There are ten frames per game. In the tenth frame you get three throws.
- In the end the person with the highest score wins.
- Remember to clean up after yourself.
- Destroy the brain, and burn the bodies in the fire pit.
- Remember that zombies will break during the game. They're brittle. These should be disposed of immediately and replaced.

Not much to this one, but there's hours of fun to be had depending on the number of zombies you have.

Zombie Skeet Shoot

If you're still freezing your ass off and have tons of ammo to waste, you could try this unique target practice sport. It's great practice on a quickly moving zombie target.

What you'll need:

- A shotgun & lots of ammo
- A steep frozen hill with a launch ramp at the bottom.
- A release mechanism
- A shot counter
- A score keeper (though the shot counter can double in a pinch)
- A large supply of frozen zombies.
- A disposal site with a fire pit

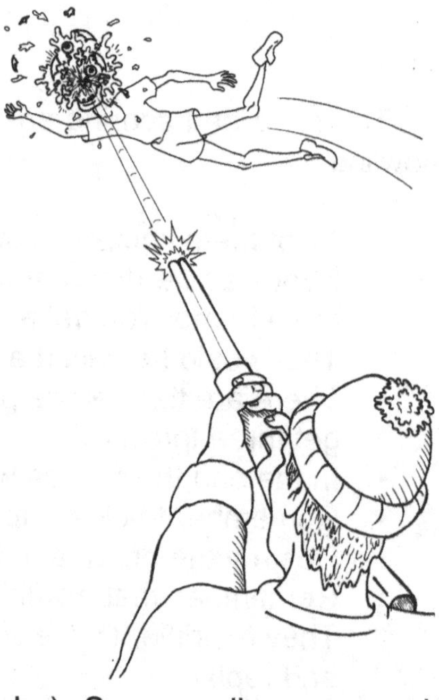

Now, this one is pretty self explanatory, but I'll go through the trouble for those of you who are already confused. Skeet shooting is target practice for hunters with rifles. Typically a shotgun is utilized here to practice bird hunting. Once you launch a flying target, your objective is to make it explode violently. Since a frozen zombie isn't likely to explode like a clay pigeon, you'll actually have to get up close to see the damage done, unless you're a REALLY good shot (or using high-powered ammo maybe). So, you pile your supply of zombies at the top of the slope, making sure they can be released accurately so that they slide down to hit the ramp and be launched by gravity alone. Someone up top loads the ramp and slides the zombie when the shooter yells pull. The object is to score the most kill shots while the zombie is in the air.

Scoring is as follows:

- 1 point for legs
- 2 points for torso and arms
- 5 points for head shots
- 10 points for headshots that cause the zombie's head to explode

Head explosion here is defined as a shot which displaces the skull in an area greater than 25 percent of the total cranial mass.

The game consists of three rounds per shooter. Once all the players have had their rounds, compare scores. The losers have to dispose of the used up corpses. Other terms must be agreed upon prior to the event's beginning.

Disposal is the standard: burn their husks in the fire pit. Remember to destroy the brain first, because fire would thaw them out and leave you with flaming death machines crawling out of your pit. If that happens, you have just increased your risk of being used in the next round of games. Try not to get bitten.

Zombie Lawn Darts

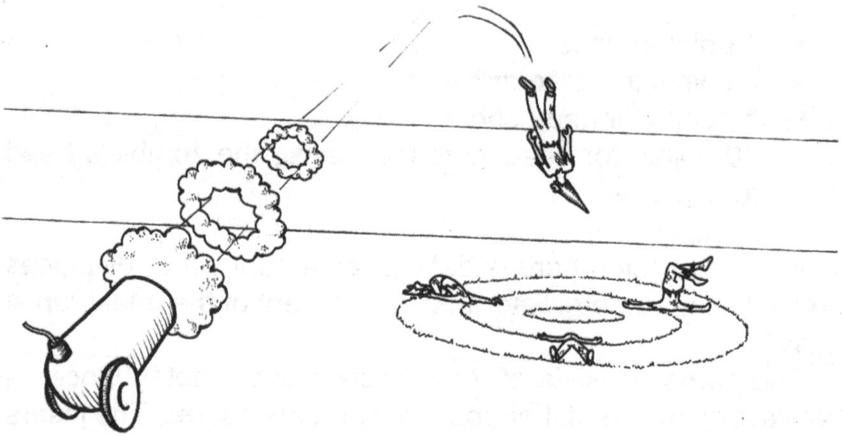

Much like traditional lawn darts, which is illegal in many states, but still fun as hell.

What you'll need:

- A large supply of frozen zombies with cone-shaped metal hats with chinstraps for "darts"
- A cannon large enough for human bodies to fit inside
- A large target painted on the ground
- A disposal site complete with fire pit

While lawn darts has become outlawed because of its inherent danger to slow-witted children, this form of amusement can be very fun and entertaining.

Game Play:

Each team is assigned three "darts" and they try to reach the most points per round.

There are ten rounds per game.

A round is played simply enough. Each team stuffs one of their "darts" into the cannon and fires it in the air.

They aim for the target, and hope to score points by sticking their dart in the ground inside a designated point area of the target.

"Darts" fired without the use of the metal cone-shaped hats that stick in the ground are worth a point multiplier of two. The reason behind this is that the ground is frozen and this will be difficult to accomplish.

"Darts" that explode on shooting count as a miss, and the team is given a new "dart" for the next round.

"Darts" that break (torso breakage only, limbs are acceptable losses) when they hit the target also count as a miss, and the team will be given a new "dart" for the next round.

The highest point total for each round determines who will "throw" first in the next round.

The highest score at the end of the game wins. The lowest score is responsible for clean-up and disposal of all "darts."

Sonny Side Up

This one will probably offend someone. But, do we care? Nope. We like offending people. In fact we aim for it.

What you need:

- Zombies (frozen is good, but fresh is OK, too)
- A set of skis
- A way to strap and prop up zombies on the skis
- A tree covered ski slope
- A judge
- A weapon to finish off possible surviving zombies

OK, so you may see where this is going, you may not. If you've made it through the other games, I'm sure you already know what I'm about to lay out in front of you. If not, get ready for squee-inducing entertainment.

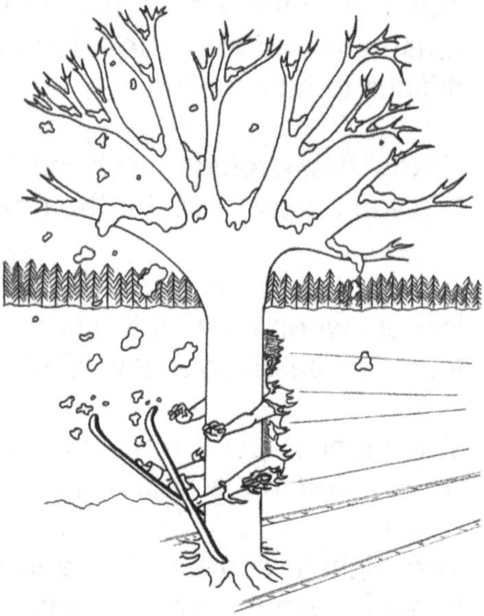

The Setup:

Affix your zombie to a set of skis. We don't care how; that's all up to you. We're doing most of the work, so you can work out the small details. Once you have done that, push him down the slope towards the trees.

Game Play:

The way to score points is for your skiing zombie to slam into trees, causing great bodily damage.

If you manage to kill your zombie with a head blow on a tree, you win instantly.

If there is a case of multiple deaths in the same game, the team that causes the most overall physical trauma to the zombie will take the win.

Now do you see why it's called Sonny Side Up?

If you don't, you're not a fan of the news and celebrity death are you?

We thought it was funny.

Zombie Hockey

Not just for winter anymore.

You will need:

- Ice skates for winter/roller-blades for summer
- A rink, either ice or concrete
- A puck, ice or street
- Scythes
- Zombies (fresh is better, makes it more entertaining)

So basically this is just a fun way to kill zombies while swooshin' around on skates.

Your team suits up and grabs the scythes and hits the rink.

Someone unleashes the zombie team to shamble around the rink. When it's on ice, it's quite funny cause they'll slip and fall. Comedy abounds at this point. On concrete, not as much fun.

Basically your team will take the game as a regular hockey game, only instead of worrying about the puck you'll use your scythe to chop the other team into bits.

Use style. Be creative. Make sure you hack and slash each and every zombie until they're pretty much goo.

I guess you could try to score a few goals in the process, however since a zombie goalie isn't going to do much other than try and eat you, it would be rather pointless.

It's all about the role playing. This one is super violent and all kinds of fun.

Remember, it's not about the game; it's how you play it.

Games You Probably Don't Want or Need Snow For

Zombie Disc Golf

This is where the Zombie Apocalypse Preparation page started for us, so this is near and dear to our little frosted-over black hearts.

If you're familiar with ball golf, then you're familiar with disc golf. If you're a sick twisted fearless bastard, you'll love zombie disc golf.

What you need:

- 18 Zombies (more would be better just in case)
- 18 Large spikes and 36 smaller spikes and/or chains
- Disc Golf discs
- Sharpened saw blades
- Beer
- More beer
- Possibly some other chemical enjoyment.
- A large field or orchard to set up your course

Map out your course, plotting hazards and various twists to make the course entertaining. Remember that your course can always be re-plotted and the holes changed around a bit. Clearing the tee areas is important for a nice smooth run up and drive. These can also be configured for both amateur and pro skill levels.

Having plotted out your course, you then take the zombies and tether them to the ground using large spikes, with the smaller spikes or chains located where you want your "basket" to be. Make sure that they're able to remain upright so that everyone has a good standard target.

Once all that is done, set the pars for each hole—these are generally based on distance—and set off on your adventure.

Each throw is counted as a stroke, and each stroke counts towards par. Traditional discs are used for driving and approach, but once you reach putting range, this is where things deviate a bit from the disc golf of old. Using a saw blade as your putter, you make your final shot.

If the blade sticks into your zombie-basket for a minimum of five seconds, then you have completed the hole and may mark down your score and move on to the next tee. Failing to stick your blade into the zombie counts as a miss and you must then take another shot.

Should your blade score a hit which amputates a limb (legs don't count and we'll explain why in a moment), despite its lack of sticking into the undead in question, it is counted as the same as having stuck the blade into the zombie in regards to the end of this hole. For the limb removal, you are rewarded with a -1 stroke bonus.

Should the blade sever the head, it's also counted as being "in the basket" or stuck, and you receive -2 off the total score, but you're then obligated to replace the spent zombie with a new one so that play can resume. Granted, you made an awesome decapitation shot, but it's only fair to the others in the group.

Now, if you happen to stick your blade into the zombie in such a way as to free it from its captivity (like cutting off it's leg or any part thereof), it's considered an out of bounds shot and you are penalized two strokes and must begin from where the zombie either wanders off the course or is violently destroyed.

If on a short hole you manage to make your regular non-bladed driver stick into the zombie, you win the round. In fact, you win every round for the rest of your days just by showing up to the course. You will be heralded as the King of Zombie Disc Golf and women will throw themselves at your feet (or men, whatever you like) wherever you go until your life functions terminate. However, should another person manage to accomplish the same feat, you must duel that person to the death for ownership of the title. There can be only one.

Just as with traditional disc golf and its variants, the person with the lowest total strokes at the end of the round wins the match.

The best part about this is that this game can be played several days in a row since you're not likely to kill the zombies in the first round. If you do manage to make some worthless, then you simply replace them with another zombie and continue.

Throughout the day, drink beer or use other mind-altering substances to enhance the experience, and enjoy the walk through the course.

Remember: friends don't let friends play ball golf. Instead, teach them this wonderful adaptation.

Armless Zombie Baseball Bat Tag

Yes, you read that correctly. Don't question; we told you we've got specially created mind reading paper in this book. This one's a bit trickier.

What you'll need:

- Armless zombies (you may have to make this happen yourself)
- Baseball bat for each player
- Teams
- Disposal site complete with fire pit

The armless zombies are harder to find, especially since they're still shambling around and trying to get your fleshy bits, but once you get them in the right place, it's time for fun.

It's just like all other kinds of tag, only you bash them until death. Choose sides and begin bashing skulls, and the team with the most armless zombie kills wins the game. If a member of your team at any time becomes "IT," then they're infected and have to be put down, and your team loses regardless of score. We would spend more time on this, but seriously it's that simple. The losing team gets to clean up.

Midget and/or Child Zombie T-Ball

This one may seem a bit cruel, but seriously, they're zombies, so don't be a pussy.

Here's what you need:

- A large supply of "smaller" zombies
- A baseball bat for each player
- Several planks of wood
- Box or two of sixteen penny nails
- A hammer
- A score keeper
- A video camera
- A disposal site complete with fire pit

We've often talked about the dangers of the "smaller" zombies. Let's be honest: most of the time, we're looking for average height people, so these little guys and gals go un-noticed. Whatever ailment they suffered from in life that made them short will add to the difficulty when they're zombies. The game is simple. Their heads are just about strike-zone level, and they tend to be pretty stable. So it's like T-Ball only far more violent.

First thing you want to do is find a group of the little tricky swarmy suckers. Then you have to trap each one individually, so you can nail their tiny feet to a plank of wood. You simply can't have your mini sports equipment meandering around on you whilst you're trying to play the game.

Then you get your videographer to start rolling. You want to make sure to capture this all on video for entertainment purposes later.

Each team sends a batter into the field, and they swing on the first little zombie in line.

If they miss the head, or the zombie all together, it's a strike. (And they should probably be slapped).

If they hit the head, but cause no damage, it's a foul.

A firm hit to the head causing noticeable damage is a base hit.

A solid hit to the head causing the skull to shatter is a double

A hit to the head which causes the eyes to pop out is a triple.

An unyielding blow to the head that causes decapitation is a home run.

If a player can hit the zombie head and cause it to fail catastrophically (blood spatter, brain, and skull chunks everywhere) that will be considered a grand slam no matter how many people are actually on base.

Fouls count as strikes; three strikes you're out.

There are three outs for each team in each inning.

Once the first side has run out of outs, the second team is up.

If any teammate inadvertently gets bitten, they are instantly out, and nailed to a board and placed in line to be "pitched."

As with traditional baseball, the game lasts nine innings.

If all zombies are dead, the team with the highest score at the time wins the game.

The losing team must clean up the bodies and dispose of any non-used zombies. Be responsible; make sure all the heads and brains have been destroyed, and then burn the bodies in your handy dandy fire pit.

Extreme Zombie T-Ball

Yeah, we have a lot of baseball themed killing methods. We're American and, in theory, this is our national past time. Though, in my opinion, eating and watching TV is possibly the real American national past time.

Here's what you need:

- Baseball bat
- Convertible car or pick-up truck
- Roads to drive down
- Teams
- Zombies
- Disposal site complete with fire pit

OK, you all know mailbox baseball right? That's where you drive around in a car and illegally bash mailboxes. Same concept here, only with zombies, and the highest number of kills wins.

Basically you load up in your open vehicle, and drive around with a "batter" at the ready to skull smash a zombie on the side of the road.

The driver may not swerve or attempt to throw off the hit. Doing so grants an automatic hit, even if the batter sucks.

If the head is crushed on the swing, it's counted as a base hit. If it explodes, it's counted as a double hit.

If you glance off and the zombie “lives,” it’s an out and the next batter is up.

Winner has the most hits at the end of the night.

Don’t do this in your neighborhood, so you don’t have to clean up the mess. However, if you do, give a hoot and all that.

Zombie Tractor Pull

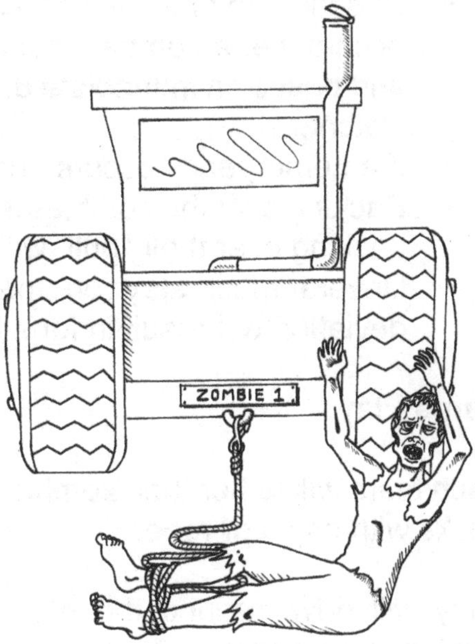

Submitted for your consideration in an effort to include our more vehemently redneck readers.

Here's what you need.

At least 2 teams of 2 people

A course judge, a distance judge, and a style judge

At least 2 trucks

At least 3 zombies per team

A length of rope or chain between 20 and 25 feet for each truck

Shotgun for emergencies

A disposal site complete with fire pit

The game is simple: you chain a still-moving zombie to the back of your truck and drag them over a pre-determined course until they are destroyed.

The Rules:

- Each driver will be allowed one pre-game lap in order to familiarize themselves with turns, grades, road conditions, and obstacles.

- Each team will have a driver and a zombie watcher in the back of the truck, and teammates will switch each round.
- Shooting zombies is not allowed unless an emergency occurs, i.e. a zombie bounces into the bed of the truck and poses an immediate danger to the driver or zombie watcher.
- If an emergency occurs, the team will forfeit the round.
- Backing over the zombies is not allowed. Players caught backing over their "pull" will forfeit the round.
- Drivers must stay on the course at all times; any deviation will result in forfeiture.

Game Play:

Each team will tether their zombies or "pull" to the back of their trucks with chain or rope.

They will drive around the pre-determined course until the zombie is no more.

The team with the least amount of laps required to destroy their zombies will win the match.

Using obstacles and parts of the course in unique ways will be rewarded with style points, which could later determine the game.

Game is a best of three system. In the case of a tie on distance, style points will be used to determine the winner.

Losing team will be responsible for course clean up and disposal of zombie chunks.

The Black Knight

No, he does not always triumph, and if he does here, that means you're probably going to be the Black Knight in the next round. (The personal favorite of David Houchins, the practical guy).

Here's what you need:

- A set of chain mail, tunic, and helm for each zombie and player
- A sword, or cutting weapon of some kind
- Supply of zombies
- A working knowledge of *Monty Python and the Holy Grail*
- A large set of balls
- Style and time judge (must be unbiased)
- A disposal site complete with fire pit

The rules are simple:

1. The chain mail and helm must be battle ready

2. Players must use a bladed weapon

3. Remove all limbs

4. The zombie must be "alive" at the end.

Game Play:

You chain the suited zombie to the game area by the ankle so it can't escape, at which point you start the clock.

The player must cut each arm and leg off, leaving the zombie as a torso only.

During the amputation of all limbs, our participant must taunt the zombie. Creative and "Pythonesque" taunts should in theory garner the most points.

The fastest time, combined with the most taunt points, wins the game.

The person with the lowest score in the game is responsible for the killing and disposal of zombies, as well as the clean up of the game area.

Also, using undead which were amputees or maybe had, like, flipper arms prior to their death and reanimation is just wrong in this case. Cheating is lying and lying is wrong. Don't be that guy.

Celebrity Look-a-Like Brain Spray

Yes, much like that movie with that guy in it.

What you need:

- A hunting rifle, or other weapon
- A perch to safely fire from
- Binoculars for spotters and observers
- A large supply of zombies; a town and/or city is your best bet for this game
- Plenty of ammunition
- A disposal site complete with fire pit

You can probably guess how this game is played by the title, but let's spell it out.

Rules:

All kills must be headshots.

All zombies must be identified and agreed upon as a celebrity look-a-like before shooting. Zombies MUST look like celebrities they've been identified with. (Otherwise, what's the point?)

Like in pool, if you call a celebrity, take the shot, and the zombie does not look like the celebrity, the shot is considered a miss.

If you take a shot without calling a celebrity, the shot is forfeited and counted as miss.

Game Play:

The players climb or get into their shooting spot and lure the zombies in.

Each player determines a celebrity look-a-like and takes the headshot.

Each viable kill is worth one point.

One extra point is awarded if the zombie is actually the celebrity called.

The game is played until all players run out of look-a-likes, or all zombies are dead.

Once there are no more look-a-likes, players must kill all remaining zombies. No points will be awarded; this is just for fun.

Lowest scorer of the game is responsible for clean up and disposal of zombie bodies.

Now, playing this sport someplace like Los Angeles or New York is likely to garner the most points, since you're likely to run into actual celebrity zombies. Any well-populated area with a lot of zombies works, and you never know who you'll run into on the road.

Amateur Zombie Dentist

This is a sadistic movie-lover's delight.

What you need:

- Supply of zombies
- Tools of pain and evil
- Nitrous oxide backpack
- Leather clothes
- Motorcycle
- Hot nurse to call you "Doctor"

This is a basic entertainment game. No points, no winner. The object of which is to extract teeth from zombies. We envision a setup much like Steve Martin had in *Little Shop of Horrors.* Bizarre tools, chairs with straps, a hot nurse, and a need to cause pain.

So you strap a zed to the chair, put on the nitrous oxide backpack, take large huffs, and start removing all the teeth. Have as much fun ripping them from the skull as humanly possible. Remember, once they have no teeth, they're much less dangerous, but until you actually succeed in pulling all the teeth, it's a game of chance. Make sure to clean up after you're done, destroy the brain, and then burn the body.

DO NOT MAKE YOURSELF DENTURES OUT OF THESE TEETH!!!

Hamster Balls o' Doom!

(Zombie Powered Vehicles)

So, you're looking for green technologies? How about shambler power!

What you need:

- A supply of zombies
- Welder
- Lots of steel
- Engineering know-how
- Someone to be "bait"

Another non-points game. Just rather entertaining, and useful for preventing the pesky global warming problem.

Basically, you make a huge hamster ball style device, throw a zombie or two into it, and power a vehicle with it.

You will have to build a seat in front of each of the "wheels" in order to prompt the zombies to move. It won't be the fastest moving vehicle, but hey it's cheap to sustain.

Just make sure you keep the grates large enough for the zombies to smell the flesh, but small enough to prevent them from getting out.

The best part of all this is, you don't have to dispose of the bodies afterward.

You just leave them in the balls until they fall apart on their own, and then replace them.

The Wishbone

You remember fighting over the wishbone as a kid? Well here's the mildly (very) psychotic adult version.

What you need:

- A zombie
- Ropes
- Two tug of war teams

Rather simple little game here. You tie the rope to the arm and leg of each side of the zombie, forming a small loop. Then tie another rope on to the loop.

Each team takes a length of rope and pulls; the goal is to rip the zombie in half.

The team with the largest chunk wins.

The team with the smallest chunk must then dispose of the zombie.

Ropes can be re-used, and the game can be replayed several times.

Simple, elegant, messy, and fun. What else do you need?

Zombie Tether-Ball

More schoolyard fun, with a deadly twist.

What you need:

- Decapitated zombie head
- Liquid latex
- Wooden peelers (those handy pizza oven scoopy things)
- Small O lag bolt
- Rope
- Duct tape
- Blowtorch
- Pole in the ground

Let's get to the setup.

First you get your decapitated zombie head. Use the blowtorch to cauterize the neck stump so as not to drip blood.

Drive the small O lag bolt into the top of the skull. Try not to kill the zombie, as it would make the game far less entertaining.

Now dip your freshly outfitted head in liquid latex. Don't ask me where you're going to get the liquid latex. Frankly, we don't know and we don't care. We came up with the game—you people need to get creative here.

Once the latex sets, attach the rope to the spiffy O lag bolt, then attach the rope to the pole.

You then use your peeler, (yes that's what they're actually called), to slap the head back and forth.

Just like in elementary school, the first person to wrap the rope completely around the pole wins the game.

If the head explodes, or is otherwise destroyed during the game, both players lose, and you must restart the whole process.

Remember to keep a gun handy just in case one player gets bitten, or otherwise becomes infected through fluid transfer. Should that happen, the sportsmanly thing to do would be to put a bullet between their eyes. Yes, it ends the sport right there, but it prevents them from having a nasty case of undeath as well. Plus, you win by default.

Zombie Jai Alai

Rather popular game played in parts of the world. Properly adapted you could have quite a fun time killing zombies with the game.

What you need:

- Cesta (hurling/ catching basket)
- Jai Alai ball (up to 140 grams, consisting of metal strands wound tightly and wrapped in goat skin)
- A huge set of balls
- A walled court to play on
- One pistol per player or designated sharpshooter

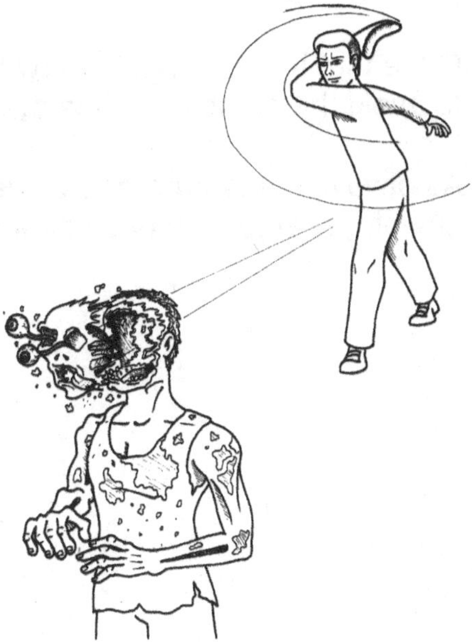

OK, so basically Jai Alai is a game typically played by teams of two people, round robin style.

The ball is hurled with the cesta, which is a hand basket curved and designed to add speed to the ball. The fastest recorded hurl with a Jai alai ball was 328 KM/H (204 MPH). With speeds like that, you can see how this would quickly turn into a zed killing bit of fun.

Let's modify the rules slightly: instead of teams of two playing round robin until one team reaches a score of seven, it'll be teams of eight people hurling and catching the ball trying to set a land speed record and explode zed heads in the process.

Since there are walls around your court, you'll slowly allow zombies into the squared circle of death and the game is on.

Hurl the ball towards another player, hoping a zombie will be between you and them.

If you can garner enough strength and speed, making contact with the zombie's skull will result in a nice explodey death shot.

Once that happens, get a new ball and start again. Make sure to avoid the zombies, since dying during a game is not fun.

As always make sure one player is packing heat, to put down any player who may become infected during the game.

Zombie Leap Frog

"So you've been watching American Ninja Warrior and believe you'll apply parkour to survival. While hopping around like a crack addicted cat will keep you from being infected, all the flips will cause you to drop supplies."
– Walking Traditionalist

Yes, finally something for you parkour/free runners to do.

The materials are rather simple:

- Zombies
- Free-running/parkour training
- Testicular fortitude

I guess this can be scored on the same premise as this "sport" is now: style and ability.

The setup is simple: you get a couple of free runners/parkour people in their pink spandex running clothes, then turn them loose on a street loaded with zombies.

They must leap, flip, and in all ways girly get around the zombies.

If one of the contestants misses and gets bitten, then that's one less free runner/parkour person the rest of us have to deal with.

Winner gets the best score.

Again, no clean up since you're not actively destroying the zombies.

So yeah, if you're into that. Enjoy.

Zombie Scuba Skip Skeet Shoot

This one is complicated and hard to pull off, but the overall effect will be damn fun.

What you need:

- A scuba diver
- Spear gun
- Speed boat
- Rope attached to spears & boat
- Large body of water
- Guns
- Beer (this sport is kinda redneck)

Put the boat in the water. Get in the middle someplace.

Send your scuba diver down with the spear gun. He spots an underwater shambler, fires, hooks the undead, and then tugs at the rope.

The driver of the boat gets the signal then takes off at full speed; yanking said zed to the surface.

Once zed starts skipping on the water, the shooter takes his shot while the zombie is in the air.

- Head = 5 points

- Torso = 2 points
- Limbs = 1 point

Most points win the game.

This can be repeated over and over. Just be good and remove the corpses from the water once you've dispatched them.

There's nothing worse than dead bodies in your swimming hole/water supply.

The following game was the winner of a contest we held in honor of our page's one-year anniversary. Our idea here was to extend an opportunity to our fans which would secure their inclusion into our book and thus ensure their printed immortality. Samantha Pictor was our illustrious winner when all was said and done, and the following submission should illustrate nicely as to why that is.

Zombie Labyrinth

Keep an Australian theme in mind. So there'll be very few guns and few large blades. Weaponry will vary, and expect a lot of weapons "cricket" style. And well, we have the idiots to use. Probably best, when proposing this game to the idiots, to replace the word "idiots" with "players"; doing so should increase participation.

Equipment Needed:

- Zombies
- Shovels, etc. for digging
- Minions to do the digging
- Razor wire
- Spikes
- Other traps (maker's choice)
- Player's weapon of choice
- Bite-proof clothing/armor
- Someone (or more) stupid enough to think this is a good idea
- Elevated viewing platform with hide
- Rope ladder
- Fuel to burn and a lighter/matches
- Noisy things

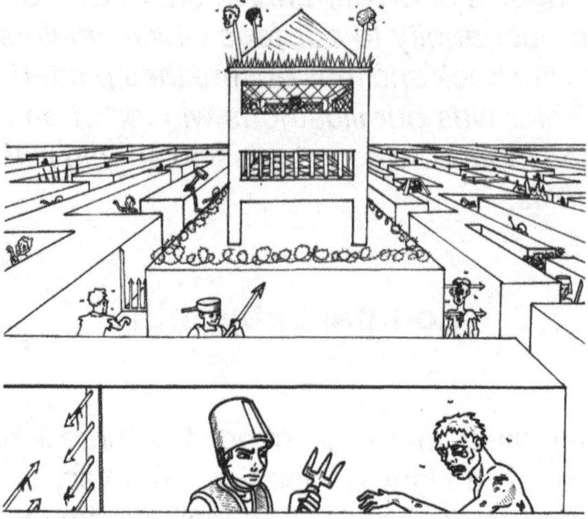

Setup:

- Have the minions dig several trenches, adding gaps in the walls in random locations (like a maze for four-year-olds). It can be as simple or as complex as your minions are strong (replaceable). Fill the "maze" with razor wire, spikes and other traps that suit your sadistic tastes
- Have the platform located in optimal viewing position
- Have your idiot dress in the armor and arm them with the weapon
- Lower the rope ladder into the maze, and then withdraw it
- Throw the noisy things into the maze
- Wait for zombies to fall into the maze
- Have the idiot hunt down the invading zombies and dispatch them
- Watch
- Replace idiot as necessary

- When fun and games are over (or it becomes too full of zombies/you're running low on idiots), fill maze with fuel and light
- Watch the bodies burn!
- Optional: You can let the idiots out of the playing field, the choice is yours

Idiot dispatches zed with the weapon of their choice. More idiots give the viewer variety. Successful idiots get the prize of living, and the illusion of respect. Maybe throw them a candy bar or beer if you feel kind.

If running multiple idiots at once, the winner is determined by most kills and most creative method of dispatch. Scoring is done at viewer's discretion.

The Inigo Montoya

Rather simple game. Those of you who appreciate classic movies will definitely know where this is going.

What you need:

- A large set of balls
- A sword
- A sense of humor
- The ability to quote movies
- Knowledge of the finer things
- Probably some whiskey
- A Sicilian to say "inconceivable"
- A large wrestler, or member of the Brute Squad

OK, this is rather simple. You are to walk around with your sword, and attack lone zombies. Doesn't sound all that hard at first, does it? Well it does have some groundwork that MUST be done first.

Each zombie you approach, you have to ask "Excuse me, do you have six fingers on your right hand?"

For all intents and purposes we're going to assume that every single zombie has six fingers on their right hand, because this bit doesn't work without it.

Having confirmed the existence of the additional digit, you must then say, “Hello. My name is Inigo Montoya. You killed my father. Prepare to die.”

Whereupon you stab the zombie once in each shoulder. Then repeat the phrase, this time with more passion and strength.

“Hello. My name is Inigo Montoya. You killed my father. Prepare to die.”

You then must slash one of the zombie’s cheeks.

Then you tell the zombie: “Offer me money.”

Since there will be no response at this time (because zombies don’t talk and you’re silly for expecting an answer), you then slash the other cheek.

And say, “Power, too. Promise me that.”

Again your foe will be silent.

Then you demand, “Offer me anything I ask for!”

You’ll get a groan, or hungry look, or lunged at.

At that point you kill the zombie, while demanding he give you your father back.

Yep, that’s it. OK, so it’s not really a game, so much as a repeatable scenario.

Remember the phrase should be repeated often, louder, with more passion each time.

In the end, you’ll feel good, and become the Dread Pirate Roberts.

The Nemesis Elimination

Everyone needs an arch nemesis. It's a rite of passage. What kind of mad scientist would you be without one?

Whatcha Gonna Need!:

- Zombies
- An overly complicated plan to take over the world
- A medical examination table complete with restraints
- A mad scientist costume
- A gun

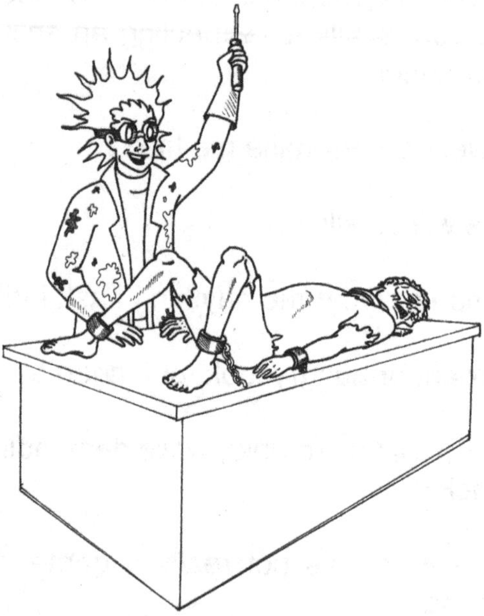

OK, simple setup.

Don your best mad scientist costume.

Take the medical examination table and use the restraints on your zombie foe.

Game Play:

Use your best recollection of a secret agent movie. You can do it. I have faith you've got at least that much imagination in you.

While your zombie struggles against the restraints, lay out your overly complicated world domination plan. Make sure to laugh manically every once in a while.

Once you've laid out the plan, look over at the zombie, refer to him as whatever secret agent you wish to use, and tell him he'll never be able to stop you.

He'll continue to struggle. You then say, "Mr. (insert secret agent name), I now expect you to die."

Shoot the zombie in the head and walk away.

I know, it's not exactly a game. It's more of a role-playing event. Also, it's not the way it ever works in the movies. The mad scientist normally has an overly complicated slow death machine that the good guy will escape from and foil his evil plan. You can play it that way if you want, but I've always felt if I was going to be an evil genius, I would at least use the genius part. Someone's out to stop me; I put a bullet in them. I am not going to let a slowly moving laser cut them in half from the junk up. I don't use a pendulum blade to slice them up, and I don't use SHARKS WITH FRIKKIN' LASER BEAMS ON THEIR FRIKKIN' HEADS! I simply put a round in the skull and move on. Score one less nemesis, and one less possible monkey wrench for the plan.

So this is how it would work in my hollowed out volcano lair. Actually I wouldn't even take the damn secret agent to my lair; a simple hotel room in a random town would be just fine. One less chance for my evil plot to take over the world to be foiled.

Grunge Rock Murder

This one is going to offend a few people. I'm not sorry about that. It's funny.

What you need:

- Supply of flannel shirts
- A double barrel shotgun
- Angry woman

Get a zombie with slightly messy hair wearing a flannel shirt.

Hand a woman a double barrel shotgun, then send her into the home where said zombie is.

She shoots him in the face.

Rather simple and to the point, right?

No, now you have to create a media blitz that makes the country believe the zombie committed suicide with a double barrel shotgun.

You also have to create a reunion album for the zombie.

Thousands of people must mourn his death, and ask, "WHY, OH, WHY DID IT HAVE TO BE THIS WAY?!"

The woman must then go on to be an incredible drug addict, get clean, and get addicted again. She must also sing very angry songs about stupid topics no one cares about. Like scuffing her Prada bag or something stupid.

The first person to do this is the winner... Wait... we have one already.

Downhill Bowling

This one can be fun, if you've got a hill to play on.

What you want:

- A hill
- Something large and destructive. I suggest tractor tires on the rims, bolted to a big pole with a few vertical pieces of steel welded to the pole. Sharpen the edges on these bad boys.
- A track for your device of destruction to roll down, plus a catching system so it doesn't roll into the next county.

Our suggestion on the design is highly recommended when you construct your tumbling death-machines. If you choose to do so, watching the rolling zombie-mauler spin its way through a group of undead would be kind of like a blender hitting slightly rotten meat.

Get a friend to lure some zombies to the bottom of the hill and into your track path.

Then you let the device, whatever you have built, go on its way. Chances are it's going to do major damage to the zombies.

It's further suggested that you build a couple of the death devices. This way you can make a second run and finish off the zed that may have survived the first round.

Best part is, once it's all done you can roll your death devices back to the top of the hill and start over. Each time will garner a different result and different deaths.

All in all, it'll be like a Kevin McCallister moment each and every time. Except, you know, funny.

Zombie Darts

We've counseled against their use, but we're going to give purpose to those useless thrown weapons like ninja stars, throwing knives, and throwing axes.

What you're going to need:

- Fenced off area
- Darts, ninja stars, throwing knives, or throwing axes—you get the idea.
- A gun per player
- Zombies
- Scoreboard
- Designated sharpshooter

Setup:

Each player will be given three of their chosen projectile weapons, and a gun.

Each player will be assigned one zombie per round.

Game Play:

It's a sick twist to a classic game of darts. You're going to need to be quick on your feet and accurate with your throws, because you're getting up close and personal with your target.

To start each round, each player is sent into the fenced

off area. A timer is set for two minutes, their assigned zombie is released, and the game is on.

The player has to throw their three projectiles into the zombie.

The shot has to be called for points, like in billiards. Once the three projectiles are thrown, the player must shoot the zombie in the head, and then tally the score.

If at any point the player falls victim to their assigned target, the designated sharpshooter will fire a headshot into both the zombie and the impending infected person in the play area.

The game is played in five rounds.

Scoring is simple and all based on called shots to specific body parts.

Scores are:

- Torso = 1 point
- Arm or leg = 5 points
- Head = 10 points
- Hand or foot = 25 points
- Toe or finger = 50 points
- Nose = 75 points
- Eye =100 points
- Tongue = 150 points
- Back of the throat = 200 points
- Kill-shot = Priceless (Actually, it's 1000 points)

At the end of the five rounds, the person with the highest score gets the glory.

Sadly, the person with the lowest score is responsible for game clean up.

The Bungee Kill

Finally a use for bungee jumping that isn't like trying to commit suicide and changing your mind.

What you need:

- Zombies
- Bungee cord
- Large bridge over heavily forested or rocky area
- Beer, whiskey, whatever you choose to drink

This one is rather simple. Strap a zombie to a bungee cord attached to a bridge and shove them off.

Now unlike human bungee jumping, you do not want to avoid obstacles.

What you want is the bungee to go into a large grove of trees, or maybe an outcropping of rocks.

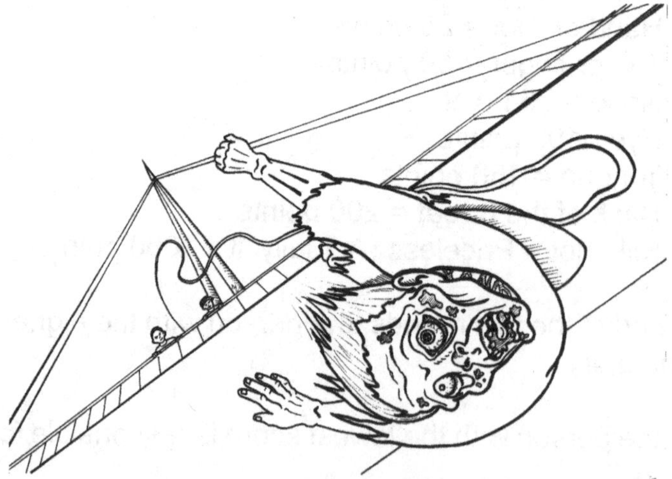

Each player gets to throw a single zombie off the bridge.

The person who causes the most damage to the zombie's body on their throw wins.

Rather simple. Quite entertaining, and all in all, damn good fun.

Punkin' Chunkin' Game of Doom

Requires a bit of engineering, but can be quite fun.

What you need:

- Homemade weapon, trebuchet, air cannon, catapult, anything you can build to fire a pumpkin at high speeds without the use of gunpowder
- 8 pound pumpkins
- Redneckitude
- Booze does not hurt the cause.
- Large area to fire weapons off in

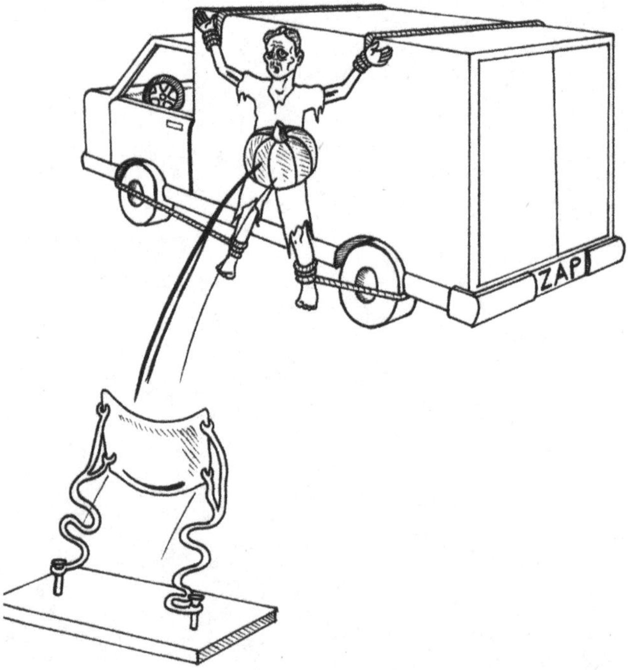

OK, you may have seen the sport, or show, called *Punkin' Chunkin'*. In order to participate in this particular game, you'll want to bone up. It's on the Discovery Channel. It's quite possibly the best use for a pumpkin outside of a pie I've ever seen.

So you build your device—air power, spring power, drop weight, whatever design you choose—the only rule for the weapon is no gun powder.

Let's lay out how it works. You take an old van, mini-vans are acceptable though slightly less masculine, and you strap the zombie to the center of the van. Then you load up your weapon of choice, whatever you've built. Fire the pumpkin at the zombie.

If it explodes upon leaving the device, you're penalized one point.

If it hits the zombie and destroys a limb, you gain a point. If you kill the zombie in one shot, you gain two points.

The game is played until one team reaches 20 points.

Now, this requires a lot of vans, pumpkins, and engineering skills, so it's one of the most in-depth games we've come up with. However, the applications of the devices, once built, are limitless. You can lob large gourds at other survivor groups as part of a friendly game of tag, and by "friendly" I mean deadly. You can use it as a way to obtain those small things you really want, like the hot blonde living in the camp down the road. Shoot the men with a pumpkin at 300 miles per hour and you'll be surprised at what you can achieve. We do not recommend these actions, even though we've come up with them. We honestly just suggest you use your cannons to kill zombies, and the random Sasquatch or other mythical beast. But if you choose to use your weapon for evil, far be it from us to talk you out of it.

The Bridge of Death

Yet again, another movie reference. Wow, bet ya didn't see that one coming.

What you need:

- A bridge over a gorge
- A unique launching device
- Unsuspecting zombies
- A list of silly questions

Ah, the Pythonesque games are always my favorite, since you can play them in any way you want, making them fun each and every time.

Basically you're going to stand around at your bridge, waiting for the occasional zombie to wander towards you.

As it nears your launching device, you ask it a silly question. When it fails to answer correctly (or at all), you trigger your device, flinging it into the gorge.

Very simple, very fun. A classic. You can never go wrong when asking, "What is the air-speed velocity of an unladen swallow?"

Relax, it's all fun and games until someone uses the Holy Hand Grenade.

Ding Dong Ditch

This is a turn on a childhood favorite.

What you need:

- Decapitated zombie head
- Gasoline
- Match
- Unsuspecting neighbor

Much like the old prank of lighting a bag full of crap on fire, leaving it on the porch, ringing a doorbell, and running off, this prank will cause all kinds of havoc.

You take your decapitated, yet still animated, head, and you place it on the doorstep of a home. Dump some fuel on it, light it on fire, ring the bell and run off.

Then hide in near-by bushes or someplace equally easy to find.

The fun is watching your poor unsuspecting neighbor try and stomp out the fire of a still very dangerous zombie head.

My best recommendation is not to place the flaming head on the doorstep of a neighbor you care about.

Also, you should be prepared to dispatch a brand new zombie, should they get bitten whilst stomping on a burning zombie head.

I mean, really it's not exactly the nicest thing in the world. But it's sure to be funny as hell.

The Pyre Pile Maker

Time for some old-fashioned k-bob fun. Vlad would approve.

What you need:

- A large vehicle, a 4x4 truck is the best choice
- A very large sharpened wooden pole
- A way to fasten the pole to the vehicle, and a quick release system to drop the pole.
- A well-built large pile of dirt, with a sheer wall.
- Several gallons of gasoline and a match.

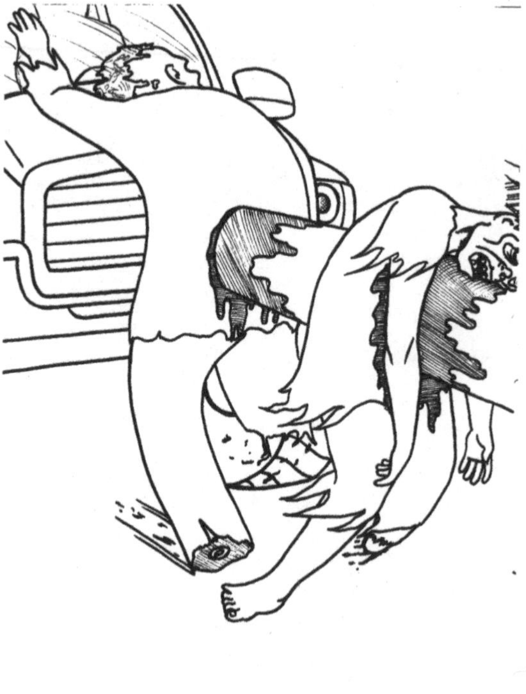

So you're one of these people who just so happens to have an affinity for fire, and you really want to set some zombies ablaze. Well, this is a game just for you. It's really simple, loads of fun, and it'll let your inner redneck and/ or sadistic Romanian ruler shine through.

First thing you do is fashion your sharpened wooden pole. The best choice for this would be an old telephone pole. You need the length. Make the end pointy.

Fasten the pole to the bottom of the truck, with the majority of it and the spike facing forward.

Now, all you do is drive around town sticking zombies with the point. The more you pile on the better. Try to set your own personal records.

Once you've gotten a number skewered you think is sufficient, drive your truck towards the pile of dirt and drive it home.

Once the pole is good and stuck, pull the quick release, which drops the pole, and back away.

Douse the pole and your k-bob'd zombies in gasoline, light them on fire, and watch them burn.

Since they're stuck on the pole, you won't have to worry about random wandering zombies bumping into things you find important. It's a great way to get your need for fuego out of your system without causing unnecessary damage to your safe house, group, or the surrounding countryside.

William Tell

Yes, just like in all the cartoons you've seen, only much more fun.

What you need:

- Zombies
- Straps
- Bow and arrows
- Some skill with a bow (only really required if you want to win)
- Some free time

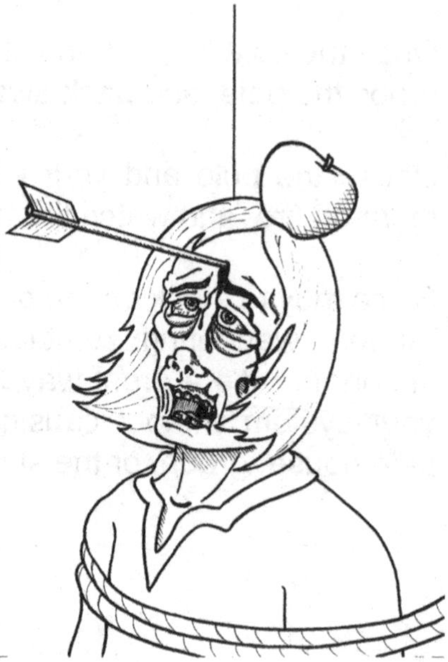

OK, so you bow masters have been hankering for some fun.

Honestly this is the best we can do for you.

It's a twist on an old story.

You strap a zombie to a tree. Bypass the apple, and shoot the shambler in the head with an arrow.

A shot directly between the eyes is worth extra points.

If the shot doesn't kill your zombie, try and best your shot. Try and hit the EXACT same spot.

Extra points added when you split the arrow Robin Hood style.

Sorry it couldn't be better. But we haven't really seen a use for an arrow other than the spear-fishing skeet shoot idea. I mean, really, who uses a bow and arrow anymore?

Aside from a few hunters who really want to keep killing after the gun season ends, and possibly those naughty Duke boys. Not much use for the bow and arrow these days.

We have gunpowder, and it makes the killing of things better, faster, and stronger. I guess this could be a fun game that may prove to be rather relaxing.

The Peek-a-Boo

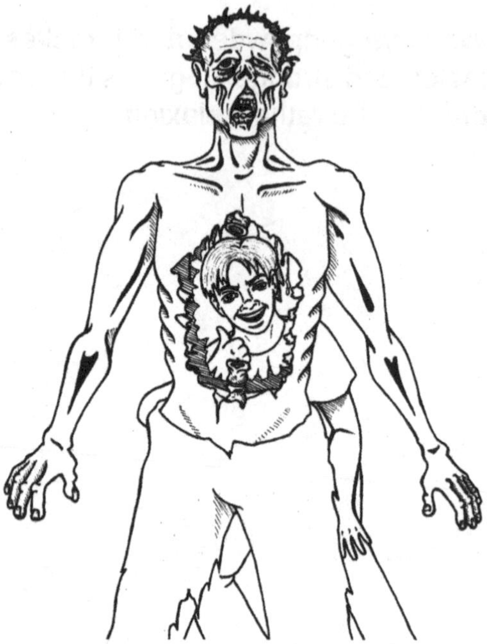

You're looking for over-the-top violence and gore? We're finally getting there.

What you need:

- A cannon
- Cannon balls
- Gun powder
- Zombies
- Camera

So you're sitting there thinking, "Damn these guys are really sick. These games, while entertaining, are very violent." Baby, you ain't heard nothing yet.

Submitted for your approval: the most violent game we could come up with.

It's rather simple; you and a partner set up the cannon.

You take aim at a zombie. Maybe it's tethered to a designated spot, maybe it isn't.

You light the fuse and blast away.

One of you quickly runs behind the now holey zombie and the other snaps a picture through the fresh hole.

Peek-A-Boo!!!

That's right. We want pictures of the gore created when a ten pound cannon ball passes through an undead body.

You'll have to be quick, because once you knock a hole in the spine, they're going to be very floppy.

You only get credit for the picture if the zombie is still standing, and you're clearly seen through the hole in the body.

It may require you to put yourself somewhat in the path of a cannon ball. That could be slightly dangerous.

We in no way advocate this action, nor do we suggest you actually participate in this game. However, if you do, we'll award you ultra-cool intarweb points. You will be deemed either the baddest of the bad, or the dumbest of the dumb. We really haven't decided. Seriously, anyone who puts their own body in the path of a cannon ball for a game should be slapped. What's wrong with you for considering it? You're just silly.

The Scavenger Hunt

It's time we stop picking on the undead. OK, not really. We're still picking on them—just not in a way that destroys them. We're going to rob their homes now that they're dead! WOO CRIMINAL FUN! You can squeal with joy now. I'll allow it.

What you need:

Homes left empty by zombies

A list of spiffy things one may find in a home

Couple of groups to run willy-nilly home to home

A weapon to fend off possible zombies

Rather simple. I'm sure you've all been on some kind of a scavenger hunt in your life. At the very least you've seen it in a T.V. show.

This gets to be fun though. Basically you can put anything you want on the list.

A vibrator from a porn star's house, Granny's teeth; wedding pictures of an ugly couple. Anything you want! You can totally be creative, and get some pretty spiffy shit in the process.

Imagine the untold treasures hidden in the homes that are vacated by the recently undead.

There could be gold, or platinum. That collection of limited edition NASCAR collector plates you've been dreaming of.

Hell, there could be FOOD. That in and of itself will be worth the trip.

Yeah, you could call it raiding for goods, but that sounds so dirty. Scavenger hunt sounds so much better. At the very least, it doesn't sound criminal this way.

Remember, always clear the home before going all crazy looking through the rooms. You never know where a zombie will be hiding.

The Cowboys' Defense

I know, "America's Team," don't pick on them. To hell with you—it's funny.

What you need:

- A field
- A football
- Football uniforms and pads
- Two referees armed with guns

The game is very simple: you place a zombie at one end of the field and throw a ball at him.

The zombie of course will ignore said ball, but that's neither here nor there. Since most Cowboys players can't hold on to a football anyway, it'll be pretty accurate.

The player on the field will then run full tilt at the zombie and tackle him.

Treat him like defensive lines treated Tony Romo and John Kitna in the 2010 season: pulverize the bastard

The first person to kill the zombie in one hit wins. Helmet-to-helmet contact is encouraged, though the zombie won't be wearing one.

The referees are to be armed and on hand just in case a player is bitten. Sadly we shall have to put them down immediately, since it's bad form to let an armored zombie run around.

The Lemming March

Time for some childhood memories.

What you need:

- A way to get the zombies' attention
- A canyon, preferably a very deep one
- Quick rope bridge
- A sense of humor

A rather simple fun time to be had here. You get one of your compadres to lure a large group of the horde.

Since they walk slowly, it's not hard to stay ahead of them, you know. Just kinda power walk to stay ahead of them.

Once you've gathered up a large number following you, make your way to the canyon.

Make sure not to get too far ahead of them, as we know zombies will meander off on their own, and the point of this fun activity is to have as many as possible.

It's IMPORTANT to watch where you walk. The game would end very quickly if you were screwing around and tripped and became a buffet.

Once you're at the canyon, shamble across the rope bridge and drop it from the other side.

Zombies are dumb. They will continue to pursue you. No bridge means a large fall for them.

It'll be kinda like a cartoon where large numbers keep falling and end up in a pile.

This game may not destroy the zombies if the canyon is not deep enough.

Another problem that could occur, if you've gathered a large enough number of zombies, is they could clog the canyon then walk across the bodies to get you. This would be the worst-case scenario.

Remember, a brisk walk will help you escape. Just make sure to watch where you're going.

Wire Fighting Attacks

This does take some set up, and a large group of people, but it's sure to be fun.

What you need:

- A wire fighting team (Don't ask me how you're supposed to get one, that's your problem)
- Sharp swords
- Random zombies
- Video camera to capture it all

OK, so you've got your wire fighting team—again no clue how you got one post apocalypse and it's not our problem to solve every issue. I know you're thinking, "Why suggest this if you don't have the answers?" Just a reminder: we do have special thought reading paper that we printed this book on. That way we can answer your questions.

The answer is, I just want to see the video later, and you work out your own technical issues. I came up with the idea—isn't that enough?

Remember the person on the wires should probably be the lightest person of your group. Not like you want to heft a 300-pound bastard around.

Then you re-create an all out battle. Flying swords, flips, and decapitations.

All while video taping it. You can go full on epic *Matrix* style fight scene, only make it good and not overly CGI or unbelievable.

A few pulls, some flight, and sword slashes. It's bound to turn out great.

I mean if Fat Bastard could have a wire fight scene, why can't you?

Operation

Just like the board game, only slightly messier.

What you need:

- A zombie
- A surgical room
- A chainsaw
- Either a wheel with organs painted on it, or a deck of cards with human organs listed
- Full surgical gear, including facial protection

You all remember the game Operation, right? You remember, right? Come on, you remember.

Well, this game is played on a much larger scale with a chainsaw!

You either spin the wheel or draw a card, depending on your choice.

Whichever organ you end up with, you must remove using only a chainsaw.

The organ must come out intact with as little damage done to the zombie as possible.

If the organ is already gone, or has been damaged by outside impact other than the game, you draw again.

Players take turns. The person who removes the most organs wins the game.

Now, since there's no buzzer to tell you when you've made a mistake, you kinda have to play on the honor system.

Remember, there will be blood and guts and other fluids flying everywhere. Make sure you're fully protected so you don't get infected.

One person not playing the game should be designated the assassin should a zombie get free or a player become infected.

A quick end to a potentially painful death is the only humane thing to do. Of course, you could just fence them off and use them in the game later if you choose to. I mean, kinda poetic justice there.

Shootout at the OK Corral

Historic reenactment is always a beautiful thing. Especially when it's a timed sporting event that ends in the mass death of zombies.

What you need:

- Zombies, lots of them
- Two old style six shooters
- Designated time keeper
- Corral or fenced in area
- Ammunition

So, this game is rather simple. Each player is given two six shooters. They are then turned loose in the corral with six zombies.

The goal is to kill all six zombies with just twelve bullets.

The fewer shots used the better.

The winner of the game will be the person who uses the fewest bullets to kill all six zombies shoot-out style.

Now, should there be a tie in the number of shots used, time can be factored in to determine a winner.

If there still is no way to determine a winner using time and number of shots taken, style points will then be used to determine the winner.

The person who can use the most flare, in the shortest time, with the fewest shots is ultimately the winner anyway. All others should bow down before their awesome skills.

The Predator

This game is just squee-levels of fun and excitement.

What you need:

- Zombies, lots of them
- Old paintball course
- Wide selection of melee weapons
- Designated assassin
- Style, determination, and anger
- Three judges

So, you think you're the baddest zombie hunter on the planet? You think you can kill anything with anything. Man have we got the game for you.

Let's lay out how it works.

You fence off an old paintball course to provide an escape-free zone for hunting. That's the game area.

You then release between three and ten zombies on the course. Each of the players must face the exact same number of zombies in each round.

The first player chooses three melee weapons. That's all they're allowed to carry.

The player must use all three weapons in the process of dispatching all zombies on the course.

The faster the time, the better the score. Remember, style will factor into the overall score.

In the case of a player being infected, that player can be added to the pool of potential targets or killed by the designated assassin.

Extra style points will be allotted to any player who has what resembles the reproductive organs of a woman with lots of teeth on their face and or dreadlocks.

A winner will be chosen by one of three ways. Fastest time: if someone is just stupid fast using all three weapons and dispatching all zeds, they win. If time exceeds five minutes per round, then it will be shifted to style points. Most creative kills and use of weapons garners the most points. Style is judged by the three judge panel, which will then combine and average scores. The highest overall score wins.

Just remember, it's all fun and games until someone breaks out the thermonuclear device strapped to their wrist. Then it's just a giant clambake.

Rock 'em Sock 'em Zombies

So you think you're the baddest mamajama that's ever walked the street. You've been watching MMA matches and think you can take down anyone or anything. You think you're the Shogun of Harlem? You think you're Sho Nuff? Well, we have the game for you!

What you need:

- Boxing ring
- Zombies
- Boxing gloves
- Headgear for the zombie (in this case, tape its mouth shut)
- Testicular fortitude
- A designated killer

This is a boxing match like you've never seen. It's man vs. killing machine in a no holds barred death match.

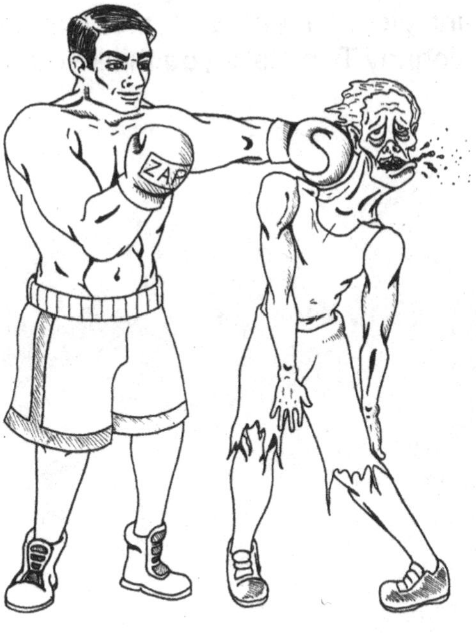

Your goal is to kill the zed by beating it to death.

Now there's none of those pussy rules about cheating involved. In fact, we encourage you to weight your boxing gloves with sand, or lead pellets, or something like that.

Since zombies don't feel pain, you really won't get a chance to kick them in the privates, or kidney punch them with any real effect or enjoyment, so dirty boxing really won't matter. Chokeholds won't work since they don't breathe, and eye gouges are right out. Your only hope is to beat their head until it explodes like day-old Jell-O left on the windowsill. That's right—you have to turn them into mush.

Use all that built up rage and anger. Bash them like they're the in-law that used to piss you off. Hell, they could actually BE that in-law. Who knows if they're going to stay zombie bite free?

Work out all that anger. It'll be better than therapy.

Remember, there aren't going to be any therapists post apocalypse. You're going to have to work out that complex somehow.

Luckily there's a designated killer on hand in case you do get infected. It'll end your problem quickly should you not be the Johnny Two-Balls you think you are.

Floppy Zombie Fun

It was a dark and stormy night when one of the admins decided to come up with a game to top Peek-A-Boo. And we did, and we were pleased.

What you need:

- A large tree or building
- A rope to trip zombies
- A large weight to drop
- A strong stomach
- Hazmat suit
- A camera

So, we thought the Peek-A-Boo would be the most violent gory game we could come up with. Then, we outdid ourselves.

That's right—we've come up with Floppy Zombie Fun. Now bear with us, because it's complicated. OK, not really.

You set your large weight up in the top of the tree, or on top of the building. Lay your rope out so you can trip your zombie victims. Once they land flat on their stomach or back, you drop the weight.

The trick to the game is to make sure the weight ONLY crushes the body from the neck down, leaving the head fully intact and uninjured.

You then have pancake zombies, or as we like to say, "floppy zombies."
This may take a bit of work as well. You may have to place yourselves in danger to get the zombie positioned just right as to avoid crushing its skull.

That means first being up close and personal with a death machine. It also means placing yourself under a heavy weight that could indeed leave you as flat as Stanley.

Once you have your floppy zombie, you will have to find a unique way to store the corpse. This may involve getting a little dirty, so be sure to don the HAZMAT suit. I suggest rolling the zombie up like a sleeping bag. Y'know, feet to head, so you got a bedroll with teeth. Calmly stack them in the corner some place and up the body count.

When you've had your fill of this kind of gore and fun, you can unroll the bodies and leave them in the sun to dry like leather. Then you can have a still alive human skin rug. Yeah it may be a little disgusting, but hey we're in the survival game, and you're smashing zombies flat with a heavy weight. Show the pride in the kill. Have a Bob throw rug. You owe them the honor of that at least.

OK, not really. But I think having a living throw rug would just be an awesome conversation piece. It really ties the room together.

Now once again you're putting yourself in mortal danger for the sake of a game, but the same rewards apply: women (and/or men), a spiffy nickname, and ultra-cool intarweb points.

Again we must admonish anyone who would literally put themselves in danger for a game. We cannot legally condone the activities listed in the above game. On the other hand, we cannot legally tell you how awesome you would be if you pulled this off and got the pictures to prove it. We can legally say you shouldn't try this because it is dangerous and could lead to injury.

The Rube Goldberg

OK, this one is going to take a lot of effort on your part. In fact you're going to have to do a lot of thinking and engineering. We're going to give a basic idea of what to do. The rest is up to you.

What you need:

- Zombie target
- Whatever your device requires to operate

This is how it works: a Rube Goldberg device is something that is super overly complicated to perform a simple task. Say like crushing a zombie with a weight or firing a gun.

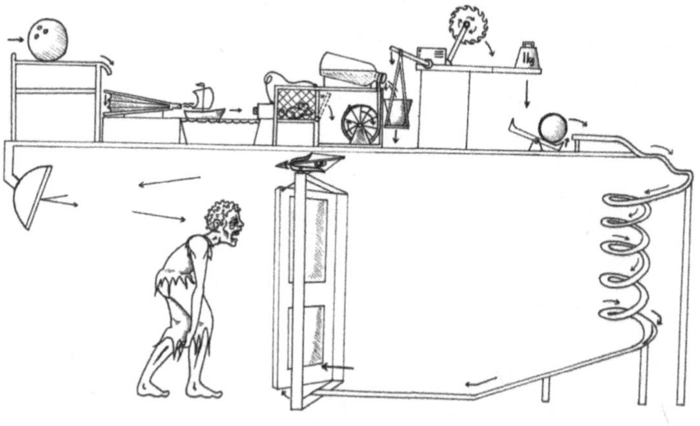

I will lay out a device to give you an idea, but you must design and build your own device to make it work.

We'll start where everything starts: a bowling ball on a set of tracks. We'll set it up to roll down the tracks onto a set of bellows.

The bellows will be aimed at a small sailboat in a washbasin of water. The bellows will blow into the sail, sending the boat across the basin to hit a button.

That button will release a mouse which will run on a wheel.

That wheel will turn a spindle that rolls up a cord.

That cord will pull a stopper on a bottle full of water.

That water will fill a bucket which will raise a lever to turn on a switch.

That switch is going to power a saw that will cut a plank of wood with a weight on one end.

The cut wood will split, causing the weight to fall onto another lever that will throw a ball into the air.

The ball will land on another set of tracks, which will in turn roll down the tracks into a door.

The door will swing open, triggering a crossbow.

The crossbow will shoot a zombie in the head.

Thus ending the Rube Goldberg Device's run.

Now, will all these things work without fail? Probably not. Making something overly complicated often leads to massive failure. However, if you make it work and pull it off, it's quite possibly the most beautiful thing you could ever hope to see in action. Like a massive domino display, this is simply poetry in motion.

Now design your own machine. See if you can make it work.

It's an extraordinarily wonderful sight to behold when it functions as it was conceived.

This ends our gaming section. By leaving you with something you have to think about, we're keeping your mind active. That's always the best way to stay alive. If you're busy thinking, you won't be getting stupid and end up dead.

SECTION THE FINAL

THIS AGAIN?

So, here we are again. You've reached the end of the manual in one of two ways again.

If you bought the first version of the book you knew not to skip to the end and read the last chapter because we call you a moron here for that. You fucking moron. But, if you read through the entire book and gained the knowledge of survival you were searching for, we're proud of you. Also, we'd like to know, did you spot the new bits and enhanced writing? If not, do it again. In fact, buy the book again. We need the money.

Another side effect of reading this whole book is you now have a far superior knowledge of weapons, tactics, and deeply regret the Red Rubber Ball. We're sorry we're not sorry about that.

There have been games, fun, comedy, and information shared along the way. We've probably offended you slightly somehow, which wasn't our intention, but nevertheless is a welcomed result. The best part of you reaching the end of this book is that we earned a bit of coin off you, and we won't be forced to destroy your walking corpse later. You're now educated enough to survive the post-apocalyptic world, or at the very least stay the hell away from the trigger happy and mildly psychopathic authors of this book.

Hopefully you've enjoyed all we wrote in this manual both times we wrote it. Don't worry once we finish this one and get our first print copies we'll likely spot more stuff we could have included in this version and will begin work on the third installment. It's like plastic surgery for some people. We just can't get it right, but we'll keep working at it until it's either a monster, or it's perfect. But uh, we pretty much nailed it.

Now it's time to give this book to someone else who needs to know how to survive. But not this copy, this copy is yours. This copy should proudly be displayed on your toilet, as to inspire toilet reading by those who need to laugh while clearing their bowels. Buy another copy to give away. Hell, buy twenty or thirty of them, make sure those people buy twenty or thirty, and if that continues, we'll finally be able to buy that island we've been dreaming of. Yes, you're invited.

You have now officially graduated from our single book course of survival. You will not only know what to do, you'll know how to enjoy yourself in the process, which in all reality is what's going to make life worth living once this is all over.

With that, your authors David Houchins and Scot Thomas offer heartfelt thanks for helping us continue to spread awareness and comedy.

Remember, it's not about merely staying alive, it's about LIVING.